THE EMERALD STONE

9-30-08

To Sidney Paige Cobb
I hope you enjoy the book

by

DJ Loomis

Edited by: Roxane Christ

Bloomington, IN   authorHOUSE   Milton Keynes, UK

AuthorHouse™
1663 Liberty Drive, Suite 200
Bloomington, IN 47403
www.authorhouse.com
Phone: 1-800-839-8640

AuthorHouse™ UK Ltd.
500 Avebury Boulevard
Central Milton Keynes, MK9 2BE
www.authorhouse.co.uk
Phone: 08001974150

This book is a work of fiction. People, places, events, and situations are the product of the author's imagination. Any resemblance to actual persons, living or dead, or historical events, is purely coincidental.

First published by AuthorHouse 2/21/2006

ISBN: 1-4259-0724-5 (sc)
ISBN: 1-4259-0725-3 (dj)

Library of Congress Control Number: 2005910866

Printed in the United States of America
Bloomington, Indiana

This book is printed on acid-free paper.

Acknowledgements

I would like to thank my husband Carl, without whom this book may never have been finished.

I would like also to thank my editor, Roxane Christ, who became a dear friend and without a doubt gave me an overwhelming amount of encouragement.

Chapter 1

Long, long ago, long before time was, as we know it to
be today, there was a charming lush forest nestled deep in
the mountains far, far away. The forest was truly enchanting
and almost magical it seemed, for everyone living within it
appeared to be untouched by evil and its dark forces. The
trees were so tall that they almost reached to the heavens
with huge trunks, some as big around as houses. Amid this
natural wonder, there was a magnificent waterfall. It tumbled
from great heights into a gentle rolling stream that weaved its
way through the forest. It was always summertime there – the
perfect place for anyone to live. Snuggled deep in the forest,
there was a small village of friendly hard working people, and
this is where our story begins.

Every day you would see the people out tending gardens,
grooming their lush green lawns or working in the quaint little
shops that lay clustered in the middle of the village, happily
helping each other to keep it all neat and clean. Everyone
helped everyone, no matter what the task; they were a very
close-knit, honest and sincere people with no trouble among
them.

One warm sunny afternoon Serina, the village shoemaker's
young daughter took a stroll down by the stream, her feline
companion, Samone, following at her feet. Samone was a
rather large Siamese cat, who liked mousing better than most
anything except sleeping.

1

Serina came upon her favorite rock protruding from the water's edge. She climbed atop it and took a seat. She dangled her feet into the cool stream below, and daydreamed of adventure while the warm sunshine caressed her face gently.

At nearly twelve years of age she lacked the ambition to do hard work, although she did her share, helping her father in his shoe shop and keeping the house tidy. She also did most of the cooking for her and her father. She did not remember ever having a mother. She had been told her mother had died right after Serina; her first, and only child, was born. Sometimes she fantasized about having a mother, to share the little secrets only a mother and daughter could share. Oh, how she wished she had known her. Everyone said Serina was a lot like her mother – beautiful, full of mischief and always looking for adventure. The resemblance between the two grew more each day – her long unruly dark hair and jet black eyes, along with her pint size frame, which was no match for a temper that was mightier than that of most twice her size, reminded the people, who had known her, of Serina's mother.

Serina slipped off the rock into the stream pulling her skirt up between her legs keeping it dry as she waded around at the water's edge enjoying the coolness on her feet and ankles.

Samone raised her head as Serina climbed down; she watched her pretty, young mistress for a moment through sleepy eyes, stood, slowly stretched her long sleek body and jumped down from the rock prancing off in the opposite direction. Of course, and unlike her mistress, she had a distinct dislike of water. She headed for the edge of the woods to look for her own adventure; maybe, if she were lucky she would run across a big fat juicy mouse.

Serina loved the water; she could splash and play in it all day long if it were not for her chores and studies. When she was not playing in the water she was wandering through the forest exploring every little nook and cranny, today was no exception. She had finished her chores early and Professor Threcher, the children's teacher, was laid up with a broken leg, so school was out for another month and a half, at least. Her best friend Koori was busy baby sitting her little brother Zeb, so Serina was left on her own to explore and do whatever she wanted to do, or as the elders would put it; "finding whatever mischief she could get herself into."

Something glittering amid the rocks caught Serina's eye drawing her back to the present. She bent down and picked up the shiny stone to get a closer look at it.

"Oh, how beautiful," Serina squealed excitedly.

It was a small green stone about the size of Serina's thumb and very lovely indeed. She turned it over and held it up toward the sunlight; its brilliant sparkles reflected the sunrays into Serina's eyes – she squinted.

As Serina gazed at the stone, the wind suddenly picked up from out of nowhere brushing a cold breeze across her face. She shivered slightly and then just as quickly as it picked up, the wind abated to a gentle stir.

A noise, a voice perhaps, from behind startled Serina, she whirled around but no one was there. She cocked her head to the left and listened for a moment but could hear nothing.

"That's odd," she said aloud.

The noise came from somewhere just inside the edge of the forest and sounded, to Serina's surprise, much like a woman's scream. She swung her head in that direction and listened, more intently this time. Again, she heard nothing, not even the rustle of the leaves from the wind gust that had been blowing cold and hard only moments ago.

She stepped out of the water and walked toward the edge of the forest to investigate the noise or voice she was sure to have heard.

Everything seemed tranquil at first, but her sense of adventure and her innate curiosity drove her farther into the woods. Still holding the green stone tightly in her fisted hand, she started walking cautiously not knowing what she would find. All the while recalling her father's warnings about her taking off on her own, but Serina loved adventure and besides, what was there to be afraid of anyway?

Serina had not gone far into the thicket when she heard the sound of running feet on the trail behind her; she turned on her heels facing the direction from which the sound came.

"Who's there?" Serina shouted, her voice echoing throughout the now silent forest. She scanned the path and surroundings, yet she saw no one nor did anyone answer.

"My ears must be playing tricks on me," she mumbled to herself as she turned back up the trail, and there, sitting proudly on a huge rock near the edge of the path, was a beautiful butterfly. Serina stopped to watch the splendid creature for a moment; her previous quest momentarily forgotten. As she eased closer to look at it, the butterfly opened and closed its large blue and yellow wings. She stopped a few feet away where she stood motionless in awe, not wanting to make a sound for fear of scaring the butterfly away.

Then, abruptly, a hand gripped her shoulder – she screamed in panic.

"Are you deaf girl? I swear; I have been calling you for ten minutes."

It was Amil, her father's young helper.

"Yo-u gave me a fright," Serina snapped. "Don't you have anything better to do than to go around sneaking up on people and scaring the begeevies out of them?"

"Your father sent me after you – seems he can never find you when he needs you." Amil spoke in haste, a little put out at having to search so long for her.

"Oh look, you scared off the pretty butterfly I was watching. You big oaf, it was just sitting there showing off for me on that big rock," Serina quirked, noticing that the butterfly had taken flight from all of the commotion. She was very annoyed with Amil for the intrusion.

"What does Papa want anyway?" she asked.

They were walking back out to the edge of the woods when Serina remembered the stone she had found. "Oh!" She exclaimed, not giving Amil a chance to respond. "Look what I found."

She opened her small palm exposing the stone and offered it to Amil.

"Isn't it just the loveliest stone you've ever seen?"

Amil took the green stone from Serina's hand and held it up to the sunlight examining it carefully. "Very nice I suppose, if you like those sort of things that is," he said handing it back to her.

Serina grabbed the stone out of his hand and held it up toward the sun. "You've got to admit it's beautiful, see how it glitters and shines when the light hits it."

"Serina you think everything is beautiful or special or the greatest," Amil said snickering. "Or is it that all girls think that way? Let me think... Oh yes, all girls think that way all right, you're just the worst of them all, Serina."

Amil's manner was nonchalant as if he was talking to himself, and before Serina had a chance to respond, he flashed a rather large grin at her, snatched the stone right out of her hand and took off running.

"You big oaf! *Come back here with my rock* or I'll beat the begeevies out of you."

Serina was no match for Amil's tall lanky frame and she knew it. He ran like the wind but she took off after him anyway. He slowed down and waited for her at the edge of the bridge laughing at the fact he could out-run her or any girl for that matter. He held out the stone pretending to throw it into the stream below as she caught up with him. She jumped up in the air, stretching her short arms up as far as she could, trying to snatch the stone. However, Amil was too tall for her so she grabbed his arm trying to pull it down closer toward her. In the shuffle, they lost their balance, fell to the ground and rolled down the slope towards the bank of the stream.

"Give me back my stone or else," Serina barked, straddling his waist and pinning his arms to the ground like the tomboy she was.

"Or else? Or else what?"

"Or else I'll black both your eyes and bloody your nose to boot, that's what."

She made a fist with one of her small hands shaking it vigorously in his face to get her point across.

"You know I'm really scared now… But, but I can't remember where I dropped it," he said with half a smile.

"You dropped it?" Serina was aghast.

"Yeah, somewhere by the bridge when you tackled me."

"Oh no, you big oaf!" She jumped up and headed back up the slope looking for the stone, her eyes focusing on the ground as she struggled up the steep incline.

Before she made it to the top though, she heard Amil chuckling. She looked over her shoulder to see him still lying on the grass laughing heartily.

"What's so funny?" she yelled.

He rolled over getting to his knees, pulled something out of his pocket then stood up. "You should see the look on your face; you really thought I dropped this little thing?"

He held up the stone so she could see it, then he tossed it high into the air toward her, she caught it with both hands as it came down.

"Good catch – for a girl," he said, and then started up the slope. When he reached the top, Serina gave him a big shove. He lost his balance once again and rolled back down to the bottom of the hill from where he had just climbed.

"That… was for fibbing to me."

Now Serina was the one laughing. She ran to the bridge rail; ready, just in case he gave chase, and watched him as he scaled his way to the top of the slope. Amil was tall, dark haired, with a dark complexion to match. He had a handsome face, very rugged looking already for a fourteen-year old. His voice was changing to a deeper more manly tone, but he was the quiet type, somewhat shy, not like most of his friends who talked nonstop; he said he always learned more by keeping his mouth shut and listening.

Serina stuck the stone in her pocket as a precautionary measure as Amil neared her; *just in case you try to take it away again*, she thought.

"What did you say Papa wanted with me anyway?" she asked again as they began walking toward the village.

"He needs an extra pair of hands this afternoon with the Muncie's order so he can finish it up."

"Oh yeah, Mr. Muncie," Serina said kindly, "with all those children he and his wife have, they are forever having to get new shoes or some new clothes for one of them. Poor Mrs. Muncie, you know she can't stitch a lick, you would think with all those children she would have learned by now, but I have seen some of her attempts and it's... Well, let's just say at least she tries hard and her cooking makes up for her lack of sewing."

"Your Papa does stay busy with the Muncie's. That's for sure."

"Mr. Muncie needs to send Jammer to Papa so he can teach him how to make shoes; that would be a good trade for him," Serina added.

Jammer was the Muncie's third child, he and Amil were good friends, he was tall like Amil, but stockier built. He and Amil were the same age and also shared the same birthday, the midwife always remarked that it was a good thing the two had been such easy births or "Ole Doc Quially would have had his hands full."

When Serina got home, she put the little stone on her dressing table before going out to the shop to help her father finish his work for Mr. Muncie.

That night after supper, Serina cleaned the kitchen then ran to her bedroom, snatched up the green stone from her dressing table and headed for the front door telling her father she was going to koori's house and promising to be back early.

Pausing, as she opened the door, Serina looked at her companion, who was curled up comfortably on a cushion near the fireplace.

"Come on Samone you lazy cat," she said, "if you're going with me, I'm in a hurry and I don't have time for your dilly-dallying about."

The cat got to her feet, slowly stretched her large body as if to say she never hurried for anyone then walked over to the door where Serina stood waiting impatiently.

Serina's father watched the two leaving.

Ah, to be young again, he thought with a big grin. He picked up his pipe and placed it in his mouth taking a deep draw, suddenly he felt old. He was getting older he thought; his hair had a hint of gray and he had put on a little weight but he was still in great health. He figured that he was staying too busy to get sick – with the shop and Serina; he did not have time for much else. He could handle the shop pretty well but it wasn't easy raising a young daughter alone.

After a moment, he set his pipe down, reclined in his chair and dozed, dreaming of Senora, his beautiful wife. Although she had been gone since Serina's birth he still missed her dearly. Ah, but in his dreams she was still with him, very much alive, very beautiful, very vibrant, yes… He still had his Senora.

When Samone saw where Serina was going, she drew back, and turned around heading back to the cottage. She was not particularly interested in being Zeb's latest new toy.

"Chicken!" Serina called out when she noticed that Samone was going home.

Koori, who was Serina's best friend, had flaming red hair that was almost as wild and unruly as her own was. With green eyes, she was a little taller than Serina and a little heavier; her creamy complexion, as did her extra weight, came from her staying indoors with her nose stuck in books day in and day out – tonight was no exception. As usual, that's where Serina found her. She was always reading and could probably quote any book or scripture ever written, if truth be told.

"Hey Serina, what are you up to tonight?" Koori said, closing her book and laying it aside. "I know you're here to tell me Amil is in love with you and wants to marry you and have lots of children, right?"

"Koori you are so silly, Amil is not in love with me, he doesn't even know I exist except to pester me."

"Sure Serina, sure. Why do you think he pesters you so all the time?"

"I don't even care Koori; I don't care about him one way or the other."

"Sure you don't."

"Oh stop teasing me, look what I found today!" Serina cut-in pulling the green stone out of her pocket and shoving it in front of Koori's face.

"Ohhhhhhhh! How pretty, where did you find it?" Koori burst out taking the stone from Serina's hand to examine it more closely.

"I found it in the stream just down from the walk bridge this afternoon. Isn't it gorgeous?"

"Oh yes, it's brilliant, it's so shiny and look at all the little cuts in it, they seem to make it catch the light and glitter at any angle."

"I know I can hardly take my eyes off it."

"It's an emerald I think and a very nice one at that," remarked Koori."

"I'm thinking I'll take it over to Mr. Nosh tomorrow and see if he can make a necklace with it, he's very good you know, what do you think?"

"Oh yes, it would make a beautiful necklace, then you could wear it all the time," Koori agreed handing the stone back to Serina.

"I'm so excited I can hardly wait until tomorrow." Serina swirled on her tiptoes holding the stone up to her chest trying to get an idea of what it would look like hanging from her neck. "You can come with me if you can take your nose out of a book long enough to get out of the house. I swear your skin is as white as alabaster, you never get out in the sunshine Koori."

Koori grimaced. "I do other things besides read, you know, I was outside just this afternoon. I helped Mother with the wash, then ran an errand for her, and took care of Zeb all afternoon, so there." She stuck her tongue out wrinkling up her nose at Serina.

Serina giggled and stuck her tongue back at her friend.

"Well, do you want to come with me or not? Then we can go exploring out to where I found the stone. Oh, I almost forgot, I heard a scream or something coming from inside the forest today so maybe we can check out the woods also."

"A scream?" Koori jumped to her feet; suddenly she was all ears and wanted to hear more. "What do you mean, 'a scream'?"

"Well, it sounded like a scream to me but I could have been mistaken, the wind picked up and started blowing real hard about the same time I heard the scream. I never felt the wind blow so hard or so cold before, so maybe it was the wind that just sounded like a woman screaming."

"Serina, you silly gnat, what would a woman be doing out in the forest all alone and why on earth would she be screaming, what woman would it have been anyway?" The questions were rolling off Koori's tongue so fast, they were running together.

"I don't know; like I said it was probably just the wind, it was blowing really hard." Serina flopped down on Koori's bed, tugging at a stray strand of her dark hair in deep thought. "Maybe it was Mrs. Muncie."

Koori laughed. "With all the children she has, I would run out in the woods and scream my head off for sure, from having to tend to that many little ones." Koori scrunched up her face as if she were in agony – Serina was hysterical... She could hardly catch her breath from laughing so hard.

"Shame on you Koori," Serina scolded lightly while regaining a little of her composure. "Mrs. Muncie is a very nice woman and her children are very helpful to her."

"Yeah, just kidding, but they do have a lot of children; its eight now isn't it?

"But it could have been..." Serina paused, her mind going back to something she had heard long ago; but on second thought, she decided to say no more.

"But, but it could have been what?" Koori asked – her curiosity peaked.

"It was nothing, I shouldn't have said anything."

This remark aroused Koori's curiosity all the more, even though she was a book bug she liked mystery and adventure almost as much as Serina did; she just chose to do her exploring through her reading.

"Serina! You've got to tell me now; it's just so unfair to start something then not to finish it. Please, please, please!"

"Okay, okay, I was going to say that a long, long time ago they say a woman was lost in the forest and never found, but I think it's just an old wives' tale."

"That's it – a woman was lost in the woods and they never found her?" Koori exclaimed, her excitement waning. "It was getting interesting for a moment there Serina, I thought there was more to the story than that."

"Well there is, but I don't know the whole story, just that years ago some woman from the village supposedly went to take lunch to her husband, who had been out chopping wood in the forest and when he came home that evening she was nowhere to be found. People got a search party together, but they never found her or any trace of her, the elders say she haunts the forest to this day."

Koori sat listening to Serina; completely entranced by what she had just heard. "How long ago was that?" Koori asked. "I don't recall ever hearing about it... Wait, I do remember hearing something like that but I never really paid any attention to it."

"It was a very long time ago, long before we were born, I think there's only a few of the elders left, who were alive when it happened."

"And they don't know what happened to her?" Koori asked astonished.

"No, they never found out."

"That's so strange."

"Yeah, I guess that's why Papa is forever warning me to stay out of the woods when I'm by myself. But I'm sure it was just an accident whatever it was that happened to that poor woman… Oh well, do you want to go with me tomorrow or not?"

"Okay, I'll go with you but let's see about taking someone else with us into the forest."

"Koori, are you afraid to go into the woods now?"

"No, just cautious, someone has to be – you're surely not."

"And that my friend is why you are my best friend, the best in the whole world," Serina concluded with a big smile.

"Well someone needs to watch out for you, you're always out exploring and getting into things without ever thinking of the consequences."

"Okay Mother Koori, if you're through scolding me I've gotta run, I told Papa I would be home early."

"Well, I'll be waiting for you outside right after breakfast in the morning," Koori said.

"Okay, see ya tomorrow."

With that, Serina was out the door, heading for home in the darkness. She did not realize that there was no moon out nor did she notice the quietness of the night. All she could think about was the pretty green stone resting deep in her pocket.

When Serina climbed into bed that night little did she know that her whole life was about to change.

She had a hard time falling asleep, she tossed and turned and kept thinking about the green stone resting atop her dressing table, the excitement of the day leaving her wide-awake.

Finally, after fighting with the covers for what seemed like hours, sleep overtook Serina and so did the dreams.

Serina dreamt that she was falling off a huge cliff toward a dark pool of water below, falling and falling but never hitting bottom. Then she dreamt of a huge black dragon with long wide wings and yellow eyes chasing her through a strange forest, shooting fiery hot flames from out of his mouth just barely missing her each time. She woke up in a cold sweat. Although it was comfortably warm, Serina was shivering. *That's odd I never dream*, she thought. She sat up staring across the room, straining her eyes in the darkness to see the dial on the big clock on the mantle; it was only three in the morning.

Serina climbed out of bed, walked over to her window and there she sat on the window seat. Her father had built it for her when she was just barely big enough to stand. He said he built it so her feet would not grow tired from standing since this was her very favorite spot in the whole house. She loved to sit on her window seat of an evening, and gaze at the forest toward the mountains beyond. She was drawn to the spot as a moth is drawn to a flame. She would often daydream that she was in danger and a lone knight in shining armor, would come riding up on his steely black stallion and rescue her away from the grips of whatever danger she had encountered. It was such a lovely spot that she sometimes sat for what seemed like hours watching the moon rise and cast down its pale glow over her small village, sending glittering shimmers of light over the mountains and across the forest right into her bedroom window. There was no moon tonight, though. Serina peered into the black sky; it was so dark she could not determine where the forest and mountains ended and where the sky began its rise to the firmament. No, there were no moonbeams shining through her window to dance across her face tonight.

Samone had wakened with Serina but after a few moments of exploring the dark room, she leapt onto her mistress's lap, curled up and fell asleep once again.

A feeling of dread came over Serina as she sat in the darkness. After a few minutes, the heavy feeling lifted, changing to one of excitement as she gazed across the darkened room to where the green gem sat upon her dressing table. She thought of how pretty it was and how she could not wait for morning to come so that she could go to Mr. Nosh's jewelry store.

With that thought, she picked up Samone and went back to bed, diving under the covers with her cat under one arm. Within moments, Serina drifted off to sleep to the sound of her beloved Samone purring contentedly in her arms.

Chapter 2

Morning came early for Serina; she hopped out of bed, ran to the kitchen making breakfast in record time. Her father was already in the shop and hard at work when she called him to the table to eat.

"What's got into you this morning Half Pint?" her father asked when she flopped his breakfast down in front of him hurriedly. "You're whizzing around here like you had a bee in your hair."

"I'm in a hurry Papa, I found this beautiful green stone yesterday and I want to take it over to Mr. Nosh and see if he can make a necklace for me," Serina replied all excited. "That is if you do not need my help in the shop. I will stay if you do, of course. I can always go later."

Her voice lost a little of its eagerness and her face took on a forlorn look unintentionally; this, of course, always melted her father's heart and that's why he had a hard time telling his little girl 'no'.

"No, no, you run along Little Bit, if I need any help I'll get Amil over here. He is a fine young man; he's always eager to help me with anything I ask. A fine young man, he is indeed, that Amil. I think he and Jammer are supposed to come this morning anyway to pick up those shoes we finished last night for Mr. Muncie."

"Papa you need to teach Jammer how to make shoes. With seven brothers and sisters his father would come out ahead for one of his own to make their shoes instead of paying you to do it for him," Serina explained as she dashed around the kitchen with a dirty pot in her hand; she was in such a flurry, she almost forgot to wash it before putting it away.

"You know if I didn't know better, I'd think you were trying to put me out of business Half Pint, why Mr. Muncie is half my business, besides he pays me in meal and vegetables most the time anyway," Mr. Zimmer chuckled.

"Oh Papa you mustn't tease me like that," Serina mused. "Have you seen my apron?"

Serina stood in the middle of the kitchen scratching her head.

"You mean the one you are wearing or, are you talking about another one?"

"Oh Papa!" Serina looked down at the apron tied around her waist then back at her father who was watching her with one eye cocked.

"Yes, that would be the one; I forgot I had it on."

They both had a good laugh then he picked up his fork digging into his breakfast with gusto. "I guess I'd better eat my breakfast before you wash the plate with my ham and eggs still on it."

After breakfast Serina finished cleaning up the kitchen then, without hesitation, she headed for her room. She cleaned and tidied it and quickly changed her clothes before heading for the door not forgetting the stone as she scurried out. She popped the pretty green stone into the pocket of her dress, reached down and patted Samone on the head.

"I'm going to town, maybe I'll go by the fish market, wanna come?"

As if she understood what Serina said, Samone rubbed against Serina's legs stretched and followed her out the door, off to town they went without a backwards glance.

Much too eager to get to Mr. Nosh's jewelry store, Serina almost forgot her friend. She had to double back at the corner down the street from Koori's house, Samone lagged behind looking for a place to wait, not wanting to follow her young mistress to her friend's house.

"What's the matter with you Samone?" Serina asked when the cat stopped by a tree at the corner of the path.

"You're just a scaredy-cat aren't you? Afraid of a little boy like Zeb – well stay here and I will be right back."

Serina left her cat sitting against a tree and hurried back to Koori's house, she ran into the house nearly out of breath rushing Koori who was not even dressed yet.

"I can't believe you're not dressed Koori, it's getting late and I want to catch Mr. Nosh before he gets too busy."

Serina was a little putout with her friend, but flopped down in a chair in the corner while Koori dressed and combed her hair.

"I had to feed Zeb his breakfast this morning while Mom ran over to Mrs. Wilber's – false labor though. She's not due for a few more weeks but she thought for sure the little tike was coming this morning, and since this is her first baby she doesn't know what to think, every time she has a pain she thinks the baby's coming."

"Poor woman, I was by there just the other day and she was in a dilemma about what to name the baby, Peter if it's a boy and Petunia if it's a girl or should she name it Joel after Mr. Wilber and so on and so on, a very undecided woman," Serina said and Koori agreed wholeheartedly.

"She's very sweet but a little slack in the head area when it comes to some things wouldn't you say... Okay I'm ready to go."

"Well it's about time," said Serina, who was already at the door. The two girls took off out the front door at a hard run Samone joining them at the corner.

They arrived at Mr. Nosh's in less than five minutes only to find a note on the door saying the shop would be closed all day.

"What?" Serina exclaimed. "Oh no!" She slid down the wall; there she sat on the edge of the windowsill with her head in her hands.

"Now what?" Koori asked in dismay. When Serina didn't answer right away, she sat down beside her on the sill. "You know," Koori said after a bit, "We could still go down to the stream so you could show me where you found the stone. Maybe we could play around in the water some too."

"Okay, but I was so hoping to show Mr. Nosh this stone, I wonder where he has gotten off to anyway." She was peering through the shop window trying to see if anyone was inside.

"Who knows, he may be helping Mr. Figgs in his field today. You know he helps him quite often when the crops are ready to harvest," Koori suggested.

Serina stood up to leave along with her friend; suddenly a smile crossed her face.

"We can go explore around in the forest, maybe we will find something interesting or we could go down to the falls; it's so beautiful there... I could just stay there forever and ever and ever and ever."

"I get the picture Serina, okay!" Koori shrieked, putting her hands to her ears.

They headed off in a skip toward the creek and to the footbridge where Serina found her treasure the day before.

"Right over here is where I found the stone." Serina hopped down into the stream by the rock she had been sitting on the day before.

"Ooh the water feels great," Koori sighed as she stepped into the cool stream just behind Serina. "Let's look around; there may be more stones in the water." Koori was trying to take Serina's mind off Mr. Nosh.

They searched around in the shallow water in hopes of finding something else; they moved and picked up small rocks that caught their eye, giving each one a good look in hopes of finding another unusual stone.

At last giving up the idea of finding any more stones, Serina asked Koori if she wanted to head into the forest and look around some. "I'll show you where I saw the pretty butterfly yesterday, its color was very unusual, I never saw one like it before, it was blue and yellow and had wings this wide." She held her hands out about eight inches apart to Koori.

The two girls took off into the forest along the trail where Serina had entered it the day before. She went into the forest so often she had her own little path worn into the grass.

Suddenly Koori remembered what Serina had told her about hearing something in there. "Now tell me again Serina, what exactly was it that you said you heard yesterday?" She had stopped walking and was waiting for Serina to start talking.

"Oh, it was nothing, I tell you, but the wind. Come on let's hurry so we can go to the falls when we're through, I want to go swimming." Koori's love of swimming overrode any fear she had about hearing some old noise.

The falls was a beautiful sight indeed the water cascaded from about a hundred and fifty feet down the side of the mountain and flowed into the stream that ran through the forest. It was the same stream that ran close by the village; the one in which Serina found her stone. There was a family of Macaws, who lived in the trees by the stream; their colors of red, blue and yellow, were so vivid that they never failed to captivate Serina's full attention, at least for a moment or two. They charmed her with their tweeting and their dancing around in the tall trees. She even gave each of them a name.

"I love it here," Serina shouted as she dipped the tips of her toes into the water testing its warmth.

"I know," Koori replied. "You could stay here forever and ever and ever and ever," she added mocking her friend's own words.

"Yes, I could, I love it so."

The girls took a long swim, splashing and playing in the water, seeing who could hold their breath the longest as they took turns plunging deep down to the bottom of the pool. Serina beat Koori by a good twenty-five seconds every time.

"When it comes to swimming Serina you're like a fish, I think you could out-swim anybody, hands down, except Amil. I think he's pretty good, you know."

Koori laughed when she saw Serina emerging from the depths of the waterfalls from one of her lengthy underwater excursions. *She is a good swimmer,* she thought, on top of the water or underneath. She could stay underwater longer than anyone around. This, she thought, must come from all the running around and exploring she does – she was always out doing something.

"In fact if the truth be known, I would think you're part fish Serina. If anyone ever checked your family heritage they would probably find out that the roots of it came right up from out of this stream," Koori went on laughing.

"You think so, huh?" Serina chuckled and then catching Koori off guard ducked her under the water, quickly swimming off before she had a chance to pop back up out of the water. She climbed up on the bank of the stream waiting for her friend. After slipping into her summer dress once again, she headed toward the edge of the trees where the family of Macaws lived.

"Come on Koori don't be so slow, let's check out this opening at the side of the mountain I found a few weeks ago, it's really neat and has a big bench like rock inside there that you can sit on."

Koori swam toward the bank where Serina had climbed out. "I wouldn't be so slow if you hadn't ducked me." Finally, she made it out of the water, following Serina into the edge of the cave.

"It's odd; no one has ever noticed this place before, as much as we play around here too... See, here right behind these bushes is the opening, and it's big inside too," Serina said excitedly.

"See..."

Samone had disappeared right after the girls headed into the forest, most likely, she went mouse hunting again but she suddenly appeared at Serina's feet, she dashed into the cave ahead of the girls eager to explore new territory.

"I don't know about this place," Koori said looking around as she entered the cave.

"It seems – well, awfully spooky to me. I feel like someone or something is watching me, don't you feel it?"

The two had made it just inside the entrance – where Koori stopped, not wanting to go any farther inside.

Serina walked over toward a rock bench and stood still for a moment. Very quietly, she looked around the dark cave listening for anything peculiar. She looked back at Koori who was still standing at the opening of the cave.

"I don't feel anything, I think you're just imagining things, you know how bad you're afraid of the dark, besides stuff like that is only in those books you read, come on in, your eyes will get accustomed to the dark in no time then it won't be so bad," Serina urged.

Koori inched her way deeper into the cave and came to stand next to Serina. She latched on to her friend's arm with both hands but refused to look around. Instead, she stared transfixed at the stone bench beside them. It was about waist high and was probably six feet long and three feet wide, it had a smooth table-like surface but the rest of the stone was very rough looking as though it had been chiseled right from the side of the mountain. Yet, someone had taken special care to flatten and polish its surface.

"Well, now that I'm in here I realize something Serina."

"What's that?"

"That I *really* do not like this cave, it's eerie."

"Oh Koori, you're so silly sometimes."

"Well, let's go anyway. My stomach is growling and it's way past lunch. Mother will be wondering what happened to me since we didn't tell her – or anyone else for that matter – where we were going."

Serina had just laid her hand on the big flat rock and was about to pull herself up on it when Koori gave her arm a hard yank pulling her away from the stone bench.

"Don't sit on that," Koori exclaimed breathlessly. "It could be some hidden altar to the Gods who will be awakened from their long deep sleep as soon as you touch it. And they will swoop down from out of nowhere to take you away, using

21

you for some evil sacrifice, or something." She still had a firm grip on Serina's arm and was now dragging her toward the opening.

"Too late, I've already touched it," Serina teased.

"Serina!"

"Okay, okay," Serina relented.

"Let's go, I'm getting pretty hungry myself, we can come back later."

Serina stopped just short of the opening to the cave where Samone had halted suddenly ahead of her. The cat's hair unexpectedly stood up on her back and she screeched loudly taking off out of the cave in a run.

"That's eerie," said Serina, still looking all around inside the cave.

"Yeah," Koori agreed. "The cat agrees with me, she thinks we have no business in this place and should get the heck out of here."

"No Koori, I just got the weirdest feeling – weird."

"What's weird?"

"Oh, it's... I don't know... It's just that, well I... Well, I just felt like I have been here before."

"You have... You said you found this place a few weeks ago, now let's go."

"Yes, but I don't mean recently, I mean a long time ago. It's strange though I don't remember ever knowing about this place before a few weeks ago but it seems so familiar all of a sudden."

"Oh, that's strange huh? But, me getting the feeling like some one is watching me is my imagination... Yeah, I can see the difference all right," Koori said in a huff, a little putout by this time.

"Oh Koori, I'm so sorry, don't be mad."

They ducked out of the cave heading back to the village. Serina stopped outside the entrance of the cave, giving it one last glance before leaving.

She found Samone at the front door when she got home and as soon as Serina opened the door, the cat ran in and disappeared under her father's large over stuffed chair.

"What's got into you, Samone?" Serina said, laughing at her cat's odd reaction. "Did you feel it too, or was it just our imagination?"

She bent down and pulled her cat out from under the chair, stroking her in her arms for a moment but Samone jumped out of her arms and headed back under the chair, not wanting anything to do with Serina.

"Oh, so now you are going to gang up against me with Koori, is that it? The both of you are nothing but big sissy-babies, that's what you are," Serina teased as she headed for the kitchen.

After lunch, her father went back to his shop and Serina set about doing her chores, which she had let slide earlier; the stone and cave temporarily forgotten.

Chapter 3

Early the next morning Serina took the green stone to Mr. Nosh leaving it with him so he could fix it up for her. She wanted it put on a leather strap of some kind, so she could wear it around her neck. He asked her to give him about three days to allow him the time he needed to make her a nice necklace.

The next few days were busy ones for Serina. She had a lot of work to do around the house and in the shop helping her father with another big shoe order. It seemed that, at this time of year, everyone needed a new pair of shoes.

The third day at lunch her father asked her to deliver a pair of shoes to Mr. Koken at the edge of the village.

"May I pick up my necklace from Mr. Nosh too? It should be ready. Oh, and after the delivery, can I go swimming? I'm through with all my chores and could sure go for a cool dip."

"Well, if you get Koori or some of your other little friends to go with you I don't see why not, enjoy the rest of the day and I will even fix supper tonight. How's that for a change?" her father offered with a big grin.

Serina jumped up from the table grabbed her father around the neck as he was putting the last bite of his apple pie into his mouth nearly knocking his fork from his hand. "That's a wonderful idea Papa."

"Why, you act like I never do anything to help around the house young lady, I should be hurt."

"Oh no, Papa… It just means I don't have to be back too early."

"Oh I see, so you really do like my cooking, and all along I thought you hated it."

"Right Papa, you're a wonderful cook and I love you very much."

In reality, her father was a terrible cook but she would not tell him so. He always overcooked everything, burning it to a crisp, except for his chicken stew, which was absolutely the best stew she ever put in her mouth. She did not know what he put in it, but it was great whatever it was.

"Maybe you could make some of your chicken stew; you know how I love it," Serina yelled back as she ran out the door.

At Mr. Nosh's Serina squealed with glee when she saw the necklace the jeweler made for her.

"Oh, Mr. Nosh it's absolutely the most beautiful thing I ever saw."

"Well I had a beautiful stone to work with my dear; I never saw one so perfect as this one before. It's absolutely flawless – a beautiful emerald indeed. Where did you say you found it again?"

"Down by the walk bridge in the stream."

"I see, well I hope you enjoy it for a long time, dear."

Serina found Koori in the bookstore after lunch; she was buying a new set of Dey Day books (her favorite author).

She wanted to show Koori her necklace, now that it was finished.

"Mr. Nosh agreed with you," said Serina, once she got her friend's attention away from the books. "He said it is definitely an emerald; he said it was the most perfect one he's ever seen. It was flawless, he said."

"Yeap, that's what I thought, it reminds me of one I read about a long time ago. I can't remember exactly what it was now, but it will come to me – something about a king of some foreign country… Oh well."

"Hey, you want to go swimming?"

26

"Not today I have to baby-sit my little brother while Mother goes over to Mrs. Wilber's, she had her baby last night and Mother is going over at one to relieve Mrs. Hans," Koori replied with a sigh. "That's why I'm getting these new books so I will have something to do while she's gone... Sorry."

"What did Mrs. Wilber have?"

"A boy; and she has decided to name him after Mr. Wilber after all."

"So we have a little Joel now huh? Is he as bald as Mr. Wilber?" Serina asked with a giggle.

"Yep," Koori replied giggling too. "Not a hair on his little pink head, maybe the two of us can go over tonight after supper and see him, he is so cute, what do you think?"

"Great idea, I'll meet you at your house, Okay?"

"Okay, I'll see you tonight. Oh, by the way, I think Jammer and a few others are down at the stream by the bridge playing around, if you hurry they may still be there."

Serina headed toward the bridge where she found the gang splashing and playing in the warm water, she joined in the fun until they all had to leave around three.

She then climbed out of the water to soak up the sun on her favorite rock – the very rock she sat on the day she found the emerald. Remembering the stone, she dug it out of her bag and held it up against the rays, watching it glitter in the afternoon sunlight. Mr. Nosh had braided thin leather straps around the stone to hold it in place then attached it to a long leather strap that went around her neck.

Serina lay on the rock for a few minutes not thinking of anything in particular while enjoying the afternoon sun and dozing off and on.

She first heard it from the edge of the forest – a low weeping sound. Instantly she sat up straining her ears to find where it was coming from. She put the stone around her neck, jumped off the rock and headed for the edge of the forest. After taking a few steps into the trees, she stopped and listened again. The sound seemed to be coming from a very large tree a little farther into the woods. Serina walked in the direction of the big tree and stopped to listen again. The sound was getting louder but still seemed to come from some distance away; *it was definitely a human sound*, Serina thought, as she crept farther into the woods. Then she saw her, standing by a large weeping-willow tree.

"Hello!" Serina spoke softly at first, but when the woman did not respond, she spoke a little louder. "Hello, are you alright?"

Before Serina could take another step, the woman hurried away without turning to face Serina.

"Wait... Don't run away... Please!" Serina ran after the woman but could not catch up with her. She soon lost sight of her as she vanished into the thick lush forest. Serina wondered around for a few more minutes looking for the woman but did not see her.

"I wonder who she is and why on earth she would up and run away like that," Serina considered as she followed the woman's trail and before she knew it, she was at the waterfalls. She stepped down to the edge of the stream of water and dipped a foot into the cool blue liquid.

"Ah," she sighed, sitting down on the bank of the stream. She stuck one foot then the other into the water and let out another long sigh. This truly was her most favorite place to be.

Across the stream up a little ways, she caught a glimpse of something moving just inside the tree line – it was the woman she saw earlier. Serina jumped up and ran down to the shallow part of the stream, where she always crossed over and jetted across the large rocks that protruded from the water to the other side, but she lost sight of the woman in the process. She ran to the tree line where she had last observed the mysterious woman but there was no sight or sound of her – nothing. Serina edged along the trees looking everywhere.

"Hello!" Serina yelled out then listened for a moment, but all she could hear, was the call of the Macaws in the overhead branches. She realized where she was as she inched her way toward the opening of the cave. She hesitated only briefly before entering the mouth of the cave.

"Hello," Serina said again hearing only the sound of her own voice echoing through the cave – apparently, it was larger than she first thought. Serina yelled out again a little louder this time, just to hear her own voice echoing off the walls.

"Hello," replied a soft voice suddenly. Serina nearly jumped out of her skin as she whirled around toward the voice.

"Hello, wh-who are you?" Serina asked in a shaky voice. She realized for the first time in her life she was actually scared. "Wh-where do you c-come from?"

The questions kept rolling off her tongue non-stop. "I don't know you, do I? You're not from my... my... v-village are you?"

Serina slowly stepped toward the woman and then stepped back, she was not certain of what to do next. The woman backed away as though she were as much afraid of Serina as Serina was of her. She was very beautiful with long black wavy hair and dark eyes.

It suddenly struck Serina who the woman looked like, HER, only all grown up.

"Do... Do I know you?" Serina asked nervously.

"Yes... I mean no." The woman spoke softly, dropping her gaze to the dirt floor.

"What do you mean?" Serina pried

"This is very hard to explain," the woman said in a tender voice, returning Serina's steady gaze.

She did not know if she could go through with this or not, it was going to be more difficult than she thought... But no, this had to be done, she had to quit fooling herself, there was no other way and she knew it.

"I knew you a long time ago."

"Really, I don't know you, where do you know me from because I have never seen you in my village before."

The woman swallowed hard and continued. "I was there the night you were born... But I, I never really knew you or spent time with you – except in my dreams," she whispered quietly.

"What are you talking about – 'your dreams'?"

"Yes Serina, in my dreams."

"How do you know my name?" Serina asked bewildered.

"This is going to be very difficult for you child but you must believe me in what I am about to tell you."

The woman paused for a long moment then continued in an unsteady voice. "I... I... a... I am..." Pausing again, she gazed at Serina with a troubled look on her face. Serina thought she noticed little beads of perspiration pearling on her forehead.

"I am your mother." She spoke so softly Serina could barely hear her, she could have sworn she heard the woman say she was her mother. Serina had to grab on to the wall to keep from falling.

"You're who?" she blurted out in shock. She was staring at the woman almost in trance by this time.

"I... am your mother Serina... you're growing up so nicely and you're so beautiful, my little Serina."

"I don't believe you, YOU'RE NOT MY MOTHER!" Serina spat at the woman. "My mother is dead. She died when I was born... how, how do... why are you saying these things?"

The woman stepped toward Serina with an outstretched hand but Serina stepped back.

"Please, don't be frightened I will not hurt you... Oh the emerald, I see you're wearing it."

Serina was backing up along the wall trying to put some distance between her and this strange woman when she tripped over a small rock. She lost her balance falling over backwards hitting her head on the hard ground – being stunned for a moment. This gave the woman time to get to Serina and offer her a hand up but Serina refused scooting back a foot, or so, away from her. The woman withdrew her hand and backed away from Serina giving her room to get to her feet by herself.

"I understand how confusing this all must be to you, but you must believe me when I say I'm your mother Serina," the woman went on in a soft floating voice. "There's so much I want to tell you – if you would only listen to me... Please."

Serina dusted herself off and shook her head to remove the dirt in her hair but this made her a little dizzy. She grabbed hold of the wall for support again, trying to steady herself, never taking her eyes off the woman.

"When you found the emerald did you hear anything?"

Serina thought about the day she found the stone. "No, why do you ask?" she lied.

"Are you sure?"

"Yes... No, I mean yes, I did hear something but it was just the wind... I think."

"A woman's scream maybe?"

"Yes, how did you know?" Serina asked, being past bewilderment and falling fast into wondering if she was dreaming... "It was the wind, howling through the trees..."

"I was there watching you from just inside the forest, you had on a beautiful blue frock, am I right?"

"I guess so, I don't remember."

"I knew when you found the Emerald that all was not lost, the Dark Lord has made his plans but now with your help we can change everything."

"What's your name?" asked Serina; although she was trying to sound strong, her voice came out squeaky and weak.

"Senora."

There was nothing but silence for a moment then Serina spoke up, her voice echoing in the cave. "I don't believe you. My father said my mother died during the night right after I was born, why would he lie about it?"

"He's right in a way... I did die the night you were born – but not like you think, not physically anyway. I died inside."

"You're not making any sense now, either you died or you didn't die. Are you a ghost?"

"No Serina, I am not a ghost. I am very much alive," the woman said with a smile. "Your father does not know that I am alive."

"This does not make any sense, why make us think you are dead, if you truly are my mother that is – not that I believe you," said Serina adamantly.

She was confused about the whole thing and certainly not believing a word this strange woman spoke.

"Please, I have only a few minutes, you must believe what I say is true or all will fail." She sighed deeply and backed up to sit on the stone bench in the middle of the room. "I know I would have a hard time believing this story also, if I were you, but what I am telling you is the truth... The night you were born I was taken away and replaced with a corpse of myself for burial purposes only." She was talking faster now her words seemed to run together – none of which made sense to Serina.

"What do you mean corpse... taken away... I don't understand what you're saying?"

"Listen to what I have to say... I know this is hard but just listen and let me finish. Your world is different now, different than it used to be. A long time ago evil lurked around everywhere and it was starting to get out of hand, the elders tried everything they could think of to stop it – to no avail. Things just got worse with each passing day... Then one day the Dark Lord offered a compromise. He offered to pull his dark forces away forever if they would do one thing – that they did, and have kept their end of the bargain and so has he – but now, now the time has come for the Dark Lord to collect his prize."

"You're talking a bunch of nonsense," Serina interrupted. "You think I believe one word of what you're saying? There is no such thing as 'dark forces' and if you call a little mischief once in awhile from some of us kids evil, well then, you're nuts," Serina concluded in a huff.

She was still standing near the entrance of the cave thinking of her quickest way of escape if she had to get away. And, judging from the way this woman was talking she had to get away, and get away soon.

"I know it's hard for you but please listen... Please."

"Okay, I'm listening but that doesn't mean a thing; I just don't want to be rude."

That really wasn't true; Serina, although scared out of her wits, for some reason, was hooked on every word this crazy woman was saying.

"Anyway what the Dark Lord wanted was the first born girl child, born on the first of May at the stroke of midnight but it had to be when there was a full moon and the baby had to come breech – you know feet first… Also, the baby had to have eyes the color of midnight. Well, the villagers were all in a tizzy. However, the Dark Lord pointed out to them how rare this occasion would be and if they really wanted to get rid of the evil in their village, this was a small sacrifice to pay indeed. So, they all agreed with his proposal, the Dark Lord pulled out his forces and disappeared. Everything went just fine for years. After a while, the people forgot about the agreement they had made with the Dark Lord – until one warm bright night almost twelve years ago, when you were born. I was having some trouble and the midwife told me you were coming breech. She was ranting and raving – pleading was more like it – with someone or something, I did not know which, at the time. She told me, that night, about the agreement with the Dark Lord; I thought it was just an old wives' tale. But little did I know how wrong I was until after you were born – at the stroke of midnight – my whole world changed in an instant…" The woman stopped abruptly.

"I can't go into it anymore right now – I have to go – but I had to see you up close just once… To see if there was any chance to change the future… To see if you would allow me to talk with you and tell you of a plan I have."

"But wait," Serina cried out. "What happened? You can't just finish your story like that; you've got to tell me." She stood still staring at the woman with her mouth wide-open.

She didn't know why, but, *she believed her*! "What… Where are… Wait… Where are you going?" Serina yelled in astonishment. "You can't just leave… Why are you leaving?"

"If I am caught all will be lost, and I will surely die this time but I will return in one week at the same time and I will meet you here at the cave... Promise me you will be here – at four o'clock, everything depends on you Serina – Please... And Serina, you cannot tell anyone, not even your father; he must not know... Promise me."

"I promise," Serina murmured.

"Now you must go and I will see you here in one week... Go."

Serina backed out of the cave and headed toward the shallow end of the pool leading into the stream, she was almost at the trees where the Macaws lived then she suddenly turned around and ran back into the cave.

"Miss... Hello..." The cave was empty, no sign of the woman – only her words echoing around her. *Where did she go?* She searched the cave but there was no other exit in the cave!

That's odd... "HELLO... WHERE D'YOU GO?"

Serina then ran out of the cave looking everywhere but no sign of the woman.

All the way home, she kept looking behind her, every so often, trying to catch a glimpse of the woman but she did not see her again. By the time she got to the bridge at the stream, she was beginning to think she had imagined it all.

"I must be mental," Serina kept saying aloud. "There's no woman back in the cave, if there was, where did she get off to when I went back in there? It makes no sense at all, and I never heard of such a story as the Dark Lord and all that rubbish... Serina you're losing your mind that's all there is to it." She kept talking to herself all the way home more to keep from hearing anything else – like *other* voices – than to try and make sense of what had happened.

At supper that night, Serina was very quiet, deep in thought about the weird events of the day – not knowing if she should broach the subject with her father or keep quiet about the whole thing. The woman did ask her not to say anything to anyone but what if she was not real, or... more importantly, what if she was this evil Dark Lord, she was talking about? Serina was surely having doubts about the whole thing.

"Half Pint... Where in this world is your mind tonight? Did you not hear a word I just said to you?" her father said loudly, snapping Serina back to the present.

"Sorry Father, what did you say?"

"You don't seem yourself tonight... Is there anything wrong, or are you feeling well, you're not getting sick are you - or is it my cooking?"

"No, the dinner is great and I'm fine... I'm just a little tired I think I over-did it today. Do you care if I turn in early tonight?"

"You go on to bed and don't worry about the dishes; I'll tidy up for you... You're not feverish are you? Come, let me check you."

Serina obediently let her father feel her forehead for any sign of fever, although she knew there was no fever. After he gave her the okay, she kissed him on the cheek, said goodnight and went to her room. At the door she turned back to face her father.

"When was I born Papa?"

"Serina you know when you were born, surely."

"No, not the year or the day, what I mean is... What time of the day or night was I born?"

Her father thought about it for a moment then said, "Late in the night, if I remember correctly. Yes, you were born at night, why all of the sudden interest?"

"Oh, no reason in particular, just curious that's all. Well goodnight again Papa..." Then Serina paused... "Was it midnight?"

"Yes, I believe it was, if I remember right, just at the stroke of midnight you came bouncing out and haven't stopped yet. Now what's with all the questions? Is it because your birthday is coming up in a few weeks?" Her father chuckled.

"No, just curious," she replied softly.

"Okay then, off with ya so I can clean up this mess."

Once in her room Serina did not go straight to bed, she paced around the room trying to figure out what her next move should be. Everything kept running through her head all jumbled together. It didn't make sense, none of it; now that she had time to think about it. *What did she mean by the 'dark forces' and such ... a full moon ... darn...* She should have asked her father if it had been a full moon. Where was he when all this took place? Her father would have to have known all about this, wouldn't he?

Serina took a quill and piece of paper from her table and sitting down on her window bench, started writing down everything she wanted to ask this strange person – if she showed up that is. She wondered if she should tell Koori, her best friend and how she would react to the story if she did tell her – but she couldn't. The woman said not to say anything to anyone.

Samone was curled up on the bed; she had ignored Serina all evening. Evidently, she was perturbed at being left behind that morning.

"I'm sorry Samone but you would have just got scared and run home to hide under Papa's chair again."

Serina finished her list then went to bed, when her head hit her pillow she found it hard to go to sleep but sleep did come eventually. She dreamt of some dark hooded man with no face carrying her off on the back of a huge flying dragon into the clouds toward the mountains over the waterfalls, where she played. He was laughing – he had an evil menacing laugh as they flew through the night. She suddenly woke up in a cold sweat with a terrible feeling of dread.

Chapter 4

Serina did not go near the forest or the stream for the next week. She even managed to keep her secret from her best friend. Although she wanted to tell her, and everyone else for that matter, she managed to keep, what happened at the cave, all to herself.

The week went along uneventfully except for the dreams. Each night the dreams were the same – this no-face-evil cloaked man on the back of a huge menacing looking dragon with bright yellow eyes was carrying her far, far away into the clouds toward the mountains in the distance. He never spoke to her. He just laughed – a demonic laugh – as he carried her away into the night.

When Tuesday came, she found herself getting more nervous than ever; forgetting stuff and dropping things. Tomorrow she would go and meet *her...* She could not bring herself to call the woman 'Mother' but she could not call her 'Senora' either. She would just call her 'the strange woman' for now, because she was strange, all of this was strange to Serina.

That night she could barely eat supper, her stomach was in knots and she had developed a rather large headache that seemed to grow more painful by the minute. Mr. Zimmer looked on his daughter with concern.

"What's with ya Half Pint? You sure you're not coming down with something?"

"No Papa, I'm fine honest... I'm just... I'm just not hungry I guess."

"Well you need to eat something to keep your strength up so you won't get sick, okay?"

"Yeah, I guess you're right, maybe a little bit of something will do me good."

Serina ate a few more bites of her Shepard's pie then shoved her bowl away excusing herself from the table.

Later that night, after the kitchen was cleaned up, Serina drew water from the barrel out-back to take a long bath. Afterwards she climbed into bed with mixed feelings about the next day. She was dreading it and looked forward to it at the same time. Her mind was just a jumble of thoughts.

Only a fool would be looking forward to meeting with a strange woman who has changed your whole world in a flash with just a few words, Serina thought as she drifted off to sleep finally, sometime after midnight.

She kept waking up throughout the night between fitful dreams and feelings of someone lurking in the shadows of her room. Once, she even thought she felt the warm breath of someone leaning just above her. She rose quickly, looking around the room for the culprit but no one was there.

"You've got to get a hold of yourself you little nitwit," she said to herself rather loudly. She uttered the words in order to convince herself that she was awake and not dreaming. She lay back down but could not go back to sleep, the clock on the mantle read 4:30AM. She shoved back the covers, stood and stretched her arms toward the ceiling – maybe a snack and a glass of milk would help her to fall back to sleep.

She went into the kitchen, made a sandwich and poured a glass of milk. She was hungrier than she realized since she had not eaten much of her supper. The food seemed to help somewhat because Serina fell right to sleep after she climbed back into bed and pulled the covers up to her nose.

She slept in later than usual the next morning and when she climbed out of bed her father already had breakfast on the table.

"Good morning Sunshine," her father piped as she walked through the kitchen door. He had all kinds of nicknames for her. He very seldom called her by her given name, most of the time it was Half Pint or Pea Wee or Little Bit.

"Good morning Papa, how are you this morning or need I ask?"

"Oh, just fine and dandy, Half Pint. How did you sleep? You look a little better this morning than you did last night I must say." He was hardly giving Serina time to answer.

"You sure are bubbly this morning, what's up?" Serina asked curiously.

"Funny you should ask, I nearly forgot, today is our annual clean out day... Ooh, by the look on your face, I see you forgot also."

Oh no, Serina thought, *'clean out day'* – that meant cleaning out the shop from top to bottom, getting rid of all the old shoes and 'mistakes' laying around. They would be dusting and cleaning anything and everything that existed in the shoe shop; this usually was an all day job. How was she going to get away to go to the forest today? She needed some excuse to get out of the cleaning early – she had to think of something fast.

"What did you say, Papa?" Serina asked snapping back to the present.

"I said Amil is bringing his cousin and Jammer with him to help out."

Taking a piece of toast and sitting down to her breakfast, Serina tried to think of some excuse to leave early so she could get out to the forest by four o'clock.

The guys did all the heavy work and the rearranging while Serina was left to doing the dusting and some light work. They worked until lunch and Serina fixed sandwiches for everyone then was left with cleaning the kitchen while her father and the boys went back to work. This was her chance, she thought – after the dishes were cleaned and put away.

It was only one o'clock but that would give her three hours before her meeting. It only took her about thirty minutes to get to the falls, so she had to kill some time before she left. She asked her father if she could be excused for the rest of the day to run some errands and go see Mrs. Wilber's new baby. She hated lying to her father. She had never lied to him before, and felt terrible about it.

"Oh sure, go on Half Pint, you worked hard this morning and there's just a few things left to do anyway, me and the boys can take care of the rest. Oh, and tell Mrs. Wilber congratulations for me, will you?"

"Are you sure Papa?"

"I'm sure, we can handle the rest of the work; you go on and enjoy yourself."

"Thanks Papa," Serina said and headed back into the house. She cleaned some of the dust and grime off herself and then changed her clothes.

Well, she thought, *it won't be a complete lie, I'll go to see the new baby, that will help me kill a little time then I'll head for the cave.* She felt a little better about the lie she told her father but the whole thing kept nagging at her. Keeping something this big from her father made her feel awful.

She made sure Samone was locked up in the house before she left, knowing the feline was going to be mad for leaving her behind again, but she knew Samone did not like going to the cave.

At the Wilber's she met Koori and her mother just leaving.

"Come by when you leave and we can go swimming or something," Koori suggested excitedly.

"Oh, I can't Koori; I have other chores to do sorry," murmured Serina not able to look her friend in the eye as she spoke – *I am lying to my best friend now!* – But she couldn't take the chance of Koori finding out about the woman...

At a little after three she bid goodbye to Mrs. Wilber and the new baby and headed for the forest and the cave, trying not to be seen by anyone, especially Koori. She took the back way out of the village and crossed the stream at a shallow spot then headed into the forest at a different place than she usually entered. Not many of the villager's came into the forest from this spot – there was no real trail to follow – so it took Serina a little more time than she planned, putting her at the cave a few minutes after four. She prayed she was not too late. She ran into the cave out of breath.

"H-hello, I'm here... Hello."

No one answered. Serina called out again but no one responded. She turned toward the entrance to leave, thinking she was too late after all.

"Hello Serina," came a soft familiar voice to Serina's ears. She spun around on her heels; the woman was standing at the back of the cave, almost hidden from view.

"Oh, I didn't see you... I thought I was too late," sighed Serina still a little out of breath.

"I was afraid you would not come, afraid you did not believe me but I see I was wrong, you have some of my inquisitiveness and sense of adventure in you. Serina I do not have much time so you need to listen to me carefully, it's of the utmost importance."

Serina took a couple of steps farther into the cave.

"I do not understand what's going on and why all the secrecy... I had to lie to my father for the first time in my life and that did not make me feel very good, so please tell me what's so important."

"Let me start at the beginning... I told you about the Dark Lord and the agreement he made with the villagers, so let's go back to the night you were born... The moment you were born, at the stroke of midnight, a dark mist filled the room and the midwife went screaming out of the room with you cradled in her arms. Your father came rushing into the bedroom and fell instantly to the floor in a deep sleep. I didn't know what was happening and tried to get out of bed but something very heavy seemed to lie over my chest preventing me from getting up... Then he appeared out of nowhere – the Dark Lord with the midwife in tow. She still had you clutched in her arms, so tightly, I feared you might not be breathing. She was still pleading with him, babbling on and on. I could not speak at first. I think I was in shock. Anyway, he moved across the room and took my hand pressing a kiss upon it and the midwife went on screaming something about the kiss of death then passed out falling to the floor beside your father, still cradling you in her arms. I feared for your life not knowing if you were dead or alive. I tried to get out of bed again, tried to get to you and your father but I could not move. Finally *he* spoke. He had an unusually deep whispering voice that gave me cold chills."

Serina stood immobile, dumbstruck with both her mouth and eyes wide open, listening, hanging on every word the woman was saying.

"He informed me of the agreement that he and the villager's had made long before... He was to take the child – you. I could not let that happen, I begged and pleaded with him not to take you but he would not hear of it... He said an agreement was made and there was no going back or his evil forces would be turned loose to reign worse than ever before over the village. I tried to convince him to take me and leave you. I made all kinds of promises, anything to save you from his clutches. Finally, he concluded to leave you and take me but there was a catch to his sudden kindness...   He would take me and let you stay behind only for twelve years, after which he would come for you at midnight on the eve of your twelfth birthday. There was no other way, I had to agree or else lose you forever."

The woman paused looking at Serina earnestly.

"He brought you here to this very cave where he placed you upon this stone bench," she went on but then paused for a moment. She stepped over to the bench placing her hand upon it then withdrew it instantly, as if touching it would burn her flesh.

Serina stood transfixed. She was staring at the woman unable to speak; her birthday was just a few weeks away.

"Once he laid you down on the stone altar he started chanting something in an unknown language, and proclaimed his rights, his right to take you as his bride when you came of age. Then the roof of the cave opened up and a brilliant light came shining down, radiating all around the altar and you. The earth started to tremble as he held his arms up toward the opening then fire shot forth from his fingertips and he fell silent. Then as quickly as it all started, it all stopped; the opening in the roof closed up and he took you and placed you back in your small cradle and took me away."

The woman stopped talking, apparently exhausted.

"If what you say is true, what happened to my father and the midwife that night? They have never mentioned anything like this before, nor has anyone else for that matter."

"The Dark Lord has a lot of powers," the woman sighed shaking her head. "He can do things no one else can do. He is very powerful, he put a hex on them that night, and he changed their memory, to think that I died in childbirth then he replaced me with a body resembling my own. After that, the Dark Lord carried me away on the back of a winged dragon. They buried my double with no one ever knowing the difference."

"Dragon?" Serina perked up suddenly. "Did you say a 'dragon'?"

"Yes, a winged dragon."

"Was it huge, black and did it have large yellow eyes?"

"Yes, very large indeed, both the dragon and its yellow eyes... Do you believe me Serina?" the woman asked softly with a hint of anxiety in her voice.

If Serina was having trouble believing her before, this cinched it, she knew the woman was speaking the truth. All of the dreams she had since she found the stone – and now this. It was all strange, very strange indeed, but she knew the woman was really who she said she was.

"Yes, yes I think I do... It just seems so far fetched."

"Well there's more still, I didn't want to tell you this until last... You were born with a special power that night; it has to do with the circumstances of how and when you were born, the full moon, at midnight, and being born breech – that's why the Dark Lord wanted the first born girl born in this particular way – you have the power to change things."

"What do you mean by *'the power to change things'*?" Serina asked curiously.

"It's in your tears. If one of your tears touches something it will change, to whatever you want it to be, as long as it is for the good. Yet, you will not receive these powers until your twelfth birthday, and now that you have the stone, you will be able to reverse things as well but only in extreme circumstances. There's more but we will not go into it all right now, there are more important things I have to tell you."

What could be more important than having special powers? Serina thought.

"Right now I need to know if I can count on you to help me – everything depends on you Serina. Can I trust you to help me, to help us? It will take a lot of courage. Do you have the courage to go up against the Dark Lord Serina?"

"And do what?" Serina asked nervously, her face suddenly showing the confusion she felt and her voice taking on a shrill tone.

"I know this is a lot to ask a young girl not quite twelve years old yet. Your life has been nothing but childish carefree happiness with no worries or fears and that's a wonderful thing but all of that is about to change, Serina. I can only try to warn you and do my best to prepare you for what's ahead of you but there is nothing I can say or do, that will change what you will soon face. It is inevitable Serina, it is up to you and you alone to stop the horrible life that awaits you, so now do you think you have the courage to go up against this Dark Lord Serina?

"I don't know, I... How? What are you talking about? What do I have to do? What can I do? I am only eleven years old like you said, I don't know anything... Maybe Papa can help, he is very strong and very brave, we can tell him and maybe he can think of something."

"NO Serina," The woman shouted causing Serina to step back in fear."

"I am sorry for raising my voice Serina," the woman said immediately in a lower tone.

It was bad enough that she was about to embark on a terrible journey, she sure did not need to have her newfound mother scaring the wits out of her too.

"It is important that no one finds out, I must warn you to keep everything in complete secrecy. I repeat no one must know what you're doing, it could be very dangerous for anyone who found out, you understand? Very dangerous..."

"Yes, dangerous, I understand," Serina said, but she did not understand anything. What was this crazy woman talking about?

"That's good, now what I need you to..."

"*Hello!*"

Serina and Senora spun around simultaneously toward the cave entrance; the voice came from just outside the cave. *What perfect timing*, Serina thought; *just when I was going to find out what it was the woman wanted.*

"Koori, what in blazes are you doing here?" she asked her friend as she stepped into the cave. Koori squinted upon entering the darkened grotto and placed her hands on either side of her face trying to shade the light from outside so she could see deeper into the cave.

"I was about to ask you the same question Serina. Who were you talking to?"

Serina turned around to face an empty cave, stunned at the disappearance of the woman. She knew she did not leave through the entrance of the cave so where did she go?

"I... I... I...was just talking to myself," she muttered while her heart was slowly returning to normal, if that were possible anymore.

"You scared the begeevies out of me Koori."

"Talking to yourself was ya?"

"Yeah, I... I like to hear myself echo. What brings you out here anyways?" asked Serina. She kept skimming the cave with her eyes while she talked to Koori, she could not imagine what happened to her 'mother', if she dared call her that. It seemed almost impossible to think, to imagine, that after twelve years of being without a mother, in an instant she could have a mother, who was alive and breathing.

"Well I went by your house to get you to come swim with me but your father said you were running errands but you were nowhere to be found, so I figured you were out here at your favorite place and I was right but I could have sworn I heard another voice besides yours in here."

Koori carefully looked around the cave thinking it was haunted or something. She still had not stepped any farther inside. Serina looked around the cave also, paying close attention to the walls, thinking there had to be another exit or something that she had not seen before, of course, that would explain it, there had to be another opening in the cave. She stuck her arm out and swung around in a circle of the cave.

"As you can see I am the only one here so you must be hearing things, maybe the sound of my voice echoing outside sounds different than it really is, I don't know... Let's go for that swim."

Serina grabbed Koori by the arm and pulled her out of the cave.

"Last one in the water has to kiss Frog," Serina yelled. Frog was a friend of Amil's, whose real name was Bud but everyone called him Frog because his voice was changing and it had a deep tone to it and creaked like an ole bull frog when he talked a lot. The two girls took off running toward the water all the while Serina was trying to think of a way to get back into that cave without Koori.

The girls swam for a few minutes then Serina begging off with a headache suggested they call it a day. At the bridge, Serina suddenly remembered her book, or at least that's what she told Koori.

"I'll go back with you."

"Oh no Koori, that's okay it's too far and besides it's getting late, I'll come by tomorrow and we can do something, okay?"

"Sure... Yeah I guess, if you're sure you don't want me to go along, then I'll head home but I don't mind walking back with you."

Serina spoke quickly. "No I'll be fine, you go on."

"Okay, see ya tomorrow."

"See ya," Serina yelled back. She was already heading back into the forest.

Once she was out of her friend's sight, she took off in a hard run all the way back to the cave. With a painful ache in her side, she entered the cave. She bent over and grabbed her knees gasping for breath. After a few moments though, she rose and began looking for some sign of an opening in the walls. Slowly she walked around the entire cave, her hand skimming the wall trying to feel something unusual or out of place. After a few minutes of searching and not finding anything that would even resembled an opening she walked to the stone bench taking care *not* to touch it, there she started looking all over the sides and top hoping to find something but there was nothing. She walked toward the back of the cave, carefully feeling the wall. When she found nothing there, she turned around and leaned up against the damp earthen wall both mentally and physically exhausted from her long run and extensive search of the cave, she closed her eyes and sighed heavily.

"It's no use," she said out loud pounding her fists against the wall and shouting, "I'll never find it."

About that time, Serina felt the earth-wall give way behind her she lunged forward to keep from falling. "What the..." said Serina astonished to see the wall moving apart so soundlessly, it stopped when it had moved far enough apart to let a single person enter. Serina stood still for an instant, not knowing what to do; she was definitely too scared to enter into the opening but if she didn't... Serina stepped toward the opening then stopped, slowly she stuck her head through the gap and what she saw was more than she could have ever imagined. It was like stepping into another world, a world so strange and different – if she dared taking a step – what would happen to her. How would she get back into the cave if the wall closed up behind her? She didn't know what to do, she wasn't even sure how she opened the wall up in the first place, or if she could do it again, for that matter. She pulled her head back and stepped back from the wall to get a better look at it so she could figure out how it opened. As soon as she stepped back, the wall started closing up again. Serina lunged forward but too late; the wall closed up so quickly, she didn't have time to stop it. She then began tapping and passing her hand over the damp wall on which she had been leaning earlier – she could not see anything different in that area of the wall than on the rest of the cave walls. She turned around and leaned on the wall, as she had done previously – nothing.

"That's so weird, why won't you open up again?" she said, slamming both her fist against the wall. Instantly the wall slid open causing her to stumble forward exposing the other side to Serina once again.

"That's it," Serina exclaimed loudly, and then quickly fell silent in case her voice carried into the other side of the cave.

"Serina!"

Oh, no not again, I can't let anyone find me in here. She ran out of the cave and ran slap dab into Amil.

"What are you doing up here?"

"Your father sent me after you, says it's getting late, seems he has to do that a lot lately. I saw Koori, she told me you were doing something and would be along later but knowing how you like to dawdle, I figured you'd be all night."

"Well you scared the begeevies out of me; you know... What if I had a weak heart or something?"

"What were you doing in there anyway?" Amil asked looking past Serina to the entrance of the cave. "What's in there?"

"Oh it's nothing, just an old hole in the mountain, it doesn't go anywhere, come on let's go it's getting late, remember?" Serina urged, grabbing Amil by the hand and dragging him toward the stream, she did not want to show the cave to Amil, it was bad enough Koori knew about it.

All the way home Serina racked her brain as how to get back to the cave and find – *her mother.* She had to meet with her again so she would know what she wanted her to do.

Chapter 5

That night Serina had to make a decision; if she met with the woman there today at four o'clock, chances were that she would be there at the same time tomorrow. She had to find a way to be at the cave the next day at the same time. Then, maybe her *mother* would be back and she would be able to tell Serina what she wanted her to do, if it wasn't too late. Serina slipped into her nightdress and slid in under the covers closing her eyes to the world outside but not to the dreams, for she knew, without a doubt, she would dream…

Sure enough, there on the back of her eyelids, as she drifted off to sleep, was the hooded man flying on the back of the huge dragon with the menacing yellow eyes, swooping down upon her trying to grab hold of her. The creature stretched his enormous claws out, taking hold of Serina. She felt the claws go deep into her back. She bolted upright with a loud scream, wide-awake, startled at the thought of being carried away by the huge creature.

Her father came running into the room, nearly tripping over the trunk at the end of her bed.

"SERINA! Are you all right? What's wrong with you?" His young daughter was shaking and had broken out in a cold sweat.

"I'm f-fine Papa; I just had a bad dream that's all." Her voice had a definite quiver to it. Her father gently took her into his arms cradling and rocking her slowly. She felt a flood of relief invading her. He made her to feel warm and protected once again.

"I'll be alright now Papa; I don't even remember what I was dreaming about anymore," she lied. She was afraid of telling him the horrible details of the dream, although she did feel better, she had not lied about that part. Her father had a magical power also, as all parents do, he could always make things better when she felt bad or was sick, and he always had the right advice for everything.

"Are you sure Half Pint? You want me to stay with you for a little while?" her father asked in his soothing 'I will make it all better' voice.

"I'm sure Papa, but thanks anyway... Goodnight."

"Goodnight Half Pint, but if you need me just call, okay?"

"Okay."

It took Serina a few minutes to fall asleep after her father left the room but this time she did not dream, it was a light uneventful sleep.

For the next three days, Serina went to the cave every day at four o'clock, making sure not to take Samone with her and waited. She would call out for the woman but refrained from opening the wall of the cave; out of fear, more than for any other reason. The woman never showed, maybe she could not come; maybe the Dark Lord found her and punished her or worse still... No... no, she did not want to think of the 'or worse still'. Each day she went to the cave and each night she dreamed the terrible dreams of the Dark Lord without a face and the evil looking dragon.

Serina went about her chores each day in a trance-like state, not paying much attention to anyone or anything, no matter what she did she could not shake the feeling of dread that hung over her like a dark cloud – of course, being unable to share this terrible burden with anyone, made things worse. She had no one to confide in, the woman had not come back to the cave, and she could not talk to her father or best friend... Well it was one thing not to tell her father maybe, but not to tell her best friend in the whole wide world; that was almost criminal. *Knowing Koori,* Serina thought, *if she thinks I'm hiding something from her she will be hurt and probably never forgive me.*

On that particular morning, Serina was sitting at the kitchen table a bowl of cold untouched porridge sitting in front of her, her appetite seemed to have vanished over the last week. With everything that was going on, it was a wonder she could get a bite down at all. Her father popped his head in the kitchen door saying: "Koori is here, Half Pint."

Serina snapped out of her daydream, looking up at her father she gave him a weak smile. When she did not say anything in reply, her father walked the distance between them and felt her forehead.

"What's wrong with you Half Pint? You've been going around this house for the last week like a puppet on a string, are you feeling okay? I sure hope you're not coming down with something."

"I'm fine Papa really."

"I don't know Half Pint, you didn't even touch your breakfast again and hardly touched your supper last night, maybe I should just tell Koori you're not feeling well and put you back to bed."

"No Papa! I'm fine, really... Tell Koori to come in here and I will eat my breakfast," Serina said anxiously. "Please Papa," Serina begged when she saw that her father was hesitating a bit.

"Well I guess it will be okay. But what I really should do is send you over to Doc Quially."

"Look I'm eating... See," Serina said scooping a large bite of porridge into her mouth.

"Okay but if you do not snap out of this gloomy mood you've been in I am taking you to see the doctor."

At that point, Koori came bouncing into the kitchen grabbed a piece of bread spreading a heavy layer of butter over it then picked up the jam. "So, what are you up to today?" she asked as she spread a generous portion of jam over her now heavily buttered bread. "You want to go swimming? Or... I know what... We can go back to the cave if you want and explore around."

"I've got other things to do today Koori, maybe tomorrow okay?"

"You've not been acting like yourself lately Serina, are you okay?"

"Not you too Koori," Serina snapped. "Everyone keeps asking me the same thing. Yesterday Mrs. Kent saw me at the market and asked me the same thing... Are you feeling well dear?" Serina mimicked the older woman almost to a tee. "You look like you're coming down with something dear? She even offered to send over some chicken soup." Serina wrinkled up her face and made a gagging noise.

"Well, if you don't want me around just say so and I'll leave Serina but you do not have to be so rude," Koori snapped back, her feelings apparently hurt.

"I'm sorry Koori, I didn't mean to hurt your feelings, but it's just that, well, I've got a lot on my mind."

"I am your best friend you know, so if you've got something bothering you... Well, you can tell me, that's what friends are for, right?"

Koori was stuffing her mouth with the rest of Serina's porridge; seeing she had pushed it away as soon as her father left the kitchen.

"It's not that easy Koori and besides it's not the kind of thing you tell anyone, it's just something I have to work out for myself."

"You've been avoiding me all week... Heck, you've been avoiding everyone all week but I've seen you head out for the forest every day at about the same time, you haven't even asked me to go along with you... So I know something's up. So now, are you going to tell me – your best friend – or not."

"I can't Koori... You just have to trust me and let me work this out myself."

"Humph, well be thatta way," Koori snarled.

She had started toward the door when she paused, glancing back at Serina. "So, I guess swimming is out of the question, right?"

"Yeah, I guess so." Serina could hear Koori muttering rather loudly; something undistinguishable, all the way to the front door. She did not like lying to Koori but she could not take the chance of her knowing what was going on, it was safer that way, at least for now anyway. She busied herself around the house for the rest of the day, pretending to have many things to do, that way she could stay out of sight, and away from Koori.

She begged off eating lunch, told her father she wasn't feeling well after all and went to her room. She sat at her window looking out over the mountain for a few minutes, and from where she sat she could look over at the stream, she could see where the bridge crossed the stream, also the path that led to the falls and the cave, and wondered who else could see the bridge and path. She knew she had to sneak out the back to avoid anyone from seeing her when she left. She could not take a chance of Koori following her.

She lay across her bed just to rest for a moment, not meaning to, but her eyes grew heavy and before she knew it she was sound asleep, no dreams, no nothing, just quite peaceful sleep, the first she had had in over a week.

At about three o'clock she awoke with a start, checked the time and jumped up off the bed, trying to get her bearings, she felt oddly out of place for a second, as though she were somewhere else, not in her bedroom at all. She took off by the back way and headed into the forest on the trail that was seldom used, going out of her way not to be seen by anyone. She kept looking behind her every so often, making sure she was not followed. *Please be there*, she thought as she neared the edge of the forest, *please*. Somehow, Serina felt that today was going to be different; she had a strong feeling… Today she would find her there in the cave waiting. This made her heart pound so hard; she could hear it beating in her chest. If she didn't know better, she would have sworn it could have been heard ten feet away it was so loud.

When she neared the shallow spot in the stream where the stones lay dotted across the water, she stopped. Was someone behind her? She turned around quickly but it was only a rabbit running across the path.

"Serina, get a hold of yourself," she muttered loudly, she turned back trying to concentrate on crossing over the stones to the other side. She was trembling so badly, she was afraid she would slip off the rocks. Once across the water she ran up the path toward the cave, stopping just outside of the entrance to catch her breath. She stood there for a moment longer than she needed to, trying to get up the courage to enter the cave.

"Serina don't be silly, you've come this far, you can not turn back now," she kept saying to herself. And somewhere in the distance, she could hear her heart beating, it was beating so rapidly, she thought, it was going to explode right inside her chest and she was shaking from head to toe.

She took a step forward then stopped. "Well here goes nothing," she said aloud then dashed into the cave.

It was dark upon entering. She could not see her hand in front of her face. She took a few steps into the cave then stopped until her eyes adjusted to the darkness. Slowly her sight adjusted to her surroundings, she was able to focus, and there she stood – at the back of the cave. "I knew you would be here today, I just knew it," Serina said when she saw the woman looking at her with a slight smile.

"I could not manage to get away before now but hoped you would remember the time we last met and come again," her mother said softly.

"I've come every day since, right at four o'clock and waited for you, hoping you would be here, I was about ready to give up."

"What about your friend?"

"No, I didn't tell her, but she knows something is up. Just today she was questioning me, and I hate lying to her."

"I understand but this is very serious and dangerous Serina, you must believe me."

"I do... I must tell you though that I have been rather puzzled at what is it you need from me? I am just a young girl as I said before; I really don't know what I could possibly do?"

"On the eve of your birthday the Dark Lord will come for you, he will come to take you back to his castle. He will put you in a room he has prepared for you. It is at the top of a tower but not to worry I have a key..."

"Wait! If he is so evil why should I go with him?" Serina asked bewildered.

"You will have no choice, there is no way of escaping him but if you put up a struggle he will make it harder on you, he will punish you and believe me you do not want him to punish you."

"When will he come? How will he co...?" Before the woman had time to reply, Serina answered her own question. "The dragon..."

"That's right; he will arrive at the stroke of midnight. You must be strong Serina, you must be brave – do you think you can do this?"

Serina thought about her dreams. "Does the Dark Lord have a face?" She asked meekly with a slight quiver in her voice. "I mean... Well in my dreams someone comes and carries me away on the back of a dragon; it's a hooded man with no face."

It was the woman who paused this time.

"Yes... He has a face, but hardly anyone sees it; he wears a hooded cloak most of the time, which is for the best, for everyone. He prefers no one to see his face."

"Why? What does he look like? Is he ... Uh ... Well, is he ugly or does he have a scar or something?"

"Sinister looking is more like it. His deeds are what make him ugly, and yes, he has a scar."

"What do I do after he comes for me?"

"Just do as I said, I have a plan but you will have to be there for it to work. He will put you in one of the towers in a room he has prepared for you, and then as soon as I can get away I will come for you with the key and a plan. Then, we can both be free of him and his evil at last."

Serina stepped forward and took the woman's hand. "Mother," she whispered in a breath full of emotions.

The woman burst into tears at hearing that single word fall from her daughter's lips. She took Serina into her arms and hugged her tightly.

"My Serina, my daughter; I have waited so long for this moment – to hold you in my arms, to look upon your face."

The woman held Serina rocking her back and forth then she gently pushed her back and held her at arms length. "You do so favor your father, with that same chin that I loved so much."

"Everyone always says that it's you that I favor. 'You are the spitting image of your mother bless her soul,' is what I always hear, or, 'why you're turning out to look just like your mother.' I hear stuff like this all the time, but no one except Mrs. Kent and a few others say I look like Papa, but if you ask me I think Mrs. Kent has a liking for Papa, if you know what I mean," Serina teased lightheartedly. She looked up into her mother's face but the woman had a strange forlorn look in her eyes, her mind drifting back to somewhere other than in that dark cave with Serina. Her face had taken on a warm glow. A smile crept across her face – she was definitely somewhere else – *deep in the past most likely*, Serina thought. Senora regained her poise and looked back at her daughter.

"Mrs. Kent always did have a liking for your father; ever since her husband was killed in a hunting accident."

Her face suddenly took on another look, one of haste.

"Enough of this for now, you must go, it's getting late and we can not take the chance of anyone finding out about our meeting, especially the Dark Lord. Please do not come back to the cave, Serina, it's too dangerous, I will not come again but I will see you at the castle after the Dark Lord has brought you... Remember, not a word of this to anyone."

Serina stepped back to leave but hesitated for a moment. "I *will* see you at the castle and nothing will separate us ever again."

Serina turned and ran out of the cave and kept running until she got to the forest's edge, not looking back once. When she had to stop and catch her breath for a moment, she sat down on the ground by the side of the path.

She still could not bring herself to look back up the path. Why, she did not know, but she felt so strongly about it that even when she heard a rustle in the leaves behind her she could not force herself to turn around, instead she got to her feet and took off running again and did not stop until she was home.

Chapter 6

Once she was safe inside her house Serina flopped down in her favorite chair in the sitting room. The next three weeks and five days will be tough, she thought – that's how long it was until her birthday. *How will I make it without anyone getting suspicious?* She could not take the chance of going back to the forest, especially the falls. Her mother said not to go back, *it seemed odd to call her 'mother'*, Serina thought. Everyone knew how much she loved to go swimming at the falls or exploring so she would just have to find a way to stay out of the forest that's just all there was to it.

Koori came over about eight o'clock pretending to come for some flour for her mother.

"Hello Koori, what's up?" Serina asked trying to make the first move toward any type of reconciliation. She could not stand having hard feelings between them, this was the first time and she hoped it would be the last. Koori, however, had a harder time coming around than Serina did.

"I just need some flour, my mother is short and the market is closed, she's in the middle of baking something and can't quit."

Baking something my foot, Serina thought; *she never baked this late at night*, at least not that she knew of.

They walked to the kitchen without speaking, once there Koori rounded on her.

"So you couldn't go swimming with me, huh? But you could go to the forest by yourself, I saw you sneak out the back way, I watched you go into the forest, to the falls no doubt. If you don't want to be friends with me anymore just say so and I will be glad to find another best friend."

"Don't be silly Koori, I don't want another best friend, I just have some problems to work out and it's something I have to do for myself, besides there is no one who could take your place."

Serina poured out some flour putting it into the container Koori had brought with her.

"I do not see why you can not tell me what's brothering you. You know they say, 'two head's are better than one' and I am very good at solving problems."

This was true, Koori was about the smartest kid she knew, maybe it was from the books she read, she could probably read a book a day, well that might be stretching it a bit but she did read a lot, in fact some of the kids called her Miss. 'Know-it-all' or Miss 'Book-worm'.

Yet Serina didn't answer. She kept looking at her friend, but couldn't bring herself to speak.

"Fine!" Koori exploded. "I can tell when I'm not wanted around anymore; maybe your next best friend won't care if you hurt her feelings and treat her like pond scum." With these words, Koori stormed out of the house without a backwards glance, leaving the flour she had come for on the table.

This was going to be harder than Serina thought, but she had to put Koori's feelings on hold for now – there were more important things to attend to, and if Koori got her backside up, well she would just have to stay like that for a while.

Mr. Zimmer sent Serina to the market the next morning for a few things but ask her to deliver a pair of shoes to Mr. Nosh first.

No one was in the jewelry store when she arrived so she killed time looking around at all of the pretty stuff he had on display. She was standing at the back counter looking at a particular piece of jewelry when she heard voices coming from the back room. The voices were muffled and undistinguishable in parts, but it was definitely a heated conversation. As their voices grew louder, Serina was able to make out what they were saying.

"...I tried but she wasn't there." One voice, a male, was not familiar to Serina but the last voice was no doubt that of Mr. Nosh's.

"You do as I tell you to do, or else you will be sorry you ever met me, understand?"

Serina dropped the stone she was holding in her hand and it made a loud clink on the countertop, the voices stopped abruptly. After a moment, Mr. Nosh appeared in the doorway with an odd expression on his face.

"Why, good morning Serina, how long have you been here?" he asked, in a pressed voice looking down at the jewelry display where the stone had fell, quite out of place.

"N-not long at a-all, I just got here, my father sent me over w-with your new sh-shoes," Serina muttered, holding up the package her father sent with her. "See!"

She was nervous and was sure it showed but as hard as she tried, she couldn't help from stumbling over her words.

"Thank you, was there anything else?" Mr. Nosh asked hastily.

"No, th--that was all, well I, I gotta run, see ya later," Serina said turning toward the door.

She fled as quickly as she could without making it look like she was as scared as she really was. Once outside the conversation she had just overheard kept running through her head.

What did he mean by being sorry he ever met him? Who was he talking to? Who were they talking about? – some woman evidently. She made it to the corner and turned up the street toward the market so deep in thought, that she wasn't paying attention to where she was going, and ran right into someone coming out of the alley.

"Oh excuse me," Serina said to the grotesque looking man. He was rather tall and thin with an enormous crooked nose that did not match his rough sun splotched face. He glared at Serina with a set of small beady eyes not saying a word then shoved past her almost in a run heading in the opposite direction. Serina shook from the chill that suddenly crossed over her body and stared transfixed after the man until he disappeared around the corner. He had an odd gait to his walk; still she could not place him, she felt sure she had never seen him before.

"Making new friends Serina?" Koori asked with a muffled giggle, she had been coming down the street and noticed the man come out of the alley bumping into Serina. She was still a little upset with her friend and decided to give her a hard time.

"Do you know that man Koori?" asked Serina, ignoring her friends little jab. She still felt odd about meeting the stranger.

"Nope, never saw him before. Is he your new friend?" Koori's voice still carried a touch of sarcasm with it.

"Knock it off Koori, I'm sorry if you're still mad at me but if you were a true friend you would understand. When I say I'm not trying to be rude or hide anything, soon you will understand, just give me a little more time." Serina was looking at her friend earnestly, silently pleading.

Koori looked back at Serina for a moment then her face took on a familiar expression.

"Sorry," she said lowering her gaze. Koori felt rather an idiot at the way she had been acting the last few days.

"That's okay. Do you want to walk with me to the market? I have to pick up some things for Papa."

"Sure," replied Koori with a smile.

The girls headed off up the street giggling and chatting without another thought given to the strange man, enjoying the rest of the afternoon together.

"There you are," Mr. Zimmer said when Serina entered the kitchen dropping her purchases on the table.

"It's a good thing you didn't have to pick up milk, it would have spoiled before you made it back you've been gone so long, what took you anyway?" her father asked.

"Oh, I stopped off at Koori's for a few minutes; we were looking at the new doll her father made for her birthday."

"Hmmm, someone else is having a birthday pretty soon; maybe she would want a new doll also," he replied pensively.

Serina cringed at the mention of her birthday. "Don't make a big deal out of my birthday; I really don't want anything... It's just another day anyway."

"Ah yes it is, but it also happens to be your twelfth birthday. A young girl doesn't turn twelve every day you know," her father said with a grin.

"So now, will it be a doll for your birthday?"

"Sure, why not." Serina however, did not sound very convincing. She was thinking what was going to take place on the eve of her birthday; suddenly she grabbed her father and hugged him tightly. "I love you Papa, so very, very much," she said, while big tears welled to her eyes. She hugged her father for a long while thinking, what if something happened and she never saw him again, that was too terrible a thought to think but...

"Well I love you too Half Pint, what brought on this sudden burst of affection?"

Serina avoided looking at her father; she did not want him to see her crying.

"Oh not anything in particular, I just felt like giving you a hug."

In bed that night, Serina kept thinking about her birthday and what was supposed to happen. If all went well she would have a mother for a birthday present and that would be the most wonderful present in the whole world but if things didn't go well... She did not want to think of what might happen if things went wrong. She didn't know if she could make it all the way to her birthday without saying something to someone, only if by accident.

The next few days came and went without a hitch and before she knew it, it was Friday, the day that all the gang got together at the stream for a swim. Koori stopped by on her way to the water.

"Are you ready?" She asked when Serina answered the door.

"Ready for what?"

"To go swimming… It's Friday, remember?"

Serina had completely forgotten about this being Friday, with everything else that had been on her mind.

"It won't take me but just a minute to get changed, wait for me okay?"

Serina hurried to change her clothes then after leaving a note for her father she left the house with Koori, headed for the swimming spot. When they arrived, the gang was already in the water, splashing and carrying on, having a blast as usual, it didn't take too long for Serina and Koori to join the fun.

"Hey! Wanna go to the falls everyone?" Jammer asked. "It's a hoot to jump off the top."

Everyone agreed except Serina, she hesitated for fear of being too close to the cave, what if some one found the cave or worse still what if Koori or Amil mentioned it and they wanted to go explore it.

"No guys let's stay here, it's too far to the falls and besides I have to leave soon, things to do and such," Serina begged desperately, trying not to sound too overly anxious.

"Let's stay here guys, the water is pretty deep there and Anna doesn't swim well," Koori piped up suddenly.

"Yeah, let's stay here; my mother doesn't want me going to the falls or into the forest for that matter," rejoined the rather small skinny blond-hair Anna.

The group went back to splashing forgetting about the falls for the moment. Koori climbed up beside Serina on the rock where she was sitting.

"You gonna tell me why you want to stay away from the falls all of a sudden," she inquired, eyeing Serina suspiciously.

"No reason, just have to get back soon that's all," Serina lied again; it seemed she was getting to be an old hand at it these days.

"What's in that cave that you don't want anyone to see? Are you keeping a secret from me?" Koori's voice had an edge to it again, she was not going to give up, Serina could tell.

"Not again! I thought we were over this," Serina said sliding off the rock and back into the water swimming away from Koori as fast as she could, leaving her friend sitting on the rock with her mouth wide open.

She didn't see Koori for two days, she didn't even see her leave the stream, pouting no doubt and if her guess was right, she would be carrying a grudge for a while. *If she would just back off and let me work this out*, Serina thought.

Sunday morning Serina dressed for church and headed out the door with her father, she dreaded seeing Koori, knowing she was still mad at her. She sat in the pew with her father looking back to the door every few minutes for her friend. When Koori did arrive, she sat in the back by her mother instead of coming to sit with Serina as she always did. *Yeap, she's still mad all right.*

After the service, she ran out quickly looking for Koori. She caught a glimpse of her walking off with Anna. The two were laughing about something. Koori looked back over her shoulder at Serina and snubbed her nose up at her then quickly returned her attention to Anna and they both started giggling again.

"Be thata way," Serina said under her breath.

The rest of the day Serina stayed in her bedroom, not coming out until supper.

When she finished with the dishes, she dried her hands on the dishtowel and went for a walk, not knowing where she was going – just walking. She headed up the path toward town. The warm breeze was floating across her face, the evening sky not quite dark yet; she could see a few clouds gathering but gave this no thought.

Before she knew it, she was at the corner across from Mr. Nosh's jewelry store.

"That's odd," Serina whispered, noticing a pale light burning at the back of the store. *He must be working late*, she thought. As she got closer, she could see movement inside the shop-front but it was too dark to tell what was going on. Remembering the strange man from the other day, Serina stepped into the shadows to watch for a moment. There were definitely two people inside the store but she could not make out who they were. The two men disappeared into the back of the shop and after a few minutes, Serina saw the light in the back room go out. She remained in the shadows for a few more minutes watching, for what, she did not know, but when she was about to leave she saw a man emerging from the back alley. He started walking down the street toward her staying close to the buildings, inside the shadows. His unusual gait told Serina that it was the same man she bumped into a few days earlier. She wasn't sure what to do. If he saw her, he would know she had been watching them. She edged along the side of the buildings toward the doorway of the herb shop. It was a deep-inset porch, into which she backed up as far as she could and leaned against the wall hoping the shadows would hide her. She held her breath for fear that he would spot her otherwise. Fortunately, he walked past Serina's hiding place without a glance and headed up the street. Serina waited until she no longer could hear his footsteps then let out her breath.

"Whew, that was close," she whispered, extremely glad he had not seen her. She waited a couple more minutes before stepping out of the dark doorway and started up the street herself. *Who was he? And what kind of business did he have with Mr. Nosh anyway?* Serina wondered. He did not look much like a jewelry person to her.

She was almost home when she caught sight of the man again; he was heading toward the path that led to the walk-bridge. It was still early enough that her father would not miss her, Serina thought. So she decided to follow him to see where the man was going. When he entered into the forest Serina decided to turn back for fear of not being able to see where she was going, and it had started to rain... She kept wondering where he was going as she made her way back home; *it's odd that he went into the forest. Where would he be going in there? What if he went to the cave and found the opening? Worse yet, what if that's where he was going, on purpose, to meet with the Dark Lord. That didn't make any sense. Why would Mr. Nosh have anything to do with the Dark Lord?* But then again remembering the conversation she over-heard in his store the other day, it made sense now – if this were true.

In her dreams that night, Serina followed the stranger into the woods to the cave where he disappeared into thin air at the mouth of the cave.

Early next morning Serina woke to the sound of the gentle rain tip tapping on her window, the thoughts of the night before still fresh on her mind. She jumped out of bed and made a mad dash to the window to look out toward the path into the forest, hoping that somehow the stranger would still be standing there. No strange man stood at the edge of the forest. She knew it before she looked but it was one of those things you just have to do.

She dressed in a hurry and headed to the kitchen. She wanted to fix breakfast for her father this morning to surprise him. She had not been herself lately and this was a way to make it up to him by making his favorite, sweet cakes.

After breakfast, she told her father she was going to Koori's for a while and would see him at lunch. Once outside she headed toward Mr. Nosh's shop. She wanted to see if she could get a glimpse of the stranger. When she noticed Mr. Nosh watching her from his store window she ducked into the herb shop on pretence of buying something.

Serina milled around the shop looking at all the different herbs and roots, smelling stuff and wondering what people did with some of the twisted ugly roots that were sitting in bins and crates. The village physician, Doc. Quially, had stepped in the shop just ahead of Serina to pick up some medicinal herbs to make his potions and solaces. He spoke to her briefly, just saying "hello," as he passed on his way to the back of the store to look at a jar of greenish goo. Just then, Serina heard a familiar voice behind her.

"I need this list filled for my mother please." Koori had come into the store.

Great! Serina thought. She did not want another encounter with her – not today. She had to watch Mr. Nosh's store and could not be distracted by Koori bugging her. Serina ducked down under the counter next to the back door. Then when no one was watching, she slipped out the door into the alley where she doubled back to the corner and watched for Koori to leave. A few minutes later Koori exited the shop and took off up the road toward the market.

Mrs. Thatcher must still be caring for Mrs. Wilber and her new baby for Koori to be doing the shopping yet again... Good, Serina thought, *it will keep her occupied and out of my hair.* She headed back to the front of the herb shop.

When Mr. Nosh closed for lunch Serina wandered back home for a bit of lunch also.

"I need you to deliver a pair of shoes to Mrs. Wilber for me this afternoon Half Pint," Mr. Zimmer said, without ever looking up from his bowl of stew. "I would do it myself but I figured you would rather do it. It will give you a chance to see that new baby again and besides, I need to get started on a new order that's just come in. I have two new orders this morning so I might need your help getting them out in time. I talked to Amil already, and he said he would come over this afternoon to help me. The next couple of days we will be busy so all the help I can get will be appreciated."

He finished his stew and leaving his dishes on the table and headed back to work.

Mrs. Wilber was in an overstuffed chair in the sitting room when Serina arrived with her package. Mrs. Thatcher led her to a similar chair and took the package from her, handing it to Mrs. Wilber.

"I haven't seen you around for a few days Serina, have you been ill? Mrs. Kent said she saw you at the market the other day and you looked under the weather somewhat, dear."

"No, I'm fine really Mrs. Thatcher, I've just been busy lately, that's all," Serina replied trying to reassure the woman.

"Koori went to run some errands for me this morning but I expect her at any moment now." Almost as soon as she got the words out of her mouth, Koori came in.

"There you are dear, look who came by?" Koori's mother said with a smile when her daughter walked into the sitting room. "Maybe you two can go play for a while this afternoon, it will do you good to get out of the house a little while... You need some sunshine, dear."

"Oh I'm sure Serina has other things to do. She doesn't seem to have time for playing these days, right Serina?" Koori said with just the tiniest hint of sarcasm, which Serina grasp readily even if the two women did not.

"As a matter of fact I do, I have to help my father this afternoon with a couple of orders," Serina replied sweetly, ignoring Koori's intent glare.

"See, what did I say, she's much too busy to play, always the little helper I say, I expect that's what you were doing last night when you headed out toward the walk bridge, huh Serina." Koori did not try to disguise the sarcasm this time.

"Just out for a walk Koori that's all, after all it was a beautiful evening, right Mrs. Thatcher?"

"Hum, oh yes dear, it was a nice night alright, loved the rain."

Koori's mother was too busy with the baby to notice the edginess between the two girls.

"I gotta run, you sure have a beautiful baby Mrs. Wilber, looks just like Mr. Wilber, see ya later Koori."

Serina was half way out the door before Mrs. Wilber had a chance to reply.

"Thank you Serina, I agree with you, the spitting image of his father."

Serina stayed busy the rest of the day in her father's shop, helping him make the soles for the new shoes and tidying up. All the while, she couldn't keep from wondering when, or if, the strange man would come back to Mr. Nosh's shop. Was she making something out of nothing? Most likely she was.

So what if Mr. Nosh talked hatefully to the man, maybe he was simple minded and did not know much... Still that didn't give him the right to treat him so unkindly. Her mind was working overtime. Remembering the look he gave her in the alleyway made her shiver, simple minded or not, he looked evil to her. Her thoughts kept running through her mind uncontrollably.

That evening Serina excused herself early, complaining of a headache. She dressed for bed then curled up on the bench at her window, wondering what her mother was doing. All of the past few weeks' events came flooding back and tears filled her eyes. She let out a sob and wiped her cheeks.

As Serina wiped her face her eyes focused on something outside her window, there, at the edge of the bridge she saw him, he stood still for a moment and then looking around, he appeared to throw something over the side. Whatever it was, it was small and it was too dark for Serina to see what the object was. But she knew it had to be the stranger from Mr. Nosh's shop, by the way he hobbled off.

She watched him straggle off toward the forest and disappearing into the woods but not without a quick backward glance toward town.

What was he up to? This was the second night in a row he went out into the woods, why hasn't anyone else noticed him, most importantly where was he from?

Serina was too busy the next day to think of much else but shoes. By the time evening rolled around Serina, her father and Amil had made three pairs of shoes completing one of his orders.

"Amil, will you deliver these shoes to Mr. Oble, on your way home? He's waiting for them," asked Mr. Zimmer when he had finished with the last pair.

"I will father," Serina said hastily, "it's out of Amil's way to go to Mr. Oble's house anyway. He lives on the other end of town." She was hoping for a chance to get out of the house and spy on Mr. Nosh, in case the strange man reappeared.

"Well, if you want to Half Pint, and I'll stir up something for supper. Thanks Amil, I'll see you in the morning, okay?"

"Yes Sir, Mr. Zimmer, good evening... Good evening Serina," Amil replied almost as an afterthought, as he left the shop.

Serina took the rather large package and left the house right behind Amil, taking the opposite direction toward town.

After delivering the shoes to Mr. Oble, Serina took a short cut toward Mr. Nosh's shop, wondering if she might catch the strange man there and follow him again but the shop was locked up and no lights were to be seen anywhere. *Oh well,* she thought as she headed back home, *it was worth a try.*

Walking by Koori's house Serina saw her friend outside playing a game with her little brother.

"Sena, ome pla too," Koori's little brother yelled.

Serina walked over to the little boy and tousled his hair. "What are you playing Zeb?" she asked the toddler, averting her eyes so as not to look at Koori.

"U pay," Zeb said, not understanding Serina. He was only two and did not talk well yet.

"Sure, I'll play Zeb... Catch." Serina took the ball and tossed it gently to him. Amazingly, he caught the ball with his forearms but dropped it as quickly as he caught it.

"Good catch Zeb," Serina said, clapping her hands. The baby held up his arms and started clapping his hands excitedly jumping up and down at the same time.

"Come on Zeb, it's time to go inside," Koori said as she took Zeb's hand leading him into the house ignoring Serina altogether.

"No, no, Koori, pa ball, pa ball."

"Tomorrow Zeb, it's late now – time for bed."

Koori swooped up her little brother and carried him, kicking and screaming into the house, leaving Serina standing there not saying a word to her.

"Whew!" Serina spouted aloud as she stomped off down the street toward home. "I don't care if she ever forgives me, she can stay mad forever for all I care. She is just hurting herself." Serina, kicked at the dirt on the path as she walked, making a small dirt cloud around her feet.

Supper was done and over with well before dark, giving Serina plenty of free time before bed so she made for the bridge hoping to see what, if anything, the stranger had thrown into the water the previous night.

Half way there Koori caught up with her. "Where ya headed? For the cave?" she asked rather casually, as if nothing had happened between them. "Can I come along?"

"Suit yourself," Serina snapped irritably still quite put out with her friend's behavior.

"What are ya gonna do at the cave so late, it's almost dark."

"I'm not going to the cave; I'm just going to the bridge," retorted Serina still disconcerted by her friend's attitude.

Koori fell in beside her, neither one spoke until they reached the bridge. "What's up with the bridge anyway?" Koori asked, mildly curious.

Serina hesitated momentarily, not knowing if she should tell her about the strange man and everything that had been going on with him and Mr. Nosh. Yet, since it did not have anything to do with her mother and the cave, or at least she did not think it did, maybe this would get Koori off her back for a while.

"I thought I saw someone throw something over into the water last night, I wanted to have a look see is all," Serina replied deciding to let Koori in on part of the mystery.

"Who was it? Did you see him?"

"I don't know who it was, a stranger I think."

"You don't think it was that man you saw the other day in the alley, do you?"

"Yeah, I think that's who it was." She was still hesitant about telling Koori anything.

"Reckon who he is, I wonder what it was that he threw in the water? How big was it anyway?" Koori asked; her curiosity aroused.

Koori could ask more questions than anyone Serina knew. She wondered if she would ever shut up. "I dunno... That's why I'm here to find out, let's climb down the bank and look around."

Both girls scaled down the levee together, paying close attention to their surroundings, forgetting all about their spat over the last week or so.

"How big was it?"

Serina held her arms out into a small circle. "About this big from what I could see, it must have moved down stream and is long gone by now."

"What gets me is why anyone would throw something into the water," Koori rejoined, puzzled over the whole thing.

"I dunno... It looked like it was wrapped up in a cloth or something."

"We better get back, it's getting late, and I told my mother I wouldn't be long... I came to apologize for the way I have been acting lately. If you don't want to talk about it, you don't have to; I've been acting like a baby about the whole thing."

That's an understatement, Serina thought, but figured it was best not to say so. If Koori was willing to make amends then the least she could do was to be big enough not to mention it, and to accept her apology.

"Don't mention it, it's all forgotten, okay? Now let's go home."

The two girls climbed up the bank and onto the bridge, walking side-by-side and chatting all the way home – friends once more.

At Serina's gate, the girls made plans for the next day then saying their goodnights. Koori headed up the street to her own house, skipping every few steps, happy to have made up with Serina at last. When she was out of sight Serina walked up her path to the front door, she stood there for a minute looking up at the starry night, briefly entranced by the beauty of the bright sparkling sky. She turned the knob and entered the house, without detecting the dark figure silhouetted inside the shadows across the way.

Chapter 7

Serina watched every day for three days and nights without a trace of the strange man until early one evening just before supper time, she was on her way home from the Muncie's, who lived on the opposite side of the village from Serina. The man was headed into the forest through what Serina called the 'unbeaten path' – the one that no one ever took. She hid behind a nearby tree watching him for a moment... His walk didn't seem right. Serina realized why – when he turned, looking over his shoulder to see if anyone had noticed his descent into the woods – it was Mr. Nosh, the jeweler.

She waited for him to disappear deep into the woods before she had the nerve to step out from behind the cover of the tree. She started in the direction of her house but after a few steps, she decided to turn back and follow him for apiece, just to see where he was going. She hurried and went into the woods at the same spot where Mr. Nosh had entered only moments before her. She made sure to stay far enough behind him so he would not notice her; it would be very hard to explain her presence in the forest so late in the evening if he were to spot her. She had only gone a little way in when she heard a set of voices coming from up the path not far from where she was. She stopped to listen but it was too hard to make out what the men were saying, so she crept-up a little closer; she still could not see them but their voices were very clear.

"It's just too risky, you've been seen enough around town to get people to asking questions, and I can't afford that."

"You still want me to come after midnight?" The other voice asked gruffly.

"No, I'll meet you in the cave instead," Mr. Nosh replied hastily. "You go now and wait for me tomorrow night, at midnight don't forget."

"Yeah, midnight don't worry I got ya."

Serina hid in the brush beside the path until Mr. Nosh passed on his way back to town.

So, they were meeting in the cave – she assumed it was the same cave where she met her mother. *Maybe that's what she meant by it being too dangerous. What were they up to,* she wondered, well whatever it was; she could bet it was no good.

Serina didn't know if she should tell her father about Mr. Nosh's secret dealings with the strange man or not. Maybe if she went to the cave and eavesdropped on their conversation then she would know if she should say anything or not. It could be nothing but a harmless excursion between the two men. *Maybe he finds precious stones for Mr. Nosh.* Serina kept thinking of reasons Mr. Nosh would be meeting with such a strange person.

After Mr. Nosh passed on his way back to the village, Serina waited for a minute or so longer – she wanted to make sure the other man was good and gone before she stepped out from under the foliage to head home. A rabbit scuttled out from the brush from somewhere behind Serina and ran up the trail disappearing back into the thick underbrush. She stood in the middle of the path holding her chest with both hands. *That,* she thought, *scared the begeevies out of me – what if it had been the strange man instead.* She didn't want to turn around and look but she knew she had to. There, standing about ten feet away in the middle of the path with his long hairy arms hanging to his sides, he stood leering at Serina so intently with those small beady eyes that she felt her body go hot all-over.

"What ya doing out here in these woods so late little girly?" The man asked brusquely.

Serina stared transfixed, immobile and unable to utter a sound.

"What's the matter? Can't ya speak little girly, I said what ya doing out here?" He muttered a little louder in the same rough tone.

"I... I...was... nothing," Serina finally managed to blurt out weakly. She was still unable to move.

"Bad things happen in these woods, especially at night." He stared at her for a minute, trying to place where he might have seen the girl before. He stepped forward a few feet, still glaring at Serina, recognition registering on his face as he drew nearer to the fear-stricken girl.

"You go home, don't come back in here... GO!" he shouted at her.

When Serina did not move he closed the gap between them in two strides, and leaned down only inches from Serina's face, he was unshaven with broken yellowed teeth and his breath was atrocious.

"GO!" he shouted again then reached out and gave Serina a hard shove.

Serina somehow managed to get her feet unglued from the path and took off running for home, not looking back once. She also took special care *not* to go by Mr. Nosh's store either.

Once she was home, she went straight to her room pleading a headache and threw herself across her bed. She could still feel the man's horrid breath on her skin.

The nightmares that night were not about the man with no face or the huge black dragon, instead she dreamt about the strange man; he was chasing her through the woods, she was running as fast as she could trying to get away when she ran right into Mr. Nosh. He grabbed her by the arm and started shaking her. He was laughing at her then his face began changing into the face of the strange man, she awoke with a start, she sat up on the side of her bed rubbing her arm while her heart slowly returned to a normal beat.

Waking up in the middle of the night is becoming a common thing these days, she thought as she climbed out of bed and headed across her room to sit at her window. She gazed out over the mountain in the distance feeling somehow closer to her mother. She suddenly realized why this spot had been so special to her growing up, for just over that mountain dwelt her mother all these years, beckoning to her. The love she had for her daughter being so strong that it traveled on the wind up over the mountaintops, through the forest and across her small village right into Serina's bedroom window.

She longed to be with her mother so deeply that her heart ached. *Soon, very soon,* she thought, they would be together and no evil Dark Lord would ever separate them again.

Chores kept Serina busy for the most part of the next day but that didn't stop her from dwelling on the events of the evening before or what was to take place that night.

Koori came by late in the afternoon to get Serina to join her at the stream for a quick swim.

"You have great timing Koori," Serina replied to her friend as she walked up to the fence where Serina was hard at work beating the last of the rugs and window hangings. This was a semi-annual chore for Serina. Her father would take everything out and hang each piece over the fence early in the morning so that Serina could proceed to beat them with a large stick and remove as much dirt and grime from them as possible. Then at night, her father would drag each item back into the house and help Serina put everything back in place. Serina didn't particularly like the chore but today she did not mind too much, she just pretended she was fighting this dark lord that held her mother captive and his entire army of evil men single handedly.

At the stream, Serina sat on the big rock, not in the mood to swim; her arms were tired from beating all the rugs and drapes. She stretched out to where she could face the forest; she wanted to keep her eyes focused in that direction in case anything unusual happened.

"Aren't you going to swim?"

"No, my arms are too tired, the rugs, you know."

Koori climbed up on the rock beside Serina, after a few minutes of playing in the water. "What's up?" Koori studied Serina for a few seconds. "You look like you're in a trance or something, staring off into the woods like that. I wish I knew what was bothering you, cause you sure have not been yourself lately."

"It's nothing; I just don't feel like swimming, that's all."

"You want to go to the falls and look around, maybe have another look at that cave huh? We have plenty of time before we have to get back for supper." Koori was trying everything to snap Serina out of her dark and moody state.

Serina turned to face her friend fear gripping her throat. "Koori I want you to forget about the falls and the cave, you hear me? I don't go there anymore and neither should you, it's too dangerous." She had said more than she had intended to but she had to keep Koori away from there.

Koori cocked a bright red eyebrow at Serina, her curiosity definitely peaked, and whispered. "Why? How is it dangerous?"

"It just is okay? So stay away from there."

"Does it have anything to do with what was thrown over the bridge the other night?"

"I don't know what that was Koori, but the man that threw it over, well, I saw him in the forest yesterday and he told me not to go back into the woods again, said it was too dangerous."

Serina proceeded to tell Koori all the details of what went on during the previous evening, deliberately leaving out the part about the meeting at midnight.

"That's so weird, why would Mr. Nosh be meeting with such a strange man?"

"I dunno... He was at Mr. Nosh's store the other day – remember when you saw me by the alley behind his store? Well, I think he had come out of Mr. Nosh's shop. I was in the jewelry shop delivering some shoes for Papa when I heard Mr. Nosh talking to someone in the back room. When Mr. Nosh came in front, he acted very strange, almost nervous like.

When I left I ran into that strange looking man coming out of the alley."

"What did he say to you?" Koori's voice trembled slightly; her eyes were glued on her friend and all thoughts of swimming gone to the wind.

"That's what was so odd, I bumped into him as he stepped from the alley and apologized to him but he just stood there, staring at me with this evil looking glare then he just pushed past me, going off down the street."

"Did you tell your father?"

"No, I still don't know if they are up to no good or what, I don't want to tell Papa and it be for nothing... You know what I mean?"

"Serina, I think you should tell him, he can make the decision of doing something about it or not but it will be off your shoulders then." Koori was positively worried.

"I tell you what Koori; if anything happens to me then you can tell my father about what I just told you, okay?" Serina said lightly, trying to abate Koori's concerns. She felt bad about telling her anything; she should have known she would react this way.

"Don't make so light of this matter Serina, you might be sorry you didn't take it more seriously," Koori scolded, evidently quite put out with her friend.

If she only knew, Serina thought, how scared she really was; if she knew everything Serina knew, about her mother, the Dark Lord... But, she dared not reveal these things for fear of what the Dark Lord would do to her mother, or to her for that matter.

"I'll let you know tomorrow if I need to worry about anything or not," Serina said evenly.

"Why? What's going to happen tomorrow?"

"Oh, Koori, you worry too much, just forget I said anything, okay? Let's go, I've got to fix supper tonight."

Koori nagged her all the way home, trying to get Serina to tell her what she had been talking about, but Serina wouldn't budge, she had already said too much.

Later that night, once she knew her father was asleep Serina climbed out of bed, she dressed in the darkness of her bedroom, daring not to light a candle for fear of disturbing her father. Very quietly, she slipped out of the house and made her way to the forest, trying to stay in the shadows the best she could, so not to attract the attention of any late niters. With no moon and only the stars to light her path, Serina had a hard time seeing where she was going. Once she got into the woods, it was even harder, at least she knew the way by heart and she could probably find the path to the cave blindfolded. Yet, her worry was not the darkness; it was running across something or someone she did not want to meet in the dark.

She was almost there when she heard a sound on the trail behind her; she spun around quickly. Startled to see Koori a few paces away, Serina stumbled.

"What in blue blazes are you doing out here?" asked Serina, horrified to see her friend out in the woods so late at night.

"I could ask you the same question, Serina," Koori retorted hastily.

Serina was still too stunned to reply.

"I'm following you... Now will you tell me *what* you're doing out here, it's close to midnight."

"I know what time it is Koori, now please go home... Please..."

"*No*, and you've still not told me yet what it is your doing out here." Koori was adamant about Serina telling her why she was out in the woods at that time of night.

"How did you know I was coming out here?"

"I didn't, not for sure anyway, but I have not been your best friend only for all our lives not to know when you were up to something, so I hid by your house and waited for you to do something, I didn't know what but I waited anyway. I was about to give up and head home when you came out of the house, and I followed you."

It was too late for Serina to turn back. She also knew she would not be able to convince Koori to go home so she would have to take her along.

"I'm going to the cave, you can come if you want to but you have to be very quiet, we're going to hide and wait for Mr. Nosh, he's supposed to meet with that strange man I told you about."

"Oh Serina, I don't think that's a good idea, what if we get caught, what will happen to us then? Maybe we should just turn around and go home."

"I'm going with you or without you Koori, so come on or go back, I don't care but we're wasting time." Serina had already started up the path, leaving Koori standing in the middle of the trail with her mouth wide open. "But I'd be careful if I were you, you may run into Mr. Nosh or worse still..."

Serina did not have to finish, Koori knew who she was talking about, and without a moment's hesitation, she bolted into a run to catch up with her crazy friend, who was already disappearing out of sight into the darkness.

"Okay, okay but remember I warned you, besides someone has to watch out for you, you don't have the sense to watch out for yourself," Koori scolded as she caught up to Serina.

"Shhhhh, would you be quiet already, we're suppose to be *sneaking* up there, or do you want to blow a trumpet and announce to them that we're coming," Serina snapped. She covered Koori's mouth with her hand trying to lower her friend's high-pitched voice.

As the girls drew near the cave Serina held out one of her arms stopping Koori from going any farther. She held up a finger and put it to her lips before Koori had a chance to ask any questions. They stepped closer to the outside entrance and there they stood very still and very quiet. Serina's heart was beating so loud that she had a hard time hearing anything else.

"What are you doing? Should we go in or what?" Koori whispered anxiously.

"Shush, I'm listening, in case they are in the cave already but I can't hear a thing for your loud mouth, so please be quiet okay?"

"Okay."

After a moment, Koori piped up. "I don't hear anything, do you?"

"I think I do, listen."

The voices were coming from farther off in the woods behind them, not from within the cave.

"It's them... Quick, in the cave..." Serina grabbed Koori by the hand and practically dragged her into the cave with her. Once inside they scrambled around looking for a place to hide, but it was so dark they couldn't see each other let alone anything else. Serina remembered a deep crevice in the wall at the backside of the grotto and pulled Koori toward it only seconds before the two men entered.

Mr. Nosh carried a lantern but the light was dim and did not carry to where the two girls stood hidden deep in the crack of the earthen wall. As long as they were silent, they may not be noticed, Serina thought, crossing her fingers for extra luck.

"Put them on the bench," Mr. Nosh ordered. He spoke brusquely to the giant man beside him. Serina thought that the big man could crush Mr. Nosh with one of his huge hands if he took a mind to it, but instead the stranger stepped forward and placed something on the stone bench then stepped back, all without saying a word. Mr. Nosh sat the lantern in the center of the bench and grabbed the bag greedily spilling its contents onto the table.

Serina and Koori were too far away and it was much too dark in the cave to see what was emptied out of the bag but Mr. Nosh's next words gave them a pretty good idea.

"Hah magnificent jewels, you did very well Thabor, very well indeed."

Mr. Nosh picked up one of the items from the table holding it near to the lantern to examine it more closely then sat it back on the table and picked up another one. He did this repeatedly until he had looked at all of the gems on the table, with each one he sighed with satisfaction.

"Still, not the quality of the stone the girl has, Thabor, I still can't believe she just found it in the stream by that bridge. Are you sure, it's the same one – the one from the royal cup? And if so how did it get there."

"Yeah, yeah it is, I swear, I seen it round her neck in the alley last week," the giant replied eagerly, but in his next breath he started losing some of his confidence. "It looks just like it anyway, I w-would b-bet my life on it," he began stumbling over his words as if he were afraid of something – of Mr. Nosh maybe.

"They're talking about…"

Serina clamped her hand over Koori's mouth to keep her from saying anything else then put a finger up to her own lips, warning her to be quiet.

They were talking about the emerald she found, she knew that but what she didn't know was why; why would they care about her necklace, Mr. Nosh's next words cleared that question up for her also.

"I have to have that stone, just think of all the things I could do if the emerald were in my hands. If I'd known that it was the royal stone when she brought it in, to be fitted into that stupid necklace, I would have replaced it with another, I almost did anyway - she would never have known the difference, the silly little twit."

"How are you going to get it?" Thabor asked apprehensively.

"You mean how are *you* going to get it, don't you?"

Thabor did not respond.

"I expect she comes out here a lot, doesn't she?"

"I dunno… I reckon."

"Well you watch for her and the next time she comes out here, you get the emerald. I don't care how you get it – understand? Do what you have to do, just don't bother me with the gory details, meanwhile you stay out of sight, I'll meet you here in three days, around midnight."

Mr. Nosh bagged up the gems, sticking them into one of his cloak pockets; he picked up the lantern and left the cave without another word, leaving Thabor in the darkness staring after him.

It was so dark in the cave without the light from the lantern that the two girls could not even see one another even though they were standing together clutching each other's hands, nor could they see the man that stood somewhere near the stone bench, but they heard him, they stood stock still, too afraid to breathe even. Serina felt sure that if the man spotted them they would be killed.

He stood there quietly for a moment until his eyes grew accustomed to the darkness. Then he walked to the back of the cave just a few feet from where the girls were hiding. They could not see him but knew he was somewhere very close. They could hear him shuffling his feet around on the dirt floor, as he looked or rather felt for something. He put his huge hands against the wall and pushed. When the wall opened up in front of him exposing a dark night sky on the other side Koori's mouth dropped open so far that Serina was afraid her bottom lip would hit the ground. She had to put her hands over Koori's mouth again to keep any sound from escaping.

After the man walked through the opening, the cave wall closed, as quickly as it had opened.

"Did you see that?" Koori exclaimed, still agape.

"Yes, I know about the opening, I found it a while back." Serina stepped away from the wall, fear still gripping her chest.

"That's why you didn't want to come to the falls with the others or with me isn't it? You were afraid one of us would find out. I wonder where it goes."

"It's not like anything you've ever seen before Koori, it's..." Serina dreaded to tell Koori any more but it was too late to worry about it now. "There's more Koori, I'll tell you on our way, but right now we have to follow him to see where he's going."

Without giving Koori a chance to respond, Serina grabbed her hand and walked over to the spot where the giant had just gone through the cave wall.

"Wait Serina… What are you talking about?" Koori dug her heels in the dirt trying to slow Serina down but there was no stopping her.

Serina pushed around on the wall until she hit the right spot and the wall disappeared, making a small opening to pass through.

Koori pulled back from Serina. "Oh, no Serina, no, no, no."

"Come on Koori, we don't have much time, I don't want him to get away."

"I'm not going in there! You're crazy, you have lost every bit of brains I thought you ever had Serina, no, no, no, we can't – we'll be slaughtered."

She was in a dreadful state of panic Serina knew; she would have to find a way to calm her down quickly.

"Koori, we have to… I haven't told you but my…mother is alive and lives in there… I have to help get her out, there's not enough time to explain everything… You just have to trust me on this… Please!"

If Koori thought she had suffered a shock earlier that night, it was certainly nothing in comparison to what she felt at that moment. Her bottom lip dropped another inch and her eyes grew to saucer size.

"Serina, you've lost your mind, I can tell, you know how I can tell, you're talking nonsense, that's how I can tell."

"And you're babbling again Koori, now come on, we're losing time."

Serina gave Koori's arm a hard yank, pulling her through the hole into the other side.

They entered into a garden of some kind, which had not been used in a very long time from the looks of it. The weeds and brambles had about taken it over, except for a narrow path where someone had been traipsing back and forth recently, someone besides her mother, that is. This strange man had been meeting Mr. Nosh, for however long Serina did not know. It was a wonder that he had not met up with Serina's mother. Maybe it was one of the reasons she could not meet with Serina anymore.

It was too dark for the two to see where they were going but Serina knew the castle lay just ahead a little ways, she just didn't know what they had to go through to get there, or who they would meet on their way.

The girls stopped at the edge of the clearing, the path led to a small footbridge, on the other side of which sat the castle, looming out in the darkness. It was huge with four large towers, one at each corner. There was a large stone walkway that led up to the front of the castle, which Serina figured was the main entrance. There were several smaller buildings, which connected to the main part of the fortress with some other outbuildings surrounding the place. A cold chill crept over Serina just looking at the menacing structure; the darkness only seemed to multiply the evil surrounding it.

Serina hesitated for a moment, trying to figure out what her next step was, thus giving Koori the opportunity to catch her breath.

"Serina, I now know, without a doubt, that you're insane, let's go back before someone catches us here – and we die."

"Koori, do you always have to be so dramatic," Serina snapped. "I swear you would make a mountain out of a mole hill, now be quiet for a minute while I figure out what were gonna do."

Koori's would-be quick retort died in her throat instantly - "Shush, someone is coming," Serina said pulling Koori into the bushes just in time to hide out of the sight of what, she was not sure, but in the gloom it appeared to be half human and half monster. He was gigantic, with long arms that almost hung to the ground, his hairy body was massive and when he turned towards the girls' hiding place, Serina gasped. His face was so grotesque that she had to look away; it frightened her so. She hid Koori's eyes for fear of her screaming at the sight of him. He looked as though nature had played a mean trick on him. His eye sockets were skewed and his nose looked like someone smashed it with a big rock. His hair was matted, and the girls could smell him from where they were crouched down in the bushes. He stunk as if he wallowed in a pigpen all day. He stopped very near to where the girls were hiding, lifted his head and took in a deep breath of air surrounding him. Then, to their horror, he grunted fiercely and lunged toward the bushes a few feet away from where they were; grabbing at the foliage with both hands pulling them up by their roots and slinging them across the garden. Serina and Koori jumped up and started running back down the path. Thankfully, the monster did not notice them. Instead he kept pulling up the bushes where they had been hiding, stopping twice to hold his head in the air sniffing loudly and making loud grunting noises. The girls hid behind a tree and watched in horror as he tore up bushes roots and all. After a few minutes of searching, he gave up and slowly turned back making a full circle of the grounds around him, inhaling deeply. Then looking confused, he took off toward an old shed that lay at the back of the grounds. The sounds he made as he wondered off were like that of a wild animal. Meanwhile the two girls stood holding one another until the monster disappeared into the darkness.

"I wonder if he could see us," Serina whispered, but Koori was too horrified to speak. She just stood there in a state of shock trembling from head-to-toe.

"Maybe he could smell us," Serina blurted out – this got Koori's attention.

"Sm-ell us, you've got to be kidding, did you get a whiff of him, how on earth could he smell anything past his own filthy self."

"Glad to see you're back to normal," Serina teased lightly.

"What was that monstrous creature? He... Did you see his hands...and his arms? His arms were enormous and he stunk. Could you smell him? I still don't believe we got away," Koori muttered disgustingly.

"I don't believe he can see, at least not very well. He must go on instinct, a sense of smell or something like that, but he sure was mad wasn't he? I'd hate to think what he would have done to us if he'd caught us."

Koori did not respond. She just stared at Serina, her mouth hanging open.

"Come on Koori let's go."

"Go, yeah let's go, I'm glad you have finally come to your senses. I'm *so* ready to go home!"

"No Koori, I have to find my mother and tell her what's going on, she's somewhere in that castle I'm sure of it, I just don't know where."

"What makes you think your mother is still alive?"

"I saw her and I talked with her in the cave. I didn't believe her at first but she finally convinced me. I know it sounds too hard to believe, but it's true Koori." Serina proceeded to tell Koori the whole story, leaving nothing out.

"That's terrible but yet wonderful at the same time."

"Yes it is, now help me look..."

"What do you mean by magical powers?" Koori asked when she finally realized the enormity of what her friend had just revealed.

"My mother said that it has something to do with my tears. She said I have the power to change things and that my necklace has a power of its own."

"Great, why don't you use some of that power to get us out of this mess?" Koori chimed.

"It's not that easy Koori, I don't know how to use my powers, and besides, I don't have them yet. She said that I would not receive these powers until my birthday. Her exact words, if I remember right, were... "At midnight on the eve of my twelfth birthday," I would receive my powers." Serina's voice trailed off as she stood there under the cover of a large willow tree, pondering the words she had just spoken.

"The same time the Dark Lord will be coming for you huh," Koori added slowly.

"Yeah..."

"What are we gonna do?" Koori asked bravely, trying to hide her fear but the slight quiver in her voice gave her away.

"I don't know, but first we have to find my mother and tell her about Mr. Nosh and what did he call that man – Thabor was it? That's if we can find her, I don't even know where to begin looking, or how to get into the castle without anyone noticing us, heck she may not even be in the castle." Serina looked at Koori with pleading eyes. "Well, are you with me or not?"

"I guess so; someone needs to watch out for you," Koori replied.

The two girls inched out from under the huge tree and started up the path toward the castle.

When they reached the small bridge they saw that it crossed a moat that appeared to surround the whole castle, only it was waterless with grass growing throughout it.

Serina stopped at the edge of the bridge rather suddenly causing Koori to bump into the back of her.

"Look up there," Serina exclaimed, "the window on the far side of the castle, there's someone's up there, quick down the slope." Matching action to words, Serina jumped down the side of the bridge onto the grassy banks of the moat dragging Koori with her as she went. She did not mean to slide all the way to the bottom but that's where she and Koori ended up.

"You think they saw us?" Koori asked fretfully.

"I don't know; I hope not."

The girls scrambled back up the bank slipping on the damp grass more than once until they reached the underside of the bridge. Once there the two climbed up to the old wooden cross boards out of sight.

"Now what?" Koori asked after a few moments of silence.

"Just stay still for a minute and let me think. If whoever it was saw us then, most certainly, they saw us jump down here... We need to get out of here as quickly as possible but not from this spot, let's go down to where those trees come up near the bank, I don't think we can be seen from there," Serina said. She rolled to the bottom of the slope before Koori had a chance to respond.

They made a mad dash for the spot Serina pointed out, trying to be quiet at the same time, although it was almost impossible.

They had a hard time climbing back up the slope; the grass was so slick with dew they kept sliding back to the bottom of the moat.

After a few minutes of getting nowhere, Koori noticed a vine of some sort that was hanging down the side of the bank a few feet away. "Serina look!"

Serina managed to get over to the vine and grab onto it, she tested its strength to see if it would hold them. It seemed sturdy enough so she began pulling herself up the slope. She was almost to the top when someone reached down offering a hand for her to take hold; Serina froze at the sight of it. The hand was hairy, huge, all gnarled and twisted out of shape. She let out a low moan as she recognized its owner. Instead of waiting for her to take his hand, he grabbed hold of her small one and with a hard yank pulled her up over the slope almost pulling her arm out of its socket in the process. He tossed her over on the ground by a tree then reached over the side of the bank and grabbed hold of Koori pulling her over the top as well, tossing her on the ground next to Serina.

The girls huddled on the ground, staring up into the face of the creature, the same one that had been pulling up the bushes searching for them earlier.

"It's okay, he will not hurt you. Thank you Zarf," came a soft voice from behind them.

Serina and Koori both whirled around in unison at the sound of the voice. The huge creature grunted, stepped back into the shadows and disappeared, away from the girls.

"Mother!" Serina cried out while running into the open arms of her mother, leaving Koori staring after her.

"Mother, thank God it's you; I came to see you... I, I. Oh Mother this is Koori my best friend."

Koori nodded at Serina's mother unable to speak. She just stared at the woman in shock and utter disbelief.

The woman stepped into the cover of the trees but the girls were a little hesitant, they kept their eyes on the creature standing behind Senora as they stepped just far enough into the shadows to be out of view of anyone and still be at a safe distance from the creature, there arms still throbbing from his rough behavior.

"Sorry for his gruff manner but he really is sweet, very loyal and protective also. Koori, how nice to meet you. Now Serina, tell me why two young girls are out here in the middle of the night? Did I not warn you it was dangerous and not to come back to the cave again... and to come here of all places... and how did you get here? I think I also mentioned, something about not telling anyone," Senora said lightly scolding Serina, she looked over at Koori then back at her daughter with some amount of disappointment on her face.

"That part is my fault," Koori piped up pulling her eyes away from the creature that stood quietly by the tree and finally acknowledging she had a voice.

"I followed her, she did not tell me anything until after I caught her coming to the cave."

"That's right," Serina added eagerly.

"I... didn't realize you were real, I mean... I don't know what I thought but..."

"It's okay Koori."

"Now, what is so urgent that you would risk dying to see me?"

"It's Mr. Nosh; he wants my necklace, the emerald." Serina held up the necklace to her mother.

"The jeweler, from the village?" Senora asked rather confused.

"Yes, he's been acting rather odd lately, having strange late night meetings and someone has been bringing him jewels from somewhere here, he said he had to have the emerald – *my emerald stone.*"

"Did you see who he was meeting with?" Serina's mother asked, her features taking on a strained look.

"Yes, he's scary looking and told me not to come back to the woods too, Mr. Nosh called him Thabor."

"Thabor, did you say?" The worried look on Senora's face deepened.

Serina told her everything; all about the meetings and how they followed Mr. Nosh into the woods and about their meeting on that very night.

"That's why I'm here; I had to tell you, I didn't know what else to do."

Serina's mother took the two girls into her arms, hugging them close to her chest. "You must not let anyone get the emerald," Senora urged. "You must keep it with you at all times. I need not tell you how important this is, if it gets into the wrong hands we will all be doomed, remember I told you that with the stone you can reverse things... If it gets into the wrong hands imagine what they could do with it," Senora pleaded with her daughter.

"I'm afraid I will lose it, why don't you keep it for me?" Serina asked.

"No, Serina you must be the one, it has to be in your possession, you're the only one with the power to make things right again."

"I don't want it; I'm afraid I will mess things up and lose you again. Please take it." Serina took the necklace from around her neck and handed it to her mother with pleading eyes.

"Oh Serina, if only I could... But you are the chosen one – no one else."

Koori stood listening to the exchange between mother and daughter, feeling utterly helpless to assist her friend in any way.

"You must leave here now; it's too dangerous," Senora said. "If Thabor was to come back and see you he would no doubt tell Takar and that would be bad for all of us. You must stay away from the cave and don't go to Mr. Nosh's shop again, make sure you are never alone when you are away from the house. Soon it will be all over; you remember what to do on your birthday right?"

Serina assured her mother that she knew what to do when it came time but she just did not know if she could pull it off or not.

"I have all the confidence in the world that you will do just fine, you have overcome a lot of your fears just by coming here tonight but you must get back."

Serina and Koori were about to leave when they stopped a few feet away.

"What is it?" her mother asked.

"Uh, I never thought about it but I was in such a hurry to get to you... I don't know how to get back into the cave."

Her mother smiled at her daughter, taking her by the hand. "Come, I will show you, then I must get back to the castle before I'm missed."

She led them back down the narrow path to where the cave entrance should be only there was no mountain; the path just dead-ended at a large tree.

"Where is it?" The girls cried out, panic gripping their throats.

"Where is the mountain, the cave, how can we get home?" All they could see, at this point, were trees, bushes and brambles.

Senora took her young daughter's hand and patted it gently trying to calm her down.

"Pay close attention," Senora said as she spread the bushes apart and exposed a small water fountain next to the tree. She cupped her hands and dipped them deep into the fountain until they were full of water then she splashed the water on the tree and before their eyes, the cave wall appeared.

"It's invisible," exclaimed Serina in disbelief.

"Yes, the water in the fountain is the only thing that makes it visible; to open it you have to press the top of the fountain like this. Senora reached over to the top of the fountain and put one hand atop the rock and gently pressed down on it, the wall opened up exposing the inside of the cave to them. She hugged the girls to her tightly, once again releasing them quickly.

"Now go, I will see you in a fortnight; remember not a word to anyone, Koori – that means you too."

"I won't tell a soul Mrs. Zimmer, I promise and I will help to watch out for Serina, I have to, you know – she *is* my best friend."

"Good girl, now you two get back home and into bed," Senora said, sounding just like a parent.

The girls slipped through the opening and as quickly as they made it through, the wall closed up behind them, cutting them off from the other side and Serina's mother.

All the way back to the village the girls talked nonstop, expressing their feelings about everything that was happening, Koori, of course, asking more questions than Serina could answer. Once in the village, Koori insisted on walking Serina to her door, making sure she was in before she headed to her own house.

Chapter 8

Koori was at Serina's house bright and early the next morning, before Serina even had the chance to get out of bed.

"Koori why are you here so early?" Serina muttered, rubbing the sleep from her eyes still half-asleep.

"I promised your mother I would watch out for you and I aim to do just that," Koori replied gleefully.

"I think I can get out of bed without your help, besides don't you have other things to do this early in the morning ... like sleep?" Serina snapped a little more loudly than she intended to, but she was so tired from being out so late and could not imagine Koori even being out of bed.

"Be hateful if you wish but I intend to keep my promise. I still can't believe your mother is still alive, it's so awesome, isn't it?"

Serina sat up in bed, stretched and rubbed her eyes again with both fists, still trying to wake up. "Yes, it's hard for me to believe it too." Serina pondered. "I keep thinking I'm gonna wake up and find everything was just a bad dream, I could handle it being a dream except for the fact I would lose my mother again... I still don't understand all of it, especially the part about me having some special powers."

"I don't know; it's hard for me to imagine not having a mother, let alone having some special powers. It's so scary too, this Dark Lord you mention, it all gives me the willies."

Serina threw her feet over the side of the bed and sat there for a moment in a sleepy haze. "Does my father know you're here? Remember you can't say anything to him."

"Yes, I know that. I'm not a complete goof you know and yes he knows I'm here, I told him we had plans to plant some flowers in the garden, don't worry."

Serina washed and dressed, and they both headed for the kitchen for some breakfast, silently. Serina was counting the days until her birthday, wondering if Koori planned to wake her every morning until then.

After breakfast, Serina's father left them and headed for his shop to finish an order for new shoes on which he had been working.

Serina enjoyed being in their kitchen more than any room in the house except for her bedroom, sitting by the window. The kitchen was always filled with sunshine, plants, and herbs sitting in pots on the windowsills. It always gave her a warm happy feeling but she did not feel so very warm and happy today. The feeling of dread hanging over her was almost more than she could take. When Koori asked Serina about something, a few minutes later, she nearly snapped her head off.

"Look Koori, I don't mean to be so hateful, I'm just tired I guess, I think I want to lie down for a little while, I'll come over to your house after I get up, okay?"

"Sure, I'm a little sleepy myself; two-thirty in the morning is an awful late hour to be going to bed anyway. See ya later. I'll lock the door on my way out."

"Okay, thanks Koori."

Serina slipped under her covers and was asleep before her head hit the pillow.

She knocked on Koori's door two hours later, feeling not much better than she had before her nap, but at least she was rested. The two spent the rest of the day together. Serina helped Koori watch her little brother while her mother went to the market. They played ball with him in the front yard until he became too cranky and the girls put him down for a nap.

They played around with Koori's new doll for a while then when her mother came back the two of them went to Serina's place and actually planted flowers in the flowerbed. Koori said that was to keep from telling a lie to Serina's father.

Serina's father had just finished the repair of a pair of shoes for Mr. Muncie when he came home to find the girls putting the finishing touch to the flowerbed, and asked them to deliver his two orders.

"Sure, just let us wash up a bit and we will go."

As soon as they were out of Mr. Zimmer's earshot Koori asked; "Where does the other order go?"

"To Frog's house, his father needed a new pair as well. Maybe Frog will be there, I know you have a yearning for him Koori."

"Oh that's not true and besides I have too much on my mind to be thinking about boys, Serina. I have to watch out for you remember?"

"Yeah right."

"But we have to go right by Mr. Nosh's shop," Koori gasped suddenly. "That's not a good idea, is there another way we can go so we don't have to pass by there?"

"Yes, but it's way out of the way, you know that. Besides, it's not like we're going to his shop, were just passing by it."

"I don't know Serina…"

Koori's looked turned pale, looking faint. She moaned and mumbled all the way to Frog's house. When they passed by Mr. Nosh's shop, Serina thought she heard Koori take in a deep breath and not let it out again until they had passed the shop and were well on their way.

"I swear, Koori you're so silly sometimes," teased Serina.

"Maybe I am, or maybe I'm just cautious, you know that word that you are not – cautious."

"But that's why I have you, Koori."

On their way back from Frog's house Serina spotted Mrs. Kent coming down the lane with her son who was about her and Koori's age.

"Serina dear!" yelled the woman, from still quite a distance away.

"Where's an alley to duck into when you need one?" Serina hissed. Koori just giggled at her friend's evident dislike of the woman and her son.

"Hello Serina, how are you doing, and how's that dear father of yours?" asked Mrs. Kent when she caught up with the two girls.

"Oh, hello Mrs. Kent, Bootie, we're doing just fine and you?"

"Me and little Bootie here were just thinking about coming around this evening to see how you and your father were doing. Since you've been under the weather and all, I thought I'd bring you some soup, and maybe fix that father of yours a good meal. He probably hasn't had a decent one since the last time I cooked one for him, isn't that right Bootie?"

The boy beside her made an animal like grunting noise but did not utter a word. He glared at the girls and continued chewing on what looked like the remains of a Blackberry tart. He was a little taller than Serina but about three times as wide, making her think that he had a hard time pushing away from the table.

"Ah... I ... I think." Serina couldn't get her words out, she felt tongue tied, because the last thing she or her father needed or wanted, were for Mrs. Kent and her pudgy son to come and visit.

"They're coming for supper at our house tonight Mrs. Kent," Koori put in just in time. Serina was so thankful to Koori she could have kissed her.

Mrs. Kent darted her eyes over to Koori for a moment, her face taking on a rather stern look. Koori took a step backwards.

"Oh, yeah that's right, I... I almost forgot, maybe another time Mrs. Kent," Serina added quickly.

The woman turned her gaze to Serina; her expression reverting to one of insincere sweetness. "Well maybe another time as you say then – when he's ready for a real meal. Well...

gotta go dear, tell your father hello for me, and Floori is it, well anyway, goodbye. Come on Bootie."

"Floori!" Koori exclaimed hotly when the woman was out of earshot. "That's *Koori* you big nitwit, my name is *Koori*."

Serina couldn't help herself; she started giggling and teasing Koori. "And *Floori* is it, goodbye *Floori*, oh *Floori*."

"Okay, that's enough of your teasing Serina," Koori retorted. Then unable to stop herself, she joined in the laughter.

"Hey thanks for saving my neck – that was quick thinking," Serina said between giggles.

"No problem, we've wanted to invite the two of you over for a while. Now, I just have to warn Mother. And, this will give my father someone to talk to besides a female at the supper table … that way I can keep my eye on you."

"You know I'm sure glad my mother is still alive, now Mrs. Kent can go find someone else to pester into marrying her. I can just see her face now; her mouth wide open, hanging to her knees. For once she will be speechless."

Koori started laughing and laughed so hard she had to stop and hold her sides.

"What's so funny?"

"Well, my mom always said Mrs. Kent was after your father to marry him and I was just imagining what it would be like for you to have Bootie for a brother."

Serina busted out laughing and the two girls laughed until they had tears coming down their cheeks.

"Heck we'd never get anything to eat, Bootie would hog it all up – 'Bootie dear try to restrain yourself dear… Save some for the others dear…' Speaking of food, what is your mother cooking for supper?"

"Were having pork roast with sweet potatoes and carrots, I know you like that, it's my favorite, and Mom was making apple strudel for dessert."

The girls laughed the rest of the way home. Serina had, for the present, forgotten her dilemma.

The Thatcher's and the Zimmer's sat down to supper that night, enjoying their meal and one another's good company.

The girls' fathers sat in deep conversation after supper while Koori and Serina helped Koori's mother with the dishes, afterwards they all sat around chatting. Koori's mother had started knitting a new sweater for the baby, throwing a word in every now and then, never missing a stitch. The three were talking about things that held no interest to the girls so they sat in the floor playing with Koori's little brother, before Serina knew it, it was time to go home.

"Thad…enjoyed the company and Mrs. Thatcher, that was a wonderful meal, don't know when I ate better," Mr. Zimmer said as he got up from the sofa.

"Probably the last time you ate here," Mr. Thatcher boomed, putting his arm around Mrs. Thatcher's rather rounded plump shoulders.

"She's about the best cook around," Mr. Thatcher added kissing his wife on the cheek.

"Ah, I'm inclined to agree with you Thad, well goodnight, coming Half Pint?"

"Yes Papa."

"Goodnight Koori, see ya tomorrow," Serina called over her shoulder as she slipped her small hand into her father's rather large one and the two of them strolled home.

Late that night, Serina woke to a noise in her room, the sound came from near her dressing table, at first she thought it was Samone but the cat lay next to her still fast asleep. When her eyes grew accustomed to the dark room, she saw an outline of someone - a man standing near her wardrobe. She lay motionless in bed, trying not to let the intruder know she had awakened. The huge shadowy form ever so quietly bent over her dressing table, passing his fingers over her things. Then she watched as he opened the drawers. Serina was in complete horror, it was Thabor, and he was looking for her necklace. Serina was sure of it. She was still wearing the necklace not wanting to remove it ever since she saw her mother.

He suddenly stopped, turned and faced the bed. Serina's heart lunged into her throat. He was standing there anticipating his next move, when her father knocked at her door and called to her.

Thabor backed back into the darkness of the wardrobe frozen for the moment. Serina knew without a doubt that if her father entered the room, Thabor would kill him, and most likely, her as well. She had to act fast. She jumped up from the bed and made a mad dash for the door pulling it open before Thabor knew what was happening and closed it behind her.

"Half Pint, are you alright? I thought I heard something," Mr. Zimmer burst out as he embraced his shivering daughter.

Serina tucked herself into her father's arms, scared out of her wits, but she could not take the chance of telling him everything. Besides, she figured Thabor climbed out the window and was long gone by now and didn't think he'd be back tonight.

"I'm fine, I'm sure it was nothing," Serina said quickly, thankful her father did not notice the slight quiver in her voice when she spoke. "But can I sleep in your room the rest of the night," Serina added, still not wanting to take the chance of having to deal with another late night visitor.

"Sure Half Pint, your little cot is still in the corner where I put it after I built your new bed." Serina climbed into the small but still comfy bed feeling safe for the first time in weeks but she had a hard time falling asleep, she kept thinking about Thabor in her room.

"Pretty desperate if you ask me," Koori remarked the next day when Serina told her about the incident. "Mr. Nosh must want that stone pretty bad."

"Bad enough to kill me if he has to," said Serina, remembering what Mr. Nosh had told Thabor in the cave a few nights back, "do whatever you have to do." She guessed that meant kill her if he had to. Why else would he tell him not to bore him with the gory details?

Koori must have felt the fear creep back up her spine, because she quickly sat down on her bed. She appeared to be deep in thought.

"I was afraid to go into my own room to dress this morning," Serina was saying. "Papa scolded me for staying in my nightdress so long. He said I couldn't get anything done in my night clothes."

"I still think you should tell him, he will know the right thing to do, and take care of that mean ole Dark Lord for us."

"Koori you heard what my mother said, we can not tell anyone, I think the powers I will receive on my birthday will be the only way of getting rid of the Dark Lord, so why put anyone else in danger? I wish you had not found out, I would feel better with you not knowing."

"Serina, I had to find out, you know that. I'm the one who does the worrying for the two of us, besides I have to watch out for you, you don't have the sense to... You're always too busy looking for a new adventure," giggled Koori.

"Well I think this one found me," said Serina solemnly. She sat looking out the window of Koori's bedroom toward the stream.

Not feeling much like company she told Koori she had a headache, which was no lie, said bye and went home.

Samone met her at the gate; she had been out mousing all morning and was ready for her nap.

"Come Samone, I'll fix you some lunch and we can both take a nap. Whatcha ya say to that?"

Samone rubbed up against Serina's leg and meowed loudly, in agreement.

The days were getting fewer and fewer for Serina, she counted them up and she let out a sob when she realized there were only eleven days before her birthday. She felt doomed, with her days being numbered until she met the Dark Lord. What fate held for her then she could only imagine.

That night Serina slept in her father's room, wanting a little more protection from Mr. Nosh's goony. She didn't feel up to fending off someone trying to steal her necklace in the middle of the night.

She slept late. When she realized what time it was, she jumped out of bed. Her father had gone to work already. She grabbed for her necklace, making sure it was still around her neck, she let out a small sigh of relief when her fingers wrapped around the emerald. She had dreamt someone was yanking it from around her neck and she put up a terrible fight to keep it. *Ten days to go,* she thought. "I wonder where I could hide until this is all over, huh Samone?"

Serina picked up the purring cat, carried her into the kitchen, and gave her a bowl of milk. "There you go sweetie," she said putting the bowl down in Samone's favorite corner. The cat happily lapped up the warm milk, stopping once to look up at Serina, silently thanking her for her breakfast.

The market was very crowded when Serina and Koori arrived. Serina had to pick up a few things for her father then Koori needed to go to the herb shop on their way home. That was the part they were dreading, knowing they had to go right past Mr. Nosh's shop. They bumped into Frog by the vegetable bins.

"Hey Serina, Koori, whatcha up to?" he asked in that deep throaty voice of his.

"Not much, just shopping," Serina replied.

"Seen ya down past the bridge the other night, what was ya up to? Looking for night fish?" He laughed heartily at his own joke.

"Yep, also thought we'd look for a few night owls, you know, those things that go hoot, hoot, in the dark," said Koori. The girls started giggling along with Frog.

"I told Amil I seen ya, he said ya had no business down there at night and he ought to tell your father."

Serina's heart jumped a beat - that's all she needed was for Amil to tell her father she had been out there, even though it was not that late, he would be worried.

"Oh that silly Amil, always the perfect one huh? I bet he never did anything wrong in his life, right?"

"Well Serina, if he had I wouldn't tell you." Frog directed his conversation to Serina but his eyes stayed on Koori.

"We gotta run, have more shopping to do, you know, come on Koori." Serina yanked Koori's arm and took off down the street toward the herb shop.

"Bye…. See ya Koori."

As soon as they were out of range, they busted out giggling.

"I think he's kinda smitten with you Koori."

"Ugh, he sounds like a frog Serina."

"But he's still kinda handsome you know."

"Do ya think he really told Amil?" asked Koori, changing the subject.

"Yep, question is, has Amil told my father yet?" Serina sounded worried; she did not like upsetting her father. He was very good to her and worried enough about her as it was.

They were almost at the herb shop when they noticed where they were.

"Can we, at least, walk on the other side of the street," Koori asked with a worried tone to her voice.

They crossed the cobble stone road just before they reached Mr. Nosh's shop, also just in time to see Mr. Nosh himself step out into the alley.

"Look!" Koori uttered franticly.

"What's that he's holding?" Serina squinted to see what Mr. Nosh had in his hands but could not make it out. "Dunno, maybe we can follow him…"

"No!" Koori exclaimed in panic, cutting Serina off. "We can't take the chance of him seeing us, he may try to take the stone. Besides, remember what your mother said about him." Koori was definitely panicking now. It was all Serina could do to get her to calm down after Mr. Nosh took off in the other direction.

"Let's get to the herb shop and get the items your mother wanted then we can start home, okay?"

Once inside the store, Koori settled down and they began collecting the things for her mother. The door jingled up front and when Serina turned to see who came in, her heart did another jump, it was Mr. Nosh.

"Quick put this in your pocket."

Serina pulled the emerald from her neck with a quick yank and handed it over to Koori.

"No, your mother said not to take it off," Koori protested.

"Never mind that - just do it."

She shoved the necklace into Koori's hand just as Mr. Nosh walked up to the girls.

"Why, hello Serina, what a surprise meeting you here, and your little friend."

Yeah, right, Serina wanted to blast out at him, he probably watched them walk into the shop and followed them, if truth be known.

"By the way, it's a good thing I found you. I need that necklace I made for you. It has a flaw in it I need to fix," he said ever so sweetly but Serina caught the acid undertone in his voice, even though he was going to great lengths to hide it.

She didn't even know if her voice would come out if she tried to speak, she was so scared, so she remained silent.

"So if you don't mind to hand it over to me, I'll take it to my shop and work on it right away, so you could have it back by - say tomorrow..." He held out a hand as he spoke, his eyes never leaving Serina's.

"I... I don't have it, I f-forgot it at home this mor-morning," stammered Serina nervously.

"Oh, I see." He looked over at Koori, and she backed up three steps before she ran into a wall. She stood there, transfixed. He returned his gaze to Serina; *if he were trying to scare them he was doing a great job of it,* she thought.

"A stone as lovely as yours should be worn all the time, what a pity, well why don't you bring it to me later then."

"Yeahs... sure," Serina replied, her eyes glued on his.

"Then later it is." He turned and walked out without making any purchases.

"I knew he didn't come in here to buy anything... See, he's headed back to his shop," said Serina, watching him through the window, as he crossed the cobblestones.

Koori finally came out of her state of shock and stepped to the window. "That was quick thinking on your part, to give me the necklace," she said as she dug out the necklace from an inside pocket of her dress.

"Here, I got the heebie-jeebies just having it in my pocket for that short a time."

She handed the necklace back to Serina with a shaking hand.

"Thanks Koori, I thought we were doomed for a minute there, did you see the way he was looking at us, I think he knew I was lying to him."

"I'd say that's a sure bet. Let's get my mother's things and get out of here before he comes back."

Serina knew Mr. Nosh would not be back, but it was a good idea to get home where they would be a little safer.

She slept at Koori's house for the next few nights, thinking that it would confuse anyone trying to steal the emerald from her in the middle of the night. Samone however would not stay with her. She had a distinct dislike of Koori's little brother but she waited for her every morning, in their kitchen for her saucer of milk, meowing and rubbing against Serina's legs - this was her way of thanking Serina.

On that particular morning, Samone was even more affectionate; she kept getting in front of Serina's feet and tripping her every time she tried to walk in any direction.

"Samone, what is your problem this morning?" Serina asked, shoving Samone out of her way with her foot, as she tried to get to her bedroom. "I'd give you more milk but you haven't finished what you have, so what do you want?"

She reached down, picked up the oversized cat, and hugged her. "Do you want a little extra attention this morning? Is that it, you think I've been ignoring you lately, don't you?"

She sat down at the table and tried to hold Samone for a minute but the cat jumped down from her lap and started for the door to her bedroom.

"What is it Samone, you want to take your nap already?"

Serina walked to her door and opened it enough for Samone to go through, but the cat would not go in, instead she pushed against Serina's legs again. "Samone, please you're tripping me."

Serina stepped away from the cat and headed back to the kitchen. Suddenly it dawned on her; what, or who was in her bedroom to make Samone act so weird? As she walked back toward her bedroom, fear gripped her chest, *what if Mr. Nosh's goony was in there again?* When she got to the door, she stopped. Her small hand trembled as she reached to shove the door open wide. She drew her hand back and felt for the emerald. She pulled it from around her neck and put into one of her pockets then slowly entered the room. At that moment Koori yelled out to her at the kitchen door. She quickly turned and ran from the room, not taking time to look around, she practically leapt into the kitchen where Koori stood holding the door open.

"There you are! I was yelling at you forever. Wanna go to the Wilber's with me to see the baby?"

Serina didn't wait to be asked twice, she ran out the door almost knocking Koori over in the process.

"Let's go," she said hastily, her voice a little quivery from her near encounter with whoever was in her bedroom.

"Well, knock me over want ya," said Koori, stumbling to regain her balance. "Dang, I didn't think you'd want to go."

"Sure, anything to get out of the house, I think someone was in my bedroom but I'm not sure, I was about to go in to check when you yelled at me. Samone was acting so strange and would not go into the bedroom when I opened the door for her."

"Wow! You really think someone was in there, that's so scary."

"I think Mr. Nosh is getting desperate and willing to take more risks to get the emerald from me. That's what I think. I wonder what plans he has to get it now."

Koori was more of a pest than ever after that little incident. Wherever Serina went, Koori was right by her side. One would have thought they were permanently attached or something.

Serina either slept in her father's room or over at Koori's, every night, more often at Koori's house though. She did not want to worry her father any more than he was. He already asked once what was up with her not sleeping in her own room.

"Is it because of the noise we heard the other night that you don't want to sleep in your room Half Pint?"

"I guess so," Serina had replied, not really lying, since her father had also heard the noise Thabor had made.

"I'm sure that was nothing, probably Samone looking for a late night snack of a big fat mouse," her father had teased, trying to lighten the matter some.

"Oh I'm sure it was," Serina had said with a big smile, trying to make light of the matter as well.

Serina had less than one week to go, only four days until her birthday. She had been marking them off on her tablet and each day she dreaded for that day to end, but there was no stopping time, she only wished it didn't tick by so fast. Each day seemed to whirl past faster than the last, leaving her a day closer to the dreaded day. The only thing that kept Serina going from day to day was the fact that she stood a chance of getting her mother back.

She had thought about the so-called *powers*, which her mother had described. If her tears could change things, then she wished they would work now, why wait until her twelfth birthday, that wasn't fair, if she had the powers now, she could get herself and her mother out of this mess. Her mother had also mentioned the necklace, she said the emerald had the power to reverse things - *what things and how did she use it?* This was all so hard for Serina to understand, still only a child. Why did it have to be her anyway, why not someone older, someone who was wiser than she was, someone who knew how to handle Dark Lords and stuff, she sure didn't know the first thing about battling the dark forces; heck she couldn't even swat a fly without missing it ten or more times.

It was hard not to be frightened of every little noise she heard, the trees brushing against the roof when the wind picked up a little, or the creak in the floor when someone walked across it and she couldn't see who it was. Everything scared her, even Samone when she would come up from out of nowhere, and would gently rub against Serina's leg or jump up into her lap suddenly. She figured she had to get a hold of herself before she went completely insane.

Tonight, she decided, she would be brave and sleep in her room. She did not want to worry her father any more than he already was and by now, Mr. Nosh and Thabor would not be back, they had to know she had not been sleeping in her room and were probably waiting to get a chance at her from somewhere else.

She was careful not to use a lamp in her room just in case one of them was watching. She changed in the semi darkness of her room, making sure, she did not go near the window then she hurriedly climbed into bed, hiding herself underneath the covers. As an afterthought she took the necklace from around her neck, got up and placed it inside a tear in the lining of her cloak, she had meant to sew it up for ages, only now she was glad she hadn't gotten around to it.

Whoever was in here before most likely looked in her cloak already, it had been hanging there for months, in the same place, maybe they would not look in the cloak again if they were to come back.

Somehow, she managed to drift off into a fitful sleep, how, she wasn't quite sure but sleep did finally come.

Very late in the night, Serina thought she heard something but it was a dream, she knew that because the Dark Lord was there also and he was not supposed to come until her birthday and that was three days away. In her dream, the Dark Lord was standing over her... No wait, someone else was standing over her first then he, the other person, was looking for the emerald but could not find it. The other person tore her room apart, throwing things on the floor, pulling out the drawers of her dressing table and throwing things out of her wardrobe. Who ever it was then walked to her bed and took her in his arms, she was being taken out of her room through the window, that's when the Dark Lord came. He filled the room with a fine mist and suddenly Serina was floating in mid air. The Dark Lord fought with the other man; it wasn't much of a fight, the other man was no match for the Dark Lord. Then, she felt herself drifting through the air and being placed back on her bed, and that was when the Dark Lord was standing over her, looking down into her eyes with great concern. That's another reason she knew it was a dream, the Dark Lord never showed his face, though for the life of her she could not remember what he looked like, all she could remember about him was a deep scar that ran down the left side of his face, she noticed it as he bent down over her bed.

The rest of the night Serina slept without dreaming, a deep restful sleep; something she desperately needed.

When she awoke, the sun was shining through her window. Serina washed, dressed, and took off for the kitchen. She stopped at the door and looked around everything was in place, proving once again that it had been just a dream. She stepped over to the wardrobe and opened it up, her cloak was hanging right where it had been all along, she reached into the lining but the stone was not there. She let out a choked sob, she started looking all through the lining - no luck it was gone! Someone had been in her room, taking her necklace with him. Serina searched everywhere but the necklace was nowhere to be found. She sat down on the floor by the wardrobe and silently began crying, softly at first but then hard heart-wrenching sobs poured out of her. She was not crying for the loss of the necklace but for the fact that she could not even take care of a stupid small green stone, so, how on earth, was she ever going to save her mother?

She was still in her bedroom when Koori came later, she did not want to leave her room. She searched and rummaged through every nook and cranny with no results.

"It can't be gone, it just can't be," wailed Koori, when Serina told her what had happened.

"Did you see who it was?"

"No, I thought it was all a bad dream, or at least part of it was anyway, I'm sure Mr. Nosh has the emerald by now and I will never see it again."

"We gotta get it back. Don't you need it for when the Dark Lord comes?" asked Koori, still confused a bit about the importance of the stone.

"I need it but I think I need it for later... I think," Serina replied still a bit fuzzy herself about the whole matter of the stone and the special powers that she was to gain on her birthday.

"What are you gonna do?"

"I'm not sure, let me think about it for a while, my mind is all jumbled up."

Serina had to figure something out. Her time was slipping away, with only three days until the day... She couldn't think about that right now though, she had to get the stone back, no matter how.

The girls took off for the village after supper, headed for Mr. Nosh's shop, with no plan in mind, just sheer determination gearing their every move.

When they arrived at the shop a short time later, it was closed, with no one in sight.

At a closer glance, Serina realized the shop door was unlocked and opened just a crack.

"That's odd, look his door is open." Serina pushed the door open a little farther and stuck her head inside. "Hello! Mr. Nosh, are you in there?"

There was no reply, so Serina pushed the door all the way open and stepped inside, with Koori in tow. Once inside she turned Koori's arm loose and walked to the counter, Koori hesitated at the door, not sure if she should follow her friend.

"Hello! Anybody here?" yelled Serina, her voice quivering slightly. She was actually somewhat afraid that someone was going to jump out and grab them.

The shop was as silent as a tomb, the outward appearance showed nothing out of place but something seemed odd; Serina got an eerie feeling just being in there.

"Let's get out of here," begged Koori, tugging at Serina's arm.

"No, let's look around while we have the chance."

Pulling away from Koori's grasp, Serina thought that Mr. Nosh's absence presented a golden opportunity for her to try and find her necklace. "We might find the emerald that would serve him right, huh?"

Koori made a halfway attempt to look for the necklace; she was too scared to do anything except watch the door but that suited Serina just fine. She figured Koori could keep watch while she searched.

"I don't like this, something seems strange about the whole thing, let's go okay?"

Serina, thinking that Koori was right, left the counter and started for the door. When they were almost there, Serina noticed a piece of paper on the floor at the edge of the doorway. The girls had been so shocked to find the door open that they had walked right over the paper, never noticing it.

"What's that?" Serina gasped. Koori looked over in the direction Serina was pointing and gasped as well. Serina picked up the paper; her heart started racing so fast, she thought it was going to pop right out of her chest as her trembling fingers unfolded the paper.

"It's a note," she uttered.

Koori stepped over to look at the piece of paper. "Read it. What does it say?"

Serina quickly began reading the note aloud; her hands were shaking as bad as her voice.

> Nosh,
> The emerald is under the stone bench in the cave. I will see you tonight at midnight.
>   T.

"So you were right Serina, now what?" Koori asked with some relief that the note wasn't directly menacing their safety.

"Now we get the emerald back – that's what! Get it before Mr. Nosh can," Serina replied as she crumpled the note and stuck it in one of her pockets

"What are you doing? You can't take that, it's not yours," said Koori in a panic.

"Well, the necklace was not Mr. Nosh's either but did that stop him from taking it? Besides he's not here, probably out running errands, Thabor most likely came by, found him gone and left this note, come on, I've got a plan."

The girls left the shop at a quick pace, trying to get home as quickly as possible without attracting any attention to them selves.

Safe in Serina's house, they breathed a sigh of relief.

"You can't go to the cave Serina; it's too dangerous; what if they catch you? You know what will happen to you?" Koori warned.

Serina wasn't listening though; she was more determined than ever to getting the necklace back.

Chapter 9

It was late, nearly ten o'clock when Serina slipped out through the back door of their cottage to make her way down to the bridge and wait for Koori. They had made plans to meet under the bridge at ten so they would have plenty of time to get to the cave, find the necklace and get back home before Mr. Nosh could ever get there.

Koori was already there when Serina arrived.

"Let's go, how long have you been waiting?" asked Serina when she climbed down under the bridge and found Koori huddled up waiting for her.

"Not long, about five minutes, I guess." Koori still sounded more worried than she admitted to being. Serina didn't want to admit it, but she was worried also.

The girls climbed up the bank and took off in the direction of the woods, making sure to be as quiet as possible as they made their way into the woods. The only noises they heard were those of an occasional night owl and the ground crunching softly beneath their feet as they walked down the path. The moon was nearly full but the forest was so thick in places that it was hard to see where they were going, still they trudged on, determined to get to the necklace before Mr. Nosh could.

When they could hear the falls ahead Serina turned to Koori, knowing how scared she was and asked her to wait in the bushes until she came back.

"Are you crazy?" She exploded. "I'm not leaving you to go on by yourself."

"It's the best way, if something happens to me, you can go get my father and tell him everything, okay?" Serina pleaded with her friend, hoping she would stay in the bushes and wait for her, if Mr. Nosh somehow found out where the emerald was.…

After a few more arguments, Koori finally agreed to stay where she was and wait for Serina to get back.

"If I'm not back in one hour… You know what to do but do not come to the cave by yourself, under any circumstances, okay?"

"Okay," Koori acquiesced reluctantly and then quickly climbed into the underbrush off the side of the path to wait for Serina.

The moon shimmering on the water made a beautiful picture, Serina thought, as she crossed the steppingstones in the stream, heading toward the cave. All of a sudden, Serina noticed it was deadly quiet. She could not hear any of the usual nighttime noises – just the sound of her heart, which was beating so loud as though it were a hundred horses' hooves, pounding the ground. *No time to panic, just get in the cave find the necklace and get out before anyone knows what's happened.*

She pulled the candle and a match from out of her pocket, struck the match on the hard rock of the cave opening, lit her candle and entered the cave. The small light flickered on the walls of the cave as she entered, illuminating the dark earthen walls around her. She stepped into the cave a little farther, her small hand shaking so hard she was afraid the light would go out, leaving her in total darkness.

"Get a grip on yourself, you big baby," she said aloud, breaking the silent hum in her ears and trying to calm her nerves at the same time. She walked up to the bench that sat in the middle of the room and held her light up over the top of it, expecting somehow, to see the necklace sitting there for the taking - of course it was not there.

"Looking for something," said a cold hard voice from somewhere in the shadows. Serina knew who it was, even though she could not see his face. She cast her gaze toward the back of the cave, not seeing anyone; she strained her eyes even harder, trying to see where the voice was coming from and then *he* stepped out into the rim of the flickering light.

"Dear sweet Serina, my, my, my, what brings a young girl of your tender age out into the woods so late at night? Could it be this?" Mr. Nosh stepped forward, his hand outstretched, holding what appeared to be her necklace.

Serina backed up a step to widen the distance between them. Fear clutched her chest to the point that she thought her heart would burst. She looked around the cave for Thabor, thinking he had to be there somewhere.

"Where's your ghoul?" Serina spat, her temper overriding her fear for the moment.

"Ah yes Thabor, well he met with a nasty little accident, a shame too, he was such a big help to me, but he did manage to get the emerald stone for me before he... uh, how would you say it? Ah yes, met with his untimely demise."

"But the note..." Serina caught herself too late; she was giving the game away.

"A clever idea I had huh? See, I figured you would come to the shop looking for the necklace, so I left the note so you would find it then I hid in the back room. I was watching you and your little friend from a small hole in the wall. I made it so I could watch anyone who's in the shop. It doesn't matter where they're standing, I can see them from that small opening. I was beginning to think you would not spot it lying in plain sight – I thought I would have to put it your hand before you noticed it was there. Your friend was even standing on it for a while, the silly little twit, she was too afraid to come very far into the shop. You should have listened to her; maybe you wouldn't be in this little predicament now."

He took a step closer to Serina; her hand was shaking so badly the candle flickered even more so, almost going out.

"Set the candle on the bench Serina, we wouldn't want to be left suddenly in the dark now would we?"

Mr. Nosh's voice was cold and callus and she saw something shimmering in the pale light – a knife. Instantly her fears multiplied a hundred fold. Her shaking hand sat the candle down and she backed away.

"Don't go too far, I want you inside the rim of light so I can keep my eye on you."

"What do you want with me? You already have the necklace," Serina demanded, fearing that she knew the answer to that question already.

"Well, I can't afford to have you babbling to everyone that I stole your necklace now can I? By the way where is your silly little friend, she was supposed to be with you so I could take care of both of you at the same time."

"She didn't come with me, I told her if I didn't come back, to be sure and tell my father and everyone else just what a cheating, stealing-no-count, evil person you are, she probably already went to my father by now."

Serina was trying to put fear into Mr. Nosh to buy a little time, knowing she had not been gone long enough for Koori to have given up her hiding place and gone for help. *She should still be in the bushes*, she thought, *waiting for me...*

In one sudden movement Mr. Nosh and Serina both turned toward the cave entrance, Serina moaned in horror as Koori stepped inside holding her hands up against her chest. *Great*, Serina muttered to herself, as all hope of getting out of the cave alive vanished.

"Serina, what's taking you so long? I've been wait..." Her voice died in her throat as she looked beyond Serina into Mr. Nosh's eyes.

"How nice of you to join us, Koori; I believe, we were just talking about you... Please step into the light by your friend."

Mr. Nosh seemed very delighted indeed, now that he had both of them right where he wanted them.

Koori came forward to stand by Serina, who exploded on her in a hushed tone. "I told you to stay put, whatever possessed you to come in here?"

"I was worried about you, I thought I could help you find the necklace," said Koori in a shaky voice, her eyes still on Mr. Nosh.

"Girls, no need to argue, you wouldn't want your last words said to one another to be in anger, now would you?"

Koori stepped in behind Serina a little, grabbing her hand, they both were afraid of what was going to happen. "It'll be okay Koori," Serina whispered, when Koori leaned into her shoulder. "I got you into this and I will find a way to get you out,"

Mr. Nosh stepped closer to the two panic-stricken girls and they both let out a whimper. Suddenly Serina got an idea, leaned over to Koori, and whispered; "When I say run, you take off."

Serina was standing next to the candle and had slowly inched her hand close to it while Mr. Nosh kept babbling about what he was going to do to them. Then Serina abruptly grabbed the candle putting the light out, burning the palm of her hand in the process – and yelled: "Run Koori! Run! She grabbed koori's hand and the two took off out of the cave, running as fast as they could. Mr. Nosh was stunned momentarily but quickly recovered and out of the cave he ran after them. They scurried to the shallow part of the water to cross the stream intending to leap quickly over the stones. Serina looked back but could not see Mr. Nosh, she wondered if he ever came out of the cave. Thinking they were in the clear, they crossed the stream and started for the path. When they reached the dense woods, the two took off in a dead run without looking back. Serina slowed down after a few minutes so that Koori, who was laboring to keep up, could catch up with her.

"I can't go on," gasped Koori, bending over and clutching her sides, panting.

"You have to, or he will catch us. I'll go slower but we have to run," Serina urged, a little out of breath herself.

"Too late," Koori exclaimed as she pointed her finger behind Serina. She spun around into Mr. Nosh's face. He grabbed both girls by an arm at the same time, causing them to scream in pain.

"Now! Back to the cave... That was very tricky of you indeed, but it was also expected. Didn't know I knew a shortcut, now did you?"

Serina had wondered how he caught up with them so fast – that was her answer, but she now wondered where the shortcut was.

Once back in the cave he threw them down on the dirt floor near the stone bench, they grabbed their sore throbbing arms immediately, unconsciously rubbing the pain he had inflected on them from his powerful grip.

Mr. Nosh lit the candle, sitting it back on the edge of the bench and then forced the girls to their feet shoving them up against the bench. He ordered them to sit on it, and walked around to the back of the cave, where he took out what appeared to be a very long knife. Koori gasped in horror grabbing Serina's arm. They both stared at Mr. Nosh – terror coursing through their young bodies.

"Let Koori go, please..." pleaded Serina in desperation. "She just stumbled into this by accident; she won't tell anyone, will you Koori?"

Koori just stared at the large knife, not saying a word.

"I can't do that, she knows too much, she would blab the first chance she got, isn't that right Koori?"

Koori suddenly snapped out of her shyness and glared at Mr. Nosh with as much venom she could muster. "That's right, you can't trust me to keep a secret, so if you're gonna kill her, you have to kill me too, that will make you a double murderer."

"Koori, keep quiet, I'm trying to save your neck," Serina spat at her friend.

"Thanks but no thanks, we will go together, that's what friends are for, remember; we share everything."

"No, she's crazy, please let her go," begged Serina.

"How touching," sneered Mr. Nosh, "true friends, willing to die for each other, so brave to be so young, what a pity." He laughed loud and deep with a chilling tone. The girls trembled with renewed horror while Serina pulled Koori close to her side.

"They will find your bodies and think that wild animals got you – as I'm sure that's what got poor Thabor. I found him in the woods this morning. He looked an awful sight – tore up pretty bad, when I looked in his coat pocket though, I found your pretty emerald stone." Mr. Nosh's smile was evil; he looked at the girls as if he were actually looking forward to the dirty deed.

Serina's mind was working fast trying to figure out their next move, when something caught her eye, just inside the shadows behind Mr. Nosh, something was there, which she had not noticed before, but she could not make out what, or who it was. Mr. Nosh was droning on and on about all the things he was going to do with the magic emerald, since he found out about all of its powers.

It happened so fast, before anyone could even know what was happening. Out of the darkness, Zarf grabbed Mr. Nosh, throwing him to the ground. He swiftly crawled away, shrinking back from the huge monster and pulled his knife flashing it at Zarf. Quick as a wink Mr. Nosh was on his feet, Zarf knocked the knife from his hand and hit the man so hard that he stumbled back and fell to the ground once again. Yet he got to his feet and stepped away from Zarf. He then reached over, grabbed koori by the hair, pulled her in front of him, and threw her at the big giant's feet, causing him to stumble and fall with a loud thud, stunning him for a moment while Mr. Nosh reached and grabbed Serina by the arm pulling her with him toward the mouth of the cave.

Zarf rolled off Koori and climbed to his feet as quickly as his bulky frame would allow leaving Koori lying motionless, evidently knocked out from the giant falling on her. Serina screamed to Koori but she lay still, lifeless on the ground. Mr. Nosh was dragging Serina with him, closer to the opening, she yanked very hard and kicked Mr. Nosh in the shin causing him to loosened his grip enough for her to pull loose. Running to Koori's side, she dropped to her knees, taking her head in her lap. Koori was alive but unconscious. There was a large bump on her forehead that seemed to be swelling by the minute. She looked up to see the two men still struggling. *No time to worry about them now*, she had to get Koori out of there and didn't know how she was going to do it. *Now*, she thought, *would be a good time to have those magical powers*. She tried to drag Koori by the arms but she was too heavy. She thought if she could just get her inside the secret opening, she would be safe for the moment.

"Koori, wake up!" Serina yelled at her but she was still out cold.

The two men were still at it and from the looks of it. Zarf was getting the worse end of it, he had the brute strength but Mr. Nosh had speed and was quite a bit smarter than the big monster-looking giant was. If she helped him, Serina thought, he would have a better chance; she just didn't know what to do. She managed to get Koori to the back wall of the cave where the secret opening was, she was about to stand up and open the wall when the wall opened, without Serina's assistance, and her mother walked through. She jumped to her feet and into her mother's arms. Immediately she started telling her everything that was going on; about Mr. Nosh stealing her necklace and what he was about to do to her and Koori when Zarf came.

Senora helped Serina to pick up Koori and lay her out of the way of the two men then she held her daughter in her arms and watched for the outcome of the incongruous fighting.

Mr. Nosh was beating Zarf around the head with a stick he found somewhere. The poor giant was throwing his hands up to his face to protect it from the blows. The smaller man was too quick for Zarf however, and before they knew it, Zarf was on the ground, bleeding. He just lay their groaning helplessly, he could not get up.

Mr. Nosh then walked the distance separating him from Serina and her mother. He was breathing very rapidly and from what little light the candle put out, they could see the evil in his eyes as he glared at the two.

"Well, the numbers just keep adding up don't they?" he sneered maliciously.

"Don't touch my daughter, or you will be sorry you were ever born." Senora spat vehemently and she pushed Serina up against the cave walls and stood in front of her.

"Ah the mother, I see where she gets her spirit, Thabor told me you were alive. Too bad you have to die again, this time for real though." He spoke in a shrilled voice, yet there was an icy undertone to it.

"Something that's puzzled me ever since my daughter told me about you and Thabor is – how did you and him meet?" Senora asked quizzically.

"That was purely by accident, I was out looking for some amethyst quartz one day and stumbled upon him, he was really quite taken aback to find someone from the village so deep in the woods. And when he found out what I was looking for, he told me he could get all the precious stones I wanted. Little did I know he was stealing them from his Masters castle, of course that did not matter to me, as long as I was getting them for next to nothing, too bad your giant here killed him I presume but I did manage to get the beautiful magic emerald I so desperately wanted." Mr. Nosh laughed viciously as he toyed with the necklace for a minute then shoved it back deep in his pocket.

"He had a bigger heart than I realized too, I told him on numerous occasions to get rid of this little twit of a daughter of yours but he just couldn't bring himself to do it. Last night I told him to get the stone and then bring the girl to me, that's what he was doing when your giant encountered him in her bedroom and killed him."

"That's not true, it was the Dark Lord, I saw him, he's the one who came into my room and attacked Thabor, he made me float in the air back to my bed," replied Serina.

"Shhhhh, Serina, it's alright, it was Zarf."

Serina gave her mother a puzzled look; she could have sworn it was the Dark Lord.

"He was supposed to meet me at my shop afterwards and he never showed up, I found him this morning in the woods where your goon carried him and left him. Enough of this though, I don't have time for this little chitchat. He took a step closer and seized Senora by the arm yanking her to the stone bench, he pulled a long piece of rope from his pocket and began tying her up, next he tied up Serina, making a loop around the two of them joining them together.

"That should do it," he said, checking the rope to make sure the rope was secure; he walked over to Koori whose body still lay unconscious on the damp earth floor.

"She's about had it already, that big ogre falling on her like that."

He bent over Koori's body to check for any sign of life when out of the corner of Serina's eye she caught a glimpse of movement.

In a huge lunging leap, Zarf was across the room attacking Mr. Nosh. Before Serina knew what was happening, he was all over the man. The jeweler was bashing and flailing his arms in a wild panic, he didn't have time to think or act, Zarf had the upper hand and in a moment Mr. Nosh lay on the floor bleeding and unmoving. It had happened so fast Serina's head was still spinning. Zarf came over to her and Senora, he was making grunting noises, shaking his head and he was still bleeding from several wounds on his head, arms and hands.

"Untie us Zarf," her mother said in her tender soft voice.

The giant reached over and with unusually gentle hands untied the two of them, Senora reached up and pressed one of her soft hands against his grotesque face and the giant let out a moaning sound that gave Serina cold chills.

"Thank you Zarf."

Serina ran over to where Koori lay and bent down beside her, checking to see if she was still breathing - to Serina's great relief, she was. Serina didn't hear him but Zarf was suddenly by her side, he bent over and swooped up Koori like she was a rag doll and laid her on the stone bench, next to the candle that was almost completely burned away. Senora bent over Koori checking her over then pulled a small vial from her cape; she raised Koori's head and put a few drops of the dark liquid into her mouth. Koori coughed and sputtered but never opened her eyes.

"She will be just fine when she wakes up Serina, the bump on her head is only minor and I can see nothing else wrong with her."

Next she eased over to Mr. Nosh to check for a pulse. He was dead, of course. Serina stared at the lifeless body, she was in a state of shock; she had never seen a dead person before. Her mother took her in her arms again and held her for a moment, assuring her everything would be all right.

"Here, you might need this," Senora said gently, handing Serina the emerald necklace she had taken from out of Mr. Nosh's pocket.

Serina took the necklace and placed it around her neck without ever taking her eyes off Mr. Nosh, she stared transfixed for a moment longer then she looked up at her mother, a question coming to mind.

"Mother, I thought I was having a dream last night. You say that Zarf came to my room, but I saw the Dark Lord and I floated in the air, while they fought. Then I floated back across the room like I was on pillows and drifted down onto the top of my bed with a soft flop, I remember it; it was a dream wasn't it, because the Dark Lord looked at me with concern in his eyes, that would make it a dream, right?"

"That was Zarf, I kinda borrowed the Dark Lord's cloak for Zarf to use and gave him some dream dust to sprinkle over you to make you think it was all a dream, I had him follow Thabor last night, I feared something was going to happen."

"But the scar – I saw the scar down his face."

"You only imagined the scar I am sure."

About that time they heard groaning noises coming from the stone bench, Koori was coming to; they rushed over to her about the time she opened her eyes.

"Koori! Are you okay? You have a nasty bump on your head but mother says you will be all right, she will, won't she mother?" Serina asked turning to her mother for some kind of reassurance then back to Koori then back to her mother again when she did not answer fast enough.

"Yes Koori you will be fine," Senora replied as both girls stared up at her.

"You may have a headache for a few days but all in all you are okay."

"You should have seen it Koori, it was awful. Mr. Nosh is dead..."

"Serina, slow down, she just came to, give her a minute," her mother chuckled.

"Whus hapning." Koori's speech was slurred but otherwise, she seemed to be all right and anxious to find out what all happened while she was unconscious.

"You should have seen Zarf, he was magnificent, Mr. Nosh had the best of him and knocked him out, mother and I thought he was dead for sure. He lay on the ground all bloody and then Mr. Nosh tied us up and when he was about to run you through with that big knife of his, well Zarf there, he came out of nowhere and pulled him away from you and killed him dead."

Koori shook her head in disbelief, she was trying hard to understand everything Serina was saying, but Serina was talking so fast she could not keep up with her. The only part she caught for sure was the part about Mr. Nosh running her through. She tried to raise herself up but was too dizzy; she laid her head back on the hard stone bench for a moment longer before she tried again.

After a few minutes deciding the two girls had had enough excitement for one night, Senora told them it was time for them to go home and for her to get back to the castle before she was missed.

"Zarf will take you back to the village; don't mention this to any one, Serina you have two more nights before the Dark Lord comes for you. Now that Mr. Nosh is no longer with us, you don't have to worry about your comings and going's, just don't come back to the cave, I have to get back before I'm missed."

She hugged both the girls and kissed them goodbye, then she walked over to where Zarf stood and handed him something, then said to him.

"Zarf; take them home."

"Arrgh!" Zarf stated.

Serina's mother walked to the secret opening, turned around and blew Serina and Koori a kiss, went through the passage and was gone.

Koori winced as Zarf picked her up; she still was unsure how to react toward him. He carried her out of the cave, grunting at Serina to follow no doubt, at least that's how Serina interpreted it. She obediently followed Zarf out into the night; she knew he had just saved all their lives but she couldn't help but feel a little afraid of the giant. As they walked, she looked up at Koori every so often to assure herself that her friend was okay.

As soon as the three were out of sight, Senora stepped back through the opening. She followed them as far as the edge of the forest and stopped, watching them disappear in the night. Zarf would sprinkle the dream dust over the two girls before leaving them, altering their memories of the last few weeks. She knew she should not have interfered with things but seeing her daughter up close and holding her in her arms was worth everything, Senora thought – just in case things did not go as planned.

She knew Serina would forget everything in a few minutes, until the Dark Lord came – everything that is, except for finding the emerald – Senora was the only one who knew about how the emerald came to be in the stream. She was the one who put it there. The emerald did have magical powers; it could reverse things as she had told her daughter but only in the hands of certain chosen ones. Serina was one of the chosen ones, the Dark Lord, well that was another matter... At least, for now, she would not have to worry about magical powers or the Dark Lord. She could just enjoy being a little girl. She could be excited about the next couple of days, marking them off, counting down like any other child who would be waiting for their birthday to arrive, instead of dreading each day in fear of what was to come.

The monstrous giant made sure the girls were safe in their own beds before he left each of them. He sprinkled a fine silvery dust over their beds and the girls fell right to sleep... But before he sprinkled the dust over Serina, she reached up, gave the giant a hug, thanked him for everything, and promised to see him soon. The giant groaned and started swaying back and forth. He reached down with one of his huge gnarled hands and touched Serina on the cheek. She saw the tears well up in his unmatched eyes before he could turn away then remembering he turned back and sprinkled the dream dust over Serina's bed.

"Goonit," the huge beast whispered.

"Goodnight Zarf," Serina whispered, as she cuddled under her bedding. She fell fast asleep before the giant had time to climb out of her window, all of the events of the past few weeks lost as she drifted off into a pleasant dreamless sleep, come morning neither Serina nor Koori would remember a thing.

Chapter 10

Serina woke up the next morning with no recollection of what had happened the night before, or for the last few weeks, for that matter. The morning rays, shining through her window and across her face, enveloped her with a warm sunny feeling all the way down to her toes. She hopped out of bed, washed, dressed and combed her long dark unruly hair, braiding it then wrapping it around her head. It was only two days until her birthday and she could hardly wait, she would be twelve years old.

All the village folks were in a tizzy about Mr. Nosh's accident when Serina and Koori got to town later that day.

The two had walked into the herb shop, doing some shopping for Koori's mother, when they had overheard Mrs. Norris, the owner, and Mrs. Kent talking.

"They say he fell out his upstairs window, what a mess, all bloody and such," Mrs. Kent was saying.

"Yes – and what a pity, he was such a nice man too."

Serina and Koori walked over to the two women, their curiosity peeked.

"Who fell from their window?" The two girls asked in unison.

"Why Mr. Nosh, the jeweler from across the street – what a shame too – my, my, my, he must have been leaning out the window or something you think," said Mrs. Kent, returning her attention to Mrs. Norris.

"He just finished making a necklace for me a couple of weeks ago," Serina put-in. Arousing the two women's curiosity, they both watched as Serina pulled the necklace from around her neck. Mrs. Norris took it from Serina, looked at it then passed it to Mrs. Kent and they both went on and on about how beautiful it was and that it was probably the last thing he made before he died, adding a few more 'what a shame's' to their chatter, of course.

Serina and Koori were almost at the door to leave when Mrs. Kent called out. "Oh Serina dear, how is your father? I've been meaning to stop by to check on him and you too, of course," she added shooting an awkward glance toward Mrs. Norris suddenly realizing how her remark must have sounded to her. Serina knew the woman didn't care anything about her. She only cared about her father.

"He's just fine, thank you, I'm going to fix him a special supper tonight, he's been working late every night this week but he's finishing up tonight and I want to surprise him."

Once outside Serina and Koori went straight over to Mr. Nosh's shop but it was all closed up with a note nailed to the front door, saying something to the effect that due to a death the shop would be closed until further notice.

"It really is a shame that he died," said Koori, matter-of-factly. "My mother said he and Mrs. Kent should have married, that way she would have left your father alone."

"Your mother thinks Mrs. Kent should marry every single man in the village, Koori," Serina snickered.

"Everyone except your father; she says he is a one time 'marrier.'"

"What does that mean?" asked Serina, her eyebrows raised in question.

"Nothing, only that; she says some people are one-time 'marriers', meaning that they only fall in love once in their lifetime and if something was to happen to their mate, they would never marry again but pine their hearts away for their lost loved one instead."

"You mean like you would if you and Bootie ever married?" asked Serina laughing at the look on Koori's face and at the thought of her friend and Mrs. Kent's porky son ever marrying. She dashed off in a trot with Koori chasing after her, yelling something about not being as bad as her – meaning Serina marrying Frog.

She caught up with Serina at the market and the two wondered through the fresh produce and meat stalls, looking for something special for Serina to cook for her father's dinner. It was true he had been working hard lately and she did want to surprise him with a nice meal.

"How about a goose?" Koori asked spying three large ones in a pen close by.

"Sounds great, he loves roast goose with thick gravy and all the trimmings."

They finished making their purchases and with their arms full, they headed back, stopping off at Koori's first then Serina left her friend and went home.

Serina opened her front door and dropped her fat goose on the floor – she was stunned. Bootie was sitting in her father's over-stuffed chair, shoving a large piece of chocolate cake into his mouth, dropping crumbs, all over himself and on Papa's chair.

"Wh-what are you doing here?" Serina asked more than a little perturbed by Bootie's presence in her house.

"Mum's cooking," he managed to blurt out, spitting even more crumbs over his chest and lap.

Serina picked up her goose and headed for the kitchen, mumbling under her breath as she went.

"Oh, hello Serina, I see you finally made it home from your playing," said Mrs. Kent in a strained fake pleasant voice as Serina walked in.

She looked around her in horror as she stepped into her once nice clean cozy kitchen. Every inch of it was now covered with pots, pans and dishes, not to mention flour, eggshells and quite a bit of other food products Serina could not recognize disgustingly splattered on the floor and counters.

"Good, you brought a goose, go out back and pluck it. I'll cook it for your father, the dear man, wasting away to nothing, he is," said Mrs. Kent, a touch of impatience in her voice, as she turned back to kneading her dough, not giving Serina a second look.

"I thought I told you I was going to cook for my father tonight, a special meal, just for me and him, remember?" Serina retorted now clearly offended by the woman's presence in her home.

"Don't be ridiculous child, that's what's wrong with him now, no one to cook a decent meal for him... Now go on with that goose like I said and don't dawdle." She was getting more impatient with Serina by the minute.

"I've never plucked a goose before Mrs. Kent, can Bootie help me?"

"Lazy are ya?" the woman replied coolly. "Well there's no time like the present to learn. It will do you good to work a little more, from the looks of this house you don't do much at all, besides little bootie is allergic to feathers, now go on with yourself."

Serina took off out the back door, goose in hand, thinking that wasn't all *little Bootie* was allergic to, most likely if it involved work in any way other than lifting a fork to his mouth, he would be allergic, probably break out in a rash and everything – no wonder he was so *fat*.

Serina sat on a stump in the yard plucking the goose; with every feather she pulled she pretended it was Mrs. Kent or Bootie's head.

After she had plucked the goose the best she could, she took it in to Mrs. Kent to cook.

"What did my father say about you cooking supper for us?" Serina asked defiantly, thinking he had been most likely hoodwinked into it somehow, knowing Mrs. Kent.

"Oh, he insisted that I not go to the trouble but I let him know it was no trouble cooking for two extra people. I wouldn't take 'no' for an answer – told him that it was too much trouble for a little girl to take care of a grown man. He agreed with me there but kept insisting for me not to bother. What does he know; he hasn't had a decent meal in so long he's forgotten what good food taste like. Now fetch me that pot then go out and see if Bootie needs anything else to snack on before supper," Mrs. Kent ordered finally ending her tirade in a demeaning tone of voice.

Serina took the big pot to Mrs. Kent but went to her room instead. She was not about to start waiting on Bootie that was for sure. If he wanted another snack then *let him get up off his lazy behind and get it himself* and besides, the last thing he needed was another snack before supper.

Serina had a miserable time at supper that night, watching Mrs. Kent shove more and more food toward her father and watching her son drag it away and pile it on his own plate when his mother wasn't looking. A few times she caught him and scolded him softly.

"Bootie dear, slow down, save some for the others... He gets like that when he doesn't get enough to snack on before meals." She cast a stranded smile in Serina's direction then promptly looked back to Mr. Zimmer, ignoring Bootie's beastly behavior.

At one point when Bootie was struggling with Serina over the bowl of potatoes, he gave her a hard kick under the table, hitting her in the shin; she let go of the bowl with a loud squeal, sending most of the potatoes flying across the table right smack into Mrs. Kent's face. Mrs. Kent let out a shriek of her own, reared back and tried to get up from her chair but its leg hung on the rug underneath the table and she flipped backwards onto the floor. Her dress, petticoat, and whatever else covered her ample belly, flew over her head. This was about the funniest thing Serina had ever seen; she burst out laughing and giggling until she cried – which was not a good thing for her to do.

Next thing she knew her father was trying to pick up Mrs. Kent from the floor, wiping potatoes from her beet-red face and scolding Serina – all at the same time. All the while Bootie never stopped eating, except to say that Serina was to blame, saying he had reached for the potatoes and Serina yanked them away from him, causing the potatoes to go flying.

"That's not true," Serina exclaimed vehemently. "He was trying to pull the bowl from me and kicked me under the table." Although, secretly, she had to admit that she did turn loose of the bowl in hopes the potatoes would fly into Bootie's face but what happened in turn was even funnier – to see Mrs. Kent getting a face full of spuds was the best.

After Mr. Zimmer helped Mrs. Kent to her feet and she managed to clean the potatoes from her face and hair, they resumed supper in silence. Serina couldn't help thinking how funny Mrs. Kent looked with parts of her hair stuck to the side of her head and her face still red in spots from the hot potatoes, especially when she would shoot Serina a scathing glance when she thought her father wasn't looking. To make matters worse Bootie kept trying to kick her shin under the table. At each kick, Serina would jump and flinch. Of course, her reactions didn't go unnoticed and her father would shoot warning looks in her direction every time she would jump while trying to avoid Bootie's boots. Overall, this was the worse night she had ever spent at the dinner table.

Mrs. Kent and Bootie stayed around after the meal chatting with her father while Serina cleaned the kitchen alone. She thought that Mrs. Kent must be the messiest cook she ever encountered from the looks of their kitchen, pot and pans, bowls and plates. She figured Mrs. Kent left the mess on purpose knowing Serina would have to clean it all up. Yet, she preferred cleaning the kitchen to being in the living room with the likes of her and her son. She only felt sorry for her father having to endure them by himself. She was about through when Bootie came in and cut himself another piece of chocolate cake, his third for the night.

"Mum says she may marry your father and when she does she's gonna teach you how to do the chores around the house and beat some of that laziness out of you," Bootie declared with a vicious little laugh.

"Oh yeah, well I got news for you," Serina snapped angrily, "my father wouldn't marry your mother if she were the last woman in this village besides he's a one-time marrier, you big lazy fat porker." She was so mad she was ready to fight him and held up her fists at him. He was just about to take a large bite of cake when she threatened him; he backed up, and tripped over a chair, falling to the floor, squashing the piece of cake right between his eyes. He then rolled over to get up displaying his whole face covered in chocolate. Serina burst out laughing for the second time that evening. Bootie got to his feet and ran into the sitting room screaming to his mother. Serina cleaned up the floor and waited for Mrs. Kent and her father to come barging in to scold her for whatever it was Bootie told them that she did. When no one came, she eased up to the door and listened to what was going on in the other room. She wasn't sure what Bootie had told them but Mrs. Kent was lecturing her father for Serina's unruly behavior.

"Really Josh, you should do something with that girl before she gets completely out of hand, why she could have hurt poor Little Bootie, it's no wonder she acts like that with no mother to teach her any better."

"Oh I'm sure poor little Bootie is just fine aren't you Bootie, no worse for wear huh?" said Mr. Zimmer smiling at the fat child who was still wiping chocolate from his face and licking his fingers. "A little chocolate cake on the face never hurt anyone and I am sure Serina didn't do anything intentional to him. Serina and I do just fine by ourselves. Oh, and I seldom have to punish her for beating up the village kids," he added with a slight chuckle.

"Well, I'm sure it was an accident. I, we, we must be going Josh. Now, come along Bootie dear, say goodnight."

Mrs. Kent yanked Bootie by the arm and pulled him out the door while he whined all the way to the gate that she was hurting his arm.

"Father you were terrific," Serina exclaimed bursting into the sitting room after Mrs. Kent and Bootie were gone.

"Not so fast my little hellion, what really happened in the kitchen?" her father asked with a sympathetic grin crossing his face.

Serina quickly explained what had taken place, including what had been said.

"Well, I'm sure Little Bootie deserved a little chocolate in the face but you don't have to be so happy about it."

They both laughed, even more so, when they recalled the spud episode at the table, although her father did scold her for laughing at Mrs. Kent's embarrassing predicament. They both went to the kitchen to have a piece of the leftover chocolate cake, and a glass of milk. When they were sitting at the table, Serina looked up at her father and asked, "Father you wouldn't ever really marry Mrs. Kent would you?"

He looked at his daughter for a long moment with a far away look in his eyes, then, replied; "Well, as a matter of fact, the thought had occurred to me,"

"Father!" Serina gasped in puzzlement. Her father couldn't help but to laugh at the look on his daughter's face. Then he took on a more serious expression and said, "No dear, I would never marry Mrs. Kent – or anyone else for that matter."

"Is that because you're a one time marrier?" asked Serina feeling as though she understood her father's feelings.

"A one time marrier huh? Well that's a new one on me but I guess you're right, I believe you need to love someone before you can marry them. I also believe you can't love two people at the same time, and I don't believe in falling out of love either, the kind of love two grown people share is very special – and no Serina, I will never marry again." At those words, Serina's father gazed into space for a moment – deep in thought. Then, turning his attention to his daughter once again he added, "It's just you and me, I guess, that is until you grow up and fall in love with some ugly, hairy legged boy and leave your father all alone." He chuckled and reaching over, he wiped off a spot of chocolate from the tip of Serina's nose. "Now who's got the chocolate face, huh?" he said, ruffling the top of her hair. "Now off to bed with you, it's late, I'll come in to say goodnight when you're dressed."

Serina stood obediently and started for the door, but half way there, she stopped and turned back to her father. "Papa, you still love my mother, don't you? That's why you can't marry again?"

"Off to bed with you Half Pint, you're talking stuff now that's too far over a little girl's head to understand," he said waving his daughter out of the kitchen.

"I'm *not* a little girl father," Serina countered petulantly. "I'll be twelve in only two days - *that* makes me a young lady."

"That's right you have a birthday coming up, I keep forgetting, you may have to remind me again tomorrow – and yes, I could see where that would make one think they were grown," he teased. "But young ladies still need their rest so it's off to bed with you."

Serina giggled all the way to her bedroom. She wondered if she *would* have to remind her father again of her birthday, he was getting older, somewhere in his thirties she thought – *anyway older people did have a tendency to forget.*

The next day, the eve of her birthday, Serina was very busy for the first part of the day, helping her father at the shop, but the rest of the day, he had told her to go and enjoy herself. So, and without waiting to be told twice, she took off for Koori's place. Once there, she helped in taking care of Zeb while Koori finished her chores. Serina and Zeb played ball in the yard until she thought her arms would fall off from tossing the ball and catching it time and again. By then, Zeb was getting cranky, probably from needing his lunch and a good nap. Not knowing exactly what to do with a young child, she took him in and right away, he ran to his mother and started howling for "bite, bite." This Serina knew, meant lunch, so she graciously left him into his mother's care and went to find Koori.

With plan in mind they headed off down the path toward the footbridge to play in the stream, this was one of their favorite places.

When they saw Amil and Frog up ahead, they hurried and caught up with the two boys.

"What's up?" Amil asked when the two girls were in earshot.

"Not much, just going to the stream, what about you two?" Serina enquired.

"Same thing, thought we'd get wet for a minute, but we have to wear clothes though," Amil grumbled dispiritedly.

Serina figured Amil would have been happier if the girls had not shown up but she was not willing to give up her swimming time for him, or any other boy for that matter.

"Yeah, too bad," Koori chimed in, casting a quick glance in Frog's direction then looking away in embarrassment upon seeing that he was returning the glance with a broad grin crossing his face. This did not pass unnoticed by Amil *or* Serina but they both silently decided to let it go at that – neither one in a teasing mood now.

"Hey, wanna go to the falls?" Frog asked excitedly.

Everyone lit up at the thought and they all headed to the cascade – the four children talking over the other, Frog the loudest of all, with his deep voice; it easily carried over everyone else's.

"The falls are Serina's most favorite place in the whole world," Koori remarked nudging her friend. "She could stay there for ever and ever and ever." Giggling, she repeated Serina's very words from just a few weeks earlier, making everyone laugh. Serina's cheeks reddened at the recollection; she secretly thought of ways to get her friend back.

Upon reaching the falls, no one hesitated; they jumped bums first into the water. It felt great to relax and play in the turquoise pool. There was a place nearby; a cliff over-hang about half way up to the top of the falls to where the boys would climb and then jump off yelling all the way down. Serina and Koori begged off from this excursion. Since Koori was afraid of heights, Serina thought it best to stay down below with her friend. It looked like it would be a real hoot though, Serina thought; to climb that high then jump into the wind, falling with the rushing falls down into the depths of the water below. She also knew she could climb and dive as good as any ole boy, anytime she wanted, if she put her mind to it.

The four of them spent the rest of the afternoon splashing and playing in the clear blue water – the boys of course, showing off their diving skills every so often. Once Frog threatened, teasingly, to carry Koori up to the top of the falls and throw her off, saying that it would cure her from being afraid of heights. She screeched and begged him not to do such a thing, saying she would surely die from fright before she ever got to the top. Serina knew this was Frog's way of flirting with Koori and joined in the teasing, because anyone could see that he was definitely smitten with her and if Serina didn't know better, she would have sworn that Koori was a little taken with him also. Of course, Koori would never admit to such a thing aloud. Serina would never admit it either, but she was a little taken with Amil. He was awfully handsome and… he was very tall and lanky, as her father would say. He was still the only one who could outrun her, and, he was the best shot with an arrow she had ever seen. Her father had told her he was a natural; give him a bow arrow and he could go out in the forest and bring home enough food for the whole village. He was the only one she knew, who was better than her father was – yet she ran a close third. Her father had been teaching her how to use a bow and arrow since she was three, all she needed was a little more strength; her aim however, was deadly.

The meadow surrounding the falls was such a lovely spot and the four stayed as late as they possibly could without getting in trouble then headed back to the village.

"Hey, I've got a great surprise for your birthday tomorrow Serina," said Amil, knowing this would get her going. He really did have a present for her but he loved to tease her. She could get riled up quicker than anyone he knew.

"What is it?" she asked, her eyes sparkling with excitement.

"Ah, but if I tell you now it will not be a surprise tomorrow, now will it." He smiled teasingly.

"That's alright, I'm sure father will surprise me with something, that's if I remind him it's my birthday."

"Well you got a point so... Naw, better not, I'm sure you can wait until tomorrow, it's not that long of a wait anyway."

"Yeah, I guess you're right," said Serina, thinking this would cause him to spill the surprise.

"You sure are gonna love it though, isn't that right Koori?" This he knew would set her off; thinking that her friend knew about it and that she had not told her – he was right.

"Koori!" Serina shouted turning an incredulous glare at her friend. "You know what my present is and you haven't even told me?"

Koori averted Serina's indignant and peering eyes to turn her attention to Amil. Not having a clue what the present was did not stop her however, and she began teasing her friend as well.

"Sure, but like Amil said, if I told you then it wouldn't be a surprise, right?"

"Oh, I can't believe my best friend knows what I'm getting for my birthday and she won't tell me," Serina said a frown crossing her brow – to Amil's delight.

About this time Frog, not wanting to be left out, joined in the fun. "You're right though Amil, she will love it," Frog's deep voice boomed - he actually knew what it was.

"You guys, I can't believe you would tease me like this, it's not fair. So, you need to tell me what my present is *now* since you've been so mean."

They all three laughed at the look on Serina's face, her lips pinned in a grimace, she was pretending to pout and was not doing a good job of it, since pouting was not one of her strong suits.

When the four got to the walk-bridge, they stopped for a moment, sitting on the huge rocks that protruded from the water onto the grassy banks. It was such a lovely spot Serina could not pass it without stopping to admire its beauty.

"This is where you found the stone in your necklace, isn't it?" Amil asked Serina, pointing to a spot in the water close by.

"Yeah, only a little farther down, right about there," she pointed. They all peered into the water ripples as if trying to imagine what she saw when Serina found the Emerald Stone.

"Wasn't that terrible about Mr. Nosh falling from his window," said Koori pensively.

"He made my stone into a necklace for me, see," Serina said holding the necklace out for her friends to admire. "Mrs. Kent and Mrs. Norris said that it was probably the last piece of work he did before he died you think?"

Serina remembered the last time she showed the stone to Amil, he had taken it away from her and had ran away with it. She wasn't going to give him the chance this time; she held it out at a distance, without taking the leather strap off from around her neck.

Frog told me he saw you two out here on the other side of the bridge a week or so ago, what were you doing out here so late?" Amil questioned, looking suspiciously from her to Koori.

Since their memories were altered by the dream dust Zarf spread over them a couple of nights before they had no memory of the incident. The two girls looked at one another, and then with a confused look, they both asked him what he was talking about, since neither one recalled being at the bridge late in the evening on any night.

"Frog said he saw you and the both of you were hanging over the bridge looking at something, maybe... Anyway, he said you then climbed down the bank and were looking around in the water. Did you lose something?"

Serina was thoroughly confused now, because she had no memory of such happening and from the look on Koori's face, she was even more confused than Serina.

"Really Amil. Maybe you saw someone else Frog, because we don't have a clue of what your talking about, do we Koori?"

"No, not a clue," Koori agreed with a bewildered look on her face.

"No, it was the two of you, I saw you with my own two eyes," Frog insisted.

"Well, maybe you can't see too good and need to have Doc Quially have a look see, huh," Koori snapped, giving Frog an indignant look. He shot a nasty glare of his own in the girls' direction, but kept silent.

"If you don't want to tell me what you were doing, then just say so but you don't have to lie about it, I won't tell your father, even though I should." Amil was getting a bit perturbed with them, thinking they were hiding something.

"*I Am* not lying to you," Serina flared, "but if I had been down here it would still be none of your business and I wouldn't tell you what I was doing anyway."

Serina's temper was mounting – Amil was calling her a liar and she couldn't understand why he was doing so. She stood up and Koori automatically stood up with her. Serina knew she had been back and forth a lot but for the life of her, she could not remember being down at the bridge late in the evening with Koori looking for something in the water – and if Koori could not remember it either, well…

"Alright, just forget I ever mentioned it," said Amil seeing that he wasn't going to get a straight answer from either one. "Come on Frog let's go, they may want to look for something else and we would just be in the way."

The two boys stood up with Amil casting Serina a very unpleasant glance. They stalked off toward the village, with her yelling out at him; "Oh yeah, I forgot, we were gonna hang around a while, we had something we wanted to look for, since *we did not find it the other night.*"

Disgruntled, Serina plopped down once again on the rock where they had been sitting. She was fuming mad and Koori was as angry about the whole thing as Serina was.

"How dare they say we were lying, who does he think he is anyway?"

"I really don't know what he has for your birthday Serina, I was just saying that to play along with them," said Koori, hoping this statement would make her friend feel any better.

"I wouldn't take his birthday present now if he begged me, the thought of him thinking such about us."

Serina and Koori waited until the boys were out of sight so they wouldn't see them then getting up and heading back to the village themselves, each one feeding the other's temper as they went.

Chapter 11

Serina went to bed that night still a little put out with Amil and Frog, she could understand Frog making a mistake in thinking he had seen her and Koori, but for Amil to think she might lie about it to him, well… She just wouldn't accept his birthday present – she would show him. The more she thought about it, the angrier she became but she was not going to let him spoil her birthday tomorrow, she was going to have a great day in spite of him…*the big galoot*. She scooted under the covers with Samone next to her, and with the blue rays of the full moon streaming across the room, and across her face, she fell asleep.

During the night Serina dreamed someone entered her room and sprinkled a misty dust in the air… Everything turned a deep purplish black, there was a heavy feeling enveloping the room… Serina felt paralyzed under the weight of her own body. She could not raise herself off the bed. She tried to cry out but nothing came out of her mouth. She lay there in silence, waiting in terror. Then there he was – a large dark hooded figure stood over her bed. There was just darkness where his face was supposed to be. Serina tried to scream but again nothing came out and fear gripped her insides as she looked up at the dark faceless figure. He fetched a small pouch from inside his cloak, pulled the drawstring and opened it, peering deep into Serina's eyes; he slowly stuck his hand inside the pouch, pulled out a small amount of a fine silvery dust and sprinkled it over her face and body.

"My prize, at last I've come for you. As it was written, so shall it be." His voice was cold and calculating; it seemed to come from all over the room, vibrating off the walls, into her ears and into her soul.

Then Serina's body was lifted weightlessly into the air above her bed; the weight of her body no longer paralyzing – she felt as light as a feather.

He took her into his arms and carried her to the window, where he climbed out into the night with Serina cradled in his arms. Once outside she struggled to get free but it was useless, she had no control over her body – she couldn't move. There was a huge menacing black dragon, with bright yellow glowing eyes, standing in Serina's back yard, trampling her beautiful azalea flowerbeds. He was waiting patiently for his Master. He turned his head and looked deep into Serina's eyes, she felt drawn toward the beast hypnotized by those big menacing eyes. She could see right through them as she felt her body going deeper into a trance. Finally, however, she managed to pull away from his stare as she was carried onto his back. Serina felt the muscles in the giant dragon's back tighten as he flapped his large wings and took flight. They rapidly gained height and soared into the air, leaving the ground far behind. They flew high up over the rooftops, speeding away, higher and higher leaving her house below. Serina looked down at the little specks dotting the ground; this was her village shrinking ever so smaller as she disappeared into the night.

The dragon was a very large one indeed; he had wings that spanned the length of at least three houses side by side. His back was ridged all the way down to the tip of his tail and he had several very large scars all over his body, leading Serina to think the dragon had been near death at least a few times in his lifetime – she wondered how he came about them. She was sitting between two of the huge ridges in front of the cloaked man, the face of whom she still could not see. There was just a dark hollow opening in the cowl where a face should have been.

They flew so high, Serina could no longer see the ground; the night sky and whiffs of clouds here and there was all there was to see. She could not remember ever dreaming such a dream as this before, yet it all seemed very familiar to her; the dragon, his big yellow eyes, the cloaked man, everything seemed familiar, she had seen it all before that night – somehow they knew each other or at least it felt as such.

She could hear his evil laugh as Serina tried to pull away from the firm grip of this cloaked faceless man. *Who is he? Where does he come from?* Serina kept asking herself as they soared through the midnight sky. She tried to wake up but it was useless, the dream just went on and on, and on... It seemed like it would last forever, when suddenly their steed started to descend, his large body changing directions as they headed down toward the earth once more.

A few minutes later, a huge castle came into view. It was as dark and menacing looking as the cloaked man sitting behind her, and although there was a full moon, the place was shrouded in darkness.

Before the dragon sat its feet on the ground, the cloaked man took out his pouch again, sprinkling more of the mysterious silvery dust over Serina, and she quickly fell asleep again. The last thing she remembered thinking was that if she was asleep already then how could she fall asleep again, without waking up?

Serina slept a deep peaceful sleep for the rest of the night – no more dreams, no nothing, just a deep, deep sleep.

Serina stirred, stretched and rolled over to her side, without opening her eyes. She felt so comfortable somehow, that she did not want to wake up. She had been in such a deep sleep that it was taking her longer than usual to awake. Suddenly remembering her dream, her eyes popped open then quickly closed again, she rubbed her eyelids hard with both her fists and very slowly lifted them again.

Where am I? She was in a large white tent it seemed. However as her eyes adjusted to her strange surroundings, she realized she was not lying in a tent but in a very large bed with four tall posts, one standing at each corner of the bed. They supported a railing from which thin white satin drapes hung and flowed to the floor.

If she thought this was a sight to behold, it was nothing to what lay outside the thin curtains. She pulled them open to step out of the bed and her breath caught in her throat. She stumbled to her feet, took a few steps, and stopped. She was standing in the middle of a very large room; the walls and windows were covered and draped in the same thin white satin material as the bed was. Serina felt like she was nestled in the middle of a cloud. There was a dressing table on one side of the room with a large mirror surmounting it. She took a step toward the dressing table and tripped. She looked down and realized she was wearing a long flowing white gown instead of her usual cotton nightdress. She walked over to the dressing table and slowly looked at her reflection in the large mirror.

"Yep, that's my face alright," Serina said aloud. She pinched her arm rather hard and let out a yelp. *No, I am not dreaming.* Looking at her arm she rubbed the spot that was beginning to turn red.

Serina felt her insides turn to jelly, as did her legs when she tried to take a step. She managed to walk over to one of the windows and look out. She took in a sharp breath at the magnificent scenery that unfolded before her eyes – just outside the window.

The vast grounds below were expertly manicured. There were flowerbeds in an array of colors, nestled under huge shade trees. Fountains and statues punctuated the lawns and the freshness and perfumes that emanated from this Eden were equally enchanting. The beauty of the garden that lay before her was incomparable to anything Serina had ever seen.

A sudden noise made Serina turn toward the door. A small rather old gray haired man entered carrying a tray. He bowed slightly in Serina's direction then walked over to a table, which Serina had not noticed before that moment. He sat the tray down, turned around, bowed again and shuffled his way toward the door.

"Wait! Who are you? Where am I?" blurted out Serina before the little gray man reached the door.

"They call me Toddle," he said in a quiet voice. "And you are here." He bowed again slightly and took another step. Serina didn't want him to leave before she obtained some answers.

"Please wait, is this a dream? Am I dreaming? Please tell me I'm dreaming."

Serina's voice was shaking as she spoke, pleading with the little man. This had to be a dream, that's all there was to it. "Well, I am wide awake... So that would make you wide awake also, so, no, this is not a dream."

He started toward the door again but Serina stopped him before he could take another step.

"Where is *here*? You said I am *here*, I don't understand. Where is my father... my house?" Serina was getting frantic.

"Here is here, there is no other place," the little man replied irritably. "And I do not know where your father is but you live here." His voice took on a sharper tone apparently annoyed with Serina for bombarding him with silly questions. He left the room without another word, even though she was begging and pleading with him to tell her something that would make sense to her.

After he left she ran to the door but it was bolted from the outside. She wiggled the knob and tried to force it to open to no avail. It was a strong sturdy door and it wouldn't budge. Serina slumped to the floor in front of the door and began crying.

She spent the rest of the morning trying to figure out how to get out of the room. She knew she couldn't get out by stepping out from any of the windows because the room was too high up. Actually, it appeared that she was a prisoner in a beautiful room at the top of a tower – a very tall tower, indeed. She looked around the room but saw no way to escape captivity.

Lunchtime brought a new servant to her room; this one was a tall skinny girl not much older than Serina.

At first, Serina did not speak to the girl. She entered carrying her tray of food over to the table, sitting it down and looking at Serina curiously. Then she shook her head and picked up the breakfast tray but stopped and turned her gaze toward Serina.

"Ya really aught a eat, no need wasting ya food like that, besides I don't wanna be a wasting me time coming up here if ya ain't gonna eat... Ya gonna eat that?" She stared at Serina as if thinking she was an unwanted addition to the place.

"No, I'd rather starve than eat," Serina replied in the same tone of voice the girl had used on her.

"Fine, suit yourself, save me the trouble of coming back up here." She was speaking more to herself than to Serina. She picked up the tray and started toward the door.

"Please, tell me where I am, and how did I get here?" Serina pleaded once more.

The girl spun around and threw Serina a long quizzical look before speaking. "Why should I tell ya anything, I don have to if I don wan to ya know," she snarled.

"I'm sorry if I made you mad, please I just want to know how I got here," Serina enjoined softly.

"Don ask me, I dunno, they just tol me to bring ya some food."

"Who told you to bring the food?" asked Serina as she stepped a little closer to the girl who in turn backed up a few steps, evidently a little afraid of Serina.

"None of your business but if ya don want it I be takin it a back with me." Then the girl suddenly scurried toward the door with the tray of food in hand and was gone before Serina could blink twice.

Since she had no other clothes to put on, Serina spent the rest of the afternoon in the beautiful gown in which she woke up.

The only other furniture in the room besides the bed, dressing table, the table for the food and a chair, was a huge wardrobe, empty of course – it was so large Serina could get inside and lie down on the floor of it and not touch its edges. At the top there was a rod to hang up clothing. At the side, there were huge drawers in which to put personal garments. The whole thing stood about eight-foot tall and was about seven-foot wide.

Late in the afternoon, an older woman unlocked the door swinging it wide to allow two men into the room. They were carrying a large wooden tub for bathing. Serina had never seen one this elaborate. They sat it in the far corner of the room. Two more men then entered carrying a large divider made of heavy wood; it folded into six sections and it was ornately carved with flowers and birds and butterflies, a very beautiful piece of furniture indeed. They sat it up in front of the tub, hiding it from view to the rest of the room. Yet again, another two men entered with a table and chair, sitting them behind the room divider. After the men had set the tub down and arranged the divider, table and chair into place, the older woman clapped her hands and they left the room and four young girls entered, their arms heavy laden with clothing, she snapped her fingers here and there at the girls, giving them orders which they carried out obediently. The girls busying themselves soon had the wardrobe full. Another girl came into the room, her arms laden with toiletries and such, filling the dressing table to the rim. She brought a beautiful silver hairbrush-and-comb set and laid them in the center of the table along with a small silver handled mirror. When they were all through, they left the room in a single file – all but the elderly woman.

"You will be getting your bath water shortly and after bathing you should dress for the party. You may pick from the three dresses I have laid out on the bed and then when you're ready, I will send Ruthie in to fix your hair."

She was a short plump woman who might have had a kind face if she smiled, but from the lines on her face, Serina thought she hadn't smiled in years.

Serina hesitated at first then rushed forward before the woman could leave.

"Please, will you tell me where I am?" asked Serina meekly. "I don't know how I got here either and no one will tell me anything, please, I just want to go home."

The woman looked Serina up and down. Serina thought she saw a glimmer of concern crossing her face; it vanished though when she spoke. "Everyone knows where this place is child, now I don't have time to play games with you, you need to bathe and dress for dinner."

"Wait, a minute ago you said something about a party, what party?" inquired Serina. She was puzzled over the whole situation and getting more puzzled by the minute.

"Your party of course," the woman muttered.

"M-my P-party," Serina stammered in bewilderment. "I don't understand, what do you mean by *my party*?"

"Your birthday party of course, now quit babbling so I can do my work."

With everything that had happened Serina had completely forgotten about her birthday. *This can't be happening, this is a dream – it's got to be a dream, that's the only thing that would explain all this weirdness.*

In a daze, Serina stepped over to the bed and looked at the clothing laid out on it. The three dresses were exquisite. They were layered in frilly lace, ribbons, and bows. *These couldn't be for wearing, could they?* One was a pale yellow with a high neck. It had very tiny buttons that started at the neckline going all the way to just below the waistline. It would take two people to fasten it because there was no way the person wearing it could button it all. The second dress, also with lots of buttons; was a deep blue with sheer white lace that covered the entire dress. The last one was lavender, it had less lace than the others did but to Serina this one was the loveliest of the three – very simply made but yet very elegant.

While she was admiring the dresses, someone knocked on the door, the woman went and opened it to let three men carrying hot water, enter. They carried their buckets over to the big tub and poured the steaming hot water into the tub, about that time three more men entered with more hot water; they kept coming until the tub was filled almost to the rim. The elderly woman busied herself putting something in the water and swishing it around then stepped from behind the big divider and said, "Miss Serina, you may go behind the dressing screen and undress for your bath now."

"I... I will not, I want to know where I am and how I got here? *Where is my father?*" Serina screamed at the woman. The latter cringed and glared at Serina for a moment and then she walked over to where she stood and looked down at her. The words Serina expected to hear did not come, instead the woman made a small attempt to smile which never made it to her eyes.

"Young lady... I do not know anything except that I need to get you ready for dinner and your party. The Master expects you at dinner by seven. It is *my* job to get you there. Now please get in the tub, we're wasting time." Her voice was as stiff and unyielding as her face was which did not faze Serina.

"Not until I find out where I am and how I got here," Serina retorted sharply.

The woman took a deep breath and both her shoulders seemed to lift up a foot then back down again.

"Very well, if that's the way you want it." She went to the door, pulled out a key unlocking it and disappeared momentarily only to return with four of the girls who had put the clothes away earlier.

Serina sensed what was about to happen. She knew her feelings were right when the girls came toward her, grabbed her and carried her fighting tooth and nail all the way to the tub. There, they stripped her naked and tossed her into the steaming hot bubbles. Serina screamed and tried to climb out of the tub but one of the girls pushed Serina under the water. She came up gasping for air but did not try to climb out again.

"That's enough Effie," the older woman snapped looking down at the near drowned Serina.

"Now you have to be down to the dining hall by seven sharp – you can't be late. So you can scrub yourself or I can get Effie here to do it, the choice is yours," added the older woman in a no nonsense tone that made Serina think twice about climbing out of the tub, instead she sunk deeper into the water until just the top of her head was poking out of the bubbles.

"Okay, I'll bathe – that's if the lot of you will leave, I would like a little privacy – and I still want to know what's going on here." With a smirk on her face, the older woman and the others stepped around the screen, leaving Serina to bathe in privacy. She sat in the warm bubbly water for a moment trying to soak in everything that had transpired since she opened her eyes that morning. It wasn't long before the gentle aroma of Jasmine and Chamomile drifted to her nostrils tickling her senses. She laid her head on the back of the tub, closed her eyes tightly, hoping it would all go away when she opened them again. This was no longer a dream, but a nightmare. She squeezed her eyes shut and lay there for a few minutes. The next thing she knew someone was nudging her shoulder roughly. She opened her eyes and looked into the face of the older woman, who handed Serina a chunk of soap that smelled just like the bubbles in which she had been soaking.

She sat up taking the soap without saying a word; finished bathing, climbed out of the wonderful water and dried off.

Everyone made a fuss over getting Serina dressed. The girl, they called Ruthie, combed Serina's hair, putting ribbons into it that matched the lavender dress she was wearing. When she finished with Serina's hair she stepped back for the older woman to give her final approval. They all clapped, smiling broadly at their handy work and then bowing to Serina, they stepped back for the older woman to lead Serina to the large mirror on the wall. She took Serina's hand, led her to stand in front of the mirror, and then stepped back. At first, Serina thought she was looking at someone else, but soon realized it was her own reflection staring back at her curiously. Ruthie had out-done herself because her hair was silky and flowing down her back in a cascade of fine curls – not the wild, unruly mess she usually saw in her mirror. The dress was undoubtedly the finest dress she had ever donned, very little lace and frills, but gorgeous just the same.

"What do you think of yourself, Serina?" the woman asked, eyeing Serina carefully, looking for any hint of disapproval.

"I... I can't believe it's me, I mean... Well, it doesn't look like me but it is most definitely me... I, it's beautiful."

"That will do girls," the woman said while she followed the servants to the door and locked it behind them. She then turned back to Serina, walked the distance between them without speaking, never taking her eyes off Serina.

Serina felt herself shrinking under the woman's intense gaze. Then as if she suddenly snapped out of a spell, the woman took a chair and seated herself, motioning to Serina to sit on the bed. Once they were both seated the woman stared down at Serina causing her to shrink back a little. She did not speak, but just stared unblinking at the young girl. For a few interminable minutes the woman continued to gawk unblinking, boring a hole into Serina's forehead, then after what seemed an eternity, the woman cleared her throat. "There are a few things I must tell you before you go down to dinner. Pay close attention to what I say, for I will not repeat them." She cleared her throat again, her tone taking on a much more serious note; she went on, never taking her eyes off Serina. "First; do not speak out at any time, only nod your head in agreement, speaking only when you are asked something directly, never disagree. Second, you will do exactly as you are told to do at all time. Last, never, I repeat, never look directly into the face of the Master, is that understood?"

Serina had been watching her closely, listening intently. She did not understand any of this and furthermore she did not want to understand, she just wanted to go home, but something in the woman's tone of voice made Serina's skin crawl.

"Who is this Master person I'm not supposed to look at and why can't I look at him?" Serina asked, curiously. "Can he tell me where I am and how I got here and how I can get back home?"

The woman looked as though she had been struck by lightening, her eyes enlarged to twice their normal size while her whole face seemed to swell, Serina felt that, maybe, she had said something wrong – no doubt of it, actually.

"The Master is our ruler; he is the one who gives us our law. He is very powerful and can be very harsh with his punishments when someone disobeys him, he *does not* like impudent children. You will mind your tongue or be taught a lesson I'm afraid." With this, the woman got up and left the room without another word, leaving Serina sitting on the bed agape.

Serina sat on the huge bed not knowing quite what to do for a few minutes. Then she began pacing the room, she walked to the far window and looked out over the gardens, it was beautiful but Serina did not care about the beauty that surrounded her, all she wanted was to find a way out of this dream world and wake up in her own bed, in her own house, in her own village.

Unexpectedly someone knocked at the door again bringing Serina back to her nightmare. She turned around just in time to see a young man enter, flanked by Ruthie, the girl who fixed her hair earlier, and the older woman. They walked over to Serina where the older woman grabbed Serina roughly by the arm trying to pull her toward the young man. Serina pulled away in a jerk and the woman stumbled backwards. To her surprise the young man stepped forward giving the older woman a stern look, silently scolding her while holding out his arm to Serina.

"Hello, my name is Ju Miss. I will accompany you down to dinner now," he said in a firm but gentle voice. His smile was faint but Serina felt it was not a good idea to give him any trouble. She stood up as he bowed slightly, took her by the arm and the two walked out with Ruthie and the old woman following close behind. They went down a long spiraling staircase that seemed to go on forever.

"Where are you taking me?" asked Serina. "Please," she added softly.

Serina's voice quivered as she looked up into the eyes of the man next to her.

"To dinner Miss, then to your party, it will be great to have a birthday party, something to celebrate around here at last." He sounded hopeful almost.

"Can you tell me where I am? And how did I get here?"

Maybe Ju will be smart enough to tell me something, she thought, *no one else seemed to know.*

"Why Miss Serina, you are at the Master's castle, your home, you live here, and today is your birthday and we're going to celebrate."

Oh great he's as dumb as everyone else! No one seems to know where here is but everyone seems to know my name and they know it's my birthday – how strange.

Serina was not paying attention to where she was being led. If she wanted to get out of this place, she would have to start paying attention to her surroundings.

"Ju, who is the Master?" Serina was still hoping he would tell her something that would be helpful.

Ju stopped in his tracks and looked down at Serina; he seemed shocked that someone would ask this question. While the women behind them stood silent, Ju pondered the question. Then he began walking again, slowly though, then he stopped again. Serina wondered if she would ever find someone who would tell her what she wanted to know.

"The Master's name is Takar. You must not be asking questions when you see him, do exactly as you are told to do Miss Serina." As he said this he looked oddly at Serina for a second then back to the women behind them, the three exchanged glances, which made Serina, feel extremely uneasy.

Ju urged Serina forward again and soon they were at a door that was to the right of them. It opened up into another long corridor that seemed to lead on forever to end into a vast room. It was a round room with a round table in the center of it and a huge tree growing out of the middle. The room had five doors in it besides the one from which they had just emerged. Each door looked exactly alike, same size, and each equidistant from the other. It would be hard to figure out which door from which to escape if you were not paying attention to it.

Ju led her to the second door to their left – it opened up into a long room, which Serina guessed was the dining room. It had a long massive wooden table that was almost as long as the room, in the center of the table sat a huge candelabrum with a smaller one at either end. There were several sconces on the walls with their candles lit, which enveloped the dining room in a warm yellowish glow. Almost immediately upon entering the room, Serina noticed that there were only three places setting at the table. She had never seen a table so long or set with such elegance before; delicate china with fine silver goblets and cutlery set upon lacy aprons.

Ju took Serina to the chair pulled out at the left of the table. "You sit here Miss – remember to be very well behaved." Serina looked up at the man with fear in her eyes, silently pleading. "I will be across the room, and remember, be good." Ju then stepped away and the older woman took his place; she looked down at Serina, an icy smile on her face.

"You, my dear will have the rare opportunity of meeting the great Lord of this castle face to face but you may not live to tell about it if you do not watch your manners tonight." At these words, she stepped back spun on her heels and left the room.

Chapter 12

Serina sat in this high-back chair stunned and confused, with the words of the older woman still ringing in her ears. Yet nothing that had been said or done had prepared her for what happened next. The door at the other end of the room opened and a large man dressed all in black entered. He walked slowly the length of the room to where Serina sat. She watched him in terror as he came closer to her. He was wearing a black hooded cloak; the hood covered his entire face, showing nothing... but something about him seemed familiar, something... what? She did not know. Serina shrunk back in dread as he stepped up to her chair.

He reached out and took a wisp of her hair into one of his hands, rubbed it gently between his fingers then held his hand to the black hole where his face should have been, she could hear him take in a deep breath then let it out slowly.

"Hmmm, Jasmine and Chamomile, such sweet fragrances, don't you agree?" His voice was low – almost a whisper, but Serina could still detect the calculating coldness in it. "At last we meet... You do not know how long I have waited for this moment. Ah but now, we have the rest of our lives together and I will not bore you with all of the tiny little details, which is something we can go into later. For now it is your birthday and after dinner we shall celebrate."

Serina pushed her chair out wanting to stand but he put a heavy hand on her shoulder. "Please stay seated," he growled, "dinner is about to be served." He then stepped around to his chair, pulled it back intending to seat himself, when Serina let go of all restraints.

"Where am I and how did I get here?" she shouted looking up into the black hollow. She was wondering if indeed, he had a face at all, not realizing the seriousness of her quandary, she charged on. "I want to go home now! My father is going to be really mad at you, besides how do you know it's my birthday? I don't know you. Who are you anyway?" Serina couldn't help herself; the questions just kept rolling out of her mouth nonstop. "I don't know where I am – no one else seems to know either, maybe you can tell me. And why are you wearing that silly hood over your face, no one can tell if you're looking at them or not, do you have a bad scar or something?"

The man stood motionless, she couldn't see his face but felt that he was glaring a hole through her. He stepped back and stood behind the chair at the end of the table, still looking at her. He then reached for the edge of the cowl and slowly pulled it back, letting it fall onto his back. Serina stared in disbelief – she was in shock at the sight of him.

He had raven black hair. His eyes were fearsome. His cheeks, his chin and forehead appeared to have been chiseled out of stone. All of these features made him brutally handsome except that the jagged scar, which ran from the top of his forehead all the way down the length of his right cheek, to the bottom of his chin, made him look very scary indeed. He quickly put the hood back over his head without saying a word.

Serina was still agape when the door at the end of the room opened once again allowing a very elegantly dressed woman to enter. She walked solemnly the length of the room to the third place setting at the table. As she came closer, Serina couldn't help but noticing how beautiful she was. She had long dark unruly hair pretty much like her own. Her eyes were dark and enticing and her fair skin only added to her beauty. She was the most striking woman Serina had ever seen and looked very much like someone Serina might have known once.

The man stepped around, greeted her with a light hug. Surprisingly though, she pulled back from the man's embrace slightly. Serina noticed the woman's reaction immediately. Then the man pulled the woman's chair out to let her sit down and then seated himself, all without one word being spoken by either the man or the woman.

From the corner of her eye, Serina caught a glimpse of Ju across the room; his eyes never left the woman except when he looked across at Serina briefly.

The woman appeared nervous, a little on edge but managed a slight smile in Serina's direction. Serina smiled back, wondering if the woman was in the same predicament as she was.

"Serina, please meet Nora," said Takar, no longer hiding the coldness in his voice.

No sooner did he seat himself that the door behind him opened. In came four servants carrying trays of food, Serina didn't get a chance to broach the subject or questions that were at the forefront of her mind again for a while. The first servant lowered his tray and began serving Takar, when he was finished he served the woman across from Serina and then he served Serina last. One servant sat several different types of bread in front of Takar, another deposited scoops of butters and jams on tiny plates in front of him while the last one sat down a tray of little sausages and meats in the middle of the table. Then each left quietly when they had finished serving their tray.

Serina sat quietly, not touching her food throughout the first course of this repast. She noticed the woman eating very little while the man ate hungrily. Every time Serina would look across the table at the woman, she would be gazing at her with gentleness. She had a forlorn look on her face but managed a forced smile in Serina's direction.

After what seemed an eternity, the servants cleared the dishes and served the second course, which Serina chose to ignore – again. The woman, once again, picked at her food and left most of her entrée untouched when the servants came to clear the dishes away.

Throughout dinner, Takar ate ravenously, paying no attention to Serina or Nora. He spoke not a word all the while – they could have been wooden statues for all he seemed to care but when the meal was over, he turned to Serina, his eyes penetrating her to the bones and said, "Now for your party, shall we?" Matching actions to words, he then stood up, pulled out the woman's chair and stepped around the table and pulled out Serina's. He held his arm out for her to take hold just as Ju had done earlier in her bedroom. Serina began to protest but thought better of it after looking across the room in Ju's direction – he stood silently against the wall and she saw the slight admonishing movement of his head. So, instead of rebelling, she stood up and took the man's arm and the three walked out the door at the end of the long room. Although as casual as it may have appeared, Serina could feel the tension in the air.

They went through the door at the end of the room from which both Takar and the woman had entered. The door opened into a sumptuous room with chairs lined up against the one wall. There were several tables arranged about the room each adorned of rich candleholders. The room was decorated in festive colored ribbons. They were retained together at the center of the ceiling by a large bow and streamed down almost to the floor in all directions. In the far corner, there was a small stage on which some musicians seemed to be waiting to play their tunes. There was also a long table standing to the side of the room loaded with all kinds of sweets, a large bowl of some pink looking drink and a very large five-tier cake decorated with sugar flowers, ribbons and bows all over it. Next to this table, there was another overflowing with fancy wrapped boxes tied with ribbons and bows to match all the other cheerful colors. However, none of this put Serina in a festive mood. More than ever, she wanted to go home and her face must have shown her feelings because not long after they had entered the room, Ju walked up to her and as he bowed he whispered softly; "Miss, you should be smiling, the Master will be most unhappy if he should cast an eye upon your face."

He then stood erect again and walked a few steps away to stand against the wall facing the center of the room.

The room was busy with servants coming and going, the orchestra was tuning their instruments and the woman Takar called Nora was standing close to Serina, looking intently at her feet. Takar had walked over to the orchestra and was conversing with one of the musicians.

As Serina was thinking if she could sneak out and... the woman cleared her throat, drawing Serina's attention to her and said, "Don't look at me... Look away, across the room or somewhere else, only, listen to my words." Automatically Serina's eyes shot up to the woman's.

"I said do not look at me, just listen to what I have to say, I don't have much time."

Serina quickly looked away in the direction of the cake across the room but her ears were straining to hear the woman's voice, which was very difficult since she was barely talking above a whisper and hardly moving her lips. "I need to talk with you tonight, understand? I will..."

Unfortunately, just then Takar came walking toward them and the woman fell silent, leaving Serina puzzled, wondering what it was the woman wanted to talk about. *Maybe she could tell me how I got here and where in the blue blazes 'here' is...*

"Please Serina, Nora, sit down, the music is about to start, as is your party my dear," Takar said as he pulled his hood back just far enough for them to see the outline of his face. His eyes cast an icy glare in Nora's direction then as not to leave Serina out he gave her the same cold hard look. Serina was thinking he must have heard them all the way across the room, for him to zoom back over to them that quickly. *He probably has the best hearing in the world.* She sat down in the chair closest to her, but she would not look Takar in the eye.

At that moment, the orchestra started playing a lively tune. Takar stood and held his hand out to Serina; she stared at it without attempting to stand. Instead, she looked up into his cold eyes. She knew everyone in the room was holding their breath, waiting. She looked over at Nora who was staring silently at her – her eyes pleading. Serina looked across the room in Ju's direction – he too, was staring at her with pleading eyes while nodding ever so slightly. Serina turned back to Takar who was still glaring down at her. His face, for what was visible of it, was tense and his jaw set in determination. Serina got to her feet slowly; she was trembling inside and could hardly put one foot in front of the other. How she managed to make it to the dance floor, she had no idea. Although Serina was a very graceful young lady when she danced with her father on occasion, here she danced like a zombie; she was stiff and gauche at every step. Throughout the whole dance, she could not bring herself to look up but she felt Takar's eyes on her the whole time, burning holes into her. *If he despises me so, why has he given me such a grand party?*

When the dance was over Takar took Serina back to the table, he made a gesture and a servant appeared, he bowed to Takar and almost instantly left in the direction of the table, which was covered, with gifts. Serina did not hear what was said but within moments the servant, along with several others, brought the colorfully wrapped packages across the room and placed them on the table next to Serina. Takar stood and everyone in the room fell silent, he cleared his throat, held his glass out in front of him and then turned to face Serina.

"To Serina, my Princess… Today begins the first day of the rest of your life; a life of such great joy, the whole world lies at your feet and with the two of us now together, there is nothing that we can not do."

He then held his glass up higher as the whole room broke out in applause. After which each person lined up just ahead of the table facing the center of the room, like they were getting ready for a military revue.

Takar held out his arm for Serina to take once more. Again, she looked for Ju but he wasn't in sight – he had gone to join the others in the line-up. So, she looked at Nora searching for support, but she motioned for her to rise. Serina wanted to protest but the words, which the old woman spoke before dinner came back to mind giving Serina second thoughts. Thus, not knowing what was in store for her, she stood up taking Takar's arm. He led her to the center of the room and again cleared his throat to speak.

"I give you your Princess... Princess Serina, meet your servants." Given half a chance, at that very moment, Serina would have bolted for the door. However, reading her very thoughts, Takar held her arm rather firmly while the servants filed past her one by one, each giving their name then bowing or curtsying. When her turn came up, the old woman who treated Serina so harshly earlier stepped up and said: "Mertie they call me, Princess Serina." Her voice was too sweet, Serina thought, for being true. The woman then curtsied and moved on. But there was something frightful about her – Serina dreaded her most of all. After each one of the servants had introduced themselves to Serina, Takar guided her back to her chair and at this point made another announcement pertaining to the gifts, Serina's birthday, and all the great things they were going to do together. Serina was still in the dark about all the wondrous things they were supposed to be able to do. She was still thinking this had to be a dream and figured she would wake up at any moment in her little bedroom, all-cozy, with Samone next to her pillow.

A servant handed the gifts to her one at a time. After she unwrapped each of them they were carried away. There were beautiful dresses, silver combs for her hair and even a live bird in a beautiful wicker cage, yet one gift stood out from all the rest, it was an ivory handled brush and mirror with matching ivory hair combs. Each item was adorned with little tiny elephants carved into the ivory. Serina did not know exactly what was expected of her so she tried to do whatever Takar said. She sensed that everyone was watching her every move. They appeared to be expecting something from her, but what? She did not know, but they all seemed as much on edge as she was herself. When she was through un-wrapping the gifts everything was removed, taken out of the room and all that was left was the enormous cake and pink punch with all the little extra pastries.

Takar stood up once again, raising his hands above his head. "If Serina will accompany me across the room we will cut the cake," he declared as he looked down at her with a large smile on his chiseled scarred face. All Serina wanted to do was make a mad dash for the door – maybe she could escape this madness, this never-ending nightmare. The only thing holding her back was that she did not know where she would go once she did escape. She had no idea where she was and no one would tell her. She didn't know how she was going to get away but she did know one thing; she was not going to put up with this charade any longer and suddenly jumped to her feet and turned on Takar.

"NO! I will not accompany you over to the cake, you can go eat it yourself, I want to go home, NOW, just tell me how to get back to my house and I will leave," Serina spat at Takar venomously. Adrenalin was coursing through her veins so fast, she felt as if she was going to pass out on the spot.

Everyone hushed their applauding and an icy silence fell over the room. Takar looked as though he had been slapped; his eyes grew wild and angry and the veins in his neck turned purple and bulged over his grayish skin. Although, the smile had vanished from his face, he recovered quickly and when he spoke again, his words were very slow and deliberate.

"I will let this slide this time – because you obviously do not know who you are talking to. You have just arrived today and everything is new and different to you but I warn you here and now… Do not raise your voice to me *ever* again, nor will you *ever* speak to me in any other way except in the most proper and respectful fashion such as one speaks to their Master, is that understood? Now, shall we have some cake and punch?"

Takar glared down at Serina with such a cold calculating stare that she recoiled and drew back from him. Nothing was said for a moment; the two just stood there staring at one another. Serina had no clue as to why she spoke out the way she did but she could not back down now, she had to stand up to him or she never would.

"I do *not* want any of your stupid cake, I do *not* want to be here, I am *not* your Princess, I want to go home, I want to see my father; he will be very worried. No one will tell me how to get out of this place or how I got here, they all act as if I have lived here all my life. I know I am not dreaming, but I don't know how I came to be in a place I've never seem before or with so many people I've never met before, where do all of you come from anyway?"

Serina was talking so fast she barely had time to take a breath. She had not noticed the music had stopped and the people were standing around with their heads bowed, looking at their feet, holding their breath for what they must have known was coming. Serina however did not know what her fate had in reserve.

Takar roared at the servants to take everything away. He turned to Nora and bellowed something incoherent to her and she left the room. Serina watched her go, she did not look back until she was stepping through the door and turned her head ever so slightly, but it was enough for Serina to see the fear in her eyes.

"You will be taken to your room and left there until you learn a few manners, you will soon find out I am not one to play games with my dear little Serina and if you know what's good for you, you will learn this lesson very soon. Do I make myself clear?" said Takar, leaning down less than an inch from Serina's face. He was so close she could feel the heat of his breath and see the beads of perspiration on his face.

Serina stood frozen to the floor; fear gripped her throat, she could not have spoken even if her life depended on it, which may have been the case at that moment. Takar snapped at

Ju and the young man, who was only a few feet from them, stepped forward immediately, bowing as he did so.

"Take her to her room and make sure the door is double locked, is that clear? Then bring the key to me. No one gets into that room without my knowing it, now get her out of my sight."

Takar turned on his heel and left the room through the closest door to him. He slammed it so forcefully that the sound echoed in Serina's ears for several minutes after he was gone.

Ju bowed to Serina then held out his arm for her. She took it without looking up. He led her out of the big party room and down a corridor to the base of the spiraling staircase, which led to her room at the top of the tower. It seemed to Serina that she had descended those stairs an eternity ago, although it had only been two hours since she had stepped out of the tower room.

They were about to start up the stairs when Ju turned to Serina; nothing had been said between the two of them until now.

"Miss Serina, you will have to be very good in order to come out of your room now. You should not have made the Master so angry. He can be very strict when someone makes him angry, you must learn not to annoy him in the future." Ju spoke softly with a hint of concern in his voice. "You will not be allowed much food for a few days, I wish you had eaten some dinner, it wouldn't be near as hard on you."

They had only taken a few steps up the stairs when Serina stopped, halting Ju as she did so.

"Please Ju, help me get out of here, I want to go home," Serina pleaded.

But Ju did not respond immediately and started climbing the staircase once again, pulling Serina with him. "You ask something that I can not do. No one goes against the Master – no one. So, please say no more and I will forget about it."

"Ju, just tell me how to get back home. If I was to get out of the castle I wouldn't know where to go, just tell me which direction to head home in, just in case – can you do that?" Ju just shook his head and kept climbing the endless stairs. When they made it to the top Ju opened the door and stepped inside, leading Serina to the center of the room before releasing her arm.

"Miss Serina, you must not cause any more trouble, I would hate to send your food to the dungeon, you would not like the dungeons, they are cold and wet and a lot of rats run freely down there."

"Ju, why won't anyone help me?" Serina asked the question out of desperation, still searching for a glimmer of hope. He stood there for a moment, pondering the question, debating whether to say something or just let it pass. Finally, he let out a long sigh then looking Serina square in the face said something that did not make sense to her.

"No one can help you now, Miss Serina... This is your destiny and there is nothing I, or anyone else, can do for you, so you need not ask again." As much as he tried to hide it in his face, he could not hide the hint of sorrow in his voice.

"What do you mean?" asked Serina in dismay.

Ju walked to the door without speaking, once there he stopped and turned around. "I've said too much already; just remember you must not give the Master any reason to punish you any further than what he did tonight."

Then, Ju left Serina standing in the middle of the room, she heard him lock the door and slowly descend the stairs, the sound of each step growing fainter until the sound of his falling footsteps vanished, leaving Serina totally alone.

Chapter 13

She paced around the room for several minutes, her mind running rampant trying to grab hold of anything that would explain what had happened throughout the day. She was as much in the dark about everything as she was when she woke up that morning. She walked to the window that looked out over the beautiful garden below; night had fallen and the full silvery moon was casting a white dusty glow giving a ghostly appearance to the expanse below her. *This place is full of evil,* Serina thought, definitely not a place she wanted to be and what did Ju mean by "no one being able to help her now?"

Serina walked back to her bed where she slowly undressed, she put on the beautiful white nightgown that had been laid out for her without giving it a second glance. Afterwards she stepped over to the dressing table and started brushing her long dark hair. She felt tired, drained, her mind just a haze when something in the mirror caught Serina's eye. All of the presents that had been given to her downstairs had been brought up to her room and were stacked on the table up against the wall across the room, laying her brush aside she walked over to the table, where she shuffled through the gifts until she found the brush and hair combs that Nora had given her. She picked each item up admiring the beauty of the hand carved ivory. When she picked up the last comb, she noticed a piece of folded paper at the bottom of the box; it was a note.

She quickly unfolded the paper, then as an extra precaution, she glanced around the room to make sure no one was watching her although she knew she was alone – Ju had locked the door behind him as he left earlier, nonetheless, she was learning to be very careful. She turned her attention back to the piece of paper in her hand and read its contents.

Serina,

These belonged to my mother, as they were passed down to her from her mother. I cannot think of anyone else I would rather have these than you, please except this gift as a beginning of a new friendship.

Love Nora

Serina abstractedly stared at the note reading it twice more. She laid it back into the box after a moment, picked up the combs and brush and walked back to the dressing table. There she sat down, turning the brush over and over in her hand looking at the delicate carved ivory. It seemed so fragile and yet so strong. She sat the brush down and picked up the combs, they were as lovely as the brush; the tiny little elephants had been carved with such detail – *how beautiful,* she thought once again. Looking in the mirror Serina ran the brush through her thick curly hair a few times then she pulled her hair back placing the combs on either side, just above her ears. She glanced at her reflection in the mirror; *nice,* she thought as she turned her head back and forth. The light color of the ivory against her dark hair only enhanced the silken ebony of her long locks. They were such an extravagant gift, why would a woman she didn't even know give her such a gift, she wondered. She took the combs out of her hair, placed them on the table, and went to bed, she did not know what she was going to do about her predicament, but she knew she couldn't do it without any sleep.

Serina had a hard time falling asleep, she kept thinking of what Takar had said to her in the party room and also of the toast he had made to her, and what did he mean by *'together they could do anything'* or something to that effect. Whatever it was she wasn't sure, but one thing she did know – he was an evil man and he scared her; he scared her very much indeed. Finally, after tossing and turning restlessly half the night, Serina fell asleep.

Sometime during the night, Serina was awakened by an odd scratching noise, thinking she was at home she sat up straining her eyes to see where the noise came from.

"Samone?" she called out to her cat before reality set in and she became conscious that she was in the tall tower of that awful castle. The room was quiet. She sat on the edge of her bed for a second listening – but nothing – no sounds whatsoever. Thinking she had been dreaming or just hearing things that didn't really exist; she laid back down on her pillow. After a few minutes of staring at the moon-streaked ceiling, she began to doze off. She was just about asleep when she heard it again - it sounded like someone was scraping something across the floor or dragging something, she wasn't sure but she lay very still with her eyes wide open, listening… All she could hear was the pounding of her heart and the sound of her own breathing. Not a sound could she hear but she got the uneasy feeling that someone was in the room with her, her heart caught up in her throat as fear gripped her chest… *yep*, there was someone in the room with her alright, she could hear *them* breathing. Serina strained her eyes as she surveyed the room as best she could without moving her head. She could verily make out an outline of someone standing in the shadow of the wardrobe.

"Who's there?" asked Serina, "Come out where I can see you, don't hide like a coward" Serina's whole body was shaking; she was so scared she could barely get the words out.

Suddenly the outline moved out of the shadows into the center of the room, it was Nora.

"W-where d-did you c-come from?" Serina stammered, yet a little of the fear gripping her throat began to ease. "H-how did y-you get in here? Did Takar send you?"

Nora stepped closer to the bed before speaking, her long dark hair casting such a contrast against the white nightdress she was wearing; *she is a very beautiful woman*, Serina thought.

"No, Takar does not know that I am here, no one knows. I told you earlier I needed to talk to you, I'm sorry if I scared you."

Serina sat up and faced the woman as she stepped closer.

"What do you need to talk to me about?"

"It's a long story and I don't really know where to start."

She paused briefly, casting her eyes around the room. She spotted a chair, pulled it over to the bed and sat down.

"Please get comfortable, this may take a long time," said Nora, in a soft lilting voice. "I guess I should start at the beginning, so bear with me as I try to tell this the best I can."

Nora thought for a moment of what she was going to say before she began.

"This will be hard for you to understand and very difficult for me to explain but please believe what I say to you is the truth." Nora paused again, she seemed to be having a hard time already, and she hadn't even begun. "You see a long time ago, before you were born, Takar..."

Just then, the door burst open with a loud bang, Takar barged in with several servants behind him. In two steps he was at the side of the bed, Nora jumped to her feet stepping back toward the wall behind her to get away from Takar, the look in her eyes revealed pure raw fear.

Takar pulled his hood back as he neared the two probably wanting them to appreciate his anger even more. He looked from Nora to Serina, Serina shrank back in total horror at the sinister look on his face and when he spoke, the icy tone of his voice had both Serina and Nora shrinking back a little farther.

"I thought you might try to sneak up here tonight, Ju will lose his life for this and you, my dear Nora, will be taken to the dungeons, what a pity."

Nora took a few steps forward and confronted Takar meekly.

"Please, do not punish Ju; he did not give me the key. I knew he had a spare key so I put something in his drink and I waited for him to fall asleep then I snuck into his room and took his key. He has no idea I came up here, he is totally loyal to you." Nora's voice trembled as she spoke.

"We shall see about that but in the meantime you will be taken to the dungeon; you know what happens when one disobeys me Nora – Omar, take her away."

Serina, not knowing what to do, sat motionless on the bed as they took Nora away then Takar turned back to face her.

"So, what did Nora have to say to you Serina?"

He had an evil twisted smile on his face and his voice had a forced calm that did not fool Serina one little bit. As hard as he may try to cover it up, he could not hide the pure evil that seemed to evolve within and around him.

"Tell me and I will let the incident that happened earlier tonight pass and you may be free to roam around the castle as you wish."

Serina stared up at him, she tried to say something but her voice seemed to be frozen in her throat.

"TELL ME!" Takar demanded vehemently. The veins were popping out in his neck again and he looked like he was going to explode, he stepped closer to the bed and leaned over Serina, causing her to scoot further back onto the bed.

"Sh- she didn't s-say anything; you broke the door down before she could, why? What could she tell me that would make you so upset?"

Bending slightly, Takar glared down at her for what seemed an eternity to Serina then he stood erect again towering over her studying her for a moment longer, all the while remaining silent.

"Very well, I will think about letting you out of your room tomorrow, tonight however a servant will remain in your room to make sure you do not have any more – late night visitors."

As he reached the door he turned back to face Serina.

"The gardens are very lovely and I am sure you will enjoy a stroll through them, think about it, and if anything Nora may have said comes to mind let me know in the morning, goodnight." With that, he pulled the door closed and Serina heard him bolt and lock it before he started down the long flight of stairs.

Serina and the servant exchanged glances without speaking then she climbed under the covers to go back to sleep. The servant who was an older short, thin, balding man sat upright in the chair that Nora had pulled over to the bedside before Takar burst through the door, only he pulled it back in front of the door.

She knew it was late but she could not go to sleep, what was so important that Nora would steal a key and risk getting caught and punished just to tell her, it had to be something very important.

Early next morning Serina heard the key turn in the door and as she raised her head just a bit to see who was coming in, she saw the guard sliding his chair out of the way, so the door could swing open. He had something shiny dangling from his hand, she watched him put the item in his coat pocket before the older woman from the previous day entered carrying a large tray of food. Serina laid her head down quickly and closed her eyes, pretending to be asleep.

"Morning Ernie, everything go alright last night?"

"Yeah Mertie, she didn't make a stir, slept like a baby she did, did ya bring me some vittles too?"

"There's enough there for the both of ya, get yours first though, before she wakes up – serves her right if she didn't get anything to eat for a day or two – but orders are orders."

"Ah, she ain't that bad is she, Mertie?"

The large woman turned on the little man with a vicious glare.

"You don't know nothing do ya Ernie? Anyone who talks and acts like she does, is trouble, big trouble and I'm here to tell ya she will be nothing but trouble, mind what I say and remember I told ya so."

"Oh here, I found this for ya, thought ya might like it," said Ernie.

"Oh, how pretty, it's for me, where did ya get it?" Mertie asked taking the gift from Ernie's thin outstretched hand.

"I found it."

"Found it huh? Well... it's alright I guess, maybe I can wear it sometimes, just to think of you Ernie."

Mertie pinched the little man's thin cheek while his face reddened with embarrassment.

Serina heard them scuffling about the room doing what... She had no idea because she still would not open her eyes. She lay very still for at least ten minutes before she finally began to stir, pretending to wake up. She didn't want to admit it, but the smell of the food was beginning to get to her, she had not eaten a bite, not a morsel of food since she entered this place the night before. She was weak and her stomach was growling so loudly, she was afraid it could be heard all the way across the room.

"Well, it looks like the little princess is awake, Ernie," Mertie said. "Maybe she will be in a better mood today..." Then addressing Serina, she added, "better get over here and eat, that is if Ernie here didn't eat it all."

Serina climbed out of bed and went behind the privacy screen to take care of her morning business and wash up a little. When she came out Ernie was gone and Mertie was making up the huge bed, she walked to the table where the breakfast sat, not caring about anything but getting something in her stomach. She grabbed a piece of toast shoving half of it into her mouth, hardly chewing, just stuffing her mouth with as much as she could get into it. She picked up the glass of milk and took a large swallow to rinse it down then stuffed the other half of the toast into her mouth. When she finished the toast, she ate the cold porridge and finished her milk before she turned around to see where Mertie was. She was standing on one side of the bed looking intently at something she was holding in her hand. Serina could not tell what it was but whatever it was; it had Mertie's full attention.

Suddenly Serina jumped to her feet, ran across the room to Mertie and in one swift movement, she grabbed the object the woman was holding, yanking it right out of her hand.

"That's my necklace, how dare you take it," Serina yelled at Mertie as she took a few steps back and held the necklace up so she could get a good look at it; she guessed that it was what Ernie had given the woman before he left.

The woman lunged for Serina, but she was too quick for her. Serina bolted across the bed in one huge leap leaving the woman stranded amid covers and pillows.

"You little imp, I'll get you and when I do you will be sorry you were ever born, now give me that necklace," spat Mertie in a hateful tone as she got up and tried again to reach for her prey.

"No way, this is my necklace, I saw Ernie with it this morning when he let you in, he stole it and gave it to you, it's mine. I had it made by the jeweler in our village," Serina shouted – all the while evading Mertie's futile attempts at grabbing her.

"So, spying on us was ya, that's one more I owe ya, now for the last time give it to me or else."

"Or else what Mertie?"

In there fight for the necklace neither one of them heard the door open. They both turned in one movement toward it and there, his massive body taking up the whole doorway, stood Takar.

The fear in Mertie's eyes matched that of Serina's as Takar walked slowly toward the bed, the woman stood motionless and speechless. *Would it be possible that Mertie is even more afraid than I am?* Serina still had the necklace clutched in her hand but she gently slid it in under the pillow and then walked to the end of the bed.

"*She* thought I had one of the spoons from the breakfast tray she brought up," Serina said accusingly pointing her index finger at Mertie. "I told her I didn't have it but she didn't believe me – said it was her job to keep count of that sort of stuff."

Takar looked long and hard at Serina then back to Mertie. The woman still had not spoken a word – she had only flashed a dirty glance in Serina's direction upon hearing the lie she had just told and then darted them back to Takar's feet.

Serina thought she had bungled that fib pretty badly but it was the best she could come up with at a moment's notice. Why she didn't tell Takar about the necklace she didn't know and the way Takar looked at the two of them gave Serina the impression that he might not have fallen for her story at all, yet his expression lightened finally.

"Mertie is a little hard nosed, that's why I gave her that job, sometimes she can get a little out of hand though, too rough with the servants, you know what I mean but we do not have to worry about that now do we? Because I'm sure you will not be doing anything to cause anymore problems, right?"

Takar's voice was cool and calculating, his stare piercing Serina like a hot poker. She was afraid to think of what he could do to someone if he were angry enough. *I've had a small demonstration of that wrath already,* Serina thought, recalling the previous night's incident.

"N-No Sir," Serina muttered. Her eyes fell to the floor as Mertie's had earlier.

"That's good, now I thought about last night and as I am sure nothing like that will happen again, I've decided to let you go for a walk around the grounds today, with me of course, then I will show you the castle from top to bottom, how does that sound?"

"Great, when can we go?" she asked eagerly.

Serina wanted nothing more than to get outside so she could figure out where she was and try to spot something that looked familiar, if that were possible, so, she was sure to be on her best behavior.

"Good, then I will have Mertie bring you down after you are dressed. Mertie I will be in my study... Oh and Mertie, I'm sure there will be no more reasons for you to threaten Miss Serina, am I right?"

Mertie raised her eyes to Takar then back down to her feet. "No Sir, no reason at all Sir."

"That's good. Then Serina I will see you in my study when you are finished and ready."

His voice had taken on a false warmness that was as chilling as his cold hard attitude. He left the room with the two of them staring after him. Once the door was closed and they could not hear his footsteps on the stairs anymore, they turned to each other, neither knowing quite what to say to the other.

Mertie broke the silence first with her gruff voice. "What ya did there, why did ya do that, saying I thought you took silver from the tray, you... you."

Mertie was having a hard time getting her words out; *she doesn't usually apologize to anyone for anything*, Serina thought.

"I don't know, I just did."

Serina felt like saying she wished Takar had punished Mertie by putting her in the dungeon but she really wouldn't wish that on anyone, even on Mertie.

"Well, you can have that ole necklace, I was gonna throw it away anyway, too big and gaudy for me."

Serina thought that was Mertie's way of thanking her for saving her from Takar's evil retribution. The two didn't say much more until Serina was dressed and ready to go downstairs. She figured with their kind of newfound friendship she would give it another try.

"Mertie, why am I here?"

Mertie stopped and looked hard into Serina's eyes for a moment then she looked away and started shuffling in a nervous half circle pattern.

"Missy, you are supposed to be here; from the beginning we all knew that... This is your place; you belong with the Master Takar."

"Why?" Serina asked again. "I don't understand any of this."

She was scared out of her wits but didn't want anyone to know. She had to figure out what was going on, and the sooner, the better. She felt the longer she stayed in this place the harder it would be for her to get home, and home was the one place she wanted to be more than anything else in the world.

"Say no more, this is your place and that's all there is to it. Let's go, the Master will be coming looking for us if we don't hurry."

Mertie unlocked the door and led Serina out to the stairway then took her by the hand and led her down the long flight of stairs to the bottom. Neither one spoke again, thus leaving Serina just as confused as she was when she woke up the morning before, finding herself in a strange place – a castle full of strangers, who had only one thing in common; they were all scared stiff of Takar.

Mertie stopped in front of a large wooden door carved from top to bottom with a giant dragon. It resembled the one she remembered from... from where, Serina wondered. She was so confused, she knew she saw a dragon like this one, but for the life of her, she could not remember where.

"Ah, I see you made it without any difficulties, no silver stuffed inside your clothing anywhere, we do not want to get on Mertie's bad side now do we?"

Takar laughed at his own joke, as he motioned Serina into a seat while he finished up with one of the servants and dismissed him with a wave of his hand. Then turning back to Serina with one of his fake smiles smeared across his face, he said, "So, are you ready for a stroll around the grounds?" he asked in one of his nicer tones.

"Oh yes, I'm ready any time you are, I am very anxious to see the gardens," replied Serina, hoping to convince him of her sincerity.

"Then let's go by all means."

He walked over to her chair and bent down holding out his right arm for her to take, revealing his arrogant expression just slightly inside the edges of his hood as he did so. Serina glanced into his dark eyes but quickly looked away as she stood. *He could never completely hide the evil inside him*, she thought, because no matter what kind of face he put on, evil would always be there glaring back for anyone to see. She took hold of his arm letting her hand rest lightly on the cuff of his cloak so as not to invite any irate rebuke from him. What she would have rather done was to make a run for it but where would she go?

Once outside she took a long deep breath exhaling slowly through her mouth, it felt good to be outside in the fresh air, out of that damp musky smelling ole castle.

Serina had thought about the woman Nora that Takar had sent to the dungeon the night before; something about her made Serina feel odd. She couldn't put her finger on it but she felt sure she had seen her or known her from somewhere, only from where, was the question.

"Serina, once you get accustomed to being here you will enjoy it and be happy here, I promise you that, and there's so much we can do, you will be surprised at the power you have and together there will be nothing we cannot do, nothing... You will see."

Serina looked up into Takar's eyes; he had a true smile on his face for the first time since she had arrived, although it was one of evil no doubt. She did not want to anger him by arguing with him about her leaving because she knew she would end up back up in that tower or even worse, in the dungeon, so she kept quiet.

The grounds were larger than she had first imagined. Looking out at them from the window in the high tower, she could see for a long way, the gardens, fountains and little streams that ran through the lawns, but standing here on the ground she felt overwhelmed by the vastness of it, she would never figure out how to get out of this place. She let out a deep sigh and headed toward a tall fountain with a statue of a mermaid at the top spouting water from her mouth.

"Ah yes, my favorite as well, I knew we had a lot in common Serina." Takar remarked when he stepped up to the fountain next to her.

"She looks lonely and scared," said Serina, thinking of how much the mermaid and she had in common. She had nothing in common with Takar except the both of them being in this dreary castle. She turned away as they walked through the lawns in silence, Takar stopped as they came upon a large barn like building.

"What's that?" Serina asked curiously.

"It's where I keep my pet, would you like to see him?"

"Pet? What kind of a pet would you keep in such a large barn?"

"Come, I will show you." Takar led the way; he seemed to be in a little better spirits than he had been earlier.

When they arrived at the door, he stopped and turned around to Serina.

"You may be frightened but don't be, he will not hurt you as long as you stay close to me and make no sudden moves, is that understood?" he warned as he opened the door not giving Serina a chance to reply.

It was dark at first until her eyes grew accustomed to the dimmer light. Then Serina saw it, he was standing in the far corner of the barn looking down at them with bright yellow piercing eyes.

"Th- that's a-a-a dragon," stammered Serina in astonishment. She always imagined dragons were not 'real' – they didn't exist; but this one surely did!

"Yes, that's a dragon, isn't he beautiful?" Takar replied with a surge of pride she had not heard before.

Serina stood there with her mouth wide open; scared was not the word to describe how she felt. When she finally got her wits about her she started backing out the door.

"Don't be afraid, he will not hurt you unless you did something to me, then he would kill you, of that – there's no doubt." Takar explained almost happily. "So whatever you do don't make any sudden moves toward me," he added with a grin.

Serina was so petrified she stood frozen to the dirt floor staring into the bright yellow eyes. Those eyes hypnotized her; she could see right through them, she felt as if she was sucked inside them. She could not pull her eyes away from his no matter how hard she tried. A loud noise from behind broke the trance suddenly. Serina spun on her heels just in time to see Takar holding a long leather whip, he had evidently popped it making the loud cracking noise that broke the spell the dragon had on her.

"JAVA!"

The huge beast backed farther into the corner and laid down. He was as afraid of Takar as she was apparently.

"See, even something as big and menacing as a dragon knows who the Master is – and obeys," said Takar in his normal cold tone.

"Let's finish our walk around the grounds, there's still much to see."

As they stepped out into the bright sunlight, Serina squinted to see where she was going, in doing so she saw something that looked familiar to her.

"Why do you have a stream without any water in it?"

"That's a moat, it goes all the way around the castle and I can flood it at will… How did you know it had no water?" he asked. It was his turn to wear the curious look.

"I don't know; it just looks empty."

She didn't know how she knew it or why it looked familiar to her, it just did.

"What about Nora? Was that her name? Are you going to keep her in the dungeon?"

"Why do you ask?" Takar studied her for a moment, was he trying to read her thoughts? Then before she herself could figure out why she asked about the woman he staggered her with his next question. "Shall I take you to see her?"

"In... in the dungeon?" Serina wasn't too sure about going down into a damp cold dungeon where rats and other horrible things lived, but she surprised herself with her reply.

"Sure, I guess so but first where does that path lead to?" She pointed in the direction of an overgrown trail that appeared unused. The grass and weeds had grown up tall, almost overtaking the path, leaving just a small track through the middle of it.

"It leads nowhere, come, let's see the dungeon." Takar's voice took on an even colder tone as he led her away from the overgrown path to nowhere.

The dungeon was dark upon entering; Takar took a lamp from the wall lighting it he led the way down a very narrow set of stone steps. Serina was wishing she had not agreed to come to this place; it was very frightening walking down a dark corridor with only a small flickering light to find their way. The walls were damp and greenish looking from the little she could see in the dim light. Serina felt sure they were very slimy.

Up ahead she could hear noises that sounded almost human, causing Serina to halt in her tracks. Takar turned back to face her, he held the light up close to his face giving him an even more eerie look than she thought possible. Serina stepped back in fear, turned and started running back toward the small light, which was the doorway from which they entered just moments ago. In her haste, she stumbled over a loose stone and fell to the cold wet floor. She tried to grab hold of the wall but it was too slimy to get a grip, thus she couldn't stand up and couldn't even see two paces in front of her. She was frightened and ready to yell, when suddenly something grabbed her, scooping her up into the air and cradling her like she were a small tot. She was so terrified she could not make a sound. The next thing she knew she was outside on the grass in the bright sunlight, she looked up to see who had carried her out of the dungeon but he, it, or whatever it was, had taken off running toward the overgrown path she had seen earlier.

Takar came running out of the doorway toward her with a bewildered look on his face. He glanced around the grounds then back down at Serina who lay on the grass covered in greenish slime.

"Who was that, who dared to shove me aside, the Great Takar? I will have his head for this, I promise him that."

Takar's black cloak was smeared with the same greenish slime that covered Serina, which brought a smile to Serina's face. Evidently, whoever picked her up and carried her outside gave Takar a hard enough shove to knock him down and this made him furious. Serina's smile broadened a little as she looked up at the GREAT TAKAR staring off in every direction looking for the culprit.

"I, I don't know, no, I'm not sure what happened or if anyone did grab me. I just know I started to run and fell over a rock or something then I ended up out here..."

Serina was not about to tell him in which direction the culprit ran because she may have just made a new best friend, whoever it, he were. She looked up at Takar; he did look a little silly with that stuff all over him like that.

"No... I'm pretty sure no one else was in there with us, maybe you just imagined someone shoved you, it all happened so fast and all."

He gave the grounds another once-over then looked down into Serina's eyes. He started to say something but then thought better of it and only grunted.

"I forget you're only a child, maybe you're not ready to see the dungeon but you should not have ran out like that you could have hurt yourself."

Serina was still puzzled as to who picked her up in that long dark corridor. Who was lurking behind them without them even knowing it, and why did 'he' pick her up? Maybe she just imagined it too... No, someone picked her up all right and carried her outside and laid her on the soft grass then ran away. Why didn't he stay or show himself to her, unless he was too afraid of Takar.

Takar took Serina back to the castle and handed her over to Mertie, giving her orders to get Serina up to her room and cleaned up and then to bring her back down for lunch.

Once out of earshot Mertie asked all kinds of questions, like did she enjoy the tour, what did she think of the Mermaid fountain, did he show her the large fishpond.

"Mertie, I saw an over grown path just across the bridge that crosses the moat, do you know where it leads to?"

Mertie thought for a moment, finally with a puzzled look on her face said she had no clue as to where it went. She always remembered it to be grown up with weeds.

"Why do you ask anyway, it's an ugly part of the grounds and the Master should pretty it up but he says to leave it alone and don't go there, so, I leave it right where it is and stay myself away from it. Better off doing what you're told around here, you'll learn that as time goes by – you will – that I'm sure of."

Mertie was more or less talking to herself than to Serina so she kept quiet while Mertie continued to babble on as she led Serina up the long flight of stairs to the tower that now was dubbed the 'Princess Tower' by all of the servants.

When Serina came down for lunch, she found Takar waiting at the end of the extremely long dining table, his look guarded. Serina felt he had something very important to discuss with someone. It didn't take her long to find out who that person was.

"Serina, please have a seat." He pulled out the chair next to his then he sat at his usual place. "Did you enjoy the tour of the grounds my dear?" he asked in and unusually kind voice, which puzzled Serina, since it was not like him to speak so kindly.

"Yes, it was very lovely," said Serina softly, not wanting to ruin his good temper.

"Good, now there's a bit of business I need to discuss with you."

Just then, one of the servants entered with their lunch and Takar fell quiet, but no sooner did the servant leave the room that he turned back to her peering into her eyes.

"Serina my dear, there's something I've been meaning to discuss with you ever since you arrived." He cleared his throat then looked away for a moment. When he turned back to her, she could see a touch of his old cold-self showing through the mask of his face.

"It has to do with why you are here."

Serina was about to put a bite of ham in her mouth and almost swallowed her fork.

"You're going to tell me how I got here?" Her voice took on a new tone and her eyes lit up brightly.

"It was destiny, my dear that brought you here." He paused only briefly then continued. "This is your home; this is where you belong – here with me. It was meant to be this way all along – from the beginning." Takar paused again for a moment seemingly in deep thought.

"But I was taken in by the tears of a beautiful woman; I have to say it was a rare weak moment for me."

His eyes took on an odd glow that Serina did not understand, she wanted to say something instead she remained quiet. Her voice was lost somewhere deep in the pit of her stomach. She sat staring into the eyes of this mad man with stark disbelief on her face.

"Ah, I see you think I'm mad, well maybe I am, nevertheless what I say is true, you belong here with me and there is nothing anyone can do about it."

Serina jumped to her feet but Takar was quicker than she was and grabbed her wrist pulling her back into her chair.

"There is more to tell but I see you are not ready to accept your destiny just yet, so I will wait, there is plenty of time… We have forever if necessary."

With this, he turned to his plate and started eating. Serina stared down at her food, thinking how could he be eating when her whole world was turned upside down? She could feel tears welling in her eyes and as hard as she tried, she could not stop them from flowing.

Takar clapped his hands together and instantly a servant appeared from one of the many doors that opened into the room.

"Take her to her room and no dinner tonight, maybe she will be a little more receptive in the morning."

Serina stood to leave; she turned around and looked him square in the eyes.

"I hate you, and I will never want to be here, and that Takar – is nothing anyone can do about it either."

She turned leaving the room without a backward glance. Once in the hall she started running, she ran all the way to the stairs, leaving the servant far behind, she ran up the stairs and into her room, falling on the bed, and there she started sobbing uncontrollably. The servant stood watching her silently then backed out of the room closing and bolting it behind him. It was a shame, he thought, for one so young to be so unhappy.

Serina spent the whole afternoon mulling over her problem; she would cry for a while then get mad at herself for being such a baby, then burst out crying again. If only she could figure out how to get out of the castle maybe then she could find out where she was and how to get back home. She knew her father must be frantic with worry by now but how was she going to get out of the castle when she couldn't even get out of her room.

During the night Serina was wakened by noises coming from somewhere outside, she climbed out of bed, headed for her window and was surprised to see Takar on the grounds near the mermaid fountain cracking his whip at the huge black dragon Java. As she watched Takar work with the big dragon, Serina thought; *he must be trying to teach him a new command.*

"You do as I bid you to do or else you will get another taste of my whip," Takar yelled as he held his hand up and cracked his mighty whip again. Fire shot out from the tip and nipped the dragon on the top of his nose, the huge beast let out a yelp and backed up about ten feet cowering down, plainly petrified of his Master.

"Everyone learns Java – sooner or later – to obey the Great Takar as you well know," he shouted while turning his gaze from the dragon and looking up to the tower window. Serina shrank back inside but she was too slow, Takar caught sight of her as she disappeared into the shadows, an evil smile crossed his face fleetingly. He made his point.

Serina heard Takar crack his whip again at which, Java yelped even louder than he did the last time. *Takar is such a cruel person*, she thought covering her head with a pillow trying to drown out the noise of the beast screaming in agony as Takar continued to crack his whip mercilessly.

Chapter 14

The next few days seemed to drag on. Serina was left alone in her room except at meals and bath time, the servants did their chores in the mornings and left without saying a word to Serina. And when she spoke, her words fell on deaf ears. Evidently, someone had warned them not to be overly friendly with her and she had not seen Mertie since Serina had been banished to her room. Serina guessed that was of Mertie's own doing though; probably so she wouldn't have to talk with her, however she had overheard Nettie and Ruthie talking earlier when they were in cleaning her room. They made pointed comments about The Master coming up and having a row with the little Princess. That's all she needed; Takar to come up and start on her again about how it was her destiny to be here and all that rubbish.

Sure enough about ten o'clock the key turned in the door and in popped Takar, his long dark robes flowing wildly as he walked rather quickly across the large room to where Serina was standing – at the far window.

"I think I have given you ample time to think about your situation now maybe you will be more receptive of me and what I have to say this time," said Takar as he pushed back the hood of his cape

Serina studied his hard chiseled face for any sign of human feelings, but all she saw was cold black eyes. He had made it a point to remove his hood lately whenever he was in her presence; Serina assumed it was to intimidate her, which it did.

"Takar, it doesn't matter what you tell me, I will not want to stay with you; I want to go home to my father and friends."

"THIS is your home now, there is no where else, do you understand me, you are special, you were born with a gift, a wonderful gift, a special power so to speak, that only a chosen few are born with. Together we will rule the world. Together we are indestructible but I have to teach you how to use this gift or it will be useless to you. Now listen to me very carefully..."

"What did you say?" Serina asked, interrupting Takar in mid sentence, suddenly something snapped in the back of her mind, something he said about having a special power, she did not know why but what he was saying sounded very familiar to her.

"Serina, you are not paying attention, I am not talking to hear my own voice."

He sounded a little put out with her but he also seemed to think she was becoming more receptive to whatever he had to say.

Serina was paying attention now for the first time. It seemed she had heard this story before, or something similar to it.

"I am listening; I just did not understand everything you said. Could you please repeat it?"

Takar looked at her for a second before continuing. "As I said, you were born with a special gift, which I will explain to you, you need me to teach you how to use this gift or you can lose it."

"You mean I have special powers?" Serina asked quizzically. Had someone already told her all of this, is this why it sounded so familiar? She peered into Takar's eyes, searching for a clue, was he the one? Maybe she did belong here, maybe this was her real home – somehow things were beginning to make sense.

"Something like that, even so with these powers you are still under my command, what I say is the last word on anything. Is that understood Serina?"

"Yeah, I, I mean yes, I understand."

Serina peered into Takar's eyes and he held her under his powerful stare longer than she wanted to be. She felt the coldness draw into her veins, deep, deep into her soul, finally gathering enough strength she managed to pull away casting her eyes to her lap where her hands were twisted so tightly together her knuckles were white, she was struggling to keep her breath flowing evenly but she was having a hard time of it.

"See Serina, no one can resist me for long, I have the power to save or destroy, and the choice is solely mine."

She would not turn back to look at him; she was so afraid, fear... She did not understand. She had never been afraid of anything. In her twelve years of life she had not been afraid of anything or anybody but now, now was different, fear gripped her very soul.

"I see we have come to an understanding my dear."

Takar fell silent and Serina could feel him staring a hole in her but still she would not face him, she knew if she did, he would be able to detect the fear she was trying so hard to hide and that would just feed his ego even more.

Takar sat silently, waiting she knew for her to look at him. Who could hold out the longest, she wondered as she sat there listening to the sound of her heart racing inside her chest. He was not going to give in and Serina knew it. So finally, she raised her head slowly but still did not speak.

"That's great Serina, when you are ready for me to teach you about this wonderful gift you have let one of the servants know and I will be glad to show you everything."

Takar spoke slowly, as if he were speaking to a small child but the coldness was still there, hidden just inside the realm of his soul, if indeed he had a soul.

"I will leave you for now, as I said let one of the servants know when you want to talk with me, I'll be waiting."

Serina stood by the window after he left her, staring down at the garden below – *such a beautiful place, how can something as beautiful as these gardens surround something so evil*, she thought, a single tear fell from her eye landing somewhere on the ground below.

Late that afternoon she heard someone outside her door but whoever it was, never entered. After a few moments, she could hear the footsteps receding down the stairway. *Whoever it was had a heavy foot,* Serina thought. 'He' also had a slight drag to one of 'his' feet. She could not place who it could have been, she had not noticed anyone walking with a limp or dragging a foot but then she was sure she had not met everyone who lived and worked in the castle.

Effie brought in Serina's dinner that night. She sat the tray on the table and left the room without a word. After eating everything on her plate, Serina dressed for bed in the long white gown that had been provided for her when she first arrived. So downhearted and not caring if she ever woke again, she climbed into the huge bed and fell fast asleep.

Late in the night Serina was awakened by a soft scraping noise, she lay still with her eyes blinking trying to get accustomed to the dark room, she heard it again, it sounded like it was coming from the large wardrobe in the corner of the room. Careful not to move she tried to look in that direction to see what could be making the noise. She figured it might be rats, a large dark shadow loomed in front of the wardrobe, Serina's voice caught in her throat, and she couldn't make a sound. She was about to speak out when the shadow moved out into the middle of the room. The moon cast its light beams across the floor of the room giving Serina enough light to see who was there, or *what* was more like it, she let out a scream as she got a better look at the creature, scaring him back into the shadows. Serina leaped out of bed not knowing what to do she yelled at the creature.

"Who are you and what do you want?"

Serina's voice was shaking as bad as the rest of her body, she stood trembling on the opposite side of the bed looking into the dark recesses of the room for whatever it was she had seen if, indeed, she had seen anything at all. One thing was for sure, though, she was not going over to the wardrobe to check it out. She reached for something, anything she could get her hands on from the bedside table and found the silver brush she had used earlier in the evening and held it high above her head as though this would scare off whatever it was she thought she saw.

She listened carefully for any sign of someone else being in the room with her, and was about to give up and sat down on the bed when she saw something move again, so she was not imagining it, there was someone or something in the room with her.

"Who's there?" She stood up holding the hairbrush up high again.

"N-N-Noa... say... come."

The creature could not speak plainly enough for Serina to understand. As he stepped out into the moonlight streaming in through the windows, Serina's voice made a funny choking sound deep in her throat, not quite making it to the surface of her lips.

"Noa... sa come," the creature said again when Serina did not respond. He stepped closer to the bed and Serina backed up a few feet.

"Who are you?" Serina asked, staring across the room at the giant. He was huge maybe ten feet tall, *well maybe not quite that tall*, Serina thought looking up at him, still keeping her distance but he was very large.

"Z-ZARF... N-Nora say come," the giant stuttered out his name apparently he was not use to talking; or at least he was not use to talking to very many people.

"Do you know Nora?"

That was a dumb question, Serina thought, *of course he knew Nora.*

"Where is Nora? I thought she was in the dungeon, besides I can't leave; the door is locked... Hey, how did you get in my room anyway, with the door locked? Do you have a key?"

The creature looked at her with a puzzled look on his face; most likely, he did not understand what she was saying. He walked over to the wardrobe and opened the door, stepping inside. Serina looked after him thinking he was truly mental.

"Where do you think your going? Get out of my clothes you big galute."

The big creature stepped back out into the room and motioned with his arm for Serina to follow him then stepped back into the wardrobe, he was so big he had to stoop over almost to his knees to get inside the wardrobe yet he was determined to go into it.

"Hey Zarf or whatever your name is get out of my wardrobe, what are you doing here and how did you get in? Where is your key?"

He did not answer her and did not come back out, Serina stood in front of her wardrobe for a long time – bewildered and waiting for the big giant creature to come back out but he must have loved staying in there because he would not come out.

Slowly Serina inched toward the armoire with her hairbrush held high overhead. When she reached the wardrobe, she paused for a moment, not knowing quite what to do. She was scared to death to reach out and open the door to the wardrobe, knowing the giant was just inside and not knowing if he would harm her if she did. With shaking hands she reached for the knob, her trembling fingers took hold of it, hesitating only briefly, she pulled the door open and jumped back toward the bed, but the creature did not come out and it was too dark inside to see him. Serina backed over to her dressing table and found one of the silver candlesticks, the ones Takar gave her as a gift after she arrived at the castle. She rummaged around the table finding a match and lit the candle quickly. Turning back toward the wardrobe, she took a few steps holding the candle out to see inside the armoire with one hand and holding the silver brush in the other.

"Zarf! Please come out." Stepping yet closer she held the candle up to get a better look inside but all she saw was her clothing and the bottom of the wardrobe.

"H-hello... Hello where are you? Where did you go?" No one was inside the wardrobe.

"Strange, did I or did I not see a strange huge creature go into my wardrobe?" she asked herself aloud. She carefully stepped around the back of the gigantic armoire but no one was there. She held up her candle to look around the room.

"Where did he go?"

Serina walked back to the front of the wardrobe and peered inside it once more. She moved the clothing around to make sure that no one was hidden in the cupboard or even in the side drawers – but there was no monster anywhere to be found!

She was seeing things or having a weird dream, that's all there was to it.

"That's odd," she said when she realized the smell surrounding the wardrobe was also familiar; *it smelled the same in the dungeon*, she thought. She had inhaled the same musky damp stench when Takar had taken her through the door that led to the dungeon. Serina stepped inside her wardrobe and bent down on her knees. She studied the floor of the clothe cupboard carefully and was about to give up when she spied a small hole in the corner of the floor, she held her candle closer to get a better look at it – it was worn and smooth around the edges. She slowly stuck her small finger into the hole, felt a knob of some kind, and pushed it down. She jumped back quickly to keep from falling into the now large opening gaping under her. She slowly shoved the board backwards and there just under the floor of the wardrobe was a set of stairs. Serina stuck the candle down inside the hole beneath her to see where the stairs were leading before heading down the steps – there was a room, *a room under my wardrobe, how strange.*

"Hello is anybody in there?" she called out, but could not hear a sound from inside the room beneath her. Hesitantly, she started down the stairs, going slowly just in case Zarf was lurking underneath the stairs. Once she reached the bottom of the stairs she held her candle up to get a better look, there was no one in the room, it was a small room with no furniture in it, there was one door and no windows. *How strange, a room with no windows...*

Serina inched her way to the door, fear gripped her body and she began trembling from head to toe, but she was determined to see where this led, could this be her way out of the castle and to home.

On the other side of the door was another staircase; a long spiraling set of stairs that seemed to go all the way to the bottom of the world. *They must have been used before the new ones were built,* Serina thought. It was difficult for Serina to climb down the narrow twisting stairway and hold her candle at the same time and she knew if she lost her candle, she would not be able to see her nose in front of her face. It was pitch dark and she had no idea how far she had gone or how far she had to go before she reached the bottom. She just hoped there was a bottom and it had a solid floor.

Finally, and perhaps after a half hour of groping her way down that interminable stairwell, Serina reached the bottom of the stairs. There, she found herself in another room with no windows and no Zarf, or whatever he was called. This room had a small table and two doors... Which one should she choose?

She sat the candlestick down and studied the surroundings. Looking around the room, she realized the room was larger than it first appeared, she picked up her half burned candle and walked to the back of the room, it was dusty and unkempt just like the one at the top of the stairs and smelled damp and musky, the same as the odor permeating her wardrobe. She studied the two doors for a moment and decided to take the one on the right, she gathered her courage, took hold of the doorknob, and gave it a twist. It opened easily enough. She pushed the door gently, far enough to get her head through.

Serina found herself looking down a long narrow corridor, one similar to the one Takar took her into leading to the dungeon, maybe this led to the dungeon as well, she slipped inside the dark damp corridor and let the door close quietly behind her.

As she made her way down the hall she noticed the unlit torches along the walls, it gave her a creepy feeling, just being there. She wished she was back home in her cozy little bed sound asleep and this was all a dream and she would wake to find her father preparing her birthday party but she could forget all of that for the time being. Now she had to concentrate on finding a way out of this horrible place and find her way home. It was quiet except for the dripping sound she could hear from somewhere farther down the hall. She held her small candle in front of her to see her way taking care not to touch the slimy walls. A large rat came running toward her and passed under her feet. Before she knew what had happened, she gasped putting her hand to her mouth to keep from screaming. She held the candle down close to the floor to see what all was at her feet. There were a few more rats running around, some as big as Serina's feet, water puddles covered the floor in places and the walls were green with moss and slime dripping to the stone floor. Finally, at the end there was a single torch lit on the wall, beckoning her forward. She stopped and took a deep breath before going on. She was petrified of what she might find at the end of the corridor.

Serina entered into a small room that had one door leading out of it, she walked over and without hesitation opened the door and went through it. She was wondering if she might get lost – all the doors and rooms, she had been through – it was a bit much to remember which was which all at once. The room opened into a larger room with two doors, it also had a stone table in the center; the table had iron bracelets attached to it – one at each corner, with a larger band hooked in the center. There was what looked like two full body harnesses hanging from the ceiling and chains, almost as big around as Serina's waist, hanging from the walls. *This must be a torture chamber*, Serina thought, looking at all the grotesque objects in the room. The sooner she got out of here the better, she concluded, as she tried to figure out through which door to go this time. Playing it safe she chose the right door again, this way if she had to get back up to her room in the tower she could remember which doors she took.

She was not prepared for what she found in the next room.

Nora sat on a small cot behind a barred wall, next to her cell stood Zarf.

"Nora!" Serina shouted as she ran toward the woman, stopping just short of the cell, and shrinking back in fear from the huge giant – ten feet tall for sure… His hair was all matted against his skull and his eyes were uneven on his face, giving him an eerie look, he was not something you would want to meet on a dark night somewhere.

"Do not be afraid of him he will not hurt you," Nora said.

That is debatable, Serina thought, as she stepped closer, setting her candlestick with the now very short candle on the damp floor next to Nora's cell

"I'm glad you came, I was afraid Zarf scared you too badly but I see you have a bit of adventure in you, just like your Mother."

"You knew my mother?" Serina asked curiously.

"Yes, I *know* your mother… very well," Nora replied almost casually.

Zarf moved a few steps away climbing on a large rock that lay near Nora's cell, there he sat, perched in remote solitude, although he did not move, his eyes kept scanning the room watching and waiting for something, or someone.

"Zarf is my guardian angel," Nora said when she noticed Serina staring at the creature. "He protects me and guards me with his life; he's been that way ever since I helped him one day but that is another story… I will tell you another day."

Nora looked at the big giant then back to Serina; she had a look about her that made Serina's heart jump a beat. Was it the fact that she was locked up down here in this old damp, stinky dungeon or was there some other reason why she felt so strange about her? Whatever the reason, Serina did feel close to her, as if she had known her for a long time.

"You're not the woman that went missing from my village long ago are you?" Serina asked suddenly. "You seem familiar to me for some reason."

"No, I am not that woman but I do know about what you speak of, I remember the tale myself."

"You do? Who are you? Why did you come to the tower that night?" Serina's voice took on renewed hope; finally, she might get out of this dirty ole castle and get back home. "Wait a minute," Serina exclaimed suddenly remembering something Nora said.

"You said, 'I *know* your mother', as in the present tense, I think you said VERY WELL if I'm not mistaking, what do you mean? My mother is dead and has been ever since I was born so how can you *know* her?"

Nora reached behind her and brought out a small leather pouch only Serina did not notice it, her attention had turned to Zarf who was still sitting on the huge rock but he had begun making a low moaning sound that shook Serina almost out of her skin.

"Why does he do that?" she asked, not knowing if she should turn her back on the creature or not. He was indeed very scary-looking, especially when he sat perched on that rock with his gnarled hands hanging over his knees – as if he was about to pounce on something – on her maybe… She could just see her body laying flat on the floor squashed like a hot potato. "Are you sure he's harmless?"

"Yes Serina, to me and you he is totally harmless, I guess I should tell you why."

"Yeah, tha-that would be good," Serina replied encouragingly glancing back at Zarf – he didn't look at all harmless to her.

"It was a long time ago, right after I arrived here, Zarf was one of the Master's ghouls, he obeyed Takar without question. I think he knew no other way but Takar's. One day Takar took me for a tour around the grounds with Zarf and a few others following along, he must have needed them to boost his ego – to make him look good in front of me... Well, we came up to the mermaid fountain and the others stepped up as well but Zarf tripped over a rock and fell taking Takar down with him to the ground. Takar was livid. When he got to his feet he lashed out at Zarf punishing him terribly, he beat him so badly it marred him for life; he looks nothing like he did before Takar left him for dead that day.

"Takar beat him?" Serina's voice shook as she spoke remembering the night Takar had the dragon down on the grounds below her window; she could still hear the creature howling. She looked over to where Zarf sat on the rock and felt pity for the giant.

"Yes, he beat him and left him for the others to carry away and bury, they dragged him out behind the dragon barn and left him, they didn't even bother to dig a hole – they just left him there."

"But he's alive, what happen that he didn't die?"

"I waited until no one was around and snuck out to the barn, I was going to try and bury him myself but when I got to him he was still breathing, just barely but he was still alive. I couldn't move him so I tried to make him comfortable. I snuck out bandages and cleaned him up as best I could. I really didn't think he was going to live but I could not just leave him there either. I made him a pillow from grass and bandaged him up and I came everyday to doctor his wounds. I would steal food from the kitchen and from the table and take to him, when he could move I snuck him into the dungeon and that's when I found out about the old stairway up to the tower. I knew I couldn't keep him in the dungeon for very long. I feared Takar would find out and kill him for sure the next time, me along with him. So I started exploring what lay behind the doors down here, when I found the stairs I climbed them to see where they went, I put Zarf in the room that connects to the corridor at the base of the stairs until he was well. He has been my loyal servant ever since."

"Does Takar know he's alive?"

"No, Zarf stays out of sight, or he would surely be put to death, there have been close calls, but so far, he has not been seen for nearly twelve years."

"That's a long time for someone to have to hide... You said he doesn't even look like he used to, so why worry about it if no one can recognize him?"

"Whether he could be recognized or not his life would be in danger, one doesn't just exist here without questions and Takar would not permit anyone to stay here, unless you are serving him and only him."

Serina glanced over at Zarf studying him, wondering what he may have looked like before Takar performed his handy work on him.

"But Zarf is not the reason I sent him for you Serina, there is something very important I have to tell you."

"Oh yes." Serina turned back to face the woman anxiously. "Like how you *know* my mother, not *knew* her."

Nora reached inside the pouch she was holding and pulled out a handful of bluish looking powder.

She hoped that this powder would refresh the part of Serina's memory, which she had asked Zarf to erase just before her birthday, then Serina would remember everything – and maybe they would have a chance once more.

"What is that stuff?" Serina asked taking a step backwards.

"This will make it easier for you to understand what I tell you. This is called memory dust. When you were brought here, Takar blew a silvery looking dust into your face and over your body. The powder made you forget certain things, such as how you woke up in the tower instead of your own bed that morning, it is called memory dust also, but it's like selective memory dust. No doubt, Takar chose to remove from your memory everything about how you arrived at the castle on the eve of your birthday. To his knowledge you had never been to the castle before, so he left your childhood memories intact, choosing to extract only your journey here."

Serina hesitated, looking from Nora to Zarf in turn. She was not sure what she should do, what if this was a trick and Nora was really a bad person after all.

"Maybe if I just wait my memory will come back on its own."

"There is only one way to get that memory back and that is through this dust I hold in my hand. So one makes you forget and the other, this bluish colored one I hold in my hand makes you remember what the other made you forget. Please don't be afraid, stand close and I will blow some of this into your face and then you will remember everything."

"How do I know I can trust you?" Serina asked hesitantly.

"You don't. Only you know what you feel in your heart Serina. Only I know my intentions, whether they are good or not, I can try to persuade you but in the end, only you can make the decision – that is where trust comes in."

Serina looked down at her feet as if they could help her decide, she was more afraid than she let on. Her insides were shaking and she felt like she was going to be sick. *Oh well, here goes nothing,* she thought as she stepped closer to the bars and closed her eyes.

"Serina!"

Serina opened her eyes and looked at Nora.

"I know you've been through a lot since you've arrived here – it means a lot to me to know that you trust me."

"I have no choice, if I'm going to find out how to get... I mean how I got here, and I must know." Serina stopped herself in time not to say why, just in case it turned out to be a trap of Takar's after all.

Nora stuck her hand through the bars holding it out flat, Serina could see the shimmering blue dust in the palm of her hand, glittering and twinkling, in the dim torch light. She held her breath and closed her eyes as she stepped closer to Nora's hand. Serina heard Nora's intake of breath and felt the dusty powder hit her full in the face as Nora blew the dust from her hand.

Serina could feel her face start to tingle but was afraid to breathe let alone open her eyes, she was sure her face was going to fall right off her head, then she would be the one needing a hooded cloak.

"Open your eyes Serina." Serina did slowly, not wanting to blink for fear of knocking any of the dust from her face.

"How long does it take before it starts working?" Serina asked feeling disappointed that it had not brought her memory back the instant the dust hit her face.

"Give it a minute to absorb into your pores."

Suddenly Zarf was at Serina's side, sweeping her up into his big hairy arms and running with her toward the door she had entered into earlier. She started to scream but he put one of his huge gnarled hands over her mouth halting the screeches in her throat. They were through the second room and into the corridor running toward the stairs before Zarf uncovered her mouth.

"ZARF! Put me down, what's going on?"

All she heard from Zarf was his unusual moan as he kept running, he was carrying Serina with one arm, her arms and legs were flopping around as if she were a rag doll. When they got to the stairs he released her, setting her on the bottom step, he was very excited, pushing her in an upward motion.

"Go!" ordered Zarf – Serina could tell he was not used to using words, he was still extremely nervous for some reason. He kept looking back and forth from the door to Serina and repeated twice. "Go?"

"Why?" Serina was puzzled about the whole incident. She tried to step around him but he blocked her. "Go," he said again more urgently now, and again he pointed to the top of the stairs and gave Serina a rough shove up onto the next step.

"Why did you grab me? Oh, it's no use; he doesn't understand what I'm saying."

She tried to push pass him again but he would not budge.

"Go! Bad! Go." It suddenly downed on Serina that maybe Zarf was trying to help her, save her from something.

"Zarf, is something wrong?"

Zarf nodded fiercely several times and pointed back to where they came from then back up the stairs, all along he was moaning, making this terrible sound.

"Is it Nora …? No, Takar! Was it Takar? Did you hear Takar coming?"

Zarf moaned louder, nodding his head wildly again, giving Serina a push as he did so.

"Okay, okay, I'm going, but tell Nora I'll be back, that stupid dust she blew on me didn't do anything but make my face twinge. I can't believe I let her talk me into something as stupid as blowing that stuff on me."

Zarf gave Serina another push up the stairs, she started climbing the hundred zillion stairs to the top of the tower, looking back every few steps to see Zarf still standing at the bottom, watching her, making sure she didn't come back down the stairs. She climbed the twisting spiraling staircase back to her room and stepped out of the wardrobe into the bedroom, being careful to put the boards back in the exact same place they had been before she went on this latest escapade. She was so disappointed however; that the dust did not work that she poured some water from the pitcher into the washbowl and scrubbed her face thoroughly. She could still feel it tingling, either from scrubbing so hard or from the dust itself - she did not know, but she would not fall for something as dumb as that again, and just to think she actually was beginning to trust Nora, *well that would not happen again either.*

Serina climbed into bed disheartened about the whole evening, why would Nora send Zarf to get her, showing her the secret passageway and where she was held prisoner if she were not on the up-and-up. It did not make any sense to her. Maybe, Nora thought, the powder would work, or she just got hold of the wrong stuff, or maybe she…

"Oh stop kidding yourself; you'll never get out of this place," Serina told herself, pulling the covers up over her head

She fell asleep after tossing and turning for about an hour, she dreamt of the strangest things, strange but yet familiar to her.

In her dreams, Nora was her mother, and there was someone chasing her, then a big black dragon swept her off and carried her away into the darkness. Serina would wake up from one dream just to fall into another one as soon as she closed her eyes. Something about her necklace, the emerald stone she wore around her neck was magic, a secret opening in a wall somewhere and Jewels were falling out of it, her friend Koori was there with her, they were running, out of breath and grabbing their sides as they ran, falling down, falling, falling.

Chapter 15

Serina woke up in a cold sweat, bolted out of bed and ran to the wardrobe, stepping inside she reached down, sticking her finger in the small hole she gave it a tug, it opened up quickly and quietly.

"It wasn't a dream," she burst out, relieved that she had not dreamed about the whole incident. "But wait, the dust, my memory... It's back, I know everything. It worked!"

Serina started jumping around the room, she was so excited she couldn't help running and jumping on the bed and yelling at the top of her lungs. "It all makes sense now, I remember everything and Nora *IS* my Mother, why didn't I figure that one out, it seems so simple now, Nora, Senora, yes, yes, yes, that's why she *knows* my mother because she *is* my mother."

Serina heard the key in the door; she quickly jumped down from the bed just as the door swung open, it was Ruthie with Serina's breakfast.

"What was all the yelling about? I could hear you clear down the stairs; they could probably hear you all the way down in the kitchens."

Serina quickly hid her excitement with a long solemn face. Although, she wanted to shout at Ruthie, and the whole castle that she would not be staying for lunch. Now that she knew everything, she would soon be going home, home to her father, her little cottage, little bedroom her cozy bed and all of her friends - no she couldn't wait to get back to her village and the peaceful life she had known.

"It's nothing, I just felt like shouting, haven't you ever felt like just shouting Ruthie... I'm tired of being cooped up here all day long, I'm going crazy Ruthie, crazy you hear me, crazy from being locked up with no one to talk to or see, but it will be okay, I feel better now.

Ruthie looked at her thinking she was in the presence of a crazed child and shook her head.

"Well if you would act more like you are supposed to maybe you would not be so lonely and could stay down stairs instead of up in this old tower then I wouldn't have so far to climb to bring you your breakfast every morning."

"That's a good idea Ruthie, I think I'll do just that, what do you think about that?"

The girl looked even more puzzled than before, if that were possible, she was not expecting the little Princess to be in such a happy mood.

Ruthie went about straightening the room and Serina sat down to eat her breakfast, she was thinking of so many things and so rapidly she could hardly keep up with all the thoughts running through her head.

If she remembered everything right, she did have a special power, and above all else, she knew how to get out of the castle and get home, this was going to be easier than she thought.

Serina finished her breakfast then quickly dressed for the day in one of the pretty frocks Takar had provided for her. *Might as well take advantage of what's offered to one in life,* Serina thought as she slipped the pretty pink dress over her head.

Not long after Ruthie left, Serina heard the key turn in the lock as she expected she would and in walked Takar.

"Well I hear you are in fine spirits this morning, glad to see you have come to your senses at long last," he said as he strode into the room.

"Yes, well one does need to come to their senses once in a while don't they Takar?" Serina replied, trying to put on her best smile but she had a slight quiver to her voice – having her memory back Serina knew exactly why also. She was very much afraid of Takar and what he could do. She also realized something else, she had no plan, no idea of how she was going to get out of the castle and back home.

"That's good to hear Serina, maybe you have decided that what I say is true and your place is here with me. Or maybe, you are playing a game, trying to play me for a fool, in which case you will lose the game Serina, trust me, no one plays Takar for a fool and lives to tell about it."

He pulled one arm from behind his back, extending it out in front of him, in it he held the silver candlestick, the one she left in front of Nora's cell the night before. In all the excitement she had forgotten all about it. She didn't know what to say and the shock of seeing the candlestick must have shown on her face too by the look on Takar's.

He walked over to the dressing table where the other candlestick stood, picked it up and held the two up next to one another.

"They appear to be a set, can you tell me how one of them ended up in the dungeon last night?" He had turned toward her and the mask of his face had taken on a demonic look. "How did you get into the dungeon last night with your door locked, tell me who unlocked your door."

Serina was trying to think of something to say but nothing came to mind.

"Tell me Serina, who unlocked this door for you last night and why did you go to the dungeon?" Takar roared, his voice was dark and cruel, the veins were starting to bulge on his face and his eyes seemed to sink in under his forehead. He covered the distance between them in two large strides and loomed menacingly over her, causing Serina to shrink back against the edge of the bed.

"I... No one... I... I mean I was asleep all, all night and the candlestick has been missing since the night I arrived. Do you really think I'm smart enough to get out of this tower by myself? And none of your servants are stupid enough to try and help me. So why would I want to go to that creepy ole dungeon? It scares me too much."

Serina was not good at thinking on her feet so this was the best she could come up with... Takar seemed to mull this over for a moment, Serina could not tell if he believed her or not for his face had taken on a guarded look.

"Why had you not told me the candlestick was missing, I would have taken care of the person who stole it."

Serina didn't think of her words as blaming someone for stealing the candlestick, she did not want to get anyone in trouble, just the thought of some unlucky servant having to face Takar's wrath gave Serina cold chills. The thought of it being her fault made her feel even worse.

"I never thought about it, I don't believe anyone stole it either, maybe it was just misplaced or something."

Takar glared at her, he had pushed his hood back when he came into the room so Serina could see the expression on his face.

"Nora says that she believed it was left there by one of the servants also... Yet, you could have set this up together, but if what you say is true then I will deal with it later."

The tone in his voice told Serina that someone was going to pay dearly for the candlestick and she did not envy that person.

He walked over to the dressing table taking the chair that was pushed up to it and carried it over to where Serina was standing, he paused for a moment before sitting, looking at Serina. *No, it was more as if he were looking through her,* she thought, such as the dragon did that day, deep into the depths of her soul.

"So now, have you thought any more about what I said to you the other day? About the castle being your home and realizing this is your world, your destiny?"

Takar's voice took on an almost friendly tone and his face actually seemed to have a hint of warmth in it.

Serina swallowed hard, eased back onto the edge of the bed, and sat down before answering his question.

"I don't understand everything about my destiny, about why I'm here, so if you could please go over everything again for me I would appreciate it."

Serina was stalling, but she didn't know what else to do, most of all she did not want to anger Takar again. She wanted to keep him in a good mood, even if it meant her playing his little game.

"When you were born Serina you were born with special powers, you were born to be with me, to live here and rule with me this place, this kingdom."

Serina remembered what her mother had told her about her powers but kept quite while Takar rambled on.

"You should have been here all along but I let you stay in your village until now, letting you grow up some before I took you to be my bride."

"Bride!" Serina choked. "What do you mean bride, I'm only twelve years old, I, I'm too young to marry."

"Yes, I know perfectly well how old you are and I have no intentions of marrying you now, you are just a child."

"That's right, just a child, too young to marry, way too young."

Serina was shocked at his words; her mother never mentioned anything to her about marriage, she had to get home and the sooner the better.

"I think when you are sixteen you will be old enough to marry. Until then you will be groomed and schooled on your behavior and manners, also you will learn to use your special powers, perfect them, then when we marry you will be ready to stand by me and rule with me and together we can take over the world."

He has flipped his ever-loving mind, Serina thought, *gone totally mad, especially if he thinks I am going to marry him.*

"Yes sixteen would be a better age to marry than twelve I think," piped Serina, managing a slight smile for Takar's benefit but inside her stomach had knotted into a ball and was rolling around to the point of making her nauseous.

"This is your destiny Serina, it was meant to be this way, long, long before you were ever born. You must understand there is nothing you or anyone else can do about it, so the best thing to do is to accept your fate and make the best of it. You will be better off for it, you will see I am right in the end," said Takar. He spoke to Serina in a manner she was not used to hearing from him; in a way a Master would talk to a prize beast – something or someone under his magnetic power.

"It's hard for a young girl to understand all of this, especially it being dumped in one's lap all at once," replied Serina speaking honestly. "If only I had known about it all along, from my birth, then it would be a simple matter of stepping into my place but like this, this throws me for a loop."

"If you need a little time to think this over I can understand, you are as you say just a child and I admit this is a lot even for an adult to absorb all at once. So, I will grant you one day, this time tomorrow I will expect you to have come to terms with everything and accept your fate and the royal blood that flows through your veins, Serina... You really have no other choice if you think about it."

"Yes, one day would be good, thank you Takar."

Takar stood to leave then reached over and patted Serina on the shoulder. "It will be great, as it should be Serina, you will see."

He left the room without another word, leaving Serina sitting on the bed in total shock, listening to his footsteps receding down the long flight of stairs.

All the rest of the day Serina pondered the conversation she and Takar had. When Effie brought her lunch Serina hardly acknowledged her presence, she was so wrapped up in her thoughts she didn't even notice Effie rummaging through her wardrobe and dressing table, nor did she notice her slipping a small object into her apron pocket before she left.

Serina did not touch a bite of lunch, her stomach was still in a knot with no sign of it getting better any time soon. If only she could come up with a plan, that's what she needed, a plan to get out of the castle so she could get to her father; he would take care of everything, including Mr. Big Bad Takar.

That evening when they brought her evening meal, a plan was forming in Serina's mind, she ate every bite of her dinner, every last crumb, she was starved and besides she needed her strength. She just needed to get back to the dungeon to her mother, she could help her, she remembered their conversations at the cave – she remembered everything... She also remembered her father could not help her after all, she had to get to her; her mother knew what to do.

Chapter 16

Serina waited until she thought everyone was sleeping then she slipped out of bed, still in her frock and shoes, and stepped into her wardrobe and through the floor panels into the room below. She paused long enough to listen for any noises then she headed for the steep spiraling stairs that had lay hidden for so many years. They were so narrow and worn; she had a hard time descending them.

At the bottom she paused again, listening for any sign of someone stirring, nothing still. *So far so good*, she thought as she started down the long corridor toward the dungeon, she kept her fingers crossed hoping her luck would not play out on her.

She hesitated at the door that opened into the dungeon, her hand was shaking so bad she could hardly hold her candlestick; the flames were flickering wildly, casting strange shadows on the walls around her giving Serina's heart one more reason to stay up in her throat.

She turned the handle, opening the door slowly so it would not creak on its hinges and just enough for her to peek through into the dungeon.

Everything appeared to be okay, so she slipped through and closed the door quietly then stepped toward the cell that Nora occupied.

"Nora, I, I mean Mother." Serina held her candle up so she could get a better look; she lay on her side fast asleep.

"Nora!" With a flutter of relief, Serina saw her mother stir and rise on her elbow – only *it was not* her mother.

Serina's heart skipped a beat, her throat constricted and her eyes grew to the size of saucers.

"What ya waking me for at this time of the night lass?"

The words came out of the mouth of the little gray haired man that brought breakfast to Serina's room the first day she arrived, and he didn't look any happier now than he did then.

"What is a young lass like you doing down in this old dungeon at this time of night? Are ya touched? It's not good for you to be down here."

"I... I... I..."

"Is that all ya can say after waking a man in the middle of the night."

Serina tried to get a grip on herself but she wasn't having much luck.

"I... I... Where's the other person that was in this cell?"

"What other person? I'm the only one in here."

Maybe Takar let Nora out of the dungeon and she was back up in her room right now fast asleep, she never thought of that but where was Zarf, he would know... Who was she trying to kid, even if Zarf knew anything Serina would not understand anything he said.

"The woman, Nora, do you know her, where is she?"

"How should I know, is that all you do is ask people questions that can't be answered?"

"She was here, last night in this very cell, I just want to know where she is, what happened to her?"

The little man scratched his head roughly, his gray hair flying around his head; he eyed Serina as if she were one of the big rats that roamed the dungeon so freely.

"I don't know anything about any one else being down here. I was thrown in here this morning because I dropped the Master's breakfast on the floor and he had to wait five minutes for another plate of food, there was no one else in here when I got here – oh, except for Rupert who lives in here. He's down there in the next to the last cell, he might know something, except he can't talk and doesn't understand a thing you say, so it wouldn't do much good to ask him."

"She has been locked in this dungeon ever since the night I arrived here, I'm sure you've known about that, I doubt that anything goes on in this castle without everyone of you knowing exactly what the other one is doing."

The little man looked hard at Serina for a moment; he started to say something then thought better of it and decided to ignore her remark all together.

Serina was really scared, what was she going to do now? She had no idea where Nora's rooms were located and in this huge castle, it could take days to find her.

"Do you know where Nora's bed chamber is? What floor does she stay on?" Serina asked, her voice reaching panic pitch.

"She stays on the fourth floor, in the north wing but I'm sure she is fast asleep now, just as I was before I was so rudely awakened."

"I apologize for waking you; I did not know Nora had been released."

"That's alright lassie," said the old man suddenly taking a kinder turn toward her.

"It's not like I have to get up before the chickens in the morning. I am old though and need my rest just to help with my aches and pains, if ya know what I mean, so if you will not be needing my services for anything else I would like to get back to sleep and you my dear should get back to the tower before something bad happens to you."

"Sure, sure, only how do I get to the fourth floor from here or into the castle for that matter, I am a bit turned around here."

"If I were you I'd go back the way I came, that would be a good start, then head up the main stairs," he said as he lay back down on the cot.

Something else dawned on Serina right then; which way was north?

"Which is the north tower?" she asked the little man, ignoring his earlier statement.

"The opposite of the south tower my dear, now goodnight," the old man grumbled, wishing Serina would be gone so he could get back to sleep. He rolled over onto his side facing the wall and whispered something incoherent while he adjusted the small pillow under his head.

"Goodnight Mister… I don't remember your name."

"Toddle, it is lass, now get on with ya."

"Grumpy aren't we," Serina muttered, more to herself than to the little man. She turned toward the door from which she had entered earlier and hurried to it wondering how she was going to find her way into the castle let alone the fourth floor.

Serina took the middle door instead not knowing where it would lead, it proved to be the very one she needed. It led her straight into a long corridor that led to a room off the kitchen; from there she took a door that opened into a large entrance area with two sets of stairs. This, she was familiar with; she had been through here before but now which way to the north tower.

Serina took the left set of stairs and started up, *still no one in sight, so far so good.* When she got to the top of the stairs, she found herself standing on a circular landing that was about fifteen feet wide and went completely around the room. The center of it opened onto the next floor up, but to top it all off, there were eight doors, making the task of finding her mother even more difficult.

"Now what," she said under her breath.

Which door would she choose; so many choices and not a clue as to which one would be the right one. All she needed was to take the wrong door and end up in Takar's bedchambers. She went to the first door – it was the most logical choice and that way, she thought, she would have an easier time remembering which doors she had opened and which ones were left.

The first two were locked, which made things simpler, the third opened onto a long corridor that had doors on either side of it – this was not the kind of complication she wanted or even needed at the moment. The fourth proved to be the right one; it opened onto another landing with a staircase in the middle of it.

Serina glanced around quickly for another candle; hers was getting desperately short. It was flickering and had burned down to the end of its wick. She knew it was only a matter of minutes or seconds before it died out leaving her in the dark. Too late, the candle flickered one last time as its small blue flame fought for its life and then died. She sat the candlestick down on the banister and started up the long stairway, feeling her way more than seeing it. When she reached the top of the stairs she found herself facing a huge man, she froze in her steps, not knowing what to do she stood there looking at the giant. He apparently did not see her, for he remained very still as she did. He was covered in an armor type suit looking every bit the part of being prepared for battle. *Maybe it was hard to see through all that stuff on his head, or maybe he was sleeping,* Serina thought. She stepped a little closer and tried to get past him without disturbing him. She edged her way carefully, her back against the wall, her eyes on *him* all the while – there was something about *him* that did not seem right. She eyed *him* more closely, studying *him*... Then suddenly a noise; someone was coming. She had nowhere to hide, she looked around franticly trying to locate something or someplace large enough to hide, she spied a rather large chest sitting by the entrance of one of the doors; she hurried to the chest and climbed in just in time. She heard the footsteps near the top of the stairs as she closed the lid, leaving it ajar to see who was up and wondering around the castle this late at night. It was Mertie. She reached the top of the stairs and looked around making sure no one was lurking about, raising her skirts to mid-calf she started to dance around on the landing humming a tune. She was holding a bottle of something in her hand and judging from her behavior Serina figured it must have been an almost empty bottle of spirits. Mertie was waltzing around the landing without a care in the world. She waltzed up to the man in the suit of armor and holding her skirts high, she curtsied awkwardly.

"Why yes your highness, I would luf to have this dance wifh you... My gown... Oh, thank youuu, I stitched it up me self, as you say it is quite esquizit."

She then clumsily grabbed the man in the armor's hand and started to dance with him. It took all of Serina's restraint to keep from bursting into loud laughter as she watched Mertie trying to dance with the man, only the man would not dance or even acknowledge Mertie's presence; he just stood there, frozen to the spot like a statue.

Feeling foolish, Serina suddenly realized the man was just that, a suit of armor, a statue so to speak.

Finally, Mertie discarded the hand of the armored man, stumbled against one of the doors, and disappeared down the corridor.

With an audible sigh of relief Serina climbed out of the chest, she looked around and listened for a moment to see if anyone else was coming or if Mertie was indeed well on her way.

There were three corridors and two doors, Serina was on the third floor as far as she could tell, and she had one more to go and hoped she was going in the right direction.

Choosing the first door, she opened it and headed down the hall toward the end of it not knowing where it might lead – if anywhere.

At the end of the corridor she found another set of stairs and from the looks of them, they were seldom used.

Serina grabbed her skirts gathering them up so she could climb the stairs more quickly. By the looks of this stairwell, she figured the servants must use it more than anyone else did. The steps were narrower than the others she had climbed and not nearly as tidy.

The corridor on this floor was only about ten feet wide and the walls were not as elaborately decorated as the ones on the lower floors. Serina wondered if this floor was not indeed the servants' quarters.

She took a deep breath, realizing how nervous she really was. Now that she was here, she did not know quite what to do. She never thought anything through – her only plan was to find Nora. Somehow, she hoped her mother could tell her how they could get out of the castle and get home. She had not expected to find someone else in her mother's cell. What's more, the time she had wasted trying to find Nora's room had made all of her escaping efforts that much harder, but at least she did not have to try to figure out how to get her mother out of the dungeon; just out of the castle and back home to her father and their little cottage.

Something suddenly dawned on her; the night she and Koori came through the cave wall into the castle grounds she remembered seeing her mother looking at them from a window high in the castle, which one was it.

"Think Serina, think," she muttered under her breath, she turned around slowly trying to remember which way they were facing the castle in regards to where she was right then. She mentally drew a picture of the castle and then tried to work out where she was. After a moment, she thought, if she had figured it out correctly, Nora's bedchamber was just ahead at the end of this corridor on the left. She took off down the hall at a trot toward the door in question – hoping in her heart that she was right, she crossed her fingers just in case, she reckoned it wouldn't hurt to have a little extra luck.

Chapter 17

Serina stood in front of the door, which she hoped was her mother's. Holding her breath, slowly she turned the doorknob. It was unlocked. She opened it just far enough to slip her slim little frame through then closed it quietly. Still holding her breath, she inched her way toward the bed. In the dim light, she thought that the person lying in bed was asleep. However, as Serina came closer she could see more distinctly the shape lying beneath the covers and realized instantly that she was in deep trouble. It was not her mother nor was *he* asleep.

"What are you doing here in my room little Princess?" the man said raising his head from the pillow.

"Ju?"

"Yes Miss?"

Serina did not know what to say, she knew she was in trouble now and did not know how to get out of it.

"Ju, I, I was looking for someone else, I'm sorry I've awakened you. I, w-will leave, I'm sorry again. Goodnight."

Serina turned and headed for the door hoping that Ju would not try to stop her. Maybe she could get out of the castle and to the wall before Ju could get to Takar to tell him she was out of the tower.

"Serina," Ju called back.

Serina stopped at the sound of Ju's voice, her feet frozen to the floor, her heart in her mouth – only two more steps and she would have been out the door and gone.

"Yes." Her voice was as shaky as her legs and her heart was pounding so fast she could hardly hear.

"If you're looking for Nora she is across the hall, I will have to let you in her room."

Serina spun on her heels, her eyes wide with astonishment, staring at Ju in disbelief. How did he know she was looking for her mother and why would he help her find her. He was very much loyal to Takar, or so she thought.

"Thank you Ju, but how did you know I was looking for Nora?"

"She told me you might come up here trying to find her."

Serina took another step toward the door then turned back to Ju with a quizzical look on her face.

"Why Ju? Why would you help me, I thought you were so loyal."

"Nora told me she is your mother little Princess… and, well I figured it would be kindly to do something nice for someone I liked really well."

"Oh I see! Well, thank you again."

Ju had climbed out of bed fully dressed; he was most definitely expecting her, Serina thought.

He walked her across the hall where he slipped a key into the door then turning back to face Serina he bent down just slightly, far enough to look her straight in the eye.

"And yes Serina, I'm very loyal…"

He pushed the door open for her then said, "Goodnight" stepping back across the hall disappearing back through his own bedroom door.

"Serina! Oh thank God you found me, I was so afraid you would not come."

"Mother…"

The two embraced with tears streaming down their faces.

"I remember mother, I remember everything, the cave, our talk, Mr. Nosh and the fight, I remember it all, now what do we do? How do we get out of here?"

"Don't worry I have a plan, where is the stone, your necklace?"

"My necklace, oh no I forgot it in the tower," Serina cried.

"We have to have the stone Serina; we can not do anything without the stone."

"Should I go back to get it?"

"No, it's too risky; let me think for a minute, I'll figure something out."

Suddenly Nora had a thought. "I'll be right back, just sit tight, I think I have a way of getting the emerald without you having to go back to the tower."

Nora left the room, leaving Serina staring after her.

How could she have been so stupid as to leave her necklace, she had not even thought about it in days, she had completely forgotten how important it was to getting them out of the castle. She wasn't sure though how it played a part in all of this but her mother was adamant about it. *How could I have just forgotten about it?*

The bedroom door opened and Nora came rushing back in with Ju in tow.

"Serina tell Ju here where to find your necklace and he will take the servants stairs to the tower and fetch it.

"It's in my wardrobe, in the pocket on the inside of my cloak; I hid it there a while back."

"I'll be back as soon as I can, in the meantime stay in here with your mother and out of sight."

"Thank you Ju."

Serina breathed a sigh of relief when Ju disappeared out the door but waiting for his return proved almost more than she could bear.

During Ju's absence, Serina told her mother how much she had longed for a mother all her life. Senora said, "I always dreamed of someday holding you in my arms… But enough of this, we'll have all the rest of our lives to talk about this, right now I need to tell you a few things you need to know, because after all Serina it's up to you and your special powers to get us out of here."

"I understand that but I'm so scared, I don't know if I will be able to go through with it."

Senora took Serina in her arms and cradled her for a moment, and then gently pushed her back to face her.

"Serina, the necklace is a powerful stone, it has the ability to reverse things and time, so one could change things – but only in your hands – or in the hands of another chosen one who has the power to use it."

"Speaking of the stone, how do you know that it can do all you say, maybe it's just a regular old green emerald."

"I know Serina, because I am the one who put the stone in the water for you to find. You see, Takar could not stop bragging about the stone being very powerful, so, one night I waited until the castle was fast asleep and while being very careful not to disturb anyone, I slipped down the stairs to the dining room. I took the royal cup from the mantle and pried the emerald out of it. I replace it with an ordinary emerald, which I found in an old jewelry box some years ago. Then the first chance I got I slipped out of the castle and took it to the stream where I knew you would find it."

"How did you know how to get out of the castle grounds if you were enslaved here?" Serina asked curiously.

"After I had been here a while Takar began to trust me out of the tower – yes I stayed in the same tower where you have been staying for a long, long time. Takar did not trust me out of the locked room or out of his sight for months after I arrived. He was afraid I might try to find a way to escape."

"How did you know about the cave?"

"I found the secret opening quite by accident actually. One day I was wandering, exploring the grounds more or less, and found the fountain. As I finished playing in the water, which seemed to flow down from nowhere, I pulled my hands away and shook them off and that's when the cave wall appeared. The water that I shook from my hands sprinkled the tree leaves and everything changed all of a sudden. The tree became an earth wall and it unexpectedly slid open as I leaned on the top of the fountain exposing the inside of the cave to me. I had no idea what had happened but I stepped into the cave and the wall closed back upon me which just about gave me heart failure."

Serina remembered the first time she opened the cave wall and how her heart leaped into her chest. "Yes I remember when I first opened it and how it scared me also."

"Anyway I started beating the wall and prying it with my fingers and it finally opened – how, I didn't know. I stepped back and it closed again as quickly as it did before. So I put my hands on the damp earth and pushed and the wall opened once more. I stepped back through and repeated the motions. I stuck my hands in the fountain shaking them off on the tree, the tree disappeared, and the earth wall was there again. I didn't go back to the fountain for weeks after that, for fear that someone would catch me, but I waited one night until everyone was asleep and slipped out again. This time I went straight to the fountain and opened the wall. I slipped through and explored the cave and its surroundings. It wasn't until later that I found out where it led to, I couldn't believe it when I realized it led to my old village and to you."

She paused to catch her breath and then finished. "That was only about a year ago. Ever since, I've been watching you every chance I got, hoping that one day I would be able to get the nerve to talk to you. I wanted to tell you what was about to happen to you, the change that was going to take place, which would affect us for the rest of our lives."

She fell silent, peering into her daughter's eyes for a moment, her brow furrowed pensively.

"Serina you know that we can not just leave this place don't you? You know if we did actually leave, Takar would just come after us again and who knows the damage that he would do then. I would not ask you to do this if there were any other way, believe me I've thought it over and over and this is the only way. You have to confront Takar, match your power against his, this is the only way we will be set free."

Serina pulled away from her mother.

"Takar? A-are you sure, I... can't do that," Serina stammered with incredulity, her eyes growing the size of saucers. *I cannot do that! And even if I could, I'll surely end up on the big ole dragon's dinner plate as his 'main course',* she thought.

At that moment, there was a light tap on the door, Serina and Senora both jumped at the sound.

"Quickly hide in the draperies and what ever you do be still and perfectly quiet."

Senora pushed Serina into the draperies then started for the door, before she reached it however it opened and Ju stuck his head in, breathing a sigh of relief Senora told Serina she could come out that all was clear.

"The emerald necklace is no where to be found, I searched your cloak inside and out, I even went through all the other clothing in the wardrobe, I searched the drawers in your dressing table and by your bed, everywhere... Are you sure you don't have it on you."

"No, I haven't been wearing it, I stuck it in my cloak pocket after me and Mertie fought over it, I'm sure of it."

"Well it wasn't there."

"Serina, you said you fought with Mertie over your necklace, what do you mean?" Senora asked.

"One night Ernie stayed in my room on Takar's orders, he stole my necklace then gave it to Mertie when she came in with my breakfast and to tidy-up the room. We fought for it and then Takar came in and I hid the necklace and told him we were fighting over her accusing me of stealing the silver and that was that. But I hid it so no one else would take it."

"When is the last time you saw it?" Senora asked.

"This morning, well I sort of saw it that is."

"What do you mean you 'sort of saw it'? Either you saw it or you didn't," Ju said with some irritation.

"Well, I felt it more than saw it. When I was dressing I kinda rubbed up against my cloak in the wardrobe and I felt it there in my pocket, I never even gave it a second thought but I remember feeling it in the pocket this morning."

Ju scratched his head and paced the floor for a moment, then returned his gaze to Serina and Senora.

"Who was in the tower today?"

Serina thought for a moment before she replied. "Well, there was Ruthie who brought my breakfast and tidied up. Later Takar came and talked with me about my destiny and stuff... Oh, and Effie came in also and was messing about quite a bit but I think that was all, why?"

"Someone took the necklace that's why – but which one? Tell me what each one of them did when they were in the tower."

"I don't know I did not pay attention to what they were doing except Takar, he was very angry with me about the candlestick I left in the dungeon last night. I had to lie my way out of that one. I thought for sure he was going to lock me up down there too, but no, he just stood in the middle of the room for a while. Then... Oh yeah, he walked over to the dressing table and picked up my other candlestick then took the chair from against the wall and sat in it by my bed... No I don't think Takar took it he never went near the wardrobe."

"Then who? What about Ruthie and Effie, what did they do, can you remember?"

"Not really, I was all wrapped up in remembering things... I really did not pay attention to anything they did."

"Think Serina, think," her mother urged. She was very nervous about the whole thing, not knowing where the necklace was, presented a big problem for all of them.

"Ruthie cleaned up the room... I didn't notice her doing anything out of the ordinary. She just cleaned and left."

"What about Effie?"

Serina was racking her brain but could not remember anything Effie did other than bringing her lunch and leave it.

"Sorry, I can't remember."

"That's okay, we'll figure something out but it would be a whole lot easier if we had the emerald."

Senora seemed worried; she started pacing the room along with Ju, rubbing her temples and biting her nails while Ju kept passing his fingers through his hair nervously.

"Wait! I remember something," Serina exclaimed suddenly. "It seems like I saw Effie going through my wardrobe and drawers... Yes, from out of the corner of my eye, I remember seeing her putting something in her apron pocket... How strange, for me to remember that now? I was so engrossed in my thoughts that I could hardly remember her leaving until now."

"Effie, that figures," said Ju, "never could be trusted that one, she will pocket anything she fancies."

"That's just great, now how do we get it back?" asked Senora.

"That will be difficult and time's running out for you and knowing Effie she's not going to give up the necklace without a fight."

"What are we gonna do?"

"We're going to get that necklace back, that's what we're going to do," said Ju. At least he sounded sure about it and that's all Serina needed.

"How are we gonna do that?"

"Simple, we're going to steal it just like she did. Now we just need to get into her room without her knowing it. It's late so I'm sure she's sound asleep, so let's go." Saying so, Ju led the way out into the corridor. Serina followed very close behind because she had no idea where they were going. Her mother brought up the rear, creeping down the hall to the stairs.

"Where are we going?" Serina asked confused as to why they were taking the stairs.

"Effie stays on the ground floor by the kitchens, only a few of us are allowed rooms above the first floor."

Ju took them through a maze of corridors, stairs and more halls and doors than Serina could even dream existed in one place. She was quickly finding out, there were more twists and turns to this old castle than she had ever imagined. When they arrived at Effie's door Ju stopped.

"Listen, if anything happens in there scramble out of here as fast as you can and don't look back, there's no need for all of us getting into hot water and that way you may still stand a chance of getting out of here, okay?"

"No, let me go in, it's my fault I didn't remember the necklace, so I should be the one to find it and besides there's no need you getting into trouble just for helping us Ju."

"No, let me do it..." Senora's words froze in her throat, Ju and Serina turned around to see what had caused the sudden shock that registered on her face.

"Takar!" Serina screamed.

"Looking for this perhaps," Takar asked a smirk visible beneath the cowl as he stepped out of the shadows holding out one hand. Serina's necklace was dangling from the tips of his long fingers; the emerald glistened as it reflected the light rays from the wall torches. Serina's breath caught in her throat.

Ju pushed Serina behind him and stepped toward Takar, that was the last thing he did for Takar threw out his other hand and a stream of light shot out from his fingertips and Ju fell to the floor.

"No!" Serina shouted as she lunged toward Takar but Senora pulled her back and stepped forward.

"You can't blame me for wanting to protect my daughter; a mother can not just let her child go without a fight Takar... Only you wouldn't know anything about that would you? You know nothing about love, all you know is evil."

"Enough! I will deal with you momentarily."

He turned from Senora to Serina, the look in his eyes was utterly demonic and his voice had a forced calm that chilled Serina's blood. She knelt down beside Ju only to see his eyes closing slowly and his arms falling limp at his side.

"How could you?" Serina cried out in outrage. "He didn't do anything to you, how could you just *kill* him like that."

"He was not loyal to his Master, I will not tolerate anyone who is not completely loyal to me, and that my dear is a lesson you should learn very soon."

He spoke in such a calm and uncaring voice it frightened Serina even more. She felt a shiver run through her body as she looked into those demon-like eyes.

Seeing a tear land on Ju's cheek and remembering what her mother had told her about the power of her tear-drops,

Serina made a wish – she wished for Ju not to be dead, and began crying harder trying to revive her friend through her tears. She really didn't know what she was doing but she kept trying… "Please Ju wake up, don't die," she sobbed but still nothing happened – Ju just laid there.

"Trying out your powers, Serina?" Takar asked derisively with a malevolent grimace. "Oh didn't I tell you that your tears will not work without the emerald stone? Too bad, it looks like you don't have any powers after all."

Serina looked up at her mother for any sign of help, but there was none. Senora knelt down next to her daughter, rueful tears coursing down her cheeks.

"I am sorry Serina, I am sorry I failed you."

"You didn't fail me Mother, I failed you but somehow, someway I will change that, I promise."

"Enough of the chatting, to the dungeons you go, Ernie! Come take these two to the dungeons. Put them in separate cells. I will be down tomorrow to deal with you both."

Ernie appeared out of nowhere, grabbing woman and child by the arms.

"Have Talbert come and remove this scum from my floor."

"Yes Sir, Master, right away Sir Master."

As Ernie was about to lead Serina and her mother away Takar added, "Now that's the way a servant is supposed to act, right Ernie?"

"Yes Sir, Master Sir, just like me, I'm the most loyal servant Sir, Master. Yes Sir, Master."

"Ernie, lest we forget," Takar uttered venomously as he walked up to the servant and reached out for one of his arms. Ernie cringed but held out his arm to his Master. Taking the little man's arm, Takar twisted it until they all heard it snap under the pressure. Ernie let out a blood-curdling scream and fell to the floor holding his now broken arm.

"Y-yes S-sir, M-master," Ernie cried out from the searing white pain that spread throughout his arm. The pain was such that he could hardly speak.

Serina and Senora stared in shocked disbelief at the cruelty of Takar.

"Get Mertie to set that arm for you Ernie after you put these two in their cells. We wouldn't want you to be unable to do your duties, now would we?"

Ernie nodded in reply. His clenched jaw would not release the words that would only show the servile weakness he felt toward his tormentor.

Outraged beyond comprehension, Serina and her mother followed Ernie in silence to the dungeon. Just before they reached the door Serina looked back at the still form lying on the floor, she swallowed hard to get the lump out of her throat. *How could a man do such a thing,* she thought, only then to realize that Takar was not a man. He was a heartless cruel individual that was capable of any evil that one could imagine. He had no feelings for anyone other than himself, he wanted to will his power over people, and using Ernie as a puppet for his demonic demonstration was a cold-hearted act of cruelty.

The dungeon was as dark and damp as Serina had left it just over an hour or so ago. Toddle was still turned with his face to the wall, sound asleep, only that didn't last long.

"What in blue blazes is it now?"

He yelled as he raised himself up from his straw cot. His voice fell short when he saw the parade of people coming in. He looked at Ernie and his obvious broken arm then turned his gaze toward Senora, and finally his eyes rested on Serina's tiny frame. He saw the fear etched on her face and for an unknown reason his heart suddenly quirked and did a little jig in his chest.

"Toddle what's the matter with ya, haven't ya ever seen others locked up in this place?" said Ernie, who was sweating profusely from the throbbing pain.

Toddle wanted to inquire about their presence but thought better of it, that's all he needed was for them to think him soft in his old age.

What did they mean to him anyway, they were just a woman and young girl, they didn't mean a thing to him, and the best thing for him to do was to lie back down and turn his face toward the wall and stay there.

"Toddle, sorry we woke you, we will try to be quiet so you can go back to sleep," said Serina softly when they filed past his cell.

The old man just made a grumbling noise and lay back down.

Ernie placed Senora in the last cell next to Rupert, a man who had been locked in the dungeon for many years. He then placed Serina in the first cell to the left of Toddle. So, there was her then Toddle's cell then an empty cell, and Rupert's cell before her mother's cell at the end of the row – Ernie had made sure the two were not next to one another.

Toddle, finding no rest, got up and rubbed his head. No need trying to sleep, he thought, with all of the racket going on, it was a wonder the dead weren't up walking about.

"You should have listened to me when I told you to go back to the tower before something happened to you Little Princess, now look at ya, you're down here in this rat infested hell-hole with the rest of us. What happened anyway?"

"It's a long story, and you really wouldn't want to know if I did tell you."

Serina sat on the edge of her straw mattress and felt something move beneath her, she jumped up letting out a shriek of surprise as a mouse leaped out of the straw and took off through the bars of the cell.

"Better check that real close before you sit back down, his wife and children may be in there too," said Toddle almost amused at the look of sheer horror on Serina's face.

"Oh great, that's all I need is to squash a family of mice in my bed."

Serina took the straw mattress off the frame and shook it vigorously and sure enough to Serina's surprise two more mice ran from the straw, not quite as big as the first one but big enough for Serina to jump back against the bars holding her skirts up in case they ran her way.

"Well, now that I'm good and awake and no chance of going back to sleep for a while, you want to tell me what's going on with you and Nora, what happened to Ernie's arm? Did the Master get mad at him or something?"

"No, he just wanted to prove a point to us, showing off the power of his mastering skills as you would say, and poor Ernie just held his arm out to him so he could break it."

Serina recoiled remembering the sound of Ernie's bones snapping in two, she told Toddle everything, not leaving anything out. She didn't care if the whole world knew anymore, she was determined to get out of this horrible place and get home where she belonged. She just had to come up with a new plan *now*, that's all there was to it.

"Ju is dead, I can't believe it," said Toddle when Serina had finished recounting the events of the night. "But he should not have interfered, the Master takes a dim view of any of his servants disobeying him, even if he was just trying to help, his loyalty should always be with our Master."

"You mean to tell me you would hold your arm out for that monster to break it also. I cannot imagine anyone being so devoted to someone like that, especially to a heartless creature like Takar. He has no heart you know, or have you even noticed, where do you people store your brains? Or, are you not allowed to have one?"

Toddle gazed sternly at Serina for a moment; he rubbed his chin then stood up and started pacing the tiny cell.

"You don't understand Little Princess he is our sole means of survival, we have nothing. He feeds us, clothes us and provides shelter for us. He gives us everything and all he asks in return is our complete undivided loyalty."

"And an arm to break every once in a while, right?"

"I understand what you say and I feel sorry for you, I do – but I still can not go against my Master and you mustn't ask me to either Little Princess."

"Remember that the next time you drop a plate of his food on the floor and he throws you down here in this God forsaken hole to fight the rats for a bed," Serina snapped, almost bitterly, at which Toddle rose an eyebrow in surprise – he didn't expect such a rebuke from someone so little.

Serina flipped her mattress over and gave it another good shake down before she placed it on the old frame; she flopped down and turned her back to the old man without another word.

Chapter 18

When Serina woke the next morning, Toddle was gone; she guessed Takar had released him so he could go back to doing his *loyal* duties. Sometime later Toddle came down with what looked like slop that Mr. Muncie fed his pigs back home and smelt about the same too. When Toddle tried to hand the bowl of garbage to her, she took one look at it and turned away, the smell alone, if not the sight of it, made her nauseous.

"No thanks, I'd rather starve."

"You might miss; you only get one helping a day."

Serina looked at him in surprise, wondering if there was anything else about Takar that would shock her.

"Then Takar can find another bride, because I am not eating that pig slop and you can tell him I said so and if he wants to come down here and break my arm for disobeying him, then that's what he will have to do, only I won't be as easy as Ernie," said Serina matter-of-factly.

"Very well, have it your way."

It wasn't until Toddle left her cell that she realized she might have gone a little too far. *Oh well everyone always said I have the temper of a redhead and it would get me in trouble some day,* she figured she just proved them right.

Serina and Nora tried to talk with one another but finally gave up. It was too hard yelling over Rupert's moaning and groaning and beating the cell bars with his food bowl. Evidently, the servants were used to him beating his dishes on the bars – they fed him out of a big wooden bowl, which looked like someone carved it out of an old log and it was big enough to feed four of Mr. Muncie's pigs.

Late that afternoon the dungeon was paid a visit by the Great Takar. He swished into the room with his robes and cloak billowing around him, appearing to be floating on air, and he wasted no time getting to Serina's cell.

"So you think the food I serve you is pig slop," Takar said scathingly, obviously enraged at Serina, she stumbled back and fell against the cot as he unlocked the cell door.

"You have the nerve to go behind my back causing one of my most faithful servants to turn against me, to try and help you escape from me – after all I've given you! I can understand Nora, she is nothing, but you, you have everything, soon you will have the world at your fingertips to do with as you please and you still can not comprehend any of it." Takar paced around the cell, his hood pulled down over his face giving him that same demonic look she remembered the night she arrived. "It does not have to be this way Serina, you know that, I will not tolerate this type of behavior from you, you will either do as I want or you will stay down here and rot with the rats, is that understood?"

"I had rather stay down here and rot than to be your bride someday, and yes, the food is pig slop."

"We'll see how you feel about it tomorrow when there is none," he hissed viciously, then in an icy tone he added; "By the way if you think the power that you have will get you out of this, think again Little Princess because you have no powers without the emerald stone."

Takar held out his hand and opened his palm revealing the emerald stone to Serina. "You are useless without it, useless without me to train and guide you in how to use what you are throwing away Serina."

"I'll show you just how useless I am," Serina replied, mustering up as much courage as possible.

"Oh, I am sure that a twelve year old silly little snip of a girl will overthrow Takar, the great Master of all." With these words, he bowed low and backed out of the cell, leaving Serina staring after him in horror.

No powers, without the necklace and of course Takar has the necklace.

She could hear her mother crying softly in her cell after Takar left the dungeon; Serina knew she had finally pushed him too far and in doing so she had left no hope for her mother.

Late that night Serina woke to the sound of something dragging along the floor, she rose just as something very large was going past her cell, it was Zarf, and he was going to Nora's cell. A few minutes later Zarf came back towards Serina's cell holding something in his hand.

"Food! Oh Zarf you're a life saver."

Serina grabbed the bread and cheese from him and started stuffing her mouth as she spoke. She was so hungry that all of her table manners disappeared instantly. All she cared about now was making sure she did not drop one crumb for the rats. Zarf began groaning incoherently, and then headed back toward Nora's cell. Serina did not know where he got the food and did not care, all she knew right then was that if Zarf had not have left she would have kissed his ugly scarred up face. When she had finished with her hearty meal, she stepped to her cell door and called for her mother.

"Mother is it true? I have no powers without the emerald?"

"No Serina, I had no idea that you were powerless without the emerald. I thought your powers were separate from those of the emerald stone but that they would work together as well as alone. I do know that the emerald is very powerful in itself and can do great things in the right hands." Senora paused, silence filling the dungeon for Rupert had became very quiet as well.

Tears fell from Serina's eyes as she listened to her mother. There had to be another way out of this and she was going to find it. Someway, somehow, she was going to find a means of escape – that was a promise she could make to herself and to her mother, only she kept the promise to herself for the moment; no need for her mother to fret again.

Early the next morning Serina was up and waiting for Toddle. When he arrived, he headed for Nora's cell. After feeding Nora and Rupert, he stepped back to Serina's cell.

"How is the Little Princess this morning? You must be starving, here take this," he said in a hushed voice, handing Serina a small napkin of bread and cheese. He then gave her a tankard of water. She eyed him carefully, wondering if Takar had sent him with the food to see if she would take it or not. Finally deciding that maybe Toddle did this out of the goodness of his heart, she took the water and drank it down instantly, spilling quite a bit on her frock in the process of quenching her thirst. Afterwards she handed the empty tankard back to Toddle, wiped her mouth and took the food.

"Is this a loyal sneaky deed you're doing for your Master? Is the food poisoned? Or is this just something someone with a heart would do?" Serina asked dubiously, stuffing her mouth with the delicious bread and goat cheese.

"Some things are just not right Little Princess. I may be a servant to the Great Takar but I do also have a heart. I fought this battle with myself all night only to come to realize that we all do things that we must pay for at some time or another. If this should be the case and I am found out then I, the same as Ju, will pay the ultimate price."

Serina stopped eating and stared at Toddle. Who else was she going to destroy before this was all settled?

"Toddle, I am truly sorry for putting you and every one else in this predicament. I never meant to cause trouble, I just want to go home, you can understand that can't you?"

Toddle looked at her long and hard for a moment, then cleared his throat and spoke in a little harsher tone.

"Little Princess, I do have a heart, as that I could not sit by and watch you starve but you must understand that I can not and will not help you and Nora escape from here."

He took the napkin from her and turned to leave.

"You're just going to let us stay down here and die with the rats," Serina called after him in a panic.

Toddle took another step, stopped, and then turned back. "My dear, the rats do not ever seem to die – they only multiply. I'm sure you will not die either."

Serina watched him walk away, her heart in the pit of her stomach. Maybe the rats didn't die down here, but she felt very strongly that if they did not find a way out of this place soon, their last days would be spent right here. She sat down on her cot with no brilliant plan of escape coming to mind, nor any hopes of one coming any time soon.

Takar came to see her late in the evening once more, only this time Serina knew what she had to do.

"I've made a decision Takar, and if you allow this I promise I will not cause any more trouble," said Serina, daring a glance at Takar's guarded features.

"Why should I listen to whatever new scheme you've come up with?" Takar asked as he peered down at his captive. Serina squared her shoulders and held her head up keeping eye contact with him. She was trying to show her bravery but inside she could feel her stomach lurching and doing summersaults.

"Because I understand my situation now; I didn't before."

Takar paced around the cell for a few minutes before coming to a stop in front of Serina once more.

"Okay, I'm listening, what is this decision you have come up with?"

"I will do as you say; I will stay here and let you train me in the use of my powers and at the right age I will become your bride."

Takar's eyes bore into Serina's, penetrating her very soul; he was searching for any clue as to the reason for this sudden change of heart.

"And what may I ask made you change your mind?"

Here comes the hard part, Serina thought. She dropped her gaze to the floor.

"This I will do willingly, if only you will let my mother go free, unharmed."

Takar was caught completely off guard by this remark. She could tell by the shocked look that registered on his face for a fraction of a second before disappearing.

"I think I should just leave you and your mother both here; as I said before, leave you here to dwell on what you have refused to accept."

"But to have me here willingly is what you wanted, am I not right?" Serina questioned him carefully weighing her words where as not to anger him into leaving without accepting her offer.

"Yes willingly, was what I had in mind."

"Then willingly you shall have. I will stay here with you and do as you bid but only if you accept my request and let my mother go free."

Takar was definitely stunned, but hid his feelings very well. He wanted her to be his little puppet, to do as he willed. Serina knew this but he had no plan of letting Nora go either.

"I will let you know of my decision tomorrow," Takar said in his usual icy tone. "Tomorrow at noon, until then you both will stay here in the dungeon... I think you still need time to think of what it will be like if you are trying to play me for a fool again Serina. Oh, and Serina..."

Serina looked up into his deep-set eyes once more.

"Yes?"

"For both of your sakes, let's hope you are not doing anything as foolish as...that."

The unspoken words told her she had pushed him about as far as she could without causing harm to herself and her mother; she felt he would kill her next.

"I understand, Takar... Until then can we at least have some decent food to eat, if not for me then for my mother?"

"I will consider it." He then turned away without looking back. He walked down to Nora's cell and after a few moments, he left the dungeon not even glancing in her direction.

"Serina, you must be out of your mind, he will never let me go. I can't believe you made such an offer to him."

"Mother, I had to, it was the only way I could know for sure that you would be alright. Don't you see if he accepts this offer you will be free, free to leave?"

Serina's voice had a certain urgency to it; it was the only way she knew to save herself and her mother.

Her mother gave up and sat back on her cot, she could not talk above Rupert's excessive banging of his food bowl across the bars of his cell anyway, besides she could tell Serina's mind was made up and at the moment, she could not come up with a better plan of getting them out of the dungeon.

Toddle arrived late with a tray of food for Serina and her mother, he served Nora first then at Serina's cell he pulled up a chair after giving her the tray of hot food and milk.

"So the little Princess has made a decision, has she?"

"Takar told you about my decision?" Serina asked in between bites, the food was still hot and delicious, and it was all she could do to talk to Toddle while she stuffed her face with the rather large chicken leg she pulled from her plate.

"Yes, he asked me to keep my eye on you to see if you were up to something, he doesn't trust you I'm afraid."

"Probably about as much as I trust him, right?" Serina managed to get out of her overstuffed mouth as she wiped it on the sleeve of her dress, and continued eating while Toddle watched the unladylike manner in which she tore at her third chicken leg.

"Even more so I fear, you can not blame him though, you have given him a terrible time since you've arrived."

Serina caught the last of his words, 'since you've arrived', and something dawned on her. "There, you said 'since I arrived', so you know when I came here. The whole castle has acted as if I have been here all my life or something, including you, but just now you said 'since I arrived', why has everyone acted like they did not know when I came to this awful castle."

Toddle looked at Serina, scratched his gray head then rubbed his chin. "Sometimes it's better to ignore than to try to explain something to someone who does not listen to what one is being told."

"Oh you're so full of philosophy Toddle, I swear, you and my father are so much alike."

"I am honored that you would consider me in the same manner as you do your father Little Princess," said Toddle.

Serina thought of what Toddle had said, he was a lot like her father, in that he always planned what he was doing, never going ahead with anything without giving it proper consideration first.

"Little Princess you have made a wise decision in doing as the Master wishes. I am sure you will not regret it later. Always remember though, you can come to me for any advice I can offer, and I will help you to understand what it is the Master wants from you from time to time."

"Thank you Toddle, that means a lot to me."

"It's nothing, that's the least I can do."

'To keep you safe' was what he wanted to say, and why, he did not know. It was as though he had become her guardian all of a sudden, and that was the last thing he wanted to do. He must be getting soft in his old age, he thought. Whatever it was, he didn't quite know how to handle it.

"Thank you again Toddle," Serina said sincerely.

"Enough of that, are you through eating?" Toddle retorted gruffly. "I need your dishes to take back to the kitchen or the cook will have my skin for it."

Serina handed him back her tray without a crumb on it, she had been so famished she had eaten part of the chicken bones before she could stop herself.

"I will be back in the morning with a good breakfast for you and Nora, until then try not to eat any rats, okay?"

Serina smiled broadly at the little man. "Okay, no rats for a midnight snack but only if you promise to bring me a verrrry large breakfast."

Toddle smiled back, feeling his heart lurch again and wondering where a girl so small put all that food.

"Goodnight Little Princess, sleep well, maybe you will be back in the tower by this time tomorrow, safe from this cold dank slimy place."

"And don't forget the rats Toddle."

"*And* the rats Little Princess, goodnight." Toddle shuffled off down to Rupert's cell with his supper, and after a few moments of conversing with the crazy loon he left without looking back.

Serina watched Toddle leave the dungeon, leaving her there to fend for herself against the rats and other unimaginable creatures that lurked there in the bowels of the castle. She drew in a deep breath and sat down on the cot wondering how someone like Toddle could be so completely loyal to the likes of Takar. Takar was utterly evil; there was no good in him at all and she doubted he was even human.

Serina was still sitting on her cot in deep thought when Toddle reappeared suddenly.

"I thought you might like to have some reading material," he said as he opened a very large book down the middle and passed it through the bars to Serina. Then from somewhere deep inside his robe, he pulled out a long, thick candle, lit it from the torch on the wall and handed it to her.

"A book, oh Toddle thank you, I love to read."

"Well I didn't know if you knew how to read or not but I took the chance that you did, and, well I had it lying around anyway you know."

"Yes, father made sure of it. Professor Threcher also taught me to count properly. I'm really good with numbers too."

"Well, the book will give you something to do down here, I'm sure you will enjoy it. Oh, there is a good spot to read on page seven hundred thirteen, very interesting – well that is if you like that sort of stuff. Might even come in handy someday, you never know... Well, goodnight, I must go now. Oh, and be sure to save your candle only for reading, it's a special candle and has a wonderful glow, I made it myself you know."

He was talking in circles, his words falling over each other, which was not like Toddle at all; Serina could tell he was very nervous, almost shy.

"Thank you again Toddle, I will enjoy it I'm sure, I will also take good care of the candle and I'll not forget it when I leave."

The book was a rather old, very large leather bound affair, tattered and worn from years of use or abuse, Serina figured, as she turned it over in her hands, examining it more closely she noticed the title.

"ZANBLAZTAMUM."

What a funny name, she thought, *it sounds made up if you ask me.* The book was so heavy Serina had a hard time holding it on her lap and turning the pages, so she laid it on the end of her cot and climbed up stretching her body out the length of the bed, lying on her stomach to get comfortable. Once settled she started flipping through the dusty moldy pages.

"Serina! What did Toddle bring you?" Nora yelled out.

"Oh just a very large old book, to keep me company while we're down here," replied Serina, never taking her eyes from the book, she did like to read, maybe not as much as her best friend Koori but nevertheless she did like reading.

"What is the name of it?" Nora asked, interrupting her concentration.

"Za-blazman, mun, or something like that I think, it's in pretty bad shape, it must be very old."

"Zanblaztamum?" Senora asked

"Yes, that's the name, have you read it before? It's very thick."

Serina started to flip to the back of the old book to read the number of pages it had.

"It's very large indeed, it has …hum."

"Thirteen hundred and thirteen pages," Senora interrupted her daughter with the exact count of pages the old book had.

Serina looked to the last page of the book. "Yes, that's right, how did you know?"

"Because, I have seen the book before; it belongs to Takar. I saw it in his study on his desk.

"Takar," Serina muttered with a degree of mounting displeasure – the creature irked her sense of decency.

At the mention of Takar's name Rupert started clinging his bowl on the bars, making a deafening racket, ending Serina's and her mothers chat time.

Why would Toddle bring her one of Takar's books to read, why not one of his, unless Takar put him up to it – THAT was the most obvious answer. There was probably some hidden incantation or spell in the book, which he wanted her to read and sending it with Toddle would ensure her reading whatever strange message he was trying to send her. What was that page number Toddle mentioned to her before he left; something thirteen … what was it, she wondered. *Well it doesn't matter anyway*, she thought, she would not read it on purpose, she would show him.

Rupert continued to bang his bowl on the bars and chanting in some unknown language, so Serina went back to flipping the pages of this enormous and incongruous volume. She looked at the funny pictures and read some of the inscriptions that accompanied them until she was too tired to hold her eyes open. Rupert had finally settled down, most likely grown tired of his own chanting and banging and all was quiet at last.

Serina drifted off to sleep a few minutes later with her head resting on top of the old book; sleeping soundly for a bit before she started dreaming. It was a very odd dream in which there was fire all around her and she was standing at the edge of a round pit filled with water. In the water was a fish that resembled an old man, he was telling her the rules of battle.

"Battle! What do you mean battle, I'm just twelve years old, I can't do battle."

Chapter 19

Serina sat up in a sudden jerk – the dream seemed so real that it woke her up completely, she was drenched in sweat but felt ice cold.

"I didn't mean to scare you Serina I was just so surprised to find you here in a dungeon of all places. Come to think of it, knowing you it makes sense though."

"What... Who?"

Serina closed and rubbed her eyes hard with both her fists then opened them again. She was staring straight into the face of her best friend, Koori. Zarf was at her side.

"Koori?" Serina jumped to her feet and ran to the bars of her cell.

"Yes, it's me, are you surprised?"

"Surprised? No silly, I'm only dumbfounded. Where did you come from, I can't believe it's you, here, let me pinch you, because I know I must be dreaming."

Serina reached through the bars toward Koori, slowly at first; almost afraid she would disappear if she touched her.

"You're real," Serina burst out excitedly, trying to hug her friend through the rusty ole bars.

"I'm real Serina and very scared, how'd you get in this ole dungeon anyway?" Koori asked with a disgusted look on her face.

"It's a long story I don't want to try to explain it all right now but I do want you to tell me how you managed to find me here at this time of the night all by yourself, knowing how you're so afraid of the dark, Koori."

Koori drew in a long breath then began; "That, is a long story also, at first I could not remember you ever existing, my memory of you and all our fun life together was gone, but something kept nagging at my brain, something was missing that was too strong to be wiped away. Then one day Zeb asked me about you and even though I didn't know what he was talking about his words stuck in my mind and that night just as I was dozing off to sleep it hit me just like dragon dung."

"It was a memory powder, he must have sprinkled it over the whole village the night he came for me that would have been the easiest way to wipe out everyone's memory of me."

"Is that your mother down in the end cell?" asked Koori, looking down the narrow walkway to the end cell through which Zarf had disappeared.

"Yes, that's her," Serina answered almost in a monotone.

"Hello Mrs...." Koori stopped and turned back toward Serina with a puzzled look on her face.

"Do I call her Mrs. Zimmer or what did you say her name was?"

"You can call her Senora or whatever you like but, come to think of it, she is still Mrs. Zimmer.

"Hello Mrs. Zimmer, remember me? My name is Koori."

Serina's mother yelled back quickly, "Yes Koori, I remember you dear. Are you okay?"

"Oh yes, just scared half to death that's all."

"How long have you been in here?" Koori asked turning back to Serina, her voice quivering as she spoke. Serina knew it had to have taken a lot of courage for her best friend to attempt such a thing as venturing out by herself, of all things, to try and find her.

"This is the third night, Takar caught us trying to escape, and put us in here to rot and I'm afraid that if Takar does not take me up on my offer we will surely die here."

"Your offer? Why is it that I don't like the sound of this offer you're talking about Serina?" Koori questioned, unsure if she wanted to know the answer to this one.

Serina pushed the lump in her throat down with a big swallow then told Koori the whole story from how Takar took her from her bed, the huge black dragon, the tower, the secret stairs from the tower to the dungeon – everything.

Koori stood there in disbelief – shocked out of her wits, her mouth wide-open and her eyes as big as plates.

"That's an awful terrible thing to do, to marry him, that monster, I can't believe it – I mean, I can believe it – but, can't your special powers help you out of this mess or something?"

"I wish they could but I'm afraid that too is useless now without the necklace."

Koori looked as gloomy as her friend did and she did not know what to do to help them out.

"If Takar catches you here he will have a fit and throw you in here with us to rot, you know that don't you?"

Koori looked a little shocked at this remark. "Should I go get your father? He can help us I'm sure of it."

"My father, as brave and strong as he is, or as any other normal man would be for that matter, is no match for the Monster Takar. He would kill him as surely as we stand here talking… No I can't take that chance; we have to figure something out ourselves."

"I was afraid you would say something like that, what can two twelve year old girls do up against a powerful man like Takar, or should I say one girl since one of us is locked up in the dungeon with no way out, or should I remind you of that."

"No, I'm well aware of that… Hey, you never did finish telling how you got here anyway."

Koori pulled up the chair she had noticed across the room when she came in and sat down.

"You know you really should blow out that candle if you're not reading or something, it's just a waste to let one burn when you have other light," Koori remarked pointing to the candle by the cot that Toddle had given Serina earlier.

"Oh yeah, I fell asleep reading and forgot about it."

"Reading? You have a book to read down here, what is it? I wonder if I have read it before?" said Koori astonished.

"I doubt it, it's not the kind of book you see everyday, it's about a foot thick and two feet long."

Serina stepped over and blew out the candle absentmindedly then rushed back to the edge of the cell and sat down. "Besides I'm sure Takar sent it down for me to read some particular paragraph about my special power and the fate of my future. You can look at the book later I promise," prompted Serina. "Right now just tell me about how you found me."

Koori pulled her eyes away from the spot where the book lay and started rattling off her story.

"Well, like I said after I went to bed that night I remembered everything. I tried to find you but no one seemed to know you; they all thought I had mush rutabagas for brains. When your father told me he had no daughter, that she died the night she was born along with her mother, I knew Takar must have done something to make everyone forget you. What that *something* was, however, I wasn't sure of but I remembered you said Takar was to take you to the castle on the eve of your birthday."

"That must have been hard for you, not being able to get anyone to listen to you, thinking you were mad or something," said Serina. "I can only imagine how you must have felt when even my father didn't believe you."

"Well, one good thing about it, Amil doesn't have to worry about *you* still being mad at him, or *him* being mad at you, because he doesn't remember you at all. I asked him and Frog if they had seen you around and they asked if I was daft or something, "who is this girl name Serina you keep asking about," they said."

"Gee Koori that seems such a long time ago, that's the least of my worries right now. Go on, tell me the rest."

"Well anyway I figured I could sneak into the castle grounds like we did that night we met your mother, but I was afraid I'd run into Takar or someone else, so I hesitated not sure what to do for two days. Hey that's ironic, my memory came back to me the same night you and your mother were locked in here in this ole dungeon, it's been three nights tonight."

Koori took in a long breath and after a deep sigh, before continuing with her account; *she could be very long-winded when she got into telling one of her stories to someone*, Serina thought.

"Anyway I knew I couldn't come in the daytime for fear of being caught for sure, so I decided to sneak in at night and hope for the best. As it turned out so far, it was a great plan, only now here you are in the dungeon and no way of escaping and no way to use your powers to get out."

"How did you find the dungeon?" Serina asked.

"Oh, I was sneaking around after I made it into the garden and ran slap dab into Zarf... Scared the begeevies out of me he did. Anyway, he took me by the hand and led me to this doorway, or rather, he dragged me in, it was very dark at first and I tried to run but he would not turn loose of my hand. Then I happened to see a faint light at the end of the corridor and thought I would at least see where it led. I guess I was just desperate enough to find you that I didn't let my fear of Zarf and the dark stop me... Besides I told you I have to look after you, because you sure can't – and this proves I'm right," Koori concluded teasingly.

"Well neither one of you can do a very good job of it if you ask me, how about you Frog."

With all the excitement surrounding the very sudden and definitely unexpected appearance of Koori into the dungeon, no one had noticed the two boys entering behind her only moments before.

"Amil, Frog, wh-what, how did you get in here, I mean where did you come from?" Serina was astonished to see them, as was Koori.

"We came in through the same place Koori did I'm sure, that is, if she came in from the wall of the cave."

Amil and Frog walked up to the cell where Serina and Koori had been talking. Koori was still speechless, staring at the two boys, agape.

"I guess, I mean how, how did you know how to get in here and I thought you did not believe Koori when she asked you guys about me," Serina asked in bewilderment.

"At first we thought she had truly gone fairy on us, but knowing Koori like we do, we thought we'd better keep an eye on her, or Frog did. He kind of has the sweets for her and he wanted to keep her out of trouble with the elders of the village, and besides she was acting so weird that I was afraid she might end up in hot-water sure enough."

"But how did you know how to find this place?"

Serina was still so shocked at seeing the boys she had completely forgot about her mother in the end cell and her trusty Zarf standing guard over her – that is until Zarf suddenly came up behind the boys and Koori.

"Oh by the way, meet Zarf, he's a friend of ours."

All three of them turned around at the same time and even as tall as Amil was he still did not come to Zarf's chest. Amil and Frog both sucked in their breath and took a step back at the sight of the giant, but Koori laughed at them taking Zarf's huge gnarled hand in hers. She gently rubbed Zarf's hand assuring the boys he was a friend.

"He's just checking the two of you out to make sure you're not here to do harm to us that's all," said Serina, snickering at Amil and Frog and remembering the night she first met up with the monstrous looking creature herself.

The two guys inched there way closer to Serina's cell not taking their eyes off Zarf. "Don't be scared, he won't hurt you, he's a friend of Serina's mother," Koori added reassuringly.

"You know a little while ago I thought that after what I've seen and heard tonight nothing would surprise me," Amil said with a slight smile, "But I guess I was wrong! What do you mean *Serina's mother*, Koori? We all know her mother died a long time ago – right? I am right, am I Serina?" Amil enquired with a question mark written across his face – *this better be good*, he thought.

"No, my mother is very much alive and in the last cell down there," replied Serina pointing in the direction of her mother's cell. "She was helping me escape when we were caught and thrown in this dirty place."

"Well I've heard it all now," Amil exclaimed throwing his arms in the air. "You mean to tell me your mother is alive, how, why, I mean… Oh, never mind." He shook his head and glanced over to Frog who was wearing the same completely baffled look as he was.

The two followed Koori down to meet Serina's mother leaving Serina alone with Zarf who was staring and scratching his head.

"I am as confused as you are Zarf but they really are my friends," said Serina trying to convince the big creature they were harmless.

When the three returned to Serina's cell, they all started talking at once.

"Wait a second," said Serina. "Amil, you never did tell me how the two of you came about finding this place, or how you knew it existed."

"We didn't *know* it existed. We followed Koori, like I said, we were keeping an eye on her and followed her here. We had no idea about the secret wall or this castle or anything else but…"

"But what?" Serina cut-in impatiently – *another long-winded one*, she thought.

"But I remembered you; it wasn't until earlier tonight… I was sitting at the dinner table with my family, when one of them mentioned my birthday, I couldn't believe it. All of a sudden everything came back to me. I remembered the last time I saw you, we argued about what you were doing out at the bridge and stuff, remember? It was the night before your birthday, I ran into my room and found your present that I made, I could not imagine why I had a… Well, you will see later."

Serina and Koori exchanged glances and a smile. "Yes Amil, I remember and all this stuff happening does not change the fact that you did not believe me and we will discuss *that* later."

"When we do, just remember how I came here to save you from what I don't know."

"I don't need saving by the likes of you, Amil Borington," retorted Serina hotly.

"That's Wellington, Miss look who's-in-a-cell-without-a-key Zimmer."

Frog and Koori both shook their heads in unison.

"Okay, now's not the time to be arguing with one another. Let him finish telling how they got here," interposed Koori with authority.

Amil stood looking at Serina for a second before continuing. "Anyways, I went to Frog's house after dinner and told him everything. It took him a minute but it finally dawned on him that what I was telling him made sense. So we took off to Koori's house and that's when we saw her sneaking out her bedroom window. We followed, not too close for fear of her seeing us. She went inside the cave and disappeared, by the time we made it to the cave she was nowhere to be seen, we searched all around inside the cave but nothing."

"If I hadn't leaned up against the back of that cave wall we'd still be looking for her," Frog piped-in suddenly – he seemed to have recovered his speech faculty, at last.

"That's right, Frog here leaned up against the wall, tired of searching for Koori and the wall moved right out from behind him and he literally fell into that garden."

"Yeah, we know how to get in but we don't know how to get out, sure hope you and Koori know how, or we're hung for sure," said Frog.

"Anyway we looked around and saw Koori entering the doorway to this place and here we are. Now do you want to tell us what's going on and why you are in a dungeon cell?"

Amil looked from Serina to Koori, and then back to Serina again. He and Frog both had a bamboozled look on their faces

– no wonder, it's not every day that you find yourself following friends into the depth of dark dungeons...

"Go on Serina; tell them what you told me, about Takar and his big dragon and about him wanting to marry you and all that rubbish."

"A dragon did you say?" Frog cried out; his interest and curiosity both peeked since he had always wanted to see a dragon first hand, yes siree.

Amil shot Frog a quick glance before turning back to look at Serina. "Yeah Serina, tell us about all that what Koori just said."

Serina recounted her story once again not leaving anything out. When she finished she sat down on her chair and put her elbows on her knees and her head in her hands.

Amil and Frog stood there looking from one to the other, not saying a word, both knowing that everything, as strange as it all sounded, must be true.

"Where's this dragon?" asked Frog, more than curious – but totally mystified by now.

"Don't worry about the dragon Frog, he would eat you for a late night snack if he saw you, but he would toast you up golden brown first," said Serina. She winced at the mere thought of the big black fire-breathing thing sleeping in the big barn just a little ways from where they were.

"So how are you getting out of here, do you have a key to these doors?" asked Amil as he yanked hard on Serina's cell door. "Or are you going to use your powers to open them?"

"No, I have no key and remember I have no powers without my necklace. What we need is a plan and I'm fresh out, do you have one I can borrow?" Serina asked despondently, eyeing Amil closely.

"Are you kidding, I don't even know how to get back home much less break you out of here," replied Amil still tugging on the bars of her cell with a flustered look on his face.

"Hey, where does this door lead to? Does it go to the dragon's lair?" Frog was walking toward the door that led to the secret stairs going up to the tower where Serina had been held captive in the first instance.

"Don't go in there, you will end up getting lost or caught, it would be better if you stayed here with all of us dear," Senora suggested in a concerned voice.

Serina's face suddenly changed, taking on a familiar look, which made Koori just a little bit nervous. She had learned a long time ago that when her friend's eyes glimmered strangely, as they did right now, it usually led to trouble and she usually ended up right in the middle of it with her.

"No Serina, whatever you are thinking, the answer is 'no', do you hear me?"

"Koori, it is the only way, I think I know how to get us out of this mess, but it will largely depend on you – at least hear me out."

Serina reached for Koori's hand through the bars, clutching it tightly, looking at her with pleading eyes.

"No, no, no – the answer is 'no' Serina." Koori was adamant. "Whatever it is that you want me to do, I'm not about to do it. So, just forget it!" She knew instinctively that whatever Serina's plan was, it would lead to a whole lot of problems and probably would get all of them killed in the process.

"But between the three of you I'm sure you could pull it off, just listen to what I'm thinking."

"At least listen to what she has to say, it may be something we can do," said Amil whose curiosity had been aroused now.

"No, on second thought she's right," said Serina to Amil then looking back to Koori she continued, "I should never ask you to do something so dangerous, I don't know what I was thinking, I guess I'm just so desperate to get out of here – just forget about it, okay?" Again, Serina sat down on her chair, put both her elbows on her knees, and leaned her head into her hands.

Koori however stood there studying her friend, thinking about what she had said. "Well at least tell us what you were thinking of, it may not be as bad as you think, and we might be able to pull it off after all."

"No, no, Koori I can't ask any of you to do it."

Koori sat back in her chair also and reached in through the bars and this time she grabbed Serina's hands and yanked them through the bars up to her elbows.

"Tell me, or I'll pull your skinny little body through these bars and you can do whatever it is yourself."

Averting a smile, Serina finally muttered, "Well, it has to do with getting the necklace back..."

"No, I knew it, I can't do it."

"Just listen Koori, it may be a good plan, go ahead Serina," said Frog who had been intently listening to every word Serina had been saying.

"Well, the three of you would have to sneak into Takar's room and get the necklace and bring it back to me so I can get us out of here and back home."

"I don't know Serina; this doesn't sound like a very good plan to me."

Koori pushed away from Serina and walked down to Senora's cell, after a few minutes she came back shaking her head at her friend.

"Your mother says that's not a good idea, she and I both think your nuts Serina, there must be another way out of here."

"You're right; I'll have to come up with something else."

"Your mother said she would help, between the five of us we're bound to come up with something that will work."

"I've got to find a way out of this cell so I can get that necklace back then I will have my powers so I can take care of the Monster Takar for good."

"Why don't you give me that book while you're trying to think of something and I can read some, maybe it will give me some ideas about how to help? Besides, you know I think better with a book in my hands."

"Yeah Serina, give her the book, we all know how she likes to read and maybe she's right, she might find a way to get us all back home by reading," said Frog, glancing at Koori with that puppy dog look he always had when he looked at Koori.

"She'll need more than her hands to hold that book it's so big and heavy."

Serina picked up the book with both hands and carried it to the bars where the three stood but the book was too thick and she could not get it through the bars.

"Open it up down the middle then slide it through that way," said Amil.

"Well one of us is using our head for something other than to hold our face on," laughed Koori.

"I forgot that's how Toddle had to pass it to me," said Serina.

Frog took hold of the book as Serina passed it through the bars.

"Begeevies, it's huge," said koori, seizing the book from Frog with both hands, she struggled to keep her balance as she sat back in the chair and placed the old book on her lap with a sigh of relief.

"I told you, good luck reading it too, it reads in circles if you ask me," said Serina.

She sat back down and resumed her earlier position with her head in her hands while Koori flipped through the pages of the old book making gleeful little sounds periodically.

Serina, Amil and Frog kept pacing and throwing out ideas at one another every once in a while, each time hoping they had come up with the perfect plan.

"There must be a way of getting that emerald back from Takar, there just has to be," Serina cried out to Amil and Frog as desperation began to roam her mind.

"We're just missing it."

After several long minutes of silence Koori shrieked and screamed giving everybody a start, she almost fell out of her chair when she tried to get up with the book still on her lap.

"Serina! I think I found a way for you to get your emerald back."

Serina looked up at Koori then she jumped from her chair as well, staring in disbelief at what Koori held in her hand.

"A key! Where did you find it?" Serina and Amil shouted out in unison.

"It was right here in the book, right here between pages seven hundred twelve and seven hundred thirteen," Koori said excitedly.

"Seven hundred thirteen! That was the page Toddle told me to read before he left."

"So you think he put the key in the book for you to find," asked Amil.

"He must have, it looks like one of the keys Ernie had hanging around his neck, the one he used to open and close the cell doors."

"See! I told you she would find a way to get us out of here in that book," exclaimed Frog, staring at the key in Koori's hand.

Koori handed the key to Serina to examine it more closely. As Serina turned the key over in her hand she felt a sudden pang of compassion for Toddle; *the little man must have had a difficult time making this decision,* she thought.

"Try it, see if it works," Koori urged.

Serina's hands shook as she reached through the bars with the key trying to place it in the lock; she kept trying to stick the key in the small opening but could not quite get it in.

"Here, let me have a go at it," Amil said taking the key from Serina's hand. "At least I can see where to put it from this side." He laughed as he slipped the key into the lock.

She held her breath as he turned the key, they all shouted when they heard the lock click.

"It opened, you're free Serina, you're free," Koori squealed with delight.

Serina stepped out of the cell and the four of them hugged tightly but quickly broke the embrace as embarrassment took over. Serina drew her eyes away from Amil's and ran the distance to her mother's cell to open her door.

"Look what was in the book Toddle brought me Mother, the key to our cell." Senora smiled and was on the verge of tears when Serina shoved the key into the lock and turned it – yet the door would not budge. She struggled with it twisting and turning, all to no avail – the key would not unlock Senora's cell door.

"Here, let me try it." Amil took the key from Serina and placed it in the lock, twisting it back and forth – the door remained immovable.

"What do we do?" she asked her mother anxiously. Her mind was spinning and her heart was pounding like a stampede of horses in her chest.

"You will have to find a way to get the stone and take care of Takar without me dear," her mother replied resignedly.

"No Mother, I can not do it without you, I have to get you out of here."

Senora reached through the bars, took Serina by the shoulders, and forced her to look at her. "Serina, you do not need me to help you, you can do this by yourself. I have confidence in you, you are brave and very strong hearted, there is no doubt in my mind that you are your father's child, and you have his same strength and wisdom. You can do this."

"Mother, I don't want to leave you down here, I will find a way to get you out, maybe there's another key, I'll go look in the book. Surely Toddle put a key to your cell in the book also."

She ran back to her cell leaving Koori and Frog chatting with her mother, while Amil followed on Serina's heels. *Maybe just maybe*, Serina thought, *Toddle left a key to her mother's cell.* If not she did not know how she would get her mother out, *maybe... No, that would not work.*

"Maybe Zarf could pull the bars off the wall, he looks very strong," said Amil, glancing back at Zarf who stood faithfully by Senora's cell.

"I was just thinking the same thing and he most likely could but we don't want to call attention to ourselves just yet

Amil, Takar would be down here and have us all in a cell or worse, dead."

"I still think you should send Frog and Koori back for your father Serina, this is not a good idea, you trying to figure this out by yourself."

"Amil, you don't understand, we can't tell my father – he would not stand a chance up against this monster."

"Like you would! Please Serina you're just a girl, a small skinny one at that – and you think you would have a better chance against this monster, you say, than your father would? I find that hard to believe."

"Of course you do Amil, to you I'm just a girl that can't do anything without the help of a boy... Well, I'll show you."

"You might find out you need more help than you think, look where you were when we found you."

"Yeah, and look who found the key, a girl, ha!"

"Oh what ever," Amil snapped, storming off to where the others were.

Serina rummaged through all the pages again and again, more roughly than she meant to but Amil had a way of making her crazy, if only she could find another key but nothing... There was no key to be found. *Now what,* she thought as she headed back to her mother's cell.

Chapter 20

Rupert had been very quiet ever since Koori arrived with Zarf. He didn't even make a fuss when the boys arrived. Maybe it was Zarf that kept him quiet, she didn't know but Serina was grateful for his silence. As she passed his cell, she noticed he was huddled in the far corner of his cot with his legs pulled up to his chest, his arms wrapped around his knees tightly. She had not really seen him before and in her excitement of getting free, she didn't even notice him when she passed him going to her mother's cell but now... Looking more closely, she noticed something – his eyes. He was watching her intently with the bluest eyes she had ever seen. Stopping in front of his cell for a second, Serina's eye's locked on Rupert's, only for a fraction of a moment, and she observed something else; he was not as old as she thought him to be. The beard and wild hair covered most of his face but his eyes were very strong and alert, he didn't have the eyes of an old man.

"What's wrong Serina, you figure you can save him too?"

She pulled herself away from Rupert's gaze.

"Oh Amil!" Serina barked a little harder than she had intended but she was still put out with him about his earlier remark. She ran to her mother's cell, leaving Amil staring after her in puzzlement.

"Mother, how long has Rupert been down here?" she asked curiously, shaking off the sudden cold chill. She could still feel his eyes on her even though she was out of his sight.

"Oh I don't know dear, a very long time I'm sure. Why?"

"I just assumed he was an old man but his eyes do not look old, and they don't reflect any insane characteristics like you would expect from someone who bangs his food bowl on the cell bars all the time and moans and groans like he does, besides what is he in here for?"

"Well, rumor has it that he refused to obey Takar, so instead of killing him Takar put him down here in the dungeon to go crazy but first he removed his voice box with that lightening bolt finger he has. That's why Rupert doesn't talk anymore, he can only make those grunting noises that we have to listen to, but never mind that, did you find another key?"

After a moment, Serina snapped back finally. "No... No, there was no other key. I searched all through the book but there was nothing... Now, what do we do?"

Senora paced the small cell floor rubbing her chin and shaking her head. Koori and Frog who were watching Senora started doing the same thing.

Koori suddenly started saying something about getting back to the village and getting help from there, but Senora and Serina both vetoed that idea knowing it would be foolish even to try and make the village people understand what was going on, besides if they could get someone to believe them, Takar would destroy them and it was getting late. It was nearly two in the morning and they were running out of time.

"No Koori, Serina wants to do this all by herself, she thinks she doesn't need anyone's help, especially a boys help, right Serina? In fact me and Frog should just head back to the village now and let her get herself out of this fix," Amil smirked sarcastically.

Serina knew Amil was just trying to make her angrier and it was working very well.

"The only option we have is for me to try and get the necklace back from Takar tonight while he is asleep – alone, and not because of what Amil says but because I don't want to put any of you in any more danger than you already are," Serina stated decisively.

All four stared at her with shocked looks on their face, with Koori and Senora sucking in their breath instantaneously.

"No, Serina that's too risky," her mother objected hastily. "You could get caught and then he would kill you for sure."

"There's bound to be another way," Koori put-in agreeing with Senora.

"How bad did you say this Takar is?" asked Frog.

"That's Takar and he's *very* bad," replied Serina.

"He can't be that bad, can he? Maybe me and Amil can take him on and feed him one of these," said Frog, shaking his fists in the air.

"You do not want to mess with Takar, he would just soon kill you as to look at you, and believe me he could do it without laying a single finger on you. All he'd have to do is to point his lightening bolt finger at you and you'd be fried on the spot – so let's think of another plan children," said Senora in her quiet whispery voice.

"I just thought of something," said Koori suddenly. "Why would Toddle bring you such a large book just to hide a key in it? Think about it, if he just wanted you to have the key he could have given it to you or put it in something a lot smaller, not a book that weighs so much you could hardly pick it up."

Serina and Senora both looked at Koori, quietly considering what she said.

"You know Koori you may be on to something at that," Senora said.

"Yeah, you said he was a little old man and that book is very large, there must be something else in it he wanted you to find or read... That's it," Koori exclaimed after a pause, "There must be something in that book he wanted you to read, which would help you escape." The two girls looked at one another then both ran toward Serina's cell at the same time.

Serina reached the cell first and grabbed up the book, Koori helped her tote it back to Senora's cell. There, they placed it on the floor where all five of them could see the pages and Serina began thumbing through it page by page.

After a short while of page flipping, Serina remembered what Toddle had mentioned... "Remember, I told you that Toddle said something to me about a certain page I might want to read, what page did you say you found the key, Koori?"

"I don't remember, I was too excited about finding the key that I forgot, I'm sorry," Koori replied ruefully.

"That's alright Koori, I can not remember what page either, but if there is anything in this book that was meant for me to see, we will find it."

"Page seven hundred and thirteen," Senora exclaimed all of a sudden. "I believe that's what you said, when Koori found the key, you said seven hundred and thirteen was the page that Toddle had told you to read."

"That's right, it was seven hundred and thirteen," Koori yelped – she too remembered.

"You're right, I remember now," said Serina; flipping the pages of the old book carefully as not to tear them. It was so old she was afraid she would rip the pages out just turning them.

"Here it is!" said Serina excitedly pointing at page '713'.

Koori leaned over to read along with Serina.

"It doesn't make sense to me, does it to you?" Serina asked the others.

"Not really, it looks like some sort of poem," said Koori.

Amil and Frog looked at one another in confusion, then back to the girls without saying a word.

"Mother, can you tell us what this means?" Serina shoved the book closer to the bars to her mother. "Page seven hundred and thirteen... Start at the top of the page and read all the way down," Serina asked her mother urgently.

Senora carefully read and reread the page quietly. She frowned, her forehead furrowed in deep thought then she lifted an eyebrow then lowered it and then lifted it again.

"Don't keep us in suspense, read it out loud, what does it mean?" Serina pleaded anxiously.

"Well, I'm not sure what it means either; maybe if I read it again it will make some sense."

Senora started reading silently, ignoring them totally. Suddenly she cleared her throat and looked up at the four children then back at the book. Serina, Koori, Frog and Amil were all waiting with bated breath as she began reading aloud the words written on the time-yellowed page.

*Its amber glow will give you unseen strength, but only for
one night's length.
First you must bathe in its warm light to gather your might.
So hurry you must and in no one put your trust.
Let the darkness be your cloak, for by the light of morn if
your deed is not done the world will for you mourn.*

"Wh-wh-what does it mean?" Serina asked, her voice trembling slightly.

"I'm not sure, Serina, it's a riddle of some sort..." replied Senora.

The five hashed over the words repeatedly but could not come up with an answer.

"It's amber glow, *what amber glow?*" Serina shouted in exasperation.

"And what does it mean to 'bathe in its light'?" asked Koori, just as puzzled as the others.

Suddenly the mad man in the cell next to Senora started chanting in a deep hoarse voice as he climbed off his cot, grabbed his cup, and began banging it against his bars.

"That's all we need is for him to start his crazy noise," Koori remarked obviously annoyed. "We're having a hard enough time as it is now trying to figure this out, now we have to put up with him and his infernal gibberish and banging."

"Listen!" Senora murmured unexpectedly. "His words are not gibberish; he's repeating the riddle, word for word." She put her finger to her lips hushing the children into momentary silence.

The five listened to Rupert as he repeated the riddle. When he ended his reciting of the verses, he also stopped banging his cup and an ominous silence suddenly enveloped the room. They looked at one another, surprised at the mad man and his ability to repeat the riddle – when all they had heard out of him, since they had been locked up, was rubbish; undecipherable words. Now all at once, he was speaking not only words but the riddle they had been trying to figure out for almost an hour.

"Mrs. Z-Zimmer," stammered Amil, embarrassed at calling this strange woman Mr. Zimmer's wife. "I thought you said that this Takar took out his voice box?"

"That's right, that's what we all heard, Takar was supposed to have burned out his vocal chords with his lightening bolt finger and all anyone has heard from him since, was confused grumbling noises."

"That doesn't make sense, if his voice box was taken out, then how can he talk? You can not talk without it," said Koori, very perplexed.

Serina walked up to the bars of Rupert's cell and stared at the man as she had done earlier. He returned the stare for a flash of a second but then jumped up on his cot and turned his back to her and began chanting his regular incomprehensible song.

"That was so weird... I wonder what made him do that," Serina asked in puzzlement.

Serina did not move, she stood there looking at Rupert through the bars, hoping he would turn back to face her, willing him to do so. Suddenly Rupert rolled over and jumped to his feet, startling Serina to the point of jumping back and losing her balance, falling over her own feet.

"Serina! Are you alright?" Senora cried out seeing her daughter tumbling to the ground.

While Koori helped her friend to her feet, Senora reached through the bars for Serina's hand. "Stay over here, away from his cell, I'm not sure if he's dangerous or not and we don't want to get him riled up again."

"There's something about him Mother... It makes me wonder if he..."

Serina looked back over her shoulder, trying to see Rupert again but he had lain once again on his cot turning his back to them all.

"We have too much to worry about to mess with him right now, we need to concentrate on the riddle."

"Yes, Mother." Serina turned reluctantly to face her mother and the five of them went back to the dilemma of solving the riddle.

"I still don't understand the part of 'bathing in its light', in fact I don't understand any part of it." Serina sighed. "Unless…"

"Unless what?" Senora and Koori repeated in unison – their curiosity mounting.

"Well, it was something Toddle said when he brought the book and candle to me." Serina stopped what she was saying, thinking back. "But, I'm sure it was nothing."

"Tell us what he said and then we can help you decide if it is nothing or not," said Senora nervously.

"I'm sure it's nothing but he said something like… *"To use it only for reading and it had a wonderful glow…"* or something like that

"What has a wonderful glow?" Senora asked quizzically.

"Oh, the candle he gave me, he said it was a special candle and that he made it himself, but I don't see what that would have to do with this riddle."

"I do," said Koori. "The riddle is talking about the candle, it has to be, and *'its amber glow'* means the candle's light."

"But *'bathe in the light'*, I don't understand," Serina said.

"Where is the candle?" Senora asked urgently.

"It's in my cell, I'll go get it." Serina scurried off to her cell to fetch the candle that Toddle had given her, while Koori, the boys and Senora waited impatiently.

"I don't know how I can 'bathe in the candle's light', do you Mother?" Serina questioned again as she rushed back to her mother's cell.

"I think I do," said Koori. "Hand me the candle, and let me read the book again."

Serina handed Koori the candle and she sat it down taking the book from Senora, sitting on her chair with the huge book on her lap, she took the candle back up into her hand and read silently for a moment.

"If I'm right, you must light the candle and stand in front of it, turning slowly in a circle."

"Do you really think it will work?"

"Well it won't hurt to give it a try, we only have our lives to lose if it doesn't, right?" said Koori urgently.

"Serina, hey, well I'm, huh, I'm... Good luck, okay?"

Amil was trying to apologize but couldn't get the words out properly. Serina rolled her eyes at him and it took all she had not to stick her tongue out at him. Instead, she ignored him totally, stepped over to the torch on the wall, and held the candle up to the flame until the wick lit with a flare. She pulled it back carefully watching its flame flicker. She cupped one hand around it so it would not go out while she stepped back over to Koori and placed the candle on the chair.

"What do I do now?"

Koori kept reading for a moment then looked up at her friend with uncertainty in her eyes. "I guess you stand in front of it and turn in circles, I'm not sure but I know it has to give you some kind of extra strength so you can go up against Takar."

"I don't know if I can do this, I'm terrified of Takar and what he can do."

Serina was having second thoughts about the whole thing all of a sudden. How could she go up against a monster like Takar? Someone who had no human feelings for anyone, surely she would die for her efforts.

"Serina, please come close for a moment, let me hold your hands, let me hug you through these bars."

Serina stepped up to her mother's cell, reaching through to her, they held each other as close as the bars would allow, without speaking, their arms wrapped around each other. Koori stepped up, Serina pulled her into their embrace, and the three stood there, not saying a word, while the two boys stood back quietly. When the three pulled apart Serina took hold of the candle, gazing at it for a moment, then she sat it back on the chair and started turning slowly in a small circle until she had completed a full circle. Feeling no different, she looked to her mother for some sort of direction.

"I don't feel any different than I did before, how will I know if it's working? How will I know if I'm doing it right?"

"Come here my child." Senora reached her arms through the bars of her cell again, Serina rushed into the arms of her mother, holding back the tears that threatened to burst forth in a gush. Senora held her daughter for a minute then pushed her back to arms length.

"You can do it Serina, I feel this in my heart, I have no doubt that you will succeed and take us home where your father waits – where we belong."

Serina pulled away, and looking into her mother's eyes, she saw the courage she needed to go up against the monster Takar.

"Serina, I think you should let me help you, let me go with you to fetch the necklace."

Serina looked at Amil, he was sincere, she knew it, but she was still hurt from his earlier stinging remarks.

"Why is that Amil, you don't think a girl can do anything but clean and cook and tend babies," she retorted, shrugging her shoulders, as she turned back to the candle. She then began walking in a circle again, her determination stronger now. She turned ever so slowly, around and around, after a few minutes, she sighed deeply, threw her hands up and started pacing the room aimlessly in frustration. "It's not working, this must not be the answer to the riddle, and I do not feel any different than before.

Serina was standing in front of Rupert's cell unaware of the man behind the bars. Abruptly and without warning, Rupert was at his cell door, he started banging his cup on the bars and before anyone knew what had happened he reached through the bars, grabbing Serina by the arm pulling her tight against the bars of his cell. Serina let out a loud scream but one of Rupert's dirty hands stifled it.

"Look deep into its light," Rupert whispered without hesitation, his voice deep and raspy – he did not stutter or falter, his speech was as steady as anyone's.

Everyone was screaming, Amil rushed to Rupert's cell trying to kick him through the bars and hitting his hands but he would not turn loose of Serina. Meanwhile Zarf had lunged toward Rupert's cell but Senora put her hand up to stop him.

"Let the light hypnotize you, then you will know what to do, listen to me carefully or you will surely die down here along with your mother and friends. If you concentrate on the light it will do what it is supposed to do."

He released Serina with a shove then ran back to his cot and jumped up on it and huddled in the far corner with his knees pulled up to his chest, his arms wrapped around them as if nothing unusual had happened.

Serina was stark still, frozen to the spot where she stood, staring at Rupert in a daze like trance.

"Serina, are you okay? Did he hurt you?" shouted her mother, so she could be heard over the frightened children.

Amil carefully walked her over to her mother's cell, all the while Serina stared back at Rupert, until she could not see him for the wall that separated his cell from her mother's.

"That crazy loon, if he were not in that dumb ole cell I'd give him what for, I would," said Frog, shaking his fists at Rupert through the bars of his cell.

"Frog, he would make mincemeat out of you if he were not in that dumb ole cell, so I wouldn't be making him angry if I were you," replied Amil, looking at his friend admonishingly.

"He could probably take us all out with one swipe from the looks of him," Koori remarked abstractedly.

"I don't know, I think we could take him, he's been in this cell for who knows how long and he's weak from lack of proper food, he doesn't look all that strong to me."

"Frog, I really think sometimes you have mutton stew for brains."

"Yeah!"

Koori agreed outwardly with Amil but silently she felt Frog was a strong capable fighter and could take on a whole army of Rupert's.

Senora had taken hold of Serina's arms holding her through the bars of her cell, trying to soothe her, although Serina had not said a word since Rupert had grabbed hold of her.

Everyone was in such a tizzy over the incident that all thoughts of Takar, the candle and the book were forgotten for the moment, until Serina suddenly snapped back into reality. *That's strange, the candle looks like it were never burned before, it's no shorter than when Toddle first gave it to me.*

"I know how to make it work now; I know what I must do," Serina murmured as she walked over to the chair where the candle stood. Trembling she picked it up and brought it up close to her face, she looked deep into its orange-yellow light, her mind and eyes focused only on its soft warm glow. Serina stared into the flickering candlelight, while everyone else looked on quietly, as if they were hypnotized from the candle's glow as well as Serina was. Serina looked past its soft flickering glow, deeper, and deeper... She felt herself being sucked into the flame.

Suddenly Serina was swept up into a whirlwind and carried away, out of the dungeon into the main part of the castle and then everything including herself moved into slow motion. She passed through rooms and halls with pictures hanging of old kings and queens with big buggy eyes looking down their pointed noses at anyone who dared pass their way. She passed the kitchens that lay silent in the dark resting before the morning bustle of activities. She went then up the stairs toward the floors that lay above the ground floor, some rooms she remembered and some she had not seen before, then as quickly as the whirlwind transported her through the castle it set her down. Serina blinked several times trying to focus her sight in the darkened room. She splayed her arms out by her sides so she could regain her balance. The whirlwind left her dizzy and disoriented and the darkness surrounding her did not help matters either. Once her eyes adjusted to the dimness she could tell she was inside someone's bedchamber. It was a very large room with several doors leading off to where Serina could only imagine... There were two windows in the room and the soft moonlight cast a pale glow across the floor, making strange shadows in the room. She could make out a large wardrobe on one of the far walls, reminding Serina of the wardrobe up in the tower and its secret stairway. There was a dressing table and chair near the wardrobe across the room between the two windows, there was a large four poster-bed – she could not tell if anyone lay in the bed though, for there was a white netting surrounding it like a cocoon, it was drawn tight all the way around the bed. She had no idea where she was but the fear gripping her chest and the eerie feeling in the pit of her stomach gave her a good idea. What she saw the next second confirmed her suspicions – there on a table next to the bed lay her necklace, shimmering in the soft moonlight. She was in the Great Takar's bedchamber, the last place she wanted to be at the moment. She could feel herself being drawn toward the bedside table, she had to have the stone but fear prevented her from moving. Serina stood frozen... She had to snap out of this but undiluted fear gripped every inch of her body, the only thing that seemed to be working on Serina's body was her pounding heart that hammered so loudly in her ears, she could not have heard the thunder in the heavens if it burst forth at that very moment. Her eyes kept darting back and forth from the emerald necklace on the night table to the huge poster-bed that lay wrapped in the soft white netting. Serina felt herself step forward then taking another step, stepping closer, it was as if someone else had taken over her body and carrying her across the room, closing the gap between her and the emerald, until she was standing beside the bed looking down at her necklace. The emerald lay within a hand's reach; all she had to do was reach down and pick it up – could she do it? Was there someone in the bed behind the netting? Takar? Was he asleep, or was he lying there watching her from behind the netting? She could feel the dread inching back through her body. This is nonsense, she told herself, she should reach down and grab the necklace and run... The longer she waited; the better her chances were of being caught. She brought her right hand out, slowly stretching it forward toward the night table and her only chance of staying alive against this monster. She was almost there, her fingers spread out and she clasped the necklace into the palm of her hand, she had made it, the necklace was in her hand, slowly Serina brought the necklace up and away from the table...

It happened so fast she wasn't sure what happened first, did she see the netting move before or after? Did she scream before or after? She wasn't sure but as quick as a lightening bolt shooting across a darkened sky Takar had Serina's wrist, she stood looking down at his cynical stare, a hint of a smile flashed across his evil face. She was completely immobilized, terrorized. Serina stared in horror as his evil hand reached out grabbing her by the shoulder.

Serina could hear someone calling her name from somewhere far away but she could not pull her eyes away from Takar's. The dark sinister, frightening eyes, peering up at her, were hypnotizing her – besides the voices were too far away, they couldn't help her, no one could help her now as Takar's grip tightened around her wrist.

"Serina!"

She heard her name called once again as she was suddenly sucked back into a whirlwind. It was transporting her speedily down through the rooms, corridors and kitchens that lay silent in the night, back through the places she had come through earlier with the pictures of the old kings and queens hanging on the walls staring quietly as she flashed back through, her secret forever safe with them.

Serina! Serina! What's wrong? Are you okay?" Amil was shaking Serina by the shoulders – she opened her eyes in a flutter to discover that she was standing in front of the candle down in the dungeon

"Serina! Serina, snap out of it. What's wrong?"

Serina pulled her eyes away from the amber glow of the candle's flame breaking its spell on her; she shut them tightly as she did so, opening them after a moment's hesitation. Amil was shaking her while the others stared at her in horror, their faces drawn tight in fear of what may have happened in the interim.

Serina felt dazed and drained while the fear that had been surging through her body relentlessly began to dissipate slowly as she realized where she was (and darn happy to be there for once), the cold damp dungeon that is, with its man size rats and overwhelming stench.

Amil was doing his best to push her toward her mother's cell but she stopped in front of Rupert's cell door gazing at the crazy loon of a man. He sat perched on his cot, balancing his lanky form on the edge as if he were about to take flight. He returned Serina's gaze and their eye's locked together for a moment. Silently she thanked him for helping her and she knew he understood. She also knew, without a doubt, that he was no more insane than she was.

Quickly Serina stepped over to her mother's cell taking her outstretched hands in hers.

"I saw it ... my necklace!" Serina exclaimed fretfully to everyone.

"Where? How did you see it? You haven't been anywhere," Koori said, looking rather oddly at her friend.

"It's up in the castle; I know how to get there too."

"Serina, what are you talking about? How did you see the emerald? You've not left the dungeon, you were just kneeling there in front of the candle like you were in a trance then you started shaking," said Amil.

"Yeah Serina, are we gonna have to put you in the cell with the loon over there," Frog asked mockingly.

"Don't say things like that Frog, that's not being very nice, can't you see she's not feeling well, right Serina?" said Koori uneasily.

"Children! Let Serina finish what she was trying to say. Go ahead dear, tell us what you saw."

"Well, as I was saying, I saw my necklace; the candle took me inside my mind down the path I need to follow to get it."

Serina told them all about what she saw, the pictures on the walls in the corridors, the rooms and the silent kitchens, deliberately leaving out the part about Takar. *No need scaring them all out of their wits, or at least not any more than they were already.*

"I know exactly where it is," continued Serina eagerly, "and I know exactly how to get there. It'll be so easy and then we can get out of this terrible place and back home where we will be safe."

"Well let's go get it, I can't wait to get out of this dungeon, it gives me the creeps," Koori piped in.

"The sooner the better," Amil agreed heartily.

"Slow down Koori not so fast," said Serina, pulling her arm back from her friend who was practically dragging her toward the door that led to the main part of the castle.

"I don't think it would be a good idea for all of us to go, in fact I think you guys need to head back to the village and wait for us there. When I get the necklace I can get my mother out of her cell and we can head back and meet you all in the village."

"Why can't we just go with you and be together and get this over with?" asked Frog rather irritated with all this delaying nonsense.

Amil flashed a glance toward Serina then turned to Frog. Although she was doing a good job of hiding her fear, Amil noticed the strain stroking Serina's face and he unexpectedly disagreed with Frog, and for that, Serina was thankful.

"Ah who wants to go with a silly girl up into an old castle anyway Frog?"

"Yeah, I guess you're right Amil but, we don't know the way back to the village so what are we going to do?"

"No problem, Koori knows the way; she can take you and my mother. I will meet you just as soon as I can get the necklace and get her out of her cell, okay Koori?"

"Well what about you? I don't want to leave you here alone."

"I won't be alone Koori, my mother will be with me and besides this will be a great way to show the boys we're smarter than they are!"

The latter remark had been said low enough for only Koori to hear. Koori thought about this, a smile spread across her face, and Serina knew she had made a point with her friend.

Senora hugged Koori goodbye and asked if she remembered how to get back into the cave then she turned to the two boys, telling them to take good care of themselves and of Koori (for good measure).

"Okay now, you guys will have to stay close to me and do exactly what I say or you could get lost," Koori ordered all at once.

Serina could tell her friend was going to love this, anything to torture them, she just hoped she hadn't made it too hard on the boys.

"What if you need help, or if something goes wrong, how will we know?" asked Koori, turning back to Serina, a worried look suddenly crossing her face.

"Nothing's going to go wrong Koori, what could possibly go wrong anyway; I'll have my necklace remember?"

"Yeah right, well whatever you say, come on guys times a wasting, see you later."

"Right," Serina said firmly.

"Serina," said Amil, he paused for a moment then decided to drop whatever he was going to say as if it was unimportant and turned to the others.

"Come on Koori show us the way outta here."

The three said their goodbyes and took off down the long corridor that led to the castle grounds and their freedom.

After they were out of sight Serina turned to her mother and with a sigh flopped down in the chair next to her cell.

Chapter 21

"Now that they're gone do you mind telling your mother where the emerald is?" asked Senora in that soft whispery voice of hers.

Serina looked over at her mother behind the bars of the dirty cell, where she had been held now for days. At this point, it didn't matter much to her whether the emerald was – on Takar's bedside table or in the huge black fire-eating dragon's mouth that lay sleeping in the big barn outside – as long as she got her mother out of that rat infested filthy cubical. On the other hand, her mother might worry just a tad bit if she knew where it lay.

"It's just sitting for the taking in one of the rooms upstairs Mother. I won't be long and I will be able to get you out of there and back home where we both belong – not to worry," Serina replied with as much enthusiasm as she could muster, knowing her mother would detect any little sign of doubt or fear on her face. It didn't work.

"Serina you might get away with that with your friends but I am your mother and although I have not been with you all these years, a mother knows things and I know you are just trying to keep me from worrying, but I will worry anyway. I know the emerald is in Takar's bedchamber because I know Takar and his evilness, so I warn you, be very careful it may be a trap."

Serina hugged her mother through the bars of the cell. *It will be so great to have a mother after all these years,* she thought.

"You're right but I did not want to worry you or the others; they would have stayed to try and help me but it will be safer for me to do this by myself. I *must* do this by myself!"

"Go Serina, you must hurry, time is running out, remember what the rhyme in the book said and do not worry about me I'm stuck down here in this cell and do not pose a threat to Takar, but please be careful."

"That's right; the rhyme said that if I do not finish by the light of day then all would be lost."

Without another word Serina turned toward the door that led to the castle, but before stepping passed the threshold, she turned to her mother once again to see her standing at her cell door staring at her with a big smile on her face. Serina's eyes then traveled over to Rupert, who was at his cell door also – he, was not smiling. He wore a look on his face that resembled encouragement. One word came from his mouth, which struck Serina as odd.

"Battle."

Serina turned and went through the door confused as to why Rupert, who always grumbled incoherently, when he grabbed her through his cell, spoke so plainly and directed her so aptly as to what she had to do with the candle – or when he repeated the rhyme earlier to everyone's astonishment and now again – plainly, she heard the word "battle." *Who was he and where did he come from?*

Serina hurried down the long corridor and through the door that led to the kitchens, still quiet, no one about, *so far so good.* Now up the stairs and to the task at hand, get the emerald and get back so she can get her mother free and home.

Serina had made it to the top of the stairs without seeing anyone but as she started toward the second set of stairs, she heard something that sounded like footsteps on the stairs below her – the very stairs from where she had just come up. She looked around to find a place to hide but there was nothing and whoever it was, was getting closer by the second.

Serina quickly shot inside the first door she came to, just as the footsteps reached the top of the stairs. She left the door ajar just enough to see whose footsteps they were. Serina's breath caught in her throat when she saw who it was.

"What do you think you're doing here?" Serina barked as quietly as she possibly could, purely enraged at her friend.

"I see that look in your eyes but don't worry Serina, I made sure Amil and Frog made it back home safely then I came back. Besides I couldn't let you do this alone, remember I have to watch out for you, or did you forget that? And besides we're best friends and best friends don't let best friends do something this stupid and scary and dangerous by themselves, right? Right – now where to? so we can get this over with."

Serina stared at Koori in total disbelief. "I can't believe you're so stupid as to come back. I told you I would meet you in the village. You can't help me do what I have to do, this is something I have to do alone Koori, it's too dangerous for you to be here."

"Not any more dangerous for me than for you right?" Koori was not giving in and was standing her ground.

"Maybe not, but this does not affect you, you could be hurt or killed then I would have to live with that. But if I do this alone, only I stand the chance of injury or death, that's the way it should be."

"Wrong! If something happened to you because I was not here to help then I would have to live with that and were wasting time so let's get going, where to?"

"Koori!"

"Say no more, you can thank me later."

Serina stomped her foot and glared at her soon to be EX-best friend. "THANK YOU?"

"I said you could do that later, now let's get going – where to?"

This was the second time in as many weeks that Koori pulled something like this on Serina. She was so mad she could see red but she could not convince Koori to go back and she was wasting precious time.

"Stay right with me and do as I say. If we live through this I will kill you later, come on..."

The two headed up the stairs to the next floor and to the necklace, when they reached Takar's bedchamber Serina begged Koori again to reconsider her actions and head back down to the dungeon, at least, and wait for her there, but she would not hear of it.

"At least wait out here in the hall while I go in to get the necklace. If I'm not out in five minutes get back to the dungeon as quickly as you can, do not wait on me, it could mean your life."

"What if I see someone, like Takar maybe, what does he look like?" Koori asked suddenly showing a little of the fear she had been trying so desperately to hide.

"Believe me if you see Takar you *will* know him but I don't think you have to worry about that."

"Why not?"

"Because, this is Takar's bedchamber and I'm sure he's in there, I hope fast asleep," said Serina irritably; pointing to the door in front of which they were standing.

"Oh," was all Koori managed to say. The look on her face told Serina that she was as scared as she, herself, was.

"Now do as I say, wait right here and give me five minutes, if I'm not back out here in five minutes you head back to the dungeon and tell my mother, is that clear Koori?"

"Yes, five minutes, back to the dungeon, got ya. Oh how will I know when five minutes is up?"

Koori's voice quivered a little but Serina knew she would be all right and hoped she would do what she asked, "Just count to sixty five times, you can do that can't you?"

"Yes Serina I know how to count."

"Okay, here I go, remember five minutes."

Serina slowly opened the door to Takar's bedchamber; her heart was in her throat as she carefully closed the door upon her. She stood quietly just inside the room, waiting for a few seconds to let her eyes get accustomed to the darkness. When she could make out the different objects in the room she started inching her way toward the bed and the table standing next to it with the emerald necklace laying there – just waiting for her to pick it up.

The sight of Takar grabbing her arm kept flashing through her mind as she closed the distance between the door and the bedside table. The look of pure evil on his face had given Serina cold chills earlier when she had been looking into his eyes but *that was a dream, right?* She was only in the room in her mind then, this was for real, she had only this one chance to get the necklace, so what was she doing thinking about ... him! But he had caught her in her mind's dream. What was that telling her? Was the candle showing her she was going to get caught? She had to force that thought out of her mind – and think of what she was doing, the task at hand, grab the necklace and run... She was so close... She kept telling herself, *don't mess it up, just keep tiptoeing toward his bed, you're almost there.* However, she could not stop the vision of Takar's hand reaching out from behind the netting and grabbing her wrist. Sweat was breaking out profusely across her brow, plus she had the worst feeling in the pit of her stomach, her legs had turned to water and she felt as if she could no longer function on her own. She stood immobile in the middle of the room, staring at the bed, all hope of getting the necklace vanishing as terror flooded her body. *I can't do this,* she thought. Turning around she walked back to the door, her legs barely carrying her. With her hand on the doorknob she began to turn it slowly, she closed her eyes on the vision of her mother in her cell and Koori waiting just outside the door for her. *She'll understand,* she thought, so would her mother, she was sure of it. Her shaking hand turned the doorknob, and then stopped, maybe they would understand, maybe they would get out of this another way, without her having to get the emerald or facing Takar but she could never face them again, nor could she face herself. She dropped her hand to her side and turned back to face the bed, she drew in a deep breath and whispered; "I'll never know if I don't try, so here goes nothing" as she made her way back across the room.

The moonlight floated across the floor as it had in the candle's light. *Everything seemed the same*, she thought, as she reached the foot of the bed. Only a few more feet, she could see the emerald necklace laying just where it had been in her vision, she took another step, then another and another – she was there. All she had to do was to reach down and take it, so what was she waiting on.

"DO IT!" She heard someone yell, in a deep raspy voice. She looked around the room quickly, startled at the voice. *It must have been my mind playing tricks*, she thought, because no one else was in the room but her and the sleeping Takar, at least she hoped with all her heart he was sleeping or dead – dead would be better.

She reached down, her trembling fingers clasped around the stone, and she slowly pulled it up to her breast, her eyes never leaving the netting surrounding the huge bed. *So far so good*, she thought as she backed up away from the table and the bed, still watching the bed she backed all the way across the room, when she reached the door she turned grabbing the knob with her free hand and swung it open just enough to slip through. She had made it!

She must have been in the room longer than the five minutes she had given Koori to wait for her because her friend was nowhere to be seen.

"Koori!" Serina whispered as loud as she dared, not wanting to wake the sleeping castle, but no reply from Koori. She could hardly believe her best friend actually did what she had requested of her without a fight, she headed for the stairs – the sooner she got back to the dungeon the better.

As she reached the stairs, Serina caught a movement of something coming from behind the suit of armor that was standing in an alcove near the stairs. She froze in her tracks until Koori came into full view.

"What are you doing here I thought I told you to go back to the dungeon if I was not back in five minutes, I can't believe you would not do as I requested of you, especially now, here when it's so dangerous Koori," whispered Serina in a stern voice. She was definitely angry with her friend.

"That's right you did," Koori replied tartly.

"Then why are you still here?" Serina snapped furiously.

"Because... My five minutes are not up yet. You said to wait for five minutes and that's what I was doing, why are you so worried about it anyway, did you get the necklace?"

"Ye-yes," Serina replied as she held out her trembling hand showing Koori the Emerald Stone.

"Let's go we have to hurry."

The two girls took off in a run down the stairs and did not slow down until they were at the bottom of the stairs on the main floor of the castle.

"Why were you hiding behind that suit of armor anyway? You scared me half to death," Serina asked after the two slowed down to a fast walk. They were entering the kitchen area now. Once through there they were almost home free, just a little farther to go.

"I was wondering if you were ever going to let me tell you, I heard someone coming so I hid there until they passed and was afraid to come out again until I saw you."

"Who was it, who did you see?"

"I don't know who they were. Remember I just got here tonight, how would I know who they were?" Koori replied wryly, a little annoyed with her friend.

"I'm sorry Koori if I sounded so hateful, I'm just a little nervous and want to get back to the dungeon and to my mother, I don't like her being down there alone."

"Yeah, me either."

The girls did not make another sound until they were safely inside the dungeon then the two of them broke into a mad run to Senora's cell.

"We got it, look I just grabbed it off the table beside the bed and got out of there without any trouble, of course Koori here had to scare me half to death by hiding behind a suit of armor."

The girls stopped dead in their tracks at the odd look on Senora's face.

"What is it? What's wrong?" Serina asked her mother, as she swooped around, looking for any sign of trouble, nothing was there, yet her mother did not utter a sound, she just stood there at the cell's door as if in a trance with a look of sheer horror on her face.

Serina felt his presence first, before she ever saw a glimmer of movement – she knew. She turned around slowly, her heart in her throat, eyes straining to see past the curtain of darkness. Then slowly he stepped out of the darkened corner into the dim rim of light. She heard Koori's sudden gasp then the hard thud as she hit the floor. Apparently, she passed out from the shock of seeing the hooded Takar.

"So my sweet little Serina I think it's time, don't you? I mean you must think it's time since I see you hold your precious insignificant little emerald in your hand. Am I wrong? Is that not what you were about to show your paralyzed mother? She *is* paralyzed you see, I thought that it would add a little flair to the scene, don't you agree?" Takar's voice dripped with sweetness.

She looked around but did not see Zarf anywhere, she wondered where he could have run off to, or had her mother sent him into hiding for his own protection. She hoped the latter was true because he may have looked like a ghoul but he had a kind heart and was loyal to her mother, for sure.

Serina stood frozen with her hand still outstretched with the emerald dangling from her fingers. *Insignificant – what did he mean by that?* It was all-powerful, it was what she was going to use against him, to win the fight that was about to be waged between the two of them, right? She sure hoped she was right, because if not...

Takar closed the gap between them with two long strides snatching the emerald from Serina's hand.

"You will no longer need this, my dear."

Serina yanked her hand back but she was too slow, Takar laughed brazenly as he dangled the necklace in front of her.

"See, I told you, you were no match for the Great Takar, besides it is of no significance to you, it would not help you against me as you foolishly think, it's just a silly little emerald."

Serina turned her head to look at her mother who stood as she had when Serina entered the dungeon; she cast her eyes on her friend who lay crumpled on the cold damp floor beside her. She had never known hate until that moment. Oh sure she hated eating her rutabagas and hated losing a foot race to Amil but the pure hate and anger, which was raging inside her presently, never existed before then – not until she met this demon personified. Who was she kidding? Even with her emerald she was no match up against his strength. She turned back to face Takar, his hooded cloak covered his entire face.

"Your little friend saved me the trouble of zapping her into eternity. How very nice of her don't you agree?"

Serina still could not speak; she just stared at the dark hole where Takar's face should be. She may not stand a chance against Takar and his demonic forces, and it was probably too late to save her mother and Koori from him, but *maybe* if she pleaded with him he would let them go. Serina slumped to the floor next to Koori who still lay lifeless to check if she was all right. Her breathing seemed normal; she had just fainted. She looked up at her mother; still standing immobile, petrified like the statue of Venus fountain in the courtyard, but the horror etched on her face gave Serina cold chills. Glancing over at Rupert's cell she noticed the man sitting on the floor near the cell door staring at her, he looked as crazed as always but then she saw it, a glint, a tiny little sparkle of recognition or realization...

Serina got to her feet and turned to Takar. She was trying to remember everything her mother told her about fighting this evil dark force. In fact she was trying so hard to remember she was getting a headache and her mind was all abuzz with jostling thoughts. All she could hear was a roaring chaos of words that did not make any sense at all. She threw both her hands to her head and cradled it between them. What was it she said about what she was supposed to do and how was she supposed to do it. Darn, she hated it when her mind drew a blank like this. She looked over to her mother again as if to will her to speak, to unfreeze herself and say something but she just stood frozen in time and space.

"Come now Serina, life here with me will not be all that bad. You will see and once you accept it you will have the whole world at your beck-and-call, the things that you and I will be able to do will be countless. With both our powers together, we will be so strong that no one will be able to stand against us," Takar was saying but Serina's thoughts were swirling around her head so fast she couldn't think let alone hear Takar's voice droning on.

What brought Takar back to the dungeon so late tonight? She wondered – when everyone was supposed to be sleeping; it was evident that he had not been in his curtained bed upstairs when she had been retrieving the necklace. How did he know? How could he have known, unless he just happened to come down to the dungeon to find her missing? Or was it something else, or someone else that led him here? Serina wondered what he must have done to her mother to make her tell.

"What brought you back down to the dungeon in the middle of the night anyway Takar?" Serina snapped nervously interrupting the tyrant in mid sentence.

"Ah yes, I was wondering when you would get around to asking that. You see I had a, what would you call it, ah yes, an inkling that someone might in fact go against me to help the poor Senora and her darling daughter, so I set a trap. I would have never believed that my beloved servant, Toddle of all people, would betray me. Just goes to show you can not put your trust in anyone these days."

It was Serina's turn to suck in a big breath of air, as she grabbed her chest. Her knees went weak and she almost sunk to the floor next to Koori, who still lay unconscious at her feet.

"No he's not dead; not yet, I want him to see my true powers unveil, unless that is you've made the decision to become my bride... I will kill him quickly and painlessly, as a present for you."

"A present for me?" Serina exclaimed outraged.

"Of course, you wouldn't want the little man to suffer would you?"

Serina stared at Takar staggered. What was it her mother said about how she could overpower this man? What did she tell her about her special powers that combined with the emerald stone, which Takar said was worthless against his powers, would win over this evil doer? Serina did not think that a twelve year old girl with a pretty little green stone necklace was much of a match in any fight against evil, let alone some one as powerful as Takar – what was her mother thinking anyway?

Serina cast her eyes around the dark dungeon in search for Toddle but he was nowhere to be seen.

"Where is he?" Serina demanded.

Takar glared at Serina for a moment before speaking, which chilled Serina all the way down to her toes.

"He is right where he should be, in his old cell... Now back to the business at hand, what is your answer Serina? What will you do? I'm tired of playing games with you, you must give me your answer now or you will end up back in the cell with Toddle along with your little unconscious friend here," Takar shouted angrily pointing to Koori lying so still on the stone floor.

Serina knew he was forcing her hand in the matter, but under the circumstances, she was glad, she had to make a decision and make one now, with her mother standing frozen in time and her best friend lying unconscious on the floor, she hoped she would make the right one.

"I will stay here as you wish Takar but only on one condition and that is; you let my mother and my friend go *unharmed*."

She figured if she could get them out of there safely it would clear her mind of all this worrying and give her time to concentrate on the job at hand – taking care of Takar; and that was going to take much concentration – without a doubt.

"I do not believe you are in a position to barter my dear Serina, so what is it going to be? Shall I put them out of their misery and lock you up with Toddle or are you going to come to your senses and do as your destiny requires?"

My destiny, my destiny, that's all she had heard since she arrived here in this dungeon of doom and she was sick to death of it. Why couldn't she make her own destiny...? But, if she did not do the right thing, her friend and her mother would surely die... She must try to persuade Takar to let them go.

"You may force me to stay here but you can not make me like it, now if you let them go free I will stay willingly, that's not asking too much Takar, just let them go."

Takar paced the floor for a moment in deep thought not saying a word when finally he came to a stop at the door of her mother's cell.

"You want me to let your mother and your silly little twit of a friend, go free?"

Takar reached through the bars and took Senora's hand; he gently rubbed her fingers with his. It was amazing how gentle he could be when he wanted to. Suddenly he withdrew his hand and started pacing again before coming to a stop once more in front of Serina.

"Look Takar, you have that memory stuff – you know you could wipe their memory away and they would not remember a thing about this place or you."

Serina looked up into the dark shadow where Takar's eyes verily visible glared down at her – his chiseled features giving him a haunting look.

"This is true little Serina, alas I would not take pleasure in killing your mother, I have grown very fond of her over the years and she has been an asset..."

Takar then began treading the floor again and took long strides down to where he held Toddle locked in an extremely small cell and in a moment came back to where Serina stood watching him closely for any sign that he would relent and let the two others go.

"Fine, I will let them go."

Serina breathed a deep sigh of relief – at last, Takar showed a small sign of being human.

"I will let them go after, and *only* after, you and I have made and signed our agreement, is that understood Serina?"

"Agreement – what are you talking about? We just made an agreement, you will let them go and I will stay here," Serina shouted in frustration as she squared her shoulders and faced Takar boldly although her insides were quivering like rapidly running water.

"Ah yes but it is not done until we sign a parchment stating such. I could not just take you at your word since you have tried to trick me on so many occasions, I would have to have it in writing, or you may consider backing out of the deal and I would not have anything to hold you to it."

Serina never intended to hold up her end of the bargain, for as soon as Koori and her mother were safe she had all intentions of confronting Takar with the powers that her mother said she had and fight him until one of them was no longer standing. It was the only way that she and her village would ever have any peace from him and all his evil. Whatever it took, she was not going to stay in this horrible castle any longer than was absolutely necessary.

"Whatever you say Takar if that is what you want then we will sign the agreement," Serina said resignedly. She was wondering how she was going to get out of signing any parchment with Takar. She did not want anything legal and binding with the man, but she did not see how she was going to get out of this one.

Takar reached inside his long flowing robes and pulled out a piece of parchment. "I just happened to have the papers with me, come, we will sign it together."

He beckoned Serina over to the small table that stood against the wall; he held out his hand producing a long feather quill and thrust it toward Serina.

"Just sign your name here and we will be done," he ordered pointing to a spot near the bottom of the document.

"What about my mother and…"

"Yes, yes, your little friend and your mother will be set free now sign the parchment," he snapped urgently.

Serina took the quill from Takar with a trembling hand. She looked down at the piece of parchment to where Takar's finger pointed – a blank space where she guessed she was supposed to sign her name.

"Go on, you can write can you not? Right here where my finger is... Just sign your full name and it will be over and your mother and friend can go home."

So many things were rushing through Serina's head that she suddenly felt dizzy the whole room was spinning around her and she had to grab the table to keep from falling.

"It will be for the better, you will see Serina – you will see."

Serina steadied herself then quickly signed the paper. No sooner had she signed it that Takar yanked it from her hand and shoved it back inside his robes.

"I thought you were supposed to sign it also Takar?"

Takar flashed his evil dark eyes at her and she could read the look on his face only too well – triumph, he had finally obtained what he wanted.

"Oh yes I forgot to do that didn't I?"

He pulled the paper out and scribbled his name across the bottom of the parchment, folded it and stuck it inside his cloak once again.

"What about my mother and my friend? You said you would let them go as soon as I signed the agreement."

"So I did." Takar clapped his hands together and from out of nowhere, it seemed, Ernie and Talbert appeared.

"Take these two back to the cave then, come back here as I have other things for you to do."

"Uh, Master Takar this one's dead ain't she? Leastways she is lying on the floor like she is," said Ernie as he was leaning over Koori inspecting her as if she were a dead rat.

"Yeah and this one ain't much better. I'm afraid if I touch her she might break up or something." Talbert was poking at Sonora through the cell bars and giggling.

Takar whipped around quickly facing Talbert, the look in his eyes was deadly.

"Never touch her! Do I make myself clear Talbert? Never."

"Yes Master." Talbert backed away from Senora's cell with stark fear on his face.

Takar stepped up to Senora's cell, holding out his right arm he spoke some undistinguishable words and Senora woke up with a scream, but fell silent as her eyes scanned the room, taking in everything and everyone, she gasped in horror when she caught sight of Koori lying on the floor at Serina's feet.

"It's okay Mother, she is just passed out," Serina said quickly noticing her mother's fearful eyes gazing in her friend's direction. She knelt beside Koori again and brushed the hair away from her face just as she began stirring.

"It's okay, you just fainted, Takar is going to let you and my mother, go home but I will stay here," said Serina.

"What's going on? Why? Oh never mind, you're going to do what you want to do no matter what any one else has to say about it, right Serina?" Koori muttered more to herself than to her friend.

"Just do as I say and don't worry about me. Oh, and Koori, will you look after my mother?"

"I guess so, that'll give me something to do in all my *free* time since I wont have you to look after any more."

"Thanks."

Serina gave Koori a perturbed look as she hugged her and then jumped to her feet and ran to her mother.

"Mother, Takar said he would let you and Koori go free, they're going to take you to the cave then turn you loose, don't worry about me, I'll be alright."

"Serina, I can not let you do this."

"It's going to be okay, I promise you, just do as Takar says and there will be a happy reunion for you when father sees you again I'm sure of it."

"Not without you Serina, I've lived all your life without you but I will gladly give up the rest of my life for you to be home with your father right this minute, alive and safe."

Takar reached into his cloak pocket, pulled out a small pouch, and handed it to Ernie.

"Ernie, you and Talbert take these two, you know what to do with this... Serina you come with me."

Takar gave Senora a long silent glance before grabbing Serina by the arm whisking her away from her mother's cell. He was blurting out orders as usual and everyone was hopping to do as he wished except for Koori.

"Why do we need help?" she yelled. "We know how to get to the cave ourselves, we don't need any help from the likes of them," she added pointing and shaking her finger at the two men coming toward her.

Serina broke free from Takar's grasp and bent down to help her friend up from the cold floor. "Koori don't talk back to him do as he says, it's healthier that way. Just go before he changes his mind, believe me you will not like it if he changes his mind."

"Truer words have not been spoken my dear Serina, now *go!*" Takar yelled at Koori pointing to the door. He grabbed Serina by the arm again pulling her along with him toward the door.

Koori managed to get to her feet and grabbed Senora's arm and the two of them headed toward the long corridor that led to their freedom closely followed by Ernie and Talbert.

After they disappeared he turned to Serina dropped his hold on her arm and held out his hand.

"Come I will walk you back to the tower and tomorrow we will move you to the same floor as mine."

As they walked by Toddle's cell Serina noticed him sitting on the old cot. He would not look up at them or even acknowledge their presence. This was painful for Serina, she knew she was to blame for whatever Takar had in store for the little man and she knew it was not going to be pleasant.

"Takar, you said you set a trap what was it? What did Toddle do?"

"I knew someone would try and help you so I let everyone know I had the emerald and laid it in plain sight for anyone to find. Then I hid in the darkness of my room and waited, I caught Toddle as he sneaked into my room to fetch the emerald so he could bring it back to you, afterwards I hid across the hall and waited for you, I knew you would come sooner or later. I watched you and your little friend from just inside the doorway, once you were in my room I made a noise to scare your little sentry friend and she hid behind the armor then I brought Toddle to the dungeon and waited for you to return."

"Oh yes I almost forgot, I said I would take care of Toddle quickly didn't I?"

Toddle stood up and walked toward the bars of his cell, when he reached them he looked into Serina's eyes and said; "Take care Little Princess."

Takar stretched out his hand with a deadly aim and shouted in some unknown language as fire flew from his fingertips and Toddle fell to the floor apparently dead.

"No! Takar why? Why did you kill him? He did no harm," Serina shouted without restraint.

"He disobeyed me, he went against me and I will not tolerate anyone who disobeys me – a lesson that would do you good to remember," he added as he grabbed Serina's arm and began pulling her toward the door again.

Serina broke loose from his grasp and dropped to the floor clinching her fingers around the bars of Toddle's cell screaming.

"Oh Toddle I'm so very sorry."

Takar grabbed Serina's wrist and pulled her back away from the cell. "He was a good servant but even good servants will be punished if they go against me, this will be a good lesson for the others."

"You beast, you did not have to kill him," Serina cried out with contempt. She wept uncontrollably for the man who tried to save her; she wondered who would be next.

"Come! You must learn to obey my orders, the sooner the better."

Takar grabbed one of Serina's arms, pulling her to her feet and dragging her along behind him. She stumbled over a loose stone in the floor falling to her knees. Takar stopped long enough for her to get on her feet again then tugged her along with him not releasing her until they reached the tower.

A tall dark haired man waited for them in her room, one she had never seen before.

"Doak will stay here tonight just to make sure nothing or no one gets in here and I will see you in the morning."

Serina glanced over at the new guard then back to Takar in puzzlement.

"Whatever Takar, just let me get into bed I'm very tired."

Remembering her necklace all of a sudden, Serina turned back to Takar. "Please, if the emerald is so useless to me as far as my powers are concerned may I have my necklace back? You know – a kind of remembrance of my mother."

Serina held her breath as Takar thought this over, when he did not answer right away she urged him even further.

"It would mean so much to me, besides you yourself said I was powerless over you... Unless maybe you're afraid after all, that I might could... possibly..."

"I am afraid of no one! The Great Takar is more powerful than anyone – you should know that by now. But to show you, you may take your silly little necklace. It has no power against me, so if it will make you happy... See; I can be a nice person when I want to be Serina."

He tossed the emerald necklace to Serina; she caught it with both hands clasping it to her chest.

Takar turned and said a few words to Doak then left without a backward glance, after a moment's silence she heard him turn the key in the lock then a few minutes later she heard the sound of his footsteps receding down the stairs.

Serina dropped into bed without bothering to change her clothing it was nearly daylight and she had failed everyone miserably but at least she had been able to free her mother and Koori and that meant more to her than anything. So what if she had to spend the rest of her life in this ole castle with the likes of Takar? It was better than being dead; leastways, she thought, it was at the moment.

After what seemed like an eternity, Serina fell into a dreamless sleep.

Chapter 22

The dawn that broke timidly over the castle was met with a flurry of activities. The Great Takar was planning a feast; he had to celebrate the wonderful news – the beginning of the long courtship, which would lead Serina to becoming his bride when she reached the proper age, of course. Yes, this was a great occasion for him indeed, for little did Serina know that Takar's powers were only half as strong as hers but once they married then his powers would be doubled to hers and that was why it was so important for the Great Takar to marry Serina.

Serina woke to the hustle and bustle of five women cleaning her room, the rough looking guard Doak was nowhere to be found. Mertie and Effie with three others were running around her room like chickens with there heads chopped off, dusting, polishing and cleaning everything that got in their way.

Serina pulled the covers over her head for she did not want to look at or speak to anyone let alone this crew.

"Up and at em Little Princess." It was Mertie, she was pulling the covers from off the top of Serina and as hard as she tried to snatch the covers back it was a losing battle with the big woman.

"Go away Mertie and let me sleep," Serina growled.

"Can't do that Missy, now you just get up from here, the girls have your breakfast ready and you need to eat while it's

305

still hot. Got a lot to do today and I don't have time to dilly-dally with ya."

"What's going on? Why the rush, I just barely climbed into bed and I'm very tired."

"Ah little one there is going to be a feast in your honor and everything must be cleaned to sparkle and shine like new silver including you," said Mertie all smiles.

Remembering the last one and the disaster it turned out to be Serina did not feel much like another feast. Besides how could she go to a feast when all she could think about was her mother and Koori?

"And not to mention your big move, the Master says Mertie is to move all of the little Princess's things up to the Floral Suite today, so that's what I am doing."

In all of last night's confusion Serina completely forgot about the move. She glanced around the room and sure enough the maids that she thought were just cleaning earlier were in fact packing up all her things, remembering something else suddenly Serina ran her hand inside her pocket where she had put her necklace the night before. *Whew! It was still there,* if only she could make everything right again, but that was just wishful thinking, nothing would be the same again – nothing.

She climbed out of bed and walked to the window. There were people all about the grounds – the lawns and hedges were trimmed, the flowerbeds manicured, in preparation for the festivities. As she stepped away from the window something from the far side of the gardens down below caught her eye she turned back just in time to see Takar head toward the dragon's lair from the other side of the lawns.

I wonder what he's up to, messing with that horrible creature, she thought, as she watched him disappear inside the barn.

Serina watched the huge doorway for a little while longer before she went to bathe and get dressed but Takar never came back out.

Later Takar came up to the tower to talk with her about the feast and to see if she was still behaving herself. Serina gave one of her best performances ever, doing and saying all the right things, convincing Takar that she was willing to stay and live in the castle with him and do all the great things he had mentioned to her so many times – he seemed happy enough. As he was leaving, Serina noticed a large nasty gash on his left hand, when she inquired about it his mood darkened, only for a fraction of a second though.

"That's just a little scratch, nothing to concern yourself with."

"Did Java do that to you?"

"I said it was none of your concern!" Takar roared as he stormed out of the room slamming the huge door behind him leaving Serina standing in the middle of the room agape.

"Touchy today isn't he?" Serina said aloud to the empty room. She swung around and headed for the bed and flopped down, still exhausted from the events from the night before, it wasn't long before she was fast asleep.

Serina slept a good part of the afternoon before Mertie woke her.

"It's a good idea to rest up afore the party so ya wont be so tired tonight huh Little Princess, but it's time to be up and stirring now and tonight you will be sleeping in your new room, you will like it much better than this ole tower.

Serina made her way down the long set of stairs while Mertie was busy cleaning and before she knew it she was at a side door that led outside and to the same side of the castle where her tower was located. Everyone was so busy with what they were doing that no one paid any attention to her or bothered to stop her, so she stepped out into the bright afternoon sun, she wandered around the grounds, with no particular place in mind, but before she knew it she was at the entrance of the huge black dragon's lair.

Petrified at the thought of being so close to the creature's dwelling, she made a dash for the castle but after a few feet, she stopped and turned back toward the big barn. Something seemed to be pulling her back. When she reached the huge door, she hesitated remembering the nasty gash on Takar's arm that she noticed earlier that very same morning. As powerful as Takar was he could barely handle the creature so why on earth was she about to enter into this darkened barn? Was she insane, marching straight to her death for surely if she came close enough to this fire eating thing, he would toast her up nicely and swallow her in one little gulp.

The barn was very dark except for the sunlight streaming in from the cracks in the boards and the stench was almost unbearable. Serina tried holding her breath but when she let it out and inhaled again, it seemed to be worse. *The poor creature,* she thought, as she inched her way forward.

She could hear his breathing in and out evenly in slumber. She dared not make any noise in fear of waking him. Serina stumbled into a pile of hay falling into it head first but she did not make enough noise to disturb the dragon. She then climbed to the top of the hay pile to have a better look around and there nestled in the far corner fast asleep lay the huge black dragon. She could barely make him out in the dimness enveloping the room. Serina lay watching the creature for a few moments marveling at his long sleek neck that he had cradled across one front leg with his tail wrapped around his body like her cat Samone would do in peaceful slumber.

Serina climbed down from the pile of hay and made her way closer, she was drawn to this dangerous creature for some reason; she couldn't explain it, as dangerous as it was, she stepped closer yet, until she was within a few feet of his head.

She stood there looking at this big black sleek shape of a dragon fast asleep thinking *he couldn't be that mean he was just big and that was probably what made him seem so menacing.* Suddenly Serina realized something – the even breathing sound that the dragon was making earlier had stopped. She turned her head slowly until her eyes met the very large yellow eyes of the now very awake dragon. Fear, such as she had never known, gripped her throat. She stood paralyzed, incapable of sound or movement. All she could do was look dead into the dragon's eyes with her mouth wide open.

The dragon raised his head slowly keeping his eyes on Serina the whole time never blinking just staring at her with those intense yellow eyes.

Serina finally came to her senses and started to back away not breaking eye contact with the dragon. When she had backed up about six or seven feet she turned and ran toward the door never looking back to see what the dragon was doing. If she made it out of the barn alive it would most definitely surprise her. Yet, for whatever reason, the dragon chose not to pursue Serina and she ran as fast as she could back to the castle for once feeling safe inside its doors.

As Serina slipped inside the kitchen door she sighed deeply. She noticed that everyone was still busy with the feast's preparation; singing and dancing and saying how there had never been a feast the likes of this one before. It was going to be so grand that people would talk about it for centuries to come, they were all so busy and happy they didn't even notice Serina as she slipped past them and headed back up to the tower.

All Serina could do was to sit at the window and watch the barn that held the dragon, feeling safe up in her tower. She could finally breathe normally again, she had been much afraid for her life and that had been too close for comfort she decided. What ever possessed her to step inside the barn, let alone go near the dragon? Well she had no plans of ever doing something that stupid again.

Serina readjusted herself on the cushions at the window and immediately began thinking of Toddle and Ju and there bravery and how they ended – they were both dead because of her. She also thought of her mother and best friend. Were they safe back in the village? How happy her father must be at seeing his wife again after so many years. Oh, how she wished she could have seen her father's face when he saw Senora again. She must think of that during the feast, it will make things a little more bearable for her.

Late in the afternoon her door swung open and in came Effie with a big smug grin on her face, she was pretending to tidy up a room that had already been cleaned and spit shined. After a few moments of doing her pretend-work, she turned to Serina with a haughty look on her face that verged on the ridiculous.

"I told the Master you couldn't be trusted but would he listen to me? No, no, but now he will, he will listen to Effie now, because I told him about you and your... great plan! That's how you got caught, what do ya say about that, huh?" Effie squeaked in her high-pitched voice.

"I think you're as loony as the loon down in the dungeon Effie but... What do I know?"

"Be that' a way see if I care," Effie shrilled quite annoyed by Serina's lack of concern. Yet she aroused her untamable curiosity with her next statement.

"I have a secret way of finding out things around here, ya know. That's how I knew where your silly little necklace was. I took it when you were not looking and gave it to my Master. He was very happy to get it as you well know, but not near as happy as he was when I told him about your little plan to escape."

When Serina did not respond, she continued.

"I bet you can't guess how I knew where you put your necklace."

Effie was trying to taunt Serina, but it was not working.

"If you're talking about the secret floor in the wardrobe Effie I already know about it. Remember, that's how I made my way down to the dungeon."

Serina left Effie thinking about that for a moment while she went to the window pretending to ignore the whiny little maid. She figured, if the maid knew anything, this was the best way to get her to spill her guts.

Serina had not reached the window before Effie began spurting at her.

"You think you're so smart don't you, well I know something that no one else knows, not even my Master and I'll never tell."

"Come on Effie..." Serina turned around to face the girl.

"I'm sure you don't know *anything* that the other servants don't know – or your Master, the Great Takar –" (Serina thought she would add a note of admiration to her speech to give Effie a sense of security.) "I'm sure you don't know anything he doesn't know; he knows everything, remember?"

Serina could see from the look in Effie's eyes; she had succeeded in pushing the girl to the limit. If she knew anything she was about to blab it all. Serina turned back to face the window, hoping the move would push the maid into revealing her secret.

"There's a secret door... There, that's all I'm telling."

The skinny little maid stood in the middle of the room with her hands on her hips glaring at Serina with a fixed grin on her face, giving the impression that she was more simple minded than she actually was, if that were possible.

"Oh yeah, where is this secret door?" Serina asked a tad too anxiously.

"Nope, I'll never tell, told ya that I wouldn't tell and I won't."

Serina turned back to face the window as if what Effie knew didn't bother her, while, in fact it was driving her crazy. How was she going to get the silly little twit to tell her anything? Then it dawned on her – yes of course, by making Effie think she knew about a door also, maybe then she would tell what Serina wanted to know so desperately.

"I know where there's a secret door also Effie, it's probably the same door as yours."

"I doubt it, mine's in the dun..." Effie stopped in mid sentence, suddenly realizing that Serina was playing her for a fool.

"Wait a minute, where's your secret door at?" Effie demanded all of sudden.

Serina had to think fast now, it sounded like Effie was about to say the 'dungeon'... Here was hoping that she was right, "In the dungeon." Serina held her breath waiting on Effie to react.

"In the dungeon you say?"

"Yeah, that's what I said, now where's yours?" Effie looked perplexed.

"But that can't be, there's only one secret door in the dungeon I'm sure of it... Just where, down there, is this secret door you know of?" Effie pressed on.

"Oh no, you don't! Now it's your turn to tell me, where your secret door is or I won't tell you anything else."

Serina was sweating now... She dearly hoped the girl would take the bait and tell her where this door was. Yet, if Effie didn't fall into her trap and wanted for Serina to show her where her make-believe door was, she would be in trouble.

Effie pondered this in her feeble brain for a few seconds before responding to Serina's challenge.

"I don't believe you know where it's at. You're just saying that to get me to tell," Effie said.

"Ah, you're probably right, but then again, how did I know it was in the dungeon?"

"Mine is a special door, what about yours?" the maid quirked. She was getting rather annoyed with Serina.

Serina walked over to her bed and sat down looking at Effie.

"It's a door – a door is a door, what's so special about that except that you can walk through it, but I guess that would make all doors special, right Effie?"

Serina stretched out across her bed and let out a deep sigh. "I'm tired, I think I'll take a nap, I'm sure your secret door is special to you Effie but I'm tired. I didn't get much sleep last night you know. Close the door quietly when you leave, will you?" *That show of total indifference,* Serina thought, *should get her to talk, if nothing else would.*

There was a long pause. In fact, Serina began to think that Effie was actually going to leave without telling her where the door was. Then the girl surprised Serina with her next statement.

"I'll show you my secret door and then you will know how special it really is, come on let's go to the dungeon."

Serina didn't know if she could trust Effie enough to go to the dungeon with her but it was a chance she had to take.

"Okay, I'll go with you but it's just an ordinary door I'm sure."

"Come on you'll see," Effie insisted impatiently.

Serina started toward the door, but Effie suggested they go down through the door in the wardrobe, claiming it would be quicker and no one else could follow them.

Once down in the little room that led to the corridor, which opened up into the dungeon, Effie halted Serina in her tracks.

"We don't go that way," Effie said pointing to the door. "We go this way."

Serina looked in the direction to which Effie was pointing but all she saw was a solid rock wall.

"There it is – I told you it was a special door didn't I?"

Serina was shocked for a second, but then she remembered the cave wall and how it opened up.

"That you did Effie, but all I see there is a rock wall, does it open up or something?"

If the wall opened up into a doorway it wouldn't surprise her, Serina thought. Nothing would surprise her any more... How silly of her to be thinking that 'nothing would surprise her' – for Effie's next action completely floored her.

The maid walked up to the solid rock wall and stepped right through it and disappeared. Serina gasped – she couldn't believe it; Effie had vanished *through* the wall! How could that be? Even the cave wall *swung open*... Still bewildered Serina stepped toward the wall. It looked solid enough, she put a hand out and touched the rocks; they appeared to be solid.

"Effie! Where did you go?" Serina yelled in dismay. She looked around the room then back to the wall, *she was alone.* Just as she was about to retrace her steps leading her back to the tower, Effie popped back into the room *through* the rock wall.

"Effie where did you go? How did you do that?" Serina demanded.

Effie stood there with a wide smile on her face. "I told you it was a special door, now do you believe me?"

"How did you disappear?"

Effie laughed and grabbed Serina's hand. "Come on I'll show you."

Serina was still a little shocked and hesitated planting her feet wide apart and stiffening her body. She was not at all sure she wanted to walk *through* a rock wall or *into it*.

"It won't hurt, see..." Effie stuck out her other hand and pushed it through the rock. "You just go right through it like it wasn't there," she added reassuringly.

Effie drew her hand back out of the wall and waved it in front of Serina's face then stuck it back through the wall.

"Come on I'll show you where it leads and that's just as special as walking through it, come on."

Effie tugged Serina's arm and Serina yielded to the temptation to letting Effie lead her *into* and *through* the wall. There was nothing to it, it was just like walking through air and once through the wall they were in another corridor with torches on the walls to light their way.

When they reached the end of the hall, it appeared to open up right into the dungeon almost in front of Rupert's cell. *That is odd*, Serina thought, *why have I not seen this opening before?* If there was no door hiding this hall or corridor, why didn't she, or any of the others, notice it? No one mentioned it.

Serina stepped through the opening, all was quiet, and Rupert was lying on his bed sleeping. There appeared to be no one else in the dungeon except Toddle's crumpled body lying on the floor of his cell.

She walked down to Toddle's cell and began weeping uncontrollably.

"I'm so sorry Toddle, to have done this to you."

She reached through the bars and picking up his cold hand she pulled it through the bars pressing it to her wet cheek silently crying for a moment then she kissed his hand and placed it across his chest.

"Too bad about ole Toddle I rather liked him," said Effie, who stood at Serina's side, "he was always kind to me and the others, we all kinda looked up to him."

Serina stood up and faced the girl. "Thanks to your horrible Master, Toddle is dead now; how can you still obey him?"

"Yes'm I sure can – if I don't, I'd end up like ole Toddle there for sure."

"Haven't you ever wanted to escape from here, to leave this horrible place?" Serina asked, puzzled by the fact that everyone, in this stupid castle, except for her and her mother, thought it was the only place in the world to be.

"Come on I want to get back to my room before someone misses me," Serina urged suddenly as she headed toward the wall from whence they came only to find there was no opening where a gaping corridor should have been. "What happened to the opening, where did it go?" she blurted out in disbelief.

She spun on her heels to face Effie, who had a gloating grin on her face.

"I told you that this end was even more special than the door."

"What do you mean Effie? I don't feel like anymore games, where's the opening – where's the hall?" she shouted, which shouting caused Rupert to stir. The man rubbed his chin and head and went back to sleep.

Effie turned her back to Serina pouting and not saying a word.

"Okay Effie I'm sorry for yelling at you; now will you *please* show me the way out of here... Oh never mind, I'll find it myself," Serina in huff turned toward the rock wall but Effie beat her to it. She stood erect against the wall so that Serina could not find the opening.

"That's fine Effie I'll go the other way," Serina said shrugging her shoulders while making her way to the other door but Effie quickly gave up and moved. By this time Serina was beyond being frustrated. She returned to the rock wall, although she had a good mind to go back to the tower using the wardrobe route. She felt along the wall trying to find the opening but it was not there, finally giving up she turned to Effie.

"Will you show me the opening?"

Effie stood there with her arms crossed over her chest wanting Serina to beg. "Can't ya say Please!" Effie berated – enjoying every ounce of power she temporarily held over Serina.

"Okay, okay… Please," Serina replied rolling her eyes towards the ceiling – she had about all she could take from this simpleton.

Bowing stupidly, Effie turned around and stepped up to a certain spot in the rock wall.

"There is a special way you have to enter through the wall, you have to turn sideways facing the right or you can't get through. Like this."

Effie turned her left side to the wall, leaned into it and disappeared and a second later popped back into the dungeon.

"See how easy that was. I learned it quite by accident one day but even more special than that, is the other side of the wall. When you're on the other side of this wall you can see right threw it, remember when we came down through it earlier, we could see into the dungeon."

"Yeah that's right I do remember."

They both stepped up to the wall. Effie went first and moved through the thick rock without a problem. Once inside the wall, Serina turned back and sure enough, she could see right through the rock into the dungeon, so, actually, you did not have to go into the dungeon, you could see the whole inside of it while staying within the secret hallway.

"Very clever Effie, whoever thought that up was a genius."

"Now it's your turn to show me your secret door," Effie challenged suddenly.

Oh how Serina was hoping Effie would have forgotten about that. She could only imagine the fit Effie was about to throw when she told her she had lied. Serina took a deep breath, deciding to tell her the truth and be done with it.

"Well the truth of the matter is I don't have a secret door, I just said that because I thought you were making up your story as well."

Effie glared at Serina without speaking for a moment, her face turned red and she started breaking into a sweat.

"But it's okay Effie," Serina said quickly before Effie could say anything. "I promise not to tell anyone, it can be our little secret Effie. You and I will be the only ones who know of its existence."

Effie was still hot but seemed to be mulling this over for a minute... "No it's not okay," she burst out finally. "You lied to me, I'm gonna tell the Master, you're gonna be in a lot of trouble."

"Please Effie..." Serina had a sudden thought and decided to test it. "Wait a minute Effie, how did you find this secret wall anyway?"

"None of your concern, you're the one's in trouble not me."

"You watched Takar use this entrance didn't you? You wanted me to believe that you found it by accident. But the truth is you were probably spying on Takar and watched him go through here and that's why you won't tell. If he knew you saw him he would be very mad huh?"

"No! You're wrong," Effie yelled. "You're wrong I tell you."

When Serina saw beads of perspiration smearing the maid's forehead, she knew she had stumbled onto the truth.

"No, I don't think so. So now I know about the entrance and if Takar knew that I found out about it he would be very upset, am I not right Effie?" Effie stared silently at Serina. "Maybe he would be so upset that you could end up like Toddle."

"You shut up you hear, you shut up right now, the Master would not care."

"Oh really, Effie you and I both know, he would be furious but I will not tell on you. Like I said it can be our little secret, OK?"

Serina felt quite sure that she had persuaded Effie to keep her mouth shut, but she was still holding her breath – *you never know with these weirdoes,* she thought.

"OK!" Effie exclaimed. "Okay, but you shouldn't trick me like that," she added pouting and then stormed off up the hall leaving Serina alone in the secret corridor.

Serina headed back to the tower exhausted from so little sleep. She lay down on her bed thinking of the secret doorway to the dungeon – *if* she ever had the opportunity to use it, it could mean another escape route for her and her mother.

Next thing Serina knew Mertie was waking her up to get dressed for the big event.

"Just let me sleep Mertie, I'm so tired and surely don't want to go to the *celebration.*"

"Well little one, one doesn't always get to do what one wants, so get up and get dressed I'll help you, remember we don't want to upset the Master."

"Oh, that's right, silly me I forgot for a moment there. Well, I'll just hop up and get dressed and try not to forget such things as upsetting the Master," said Serina acidly.

"Don't get smart with me little one I won't put up with it. Now come on and let's get dressed."

Serina took the gown that Mertie was holding out for her and preceded to get dressed. It was a beautiful gown of pale lavender but Serina didn't notice how exquisite it was – she just got dressed and sat down so Mertie could fix her dark unruly hair. When she was finished she stood back to marvel at her handy work.

"Well Little Princess I have to say you look beautiful, as a little princess should look, not anything like the little munchkin that's been running around here lately snapping every one's head off when they would speak to her."

Serina only glanced in the mirror when Mertie asked what she thought of the hairdo, but when she didn't say anything

Mertie grunted and then snapped, "What's the matter? Forgot your manners?"

"No Mertie," said Serina duly. "It looks nice, thank you."

Well off you go but remember the rest of your things will be in the Floral Suite after the party so you will be going there instead of up here to the tower."

"Why do I have to move into another room? Why can't I just stay here, I've kinda gotten use to the tower, maybe Takar will let me stay here if I ask him."

"This ole tower is awfully drafty and not near as pretty as the Floral Suite, trust me you will like the Floral Suite much better than this ole tower," said Mertie. "Now scat the Master is waiting at the bottom of the stairs for you."

Takar was waiting for Serina at the bottom of the stairs, just as Mertie had said. He bowed to her as she stepped off the last stair never taking his eyes off her. His eyes were clouded revealing nothing of his mood making Serina wonder just what was on his evil mind.

"Just as lovely as I pictured you would be this evening Serina and without the sarcasm, I'm impressed to say the least."

"Thank you Takar," said Serina, just as sweetly as she could muster taking care to keep her loathing in check.

"Now before we go into dinner we have a few minutes so come and I will show you your new rooms."

Serina followed Takar up the stairs to the third floor; he stopped just beyond his own bedroom door at another door and turned the knob, swinging it open for her to step in. Takar stepped aside letting Serina enter into the suite of rooms ahead of him. There were three rooms in all. The sitting room, in which they were standing; to the right, there was the bedchamber and a small dressing room with a huge wooden bathtub in the center of it. Serina also noticed that most all of her things had been brought here and put away.

"It's very lovely Takar," Serina managed to say without any note of distaste in her voice.

"So you are pleased I take it," asked Takar watching her intently for any sign of deceit on her part.

"Yes, it's very lovely." And it was, and in any other circumstances she would love to have this as her own but she kept that to herself.

"Great now that you have approved of your rooms we can go down and join the others and of course you will be coming here tonight after our party, there will be no need for you to go back to the tower. Mertie and the others will have the rest of your things brought up here. So shall we?"

At these words, Takar held his arm out to her. As they left the room and headed back toward the large stairway, Serina hesitated for only a fraction of a second before dropping her hand on his arm but it was long enough for Takar to have noticed. Yet, he remained silent.

Chapter 23

The party was more lavish than the last one, if that were possible. Everyone who lived in and around the castle was in attendance dressed in their finest including all of the servants – the party was a huge success in fact. Serina played her part so well she caught herself being wrapped up in all of the excitement a time or two, but every time she did, she would remember something Takar had done and it would bring her back promptly to reality.

Close to the end of the feast, Takar stood clicking his glass with a fork to get everyone's attention.

"If everyone would allow me I have an announcement to make." He turned to face Serina then back to the crowd.

"Tonight Serina and I start our long journey; it's a journey of courtship that will end in marriage when Serina turns of age. This of course calls for a special toast."

Takar motioned to one of his servants, the one who had stayed in Serina's room the night before – Doak. Doak disappeared and returned quickly with something in his hand, which he handed to Takar.

"With this cup Serina and I will drink to our courtship and coming wedding in front of all of you so you will know and bear witness that we are bonded together for life and no one shall revoke our vows."

Another servant entered the room with a large bottle; he came to Takar's side and poured the crimson liquid into the cup, which Takar held in his hand. The cup appeared to be made of gold and was covered in rubies and emeralds; it had a rather large emerald in the center of the cup with smaller ones surrounding it.

Suddenly Serina remembered something her mother had told her – how she came about getting the emerald that was in her necklace. Serina's heart leaped into her throat her eyes frozen to the cup and the large emerald, she could hear everyone applauding and cheering. Serina's mind was racing. *This is not good; this is not good at all*, she thought, her eyes transfixed on the cup. *If Takar notices that the emerald has been replaced he will surely kill me.* What was she going to do; her mind was a total blank.

Takar took Serina's hand beckoning her to stand, and when she did not move quickly enough, he tugged at her arm and pulled her to her feet. As she pulled her eyes away from the cup and looked up into his eyes, she noticed just a trace of annoyance but it disappeared quickly.

"This is a special potion that has been passed down from my ancestors for generations. It contains the power and strength from the blood of a dragon and the pure and magical blood of a unicorn, which gives one, immortality." He then turned to Serina handing her the cup of thick red liquid, he paused briefly looking deep into Serina's eyes.

"Now, with this drink, you will be bonded to me for ever so, please Serina drink generously."

Serina took the cup but did not raise it to her lips; instead, she just stared at Takar. Her whole body was trembling and she could feel perspiration pearling on her brow.

"Serina I know you are nervous and with good reason, you are young, you see things through a child's eyes but trust me this is your destiny."

Serina had heard that enough times before now and knew how easy it would be for Takar to get his hands on her mother again if she did not do as he wished but she still hesitated, the last thing she wanted was to be bonded to this creature for the rest of her life.

Takar's eyes took on a demon like glow as he stood there watching her with the cup in her hands. He reached out and placed his hands around Serina's guiding the cup to her lips. Serina took a deep breath and placed the cup to her lips *pretending* to take a sip. Takar, noticing what she was up to, pushed the cup up higher spilling the dark red liquid into her mouth and onto her dress. Serina choked on the substance as it slid down her throat, she tried to cough it out but it was too late, the potion was now inside her and she was doomed to a life with this crazy mad man.

Takar took the cup from Serina's shaking hands to take a drink himself but just before the cup reached his lips the servant standing next to him turned quickly toward Serina knocking the cup of potion from Takar's hand to the floor spilling its contents and enraging the Dark Lord. "You clumsy fool," roared Takar but the whole room was watching Serina now.

Her legs had begun shaking badly. She was afraid they would not hold her. Her eyes rolled back, her knees finally giving out she collapsed to the floor like a wilted flower. A cloud of blackness engulfed her, as she lay slumped on the floor. The humdrum of voices that was swirling around her head vanished leaving nothing but silence, sweet, sweet silence.

Serina awoke late the next afternoon feeling drugged and sluggish. At first, she did not recognize where she was, but as all of the events of the last few days slowly dawned on her, she closed her eyes hoping to make it all go away. She was hoping to open her eyes in the safety of her little bed at home, in her father's house, in the tiny village where she grew up. Serina opened her eyes just a slit, slowly taking in her surroundings, she was not in her little bed back in her village; she was in the Floral Suite tucked in the huge bed that would make three of her one at home, and remembering everything that had taken place the night before, Serina suddenly felt sick to her stomach.

The potion, she thought, as she clutched her stomach with both hands. "What did he say was in that thing anyway? Something about dragons and what else was it... Oh yeah, dragon's blood and unicorn's blood for immortality," Serina said aloud feeling uncomfortable just at the thought of what she had been forced to drink. She sat up in the big bed her hands still clutching her stomach and added, "I feel more like I could die at any moment instead."

She reclined her head on the pillows and closed her eyes tightly as if by doing so it would change things back to the happy life she once knew.

It was a few more minutes before she managed to drag herself out of bed and get dressed. She searched through her clothing from the night before looking for her necklace since it was not around her neck. She could have sworn she was wearing it when she went down to the party... At last; there it was, tucked in with the discarded clothing on the floor. She slipped it around her neck feeling a little safer with it next to her body.

Hating the thought of seeing any one, especially Takar she slipped out of her room into the hall and proceeded down to the back servants' stairs. As luck would have it she didn't see anyone until she reached the kitchen, three of the kitchen helpers were busy preparing the evening meal. Doak, the huge guard, was also in attendance. Trying to slip past him, she headed toward the door leading to the back of the castle... Too late, he spied her and came walking toward her with a dark expression on his face.

"So the little Princess is finally awake and about time huh?"

Serina tried to ignore him but he wouldn't have it.

"What's the matter, cat's got your tongue?" he said with menace in his voice.

"No, I just have nothing to say, excuse me please."

Serina tried to get past him but he kept stepping in her way.

"Oh I get it; you think you're too good to talk to me, well let me tell you I'm not a servant I am a loyal guard to Takar and he values me very highly," Doak declared with pride. "I am the one he sends for when he needs something important taken care of. So don't forget it I may have to guard you again so it would do you good to be nice to me little one," he concluded as he glared threateningly at Serina who instantly melted with terror coursing down her spine – yet, she dared not show fear on her face or she would surely regret it.

"Well I'll try to remember that okay? Now if you will excuse me I have better things to do than to stand around talking with you." Serina slid past him before he could grab her arm and headed out the kitchen door.

She walked as fast as she could toward the back gardens so she could be alone for a while. She had so much on her mind, she just wanted to sit in the peaceful flower garden, smelling the enticing scents of the roses – this was the one place where she could find refuge while trying to forget everything around her.

Serina found an old wooden bench toward the back of the garden and slumped down onto it taking a deep breath and letting it out slowly, she closed her eyes, sitting without thinking of anything in particular, just sitting, and enjoying the warm sunshine on her face and the fragrant flowers that populated this tranquil landscape.

Serina had no idea how long she had been there when she was awakened by the distant sound of voices. Opening her eyes and sitting up straight she listened more closely to the vaguely familiar voices. It was Ernie and Talbert, the two men who had taken her mother and Koori out of the dungeon to safety two nights before. They were walking through the garden's hedge.

Serina could barely make out their words but one word did reach her ears. "Nora!" Serina leaned in the direction of the sound enabling her to listen to what they were saying a little better. Then as they came closer, she could hear them very well.

"And did ya see the look on the little one's face when she found out she wasn't going home like she thought?"

"Yeah and Nora she knew I think that's why she hushed the girl up, where she wouldn't get in more trouble, smart woman, huh."

"Yeah well not too smart she ended up in the tower anyways, now they have Doak guarding em and they bettered be watching themselves, ole Doak will give em what fer if they don't."

Serina could hardly believe her ears; her mother and Koori didn't get to go home as Takar promised – they were in the tower being held prisoners. She should have known better than to believe anything Takar told her, not only was he evil he was a liar as well.

Not wanting to alert the two of her presence Serina waited until they were clear out of sight then took off at a mad dash for the kitchen and the back stairs to her room. In her room feeling assured, no one saw her she paced her sitting room trying to think of what to do next. She knew if she tried to get into the tower through the hidden door in the floor of the wardrobe, it would have to be late at night when she felt almost certain Doak would be asleep or... Hey, he was just down in the kitchen earlier; maybe, just maybe, he will still be down there.

Serina rushed out of her room intending to make her way quickly toward the stairs again, but just outside her door she ran slap dab into Takar, he was coming out of his rooms.

"What's the rush?" Takar asked eyeing her with a hint of suspicion on his face.

"Oh nothing, just, uh, I haven't had anything to eat and thought I would head down to the kitchen for a quick bite of something," said Serina quickly avoiding his gaze and trying to sound nonchalant, hoping he would not notice the anxiety that was raging inside her.

"Oh, well then by all means go right ahead."

Serina quickly took off toward the back stairs, trying to get out of Takar's sight as fast as she could.

"I was just headed down that way myself, I would be pleased if you walked with me instead of taking the servants' stairs."

Serina stopped dead in her tracks and slowly turned around and walked back toward Takar.

"Sure, why not," said Serina just barely keeping her loathing in check. Oh, how she hated this man but she must not let on how she felt or she would end up in the tower along with her mother and Koori and that would not help her to free them.

"Really Serina, you must realize your place here. One day you will be queen of this whole kingdom and a queen does not take the servants' stairs," said Takar

The two headed down the main stairs to the ground floor together in silence much to Serina's surprise for she surely expected him to say something about the events of the night before but not a word fell from his mouth or hers.

Takar followed her all the way into the kitchen pretending to be a little hungry himself. He gave orders to one of the servants to put together two lamb sandwiches while Serina walked around pretending to look at all the kitchen gadgets hanging from the walls and on the shelves but in reality she was looking to see if Doak was still hanging around somewhere.

The two sat at the long table and Serina tried to eat the sandwich but she had no appetite. Knowing her mother and Koori were up in the tower being held prisoner made her stomach churn.

"What's the matter? I thought you were hungry?" asked Takar.

"I still don't feel too well Takar, so if you don't mind I think I will go back to my room."

Takar stood up as Serina got to her feet. "Maybe you will feel better by dinner time if not, I can send your dinner up with Mertie," said Takar with a guarded look on his face.

"Sure, that would be fine, th-thanks."

Serina left the kitchen and headed back to her rooms as quickly as she could without looking anxious because the last thing she wanted to do was to draw suspicion to her.

At about six thirty, Mertie arrived with a tray of food, which she deposited on the small table in the sitting room.

"So the little Princess is not feeling too well is it?" Mertie stated rather than asked as she sat the food down.

"Yeah, I must be catching something," murmured Serina, pretending to feel bad, she was sitting in the big overstuffed chair watching Mertie setting the table for her to eat hoping she would hurry and leave the room because smelling the food made Serina realize how hungry she really was since she had not eaten since the night before.

"Well maybe this will make you feel better; a little food never hurt anyone."

"Thank you Mertie, I will try and eat something, you're a dear for bringing it up to me."

"Oh don't make such a fuss, I'm just doing my job, you know we all have our jobs to do around here even you. Yap, we all have our own jobs to do, just doing my job... Oh well, there ya go Little Princess, ya table is all ready for you. Come sit down and eat a bite while it's still hot."

Serina pulled herself out of the big chair, made her way to the table, and took a seat. She was so famished she dove into the food immediately.

"Well you must already be feeling better, with an appetite like that, you need to slow down and taste what you're putting in your mouth, in other words eat like a young lady not like a little urchin."

"Sorry Mertie, I'm just hungry – must be the smell of good food that fixed my stomach right up."

"Well don't choke on the bones as they go down," said Mertie with a half smile on her face.

"I will see you in the morning ... goodnight Little Princess."

Mertie was already headed out the door as she spoke.

"Goodnight Mertie."

Serina hurried up with the last of her dinner, washing it down with a huge gulp of milk, wiping her mouth with her napkin, she shoved her chair out from under her and ran to the door to listen. She listened for any sign of activity in the hall – nothing, not a peep from anyone but it was still early, much too early to go slipping out and down the back stairs, she had to wait until she was certain everyone was in bed for the night before she dared slip out of her room.

Serina lay across her bed to wait until it was safe to leave and before long she drifted off to sleep not to wake until about two in the morning. Suddenly realizing how late it was, she jumped to her feet and ran to the door. She listened for a moment before she opened the door and stuck her head out looking up and down the hall but no one was about and everything was quiet. She listened for a moment longer then not hearing anything, she slipped out of her room closing her door softly as she went.

Serina headed for the back stairs and was soon at the bottom of the long spiral staircase that would lead her to the hidden door in the wardrobe in the tower.

She slowly made her way up the stairs to the hidden trap door, she listened for a moment for any sign of activity, she could not hear any noise but she waited for a few more minutes before she tried the door.

The door slid open above her without any effort, Serina slipped her tiny frame up through the opening, and when she was in the wardrobe, she slid the trap door back into position without a sound. She listened but heard nothing except the heavy sound of breathing from someone in deep slumber. She waited for a moment more then slowly opened the wardrobe and stepped out into the familiar room.

Serina's heart was in her throat. She stood motionless inside the shadow of the wardrobe not wanting to leave the security that the darkness offered. Once she got her fear under control, she stepped out into the moonlight that streamed in from the tower windows and slowly headed toward the bed where her mother and Koori lay sound asleep. She was almost to the middle of the room when she realized that the deep even breathing she had been hearing was not coming from the bed, but from the other side of the room – there was someone else in the room besides her mother and Koori.

Doak was leaning back in his chair and had fallen asleep, his mouth slack in peaceful slumber – *most likely dreaming of torturing some poor soul* – Serina thought while she had expected him to be outside the door, so now she would have to be utterly quiet.

She lowered herself to the floor and crawled the rest of the way to her mother's side of the bed. Once there she tapped her mother gently on the shoulder. Senora opened her eyes and was startled to see her daughter at her bedside.

"Shuuu," Serina whispered to her mother.

"It's me Serina, I came to get you out of here come on, I'll wake Koori."

"Serina," her mother whispered, "No."

"What?" Serina asked startled at her instant denial.

"You can't free us we're chained."

Senora pulled backed the covers and revealed the chains around her ankle.

"Koori is chained as well and besides Doak is across the room guarding us, there's no way we can get out of this, except for you... You are the only way to freedom – freedom for all of us."

"Oh Mother, I'm so sorry," Serina cried softly

"What happened anyway? I thought Takar told Ernie and Talbert to take you to the cave and let you go, he promised."

"He only told them that in front of you, he never had any plans of letting us go, we are his hold on you, don't you see? As long as we are captive, he can use us as leverage against you whenever need be. If you show sign of not succumbing to his will then he will show you that we're still his prisoners, forcing you to do as he wishes."

"But he prom... Of course, he did – he never meant to let you go. I see it now, I just don't know why it took me so long to realize it. I guess it was just wishful thinking on my part."

"Serina you have to confront him, battle him with all your might or he will forever hold us in captivity."

"Battle."

"That's what Rupert said, remember? Back in the dungeon before I took out of there to get my necklace from Takar, he looked into my eyes and said just one word – 'battle'."

Serina remembered the look in Rupert's eyes, those deep blue eyes, they were not eyes of a crazy man – they were the eyes of wisdom and strength."

"That's right, BATTLE." Serina said a little too loud causing Doak to stir in his sleep. Senora hushed her daughter placing a gentle hand over her mouth keeping Serina from any further outbursts.

"I just don't know how I'm going to battle it out with the mighty Takar when he can shoot fire from his fingers and kill someone on the spot, that's mighty powerful if you ask me - and me with my little green emerald... Yeah I can see where I can go up against something like that... Oh, not to mention that I don't even know how to fight anyone or use this dumb necklace in the first place... Are we supposed to use swords or what?"

Serina was starting to get worked up and her voice was getting louder once again.

"Shuuu, Serina you will wake Doak and then we will all be in chains."

"Okay," Serina whispered.

"But I can't help it I don't know what to do. I don't know how to do battle."

"Just think of him as Amil, you're always outwitting Amil aren't you?" Koori whispered, as she raised herself up on one elbow. She was now fully awake and looking at her friend quizzically. "I was wondering how long it would take you before you found out we were up here."

"Koori! Outwitting Amil is one thing, taking on this powerful monster is another." Serina reached over her mother and thumped her friend on the forehead.

Koori reached over and thumped Serina back.

"What I mean is, use your head; you do not have to be more powerful than he is necessarily to win the battle Serina. If you can out-wit him, then you will have beaten him, just like you always do with Amil or anyone else. Use your noggin that's what it's up there for, gees do I have to do all the thinking for you?"

"If you're so smart you go battle him for me."

"Well Serina you're the one with the power and the necklace so I guess that leaves me out and besides I am a little chained up at the moment."

Koori pulled back her side of the covers pointing to her leg revealing her chains as well.

They all hushed at the same time turning to look across the room where Doak was stirring in his chair, he straightened for a second rolled his head around making a loud pop in his neck then leaned his head back up against the wall.

The three waited for what seemed an eternity before anyone of them spoke again.

"Serina you had better go before you get caught, I can only imagine what would happen to you, please go – go now," Senora pleaded with her daughter quietly.

"Yeah Serina you can't fight ole Takar if you're locked up in here with us," Koori whispered.

"You're right, I will figure this out one way or another and I will beat him at his own game, you watch and see, just watch."

Serina raised herself from the floor where she had been kneeling next to the bed.

"You must be strong Serina and keep your wits about you, don't let him get into your head or he will overpower you for sure."

"Thanks Mother, I will and I will be back for you soon, Koori watch out for her okay?"

"I will Serina, don't worry about us we'll be right here waiting for you."

Then, without another word, Serina crawled to the wardrobe and slipped inside and through the trap door before she would allow herself to take a deep breath. What was she going to do? And how was she going to do it?

She silently climbed the servant's stairs to the third floor and into her rooms while the castle lay in slumber but instead of climbing into her bed she walked over to the window and gazed onto the shadowy sleeping castle grounds, her mind in terrible turmoil.

Chapter 24

Serina waited to go down to breakfast the next morning until she felt certain Takar had finished his breakfast and was gone. She surely did not want a confrontation with him, not knowing if she would be able to keep her knowledge of her mother and Koori chained in the tower from him. She had to avoid him as much as possible until she figured out how she was going to face him.

When Serina reached the bottom of the main stairs, she overheard voices coming from a closed door to her left. Curiosity getting the best of her she eased over toward the door. As she got closer, she could make out the voices and recognized one of them as Takar and the other man's deep rough voice was none other than Doak the *loyal guard* that Takar used for *special occasions* as she remembered him saying to her the day before, if her memory served her correctly.

The two were in a deep conversation about something or someone from what she gathered, but the voices were too muffled for her to understand what was said. She then stepped closer to the door so she could hear them better.

"Never mind what I said earlier, I'm telling you now she is to be watched at all times until I say otherwise, do I make myself clear?"

"Yes Sir, perfectly clear."

"Will you need me for your little midnight ride tonight or do you want me to stay in the tower again guarding the two women?"

"Stay in the tower, I will not be needing any help for what I have to do."

"As you wish, Takar."

"Good, now leave me I have to go check on the new batch of potion. I can not believe that imbecile knocked the whole cup of potion from my hand, spilled every last drop but he will not have the opportunity to do that again," said Takar darkly, still very perturbed by the whole incident.

"Yes of course."

So, Takar was making another batch of that awful potion! What else was he up to that would be taking him out at midnight? Serina ran back to the stairs climbing up several steps at once so as not to be noticed when Doak came out of the room. She pretended to be just coming down when the man emerged from the room; he strode off through another door without even noticing her standing on the stairs.

As soon as he was out of sight, she made a run for it, down the stairs and to the back into the kitchens before Takar had a chance to catch her out in the foyer plus she was hungry and was hoping she could get some breakfast before it was too late.

Mertie spied her and ambled over to her.

"Well is the little Princess late for breakfast? Did ya sleep in a bit this morning?"

"Yes Mertie. As... as a matter of fact I did, still feeling a little poorly but I thought one of your wonderful breakfasts would make me feel all better."

"Oh ya did, did ya?" Mertie laughed and patted Serina on the shoulder.

"Child I just deliver the food I don't make it, they do."

She pointed to the four women working around in the kitchen, one was hanging up a huge stew pot and another was cutting up vegetables on a worktable the other two were washing up the breakfast dishes in two huge wooden tubs.

"Oh, is it too late to get something to eat?" asked Serina.

"I just so happened to have a little put away for a little Princess who, I noticed, was not at breakfast."

Mertie walked over and picked up a tray covered with a large white napkin and brought it over to Serina,

"Thank you Mertie."

Serina took the tray, sat down at the servants table, and uncovered the food. Suddenly remembering her manners she took the napkin, placed it on her lap, picked up her spoon, and proceeded eating in such a mannerly fashion it surprised even Serina herself.

All the while Serina ate she was wondering where Takar was going so late at night after everyone was in bed asleep. What was he up to?

She was almost finished with her breakfast when Doak came strolling into the kitchen. Not noticing her at first he walked over to one of the servants and started instructing them in some special something he wanted done then as he turned to leave he noticed Serina sitting at the table in the back up against the wall.

"Well, well, well look at what we have here, the little princess eating her breakfast in the kitchen with the servants."

He walked over to where Serina sat and pulled up a chair and sit down next to her, he had a nasty grin on his face, kinda like he was up to something sneaky.

"How's our Little Princess today?"

Serina wanted to ignore him but was afraid that would only make matters worse.

"Just fine."

She glanced up but she would not look him in the eye instead she turned her attention back to her nearly empty bowl stirring her spoon around in what was left of her porridge.

"So, you had a late night last night?"

Serina whipped her head around so fast it made her dizzy.

"Maybe you were out roaming the halls, you know just couldn't sleep... Or... maybe you were just out up to something sneaky."

"What are you talking about?" Serina flared. "I was..."

"...out wondering about in the halls," Doak interrupted her in mid sentence, forcing her to look at him.

Serina glared at him not knowing what to say.

"I have my little spies Serina, there's not much you can do without me knowing about it, I even know things that Takar doesn't know about."

Serina still had not spoken another word she just stared at him in disbelief.

"So, you must be verrrry careful around this castle, that is, if you're up to no good, going around sneaking into places you shouldn't be, it could end up being very dangerous for a young girl such as yourself, who knows you might run into a monster or something."

"Well... There are plenty of those around, right Doak?"

"If I were you, I would mind my tongue, it could be very harmful to you, you little bit of nuisance," Doak snickered.

"Having a little bit of a chat you two... Ah Serina, I see you finally came down for breakfast."

The two had been so engrossed in there little conversation that neither one of them noticed Takar walking up behind Doak.

"Yes, I slept in this morning, still a little bit out of it I guess."

Serina was even more afraid than before, not knowing how much, if any of the conversation Takar might have overheard. She peered into his eyes searching for some clue but his expression was guarded as usual.

"Serina when will you learn, your place is not in here with the servants. I will not have you eating in the kitchen again, is that understood?"

"I'm sorry Takar I just didn't want to eat in that big dining room by myself and I didn't see the harm in coming back here to eat."

"You could have sent one of the servants for me, I would have gladly come and sit with you so you would not have been alone. So, now there is no excuse for you to be hanging around the kitchens any more."

"Yes Takar, I will remember that."

He turned his gaze toward Doak then while Serina breathed a small sigh of relief, she returned her attention to the bowl of now very cold porridge and stirred it slowly with her spoon. She was confused about Doak's statement. Had he seen her last night in the tower, or had someone else seen her in the halls and reported it back to him? If so, why reporting to Doak and not to Takar and if it had been someone else – then who – she wondered. She let go of her spoon and stood up wanting to get as far away from these two as she could without being obvious about it.

"Takar and Doak had stepped a few feet away and were deep in conversation so neither one saw Serina slipping out the back door. She headed out toward the back garden again so she could be alone to think, she had a lot of thinking to do.

Serina almost reached the garden when she saw someone going into the dragon's lair. She stopped and watched for a moment to see if she could recognize who it was. She knew it was not Takar because she had just left him and Doak in the kitchen. So who would be going in there? She made her way toward the big barn curiosity getting the best of her as usual. When she got there, she poked her head through the door but it was so dark inside that she couldn't see anything clearly. She looked around to make sure Takar, or no one else had observed her then eased herself just inside the big doors quickly stepping side ways into the barn so to remain in the shadows. She waited until her eyes grew accustomed to the semi darkness then inched her way further into the barn to get a better look at the man and at what he was doing in the dragon's den.

Serina crept up to a large pile of hay that lay on the floor not too far from where the dragon lay snoozing. She looked around for the man but did not see him at first. Then from the corner of her eye, she caught a glance of someone moving toward the dragon from the far back corner of the barn. It was *he*, the man she had seen entering the barn a few minutes earlier. She dove into the pile of hay to hide from his view but then realized that she could no longer see what was going on – she wiggled through the hay noiselessly just enough to poke her head up and peer out through the straw without being seen.

The man was dragging some type of animal carcass over toward the dragon. *He must be the dragon's keeper,* Serina thought. She had seen the man before but never thought about what his duties were at the castle. She watched him as he fed the huge animal; he was singing an old tune and talking to the dragon as if he were talking to a young child.

"Don't ya worry none, now you know ole Deeker will take good care of ya, don't ya?"

The dragon rose to his full height and for a moment Serina thought ole Deeker was going to be part of the Dragon's lunch but then the huge beast reached down and grabbed the whole animal carcass into his mouth and began chewing.

Serina lay in the hay watching the dragon munching the dead animal, bones and all. He was definitely huge reaching almost to the roof of the barn but he was also very beautiful. His long wings tucked in behind his front legs while his tail curved out into an S shape behind him. This was the first time Serina had a chance really to look at him and he was a magnificent creature, dangerous but magnificent.

She had no idea how long she lay there in the hay watching the dragon and the man when she heard a familiar voice coming from the doors behind her.

"Deeker!"

"Yes, I'm over here your highness."

Serina scooted back into the hay a bit making sure she was covered for fear of being found but not before she noticed that Doak was with Takar.

"Have you fed him up real good?"

"Oh yes sir, he has just finished his breakfast sir and I might add I threw in a little extra treat for him," said Deeker as he bowed before Takar.

"Excellent, I don't want you to feed him this evening I am going to take him out sometime later tonight and he doesn't fly as well on a full stomach, make sure he is clean you know how I hate getting my robes dirty from riding."

"Yes sir your highness, I will get right to grooming him as soon as he's had a chance to let his food settle."

"Oh Deeker be careful he doesn't toast you up for an afternoon treat, you know how he gets if he misses a meal."

"Oh sure Master, I won't forget, I'll be careful and I will have him some nice supper waiting for him when you return. Oh might I ask the Master where he is off to tonight?"

"Never mind where I'm off to Deeker just have him ready."

Serina heard Doak sneaker at Takar's remark.

Takar and Doak left the barn leaving Deeker staring after them. As soon as they were out of sight he turned his attention back to the dragon, who was curling up for his morning nap. Then the man went back to singing and talking to the beast. He picked up a large grooming brush and began stroking the dragon as he sang.

Oh come with me to the dragon's lair
And I'll show you something special there
Oh no, no don't you worry none
He's just a wee little dragon.

So whatever Takar was up to, he needed to ride his fire eating dragon to do it. *He must be going far away to ride the dragon. Where then was he going? What was he going to do?*

Serina lay quietly in the hay pondering her thoughts for what seemed like hours on end until finally the man left the barn, leaving the now sleeping dragon curled up in his bed of straw.

Waiting for a few more minutes making sure no one was around; she eased out of the hay very carefully as not to wake the dragon and slipped out of the barn through a loose board she had noticed earlier. Once outside she glanced around looking for anyone who might be near – there was no one in sight so she crept along the back side of the barn until she reached the corner of it. There, she once again checked for anyone who might be wandering about the grounds. She preferred to be by herself with her thoughts. At the back of the barn she was not in sight of the castle and hidden from anybody wandering the grounds – that's what she wanted. She took this opportunity to explore something, she had never really noticed before – all of the little buildings scattered around the castle grounds, she had seen several but had not paid attention to what they were.

At a closer glance, she noticed that some were houses. *Funny*, she had assumed that everyone lived inside the castle but now she realized that some of the servants actually lived out here in these small shabby shed like houses.

You would think, Serina thought, *that as big as the castle was Takar would at least let them all live in it too.*

She watched a couple of small children playing near one of the old run down houses. They seemed happy and content while they ran and played with an old ball someone had fashioned from a piece of wood.

Serina found a large rock at the edge of a clearing farther away yet from the barn and the houses. She climbed over the top of it, stretched out and while using her arm for a pillow, she let the warm afternoon sun gently caress her. Here finally, she could be alone with her thoughts and try to figure out what she was going to do.

She was so confused that she didn't know where to start first. She had to get her mother and Koori out of that tower and she knew that she had to confront Takar but how, when and where was beyond her at the moment. What was Takar up to that was going to take him away from the castle in the dead of night? It had to be something sneaky and evil knowing him.

She remembered when he came to her village, taking her in the middle of the night; was he going to do something like that again or was he up to something worse. With her mother locked up in the tower, she could not even get to her to tell her about it. She knew she was watched, so sneaking up to the tower to talk with her was out of the question; she had to figure this out on her own.

The birds overhead were chirping and singing, they were so happy, there only concern was where to get their next worm for dinner. Serina wished that was all she had to worry about, if only she were a bird then she could fly into the tower and free her mother and friend and they could all fly away together, happy forever more.

Oh well so much for wishful thinking, she thought. Then something suddenly dawned on her – the night Takar took her from the dungeon he made the remark that he was not afraid of her and her silly little necklace – well that must be because he thinks the necklace is not powerful, he has no clue that the stone in her necklace is actually the stone from his scepter. He did not know that Senora had changed the stones. "Outsmart him," that was what Koori said and if he thought her emerald was worthless then maybe she did have the advantage over him. She jumped off the rock making a mad dash back to the castle; a plan was already forming in her mind. "It just might work." She shouted gleefully. "It just might, by gollies, work."

Serina asked if she could have lunch in her room instead of the dining room not wanting to give Takar a chance to figure out what was on her mind. She didn't think she could pretend to be happy, plus it gave her a chance to be alone to go over her plan, it had to work, this could be her only chance and she had to take it.

Sometime after dinner, Takar knocked on her door just as Serina thought that he might. When she did not answer, he knocked again rather loudly then entered the room in a rush.

Serina pretended to be asleep and rose slightly from under the cover as he entered her bedchambers.

"Yes Takar, what is it?"

He stared at her for a second not knowing what to say; she knew he did not expect to find her in bed let alone in her rooms at all, this of course gave Serina one up on him and she smiled inwardly at his confusion.

"I... came to see how you were feeling, are you sick? Is there something you need? You know; medicine or something."

"No, I'm fine."

He probably thought she was dying and his chances of becoming more powerful were fading along with her, because she knew he was not genuinely concerned for her health other than for his own selfish reasons.

He bent down close to Serina revealing his scarred face and touched her forehead, checking for a fever she reckoned. Then he drew his hand back and standing to his full height declared.

"You do not feel feverish."

"No, no Takar I'm just a little tired I guess all the excitement of the last few days has gotten to me and I just need to... Well, rest, I should be better by tomorrow."

"Well then if you are sure I will leave you be and hopefully you will be joining me for breakfast in the morning."

He stated this last remark more as an order than a request. With that, he spun on his heels and left her chambers his robes billowing out around him like a cloud of blackness leaving Serina staring after him with her mouth agape.

She yanked off the covers, leaped off the bed fully dressed and ran to the door after him listening for any sounds outside the door but all she heard was silence.

"Yes sure Takar, right after I free my mother and Koori and take care of you for ever," said Serina feeling brave now that she was alone again.

Chapter 25

Waiting until just before midnight and to ensure everyone was tucked in for the night, Serina stepped to her door and opening it just enough to look up and down the passage just in case anyone was up and wandering the halls. There was no one in sight so she eased through her door and headed for the servants stairs. Finding no one about she slipped down the stairs and headed for the dragon's lair hoping to get a clue as to where Takar was going then she could go back up to the tower and get her mother and Koori out of there and home before Takar came back. After which she could deal with him without worrying about their safety.

Serina made it to the barn safely without anyone detecting her. She eased her way around to the back of the barn and slipped in through the loose board she had used earlier in the day. She listened carefully for anyone who might have heard her sneaking in. There were three men in the barn Takar, Doak and Deeker. They were all three busy getting the dragon ready for Takar's little nighttime excursion and did not hear Serina. She found her way to the large pile of hay where she had been hiding that morning and buried herself deep into the straw out of sight. There she listened, straining her ears to catch a phrase or a word that would give her a clue as to where Takar was going and how long he would be gone, surely one of them had to say something.

The dragon was laying down on his belly while Deeker finished wiping him down, he shone like black glass in the dim light, he was a magnificent looking creature; even if he was dangerous Serina could not help admiring him.

"Hurry up Deeker, you're wasting my time, I told you to have him ready by midnight."

"Yes Master, he's almost ready, I wanted to make sure he was clean – to keep from soiling your robes, Master."

"Yes, yes, well hurry up."

"Yes, Master."

Deeker went back to rubbing down the dragon and Takar turned to Doak.

"Make sure you watch the tower closely; I don't want to take a chance of Serina finding out that I have her stupid little friend and her mother locked away up there. I want it to be a surprise for later in case I have to use it against her."

Serina lay there quietly under the hay listening to the two men talking.

"Too late Takar," Serina whispered to herself.

"How long will you be gone?"

"I should be back in a little while, it doesn't take long to burn a village to the ground and when I'm done there will be nothing for Serina to go back to and with her mother and friend held captive, there will be nothing she wouldn't do to keep them safe. I will show her who she is dealing with, I will have her at my beck-and-call."

So that was what he was up to, he was going to burn her village – destroy it along with everyone in it!

"On second thought Doak, go fetch Serina from her room. I think I want her to see this first hand – then there will be no doubt in her mind and she will know that all she has to cling to is her mother and little friend and if she doesn't want something to happen to them – she will do as bidden, so hurry go fetch her for me."

Serina took hold of the necklace that hung around her neck, clutching it tightly, giving herself a little more courage and, without another moment's hesitation, she came out of her hiding place.

No need for that Takar, I'm right here," said Serina stepping out into the middle of the barn startling Takar and the others.

All three men spun around in one movement to see the small girl standing before them. She had straw in her hair and clinging to her clothing from hiding in the hay. She looked like a scared little street urchin.

"Well, well, well, looked who we have here and just in time my dear I want to take you on a little trip."

"You're not taking me anywhere an, an, and you're not go, going either," Serina spluttered nervously. Her heart was in her throat making it difficult to speak.

"Oh, and just who is going to stop me? You? You and your silly little useless necklace, seriously Serina you make me laugh."

"That's right, me Takar."

Serina was shaking so hard she knew she had to get a grip on herself or else she would be useless against him.

"I heard what you said about destroying my village, I heard everything and I'm afraid I can't let you do that, you will not have a hold over me like you do over everyone else here."

Takar took a step toward Serina, she edged back a foot or two, and her hand automatically flew to her breast seeking her necklace – double-checking. She knew it was there but she was just making sure it had not vanished by some unforeseen something. She knew she had no chance against Takar without it. Her fingers felt the emerald close to her heart and she drew in a deep breath to steady herself.

Doak and Deeker were standing there watching Serina and Takar. Doak had an evil smile on his face but she was unable to read Deeker's expression.

"Come now Serina do not make me angry, I get very upset when I get angry as you should very well know by now."

"Oh I know how evil you are Takar. I should not have believed you when you said you would free my mother and

Koori – silly me I thought for once you were actually going to be good at your word, but I know now that you are incapable of doing anything nice or good. You would have to have a heart to be able to be nice and we both know that is one thing in this world that you do not possess."

"That's right Serina, now come to me; I am tired of fooling with you."

He lunged for Serina but she backed away. From the corner of her eye she saw Doak moving behind her so she skirted around so as to have Doak and Takar in front of her again. Takar put up his hand toward Doak.

"Leave her to me Doak, I do not need any help with a wee little brat as this."

"You will regret ever trying to go against *The Great Takar.*" He yelled the last few words at the top of his lungs causing both Deeker and Doak to step back in fear. Serina trembled but held her ground staring at Takar watching for his next move. Whatever it may be she had to be ready and she would have to be quick.

Takar raised his right arm and stretched out his hand but Serina knew what to expect. When he shot a fiery bolt from his fingertips, she dropped and rolled to one side just barely missing the hot flame as it hit the ground where Serina had just been standing. She quickly jumped back to her feet ready for his next shot.

"Outsmart him, out think him," her mind was racing but she didn't have time to plan her next move, she barely had time to jump out of the way again as Takar shot another bolt of fire at her feet. This was not exactly the way she imagined the battle between her and Takar would be.

"You are very quick Serina but you will wear down soon letting your guard down out of exhaustion then I will finish this little game up and we can be on our way, I still have a village to destroy you know."

He was toying with her as a cat would a mouse before he sat in for the kill, how much longer she had before evading him became useless, she did not know.

From somewhere behind a pair of hands grabbed Serina around her waist; she had been so busy jumping out of the way of Takar's fire blasts she had not noticed Doak sneaking up behind her. She fought him but he was much too strong for her. He was laughing as he dragged her over to Takar shoving her into his Master's arms.

"Now we can finish this Serina the easy way or the hard way it is up to you."

"I don't think so Mister, let her go!"

Takar whirled around slinging Serina with him to look upon the intruder or intruders, as it turned out to be.

Amil and Frog stood just inside the doorway of the barn. In the midst of all the commotion, no one had heard the two of them coming in.

"What now? And who might you be? I need to know these things before I kill the both of you."

"Never mind that; just let her go," said Amil authoritatively – Serina had never seen or heard that side of Amil before now.

"Yeah or we might have to hurt you," Frog threw in rather matter-of-factly.

"Ohhhhh, I see," said Takar derisively grimacing in despise.

"Run you two before he kills you," Serina blurted out.

"Ah, see Serina, you are getting smarter by the minute."

"We're not afraid of you, you big ugly troll," Frog shouted.

"You should be," were Takar's only words. The next thing Serina knew he was flinging her from his right hand to his left. She knew what he was about to do and forced herself free of his hold grabbing his right arm and pulling it down toward the ground screaming at the two boys at the same time.

"Run!"

Takar threw her away from him and turned back toward Amil and Frog but they were already out of sight.

He turned to Doak who was standing nearby. "Find them and bring them to me."

Doak took off toward where the boys had been standing; but he had not noticed where they had gone because he had been too busy watching Takar instead of the boys.

Takar turned his attention back to Serina who was crawling away trying to hide. She scrambled to her feet and turned to run but she ran right into the huge dragon, which was on his feet now and watching her very closely.

She quickly ducked under the dragon's legs and out of Takar's sight. The dragon turned his head in Serina's direction, keeping his enormous yellow eyes on her, all the while quietly watching her, and that's when Serina noticed for the first time that one of the dragon's legs was held by a huge chain, which was securely fastened with a bolt to the ground. She had never observed this before because every time she had been in the barn the dragon had been lying down or its paws had been hidden under the straw. Serina backed up a few feet keeping eye contact with the dragon in fear he might roast her up like Takar was trying to do.

She made her way around to the dragon's tail, trying to keep her eye on the beast while watching Takar's every move at the same time. She stepped backwards carefully toward the rear of the barn; her heart was pounding so loudly she could not hear anything else.

The dragon kept staring at Serina, his head following her, watching her curiously.

"Please, please do not eat me Mr. Dragon," Serina pleaded silently as she made her way ever so cautiously to the back of the barn and out of Takar's sight.

To her surprise the dragon just watched her and did not move. Except for his roving eyes, he stayed motionless staring after her as she crept into the darkness and out of the realm of dim light that shone from the torches hanging sparsely along the barn's walls.

Serina was in complete darkness now out of sight of everyone but she knew the dragon could still see her and she could hardly swallow for the huge lump in her throat, which was her heart.

She could hear Takar on the other side of the dragon shouting at Doak and Deeker and from the sound of his voice; they had not found Amil and Frog. *Now if they would just stay hidden, out of sight… What were they doing here anyway? Doesn't anyone listen anymore?*

They were supposed to wait for her in the village along with Koori. Of course, it had been a few days since they left the dungeon so maybe they got tired of waiting but their timing could not have been worse, Serina thought. Now she had to watch out for the both of them as well.

"Serina!" Takar shouted. "I know you can hear me so I will make myself very clear and I will only give you this one last chance," Takar continued.

Serina listened but did not move from where she stood for fear of being seen.

"If you would like I can go to the tower and fetch your little friend or perhaps your mother, maybe one of them can persuade you to listen to me… If you heard one of them scream a time or two, you would be more receptive and willing to do as I say. As I said earlier I am tired of playing these little games of yours."

She could hear the cynicism in his voice and she knew he would not hesitate in killing one of them to make his point clear. She just hoped that Amil and Frog had gotten away safely.

"You have to outwit him" was what Koori said; *yes, outwit him, but how?* Well she didn't have time to think now because if she didn't show herself soon Takar would send someone to the tower.

"Okay you win Takar," said Serina as she emerged from out of the darkened corner of the barn.

"You do not have to send for my mother, I am here." Serina walked slowly toward the dragon keeping her eye on him as she went for fear of being swallowed up since she just remembered that the poor beast had not been fed since breakfast.

When she emerged out from behind the dragon, Takar stood waiting for her.

"A wise move Serina, a wise move indeed," Takar sneered. "Now come to me."

He held out his hand but Serina hesitated, she knew if he took hold of her she would have no chance. *No,* Serina decided silently, she must keep her distance and fight him with all her might. If she lost then she would know that at least she had given it her best shot.

"I don't think so Takar, I will not bow down to you and I will not give in."

Takar raised both his arms in the air and roared like a wild animal caught in a trap causing both the dragon and Serina to jump back a step.

The dragon turned his gaze on Takar momentarily, curiously watching him then he backed up a few more feet; Serina was thinking that the dragon was thinking he best get out of the way and so was Serina, she backed up a few more feet along with the dragon.

"Serina you have tried my patience long enough now you will pay for it."

Takar was quick with his next step, shooting a fiery bolt from his fingertips but Serina was a little faster. She jumped into the side of a hay pile just in time to miss his deadly torch as it hit the ground where she had been standing, catching some straw on fire. She knew she could not hide in the hay any longer for fear of burning with it. Quickly she crept out from under the hay and crawled on her hands and knees to get behind some old wooden crates that stood not far away.

"Come out, come out from wherever you are Serina, I am tired of these little games you play; you can not hide from me forever."

She knew this but she did not know what to do next. Takar solved her dilemma a few minutes later when he caught the pile of hay on fire where she had been hiding. It started burning quickly and before she knew it, it was completely ablaze, causing the dragon to go utterly berserk. The huge beast started flailing around, and his long tail whirled about knocking things down in panic.

"Java," Takar yelled at the beast trying to settle him down some but the dragon did not listen, he kept pulling at his chain trying to get loose, the animal was definitely afraid.

Takar saw Serina hiding behind the crates and he ran toward her. Escaping capture, she ran from behind the crates toward the back of the barn and into the shadows again, hoping Takar would not see her. Unfortunately, she tripped over something on the floor and stumbled to her knees. She tried to get up but Takar had spotted her and was rushing toward her. She felt she could not get away in time but she bravely climbed to her feet and began running again as fast as she could. She could not see anything in front of her but a wall of darkness – smoke was invading the barn rapidly.

Serina had run only a few more feet before she ran into something else, something big – Deeker. She gasped and he shoved his hand over her mouth quickly preventing her from screaming. Then he grabbed her by the arm and pulled her in the direction of the other side of the barn, deeper into the darkened shadows. Serina didn't utter a word she just let Deeker pull her along and wondered what he was doing. Was he taking her to Takar, if so he was headed in the wrong direction?

Deeker stopped running suddenly and grabbed Serina by the shoulders.

"Listen to me, your friends are hiding in the back of that old cart over by the door. Go get them and get out while I divert the Master away from you."

Serina stared up at the old man in the darkness not sure what to say, she could not see his face just the outline of him standing there before her.

"Why are you...?"

"Go!" he whispered shoving Serina with both hands. "Go before I get my wits back and turn ya over to the Master." He shoved her again harder this time and Serina took off in the direction he had pointed. She turned around to thank him but since she could not see him in the darkness, she turned back and headed toward the old cart and the door to freedom.

She heard a loud commotion behind her and she stopped running to listen.

"Deeker what are you doing back here I thought you were out helping Doak look for those two boys?"

"Yes Master. I thought I saw one of them run back here."

"You stupid twit that was the girl don't you know the difference between a boy and a girl."

"Ye, yes Master. I guess I was wrong."

"Get out of my way," roared Takar.

Serina heard a loud noise and knew Takar had shoved Deeker into something, most likely knocking him down in the process.

When she got to the cart she climbed up its side looking over the edge hoping to see something – anything. Suddenly, a hand grabbed her, yanking her into the cart. It was Amil.

"What are you two doing back here I thought I told you to stay in the village and wait for me there," scolded Serina. She was rather put out with the two and for good reasons.

"Well, we got tired of waiting. We've been here for two days trying to find you. We've been hiding out behind one of the old houses near the woods staying out of sight. Besides, I never did like taking orders from a girl," said Amil, he was a little angry with Serina for not even thanking him for saving her life from 'that thing in the hood'. *Ungrateful little imp she is,* he thought.

"Have you seen Koori, did she come back?" asked Frog

"Yes Frog she's here, you two should have listened to me, now you're in more danger than before."

"You know you could at least thank us for saving you from that ogre that was holding you when we got here... Talking about being in danger, well it looked to us like you were the one in danger, or were the two of you just playing around?"

"Urg, you, you make me so mad, sometimes I think you two have mutton stew for brains and... Oh forget it," snapped Serina.

"Forget it?"

"Yes?" Serina demanded.

"We don't have time to sit around in this cart discussing it, we gotta get out of here now so come on and I will show you a place to hide."

"Hide? We are not going to hide and let a little girl do the fighting, we are men and men do the fighting not girls," Frog boasted sharply.

"Frog, you are no match for Takar. If he catches you he will surely feed you to his dragon after he is through toying with you, so please you have to hide."

Serina started to climb out of the cart but Amil drew her back in.

"Serina I know you are supposed to do battle with this mad man but he will kill you for sure, I just got a glance of what he is capable of, so let's get out of here together."

"No Amil, I have to do this or we will all die, my mother and Koori are chained up in a tower. I thought he let them go but he hid them away instead. You and Frog would be there too, if not dead, if you had not left here when you did."

"Serina."

"No! Listen to me you've got to get out of here while you can, come on."

She turned around and crawled out of the cart and into the waiting arms of Doak.

"I found them Master there over he…"

Both Amil and Frog jumped on Doak's back knocking him to the floor and Serina kicked him in the shin. Frog found an old bucket and shoved it over the top of Doak's head. Then, all three ran as fast as they could out of the barn around the side into the thick trees. They squatted on the ground once they had ran about ten or fifteen feet beyond the dense tree line.

"I'm gonna tell you how to get into the tower and get my mother and Koori out, listen carefully. Since Doak is here there may not be anyone guarding them but if there is someone, he might be asleep and you can take him by surprise."

"Serina I can't let you do this, without at least helping you," said Amil.

"You would be helping me Amil if you would get my mother and Koori free."

"We will be back as quickly as we can. Oh, and Serina, save some of the fighting for us, you know, so we will not lose face when this tale is told later."

"I will Amil, I promise." Serina smiled.

Serina, Amil and Frog ran to the back of the barn, once they were there and out of sight, Serina told them how to get into the castle and into the secret entrance to the tower then she left them. Serina headed back into the barn through the loose board she had used earlier, she had to find Takar before he found her.

Chapter 26

The fire had spread and now included the old crates and several other items that lay close by. Serina just barely made it past the edge of the fire to get to the rear of the barn where she could hear the dragon blaring in fear. Fortunately, she did not see anyone around. At the back of the barn and through the smoke she saw the dragon pulling on the chain trying to break loose. She knew it was just a matter of time before he broke his bonds and escaped but would he obey Takar when he was free?

The blaze was burning so brightly that the whole front of the barn was alight making it easier for her to spot Takar. He was lurking behind some boards that were leaning up against the side of the barn, looking to see if she may be hiding there.

"Looking for me Takar?" Serina stepped out into view so he could get a good look at her.

Takar spun around at the sound of her voice, quite startled at seeing Serina standing so close to him.

He didn't utter a word, instead he threw out his right arm shooting a blue ball of fire toward her, Serina darted out of the way just in time, the flame landed only inches from her feet.

"Give it up Serina, you cannot out run me or out last me, I am the Great Takar, there is no one more powerful than me, you can not beat me – you will see."

Serina could hear the creature screaming and roaring from somewhere behind her, he was still fighting trying to free himself.

"Why don't you free Java, get him out of here can't you tell he is afraid."

"He will be fine Serina."

Takar yelled something in some unknown language to the dragon and the beast instantly hushed his roaring and screeching.

"See Serina even the dragon, as big and ferocious as he is, knows to listen to me."

She looked behind her at the dragon; he was hunched down on his hind legs staring at them. Even though he was quiet now, Serina could not help but feel the tension in the huge beast. He was quiet yes, but that did not say much for his mood.

Takar, catching Serina off guard, shot another bolt of orange blue flame at her, this time sparking a fire on the hem of her dress. She fell to the ground and proceeded rolling around on the dirt floor trying to put the fire out, thus giving Takar another chance at her. Before she could get to her feet, he shot another lightening bolt at her hitting her in the chest knocking her to the ground.

Serina gasped as she hit the dirt, her eyes felt like they had been knocked to the back of her head as everything went black on her.

"So finally you are at my feet like you are supposed to be Serina."

She could hear the evil in Takar's voice as he stood over her but she lay silently in the dirt for she had this searing pain in her chest and still could not see a thing.

Takar reached down grabbing Serina's arm but she wrenched free scooting back away from him.

"Don't touch me, you, you evil monster."

Takar just laughed at her with that wicked evil laugh of his, giving Serina cold chills.

"I mean it; don't touch me again or you will regret it, I promise you."

"Big words for such a small girl," Takar snarled.

Meanwhile Serina's sight was slowly coming back. It was still fuzzy and she could see three of Takar now. *That's all I need; two more of him.* She kept crawling away but at every move she made, Takar took another step toward her, staying just a step or so away.

Suddenly Serina backed into something large. She felt behind her to get a grip and pull herself up only to find out that she had backed right into Java. The big dragon was still sitting on its haunches watching their every move.

"Oh, I see you have backed yourself into my dragon, you know he has not had his supper yet and you would make a nice little treat for him, so I would be very careful if I were you Serina," Takar threatened icily.

What a fine mess I've got myself into, she thought, as she got to her feet.

"I am intrigued though Serina, how you survived my lightening bolt... Maybe you are more powerful than I thought, not powerful enough to beat me but, you have surprised me."

He had not actually meant to hit Serina – he had only wanted to scare her, but he was astonished that she was still alive, let alone standing.

"There's more from where that came from," spat Serina defiantly, still feeling the pain in her chest, she too wondered how she survived Takar's fiery blow.

"Oh, are you trying to frighten me Serina?" Takar sneered. "If so let me warn you, I do not frighten easily."

Serina's vision was almost back to normal now and she could only see one of Takar, which was a relief; the pain in her chest was also easing somewhat.

The fire was blazing all around behind Takar setting alight everything in its path. Serina wished Deeker would come and unlock the chains on the poor dragon or, maybe he could break free before it was too late but she had no idea where Deeker was or if he was alive.

"Serina, stop fooling around and let's get out of here before we are consumed in this fire."

"What about the dragon? Unlock his chains," said Serina.

"I will take care of the dragon; come let us get out of here."

"Not until you free the dragon," snapped Serina.

"Oh very well, I'll free the stupid animal."

Takar feigned to unlock the dragon's chains while grabbing Serina by the arm, catching her unaware. Yet, she quickly wrenched free of him and ran, which provoked a string of loud curses to come out of Takar's distorted mouth.

He turned around and ran after Serina but she was too quick for him. She made it to the far side of the barn where the loose board was and tried to slip through the opening. In her haste, however, she caught her dress on the boards keeping her from getting through.

Takar's hand reached and pulled her back into the burning barn with such force that Serina went flying across the floor landing on her backside in the dirt. She scrambled to her feet but Takar was on top of her before she had time to make her escape. He grabbed her and flung her up against the old cart where she had found Amil and Frog, which allowed her, in an instant to be on her feet, and making a mad dash under the cart before Takar could reach her; she scrambled out on the other side of it and stood up.

"You will not get away from me Serina," Takar roared as he darted around the cart after her.

Serina took off hoping she could make it to the door safely, but Takar had other plans for her.

"Not so fast Serina," Takar yelled after her. She knew he was close behind her but she could make it – her breath was laboring as she ran as fast as she could toward the open door. If she could just get him out into the open and away from the burning barn then she could concentrate on what she had to do.

She also knew she was still alive because Takar did not want to kill her. However, he would not hesitate to kill her mother and the others if they stood in his way to get what he wanted. Nothing or no one meant anything to him except in Serina's case – it was her powers he wanted.

"Serina!" yelled Takar just as she cleared the barn door.

She slowed to a stop and turned to face him, she was nearly out of breath and her sides were hurting from all her running anyway.

"That's better," he said as he took another step toward her.

He did not even look winded from all the running around he had been doing. *What is it*, she thought, *that gives him all his strength and vigor.*

She looked up at the black hole where his face was hidden, just inside the edges of the cloak – in the dark of night he seemed even more menacing than he looked in the light of day and she knew he would stop at nothing to get what he wanted.

"Takar! You will have to kill me because I will never give in to you, I will never let you own me."

With that Serina reached up and yanked the emerald necklace from around her neck clasping it in her hand. She stepped back a few feet, hoping the emerald would do its job. She held it up and closed her eyes.

"What is this?" laughed Takar. "You think that little necklace is going to defeat me?" He laughed harder glaring down at her. He kept laughing at her as though she was something made for his amusement. "Look at you, standing there with that silly little necklace in your hand. You think that a small little snip of a girl, not even a woman yet, is going to defeat the Great Takar? Honestly, Serina, I thought you had more wits about you than that. As I told you before that is nothing but a silly little emerald that your mother found. With it and your minimal little nothing powers, you do not stand a chance against a croaking bull frog, let alone against the Master."

Serina glared at him in silence, her whole body was trembling inside. She knew he was probably right but she was going to give her all, she would not go down without a fight.

"So what is it going to be Serina, are you tired of playing this stupid little game? If you come with me now I will leave your precious little village alone as a token of good faith, what do you say Serina?"

"Do you honestly expect me to believe you, after all the lies you have told?"

Takar laughed as he stepped a little closer to Serina. "I have had enough, so shall we stop playing and go back to the castle."

"I told you Takar I will not give in to you."

"Fine, have it your way but remember I warned you."

Serina took another few steps away from him to get a little distance between her and Takar but he surprised her with his next move. Instead of shooting one of his fiery lightening bolts at her, as she expected him to do, he turned around headed back to the burning barn.

She stood in puzzlement at this odd turn of events. Why was he going back to the blazing barn? Did he have a heart after all and was he going to free Java? She could hear the animal from somewhere deep inside the barn; he was roaring.

Takar was almost to the barn door when everything started happening so fast; one second she was standing there staring after Takar, the next she was diving for the ground trying to miss the huge lightening bolt Takar was shooting her way. Takar had thrown her off-guard by making her think he was going back into the barn after Java. She should have known better than to think he cared for what happened to the dragon. He did not care about anything else so why should he care about Java?

From the corner of her eye, Serina saw Frog emerging from the side of the barn.

"Frog, quick, go around the side of the barn through the loose board and unchain Java," yelled Serina as she rolled on the ground dodging another lightening bolt from Takar.

"Who!" Frog yelled back at Serina.

"The dragon; he's chained inside the barn. Hurry get him out."

Takar turned in Frog's direction throwing a lightening bolt that way just missing him by inches and hitting the front of the barn instead, Frog jumped back and disappeared around the side of the burning barn.

Frog's momentary distraction gave Serina just enough time to get to her feet before Takar's next attack, this time she was ready.

Takar turned back to Serina, throwing both his arms out, he yelled some undistinguishable words and a blue and white fiery bolt of lightening flew from his hand toward Serina. She stood her ground holding up the Emerald Stone, and like a magnet, it drew the lightening strike straight to it, consuming the fire within it, knocking Serina off her feet in the process.

Takar stood staring in shocked silence; he appeared astounded at what had just happened. Serina, on the other hand, rose to her feet steadying herself for Takar's next shot.

She glanced at the Emerald Stone in her hand. *Funny,* she thought, *it didn't even feel warm and it looks the same as always.* Yet, it had most definitely absorbed the whole fiery bolt of lightening Takar had just shot at her.

"Well, it appears I may have been wrong about your emerald Serina, I wonder where your mother found it?"

"Just lying around somewhere Takar."

The barn was completely enveloped by the flames now; Serina was hoping Frog had gotten Java out in time, since she could not hear his screams anymore – she was taking that as a good sign.

Takar moved slowly in a circle around Serina never taking his eyes off her nor speaking, just gliding around her giving the impression he was floating on air. Serina pivoted with him ready for whatever his next move would be.

Takar was in the shadows now making it harder for her to see him in the moonless night. Serina realized that this was his plan; if she could not see him then he had the advantage over her. She stepped closer to him, keeping him in sight. She had to be able to see his hands in order to know what his next move was going to be.

He played with her as if she were a toy, watching her like a feline ready to pounce on its prey. Serina was trembling from head to toe – even more than before, if that were possible. Shaking, she stepped closer to keep him in full view but suddenly Takar jumped toward her. Serina stumbled backwards and in that quick second Takar grabbed one of her arms pulling her to him so roughly that Serina dropped her necklace in the dirt. She wiggled around trying to free herself but he tightened his grip causing her to scream out in pain.

"Give me the necklace and I will release you."

"No!" yelled Serina as she tried wrenching her arm free but it was useless, he just squeezed tighter as she let out another scream.

"It does not have to be this way Serina if you would just give me the necklace."

"Never! I said."

As Takar reached down to grab her other arm, Serina closed her teeth down as hard as she could on his hand – fiercely biting him until he pulled back in pain, blood already dripping from the wound.

"You little wench you will pay for that," Takar shouted as he swung his bleeding hand at Serina's face so hard that it split her lip opened. She could taste the warm blood in her mouth and tears sprang to her eyes as she fought him desperately trying to free herself from his grip.

From somewhere behind them, all of a sudden she heard a horrible sound. Both she and Takar spun around but she could not see what made the sound. Takar tightened his grip on Serina's arm while backing up, dragging her with him.

Then all at once, Takar yelled out in pain loosening his grip on Serina's arm. She pulled away falling to the hard ground free at last. Just as she got to her feet, she felt Takar's hand grabbing hold to her arm again, pulling her back to him. She pushed against him fighting him and managed to get free from his grasp but fell to the ground once again almost knocking the wind out of her. She scrambled to her feet just in time to see Java flipping Takar through the air. He landed with a thud but was on his feet instantly. The dragon whipped his tail around knocking Takar off his feet yet again. This time when Takar got to his feet, he yelled something at the dragon causing Java to screech an ear-splitting sound. The dragon swung his huge head from side to side as he roared but he did not heel to Takar as Serina thought he would, instead he swung his tail around knocking Takar backwards to the ground once more. Yet, Takar was fast on his feet this time shooting a large ball of fire at the dragon from both hands. The dragon met his fiery blaze with one of his own. The two seemed to hold each other at bay for awhile, the dragon blowing his stream of fire at Takar and Takar holding both his hands outstretched, matching the dragon flame for searing flame.

Serina dropped down on the ground searching for her necklace, all the while keeping one eye on the dragon and Takar. She felt around in the dirt searching desperately. When her hand finally came across the emerald, she breathed a deep sigh of relief and clutched it to her chest.

The dragon and Takar were still going at it fighting fire against fire when Serina stood up to watch the endless bout. It was strange watching man and animal battling against one another, brute strength against unmatchable wit and power. Serina knew, however, that it was just a matter of time before Takar grew tired of the game and killed Java. Now that the animal had turned on him, Takar must have known he could not trust him again. He had no control over him so there was no other alternative, for this Serina wept, she pleaded with Takar not to kill the dragon but she knew she was pleading in vain.

"Takar, please, stop – you will kill him, leave him alone," Serina begged.

Takar paid no heed to Serina; he instead forced his fiery flame harder at the dragon, refusing to listen to her plea for mercy.

Serina had to stop him before he killed Java; she clutched her necklace to her breast and plunged forward toward Takar and the dragon. She came up behind Takar and with all her might shoved him with both her hands until he lunged forward breaking his contact with the dragon. They both fell to the ground; Serina on top of Takar and the dragon's flame blew past both them hitting the ground just next to where they had fallen.

Takar rolled over getting to his feet shoving Serina over on the ground, the dragon sucked in his breath, backing up a foot or two watching for Takar's next move. Takar was furious and shot an evil glare in Serina's direction.

"I will deal with you in a moment... First, I must slay me a dragon – no one, or nothing goes against the Great Takar, not even my own dragon," he spat viciously. "No, he must pay for his disobedience now."

He turned his attention back to Java leaving Serina weeping on the ground at his feet.

He roared out at the dragon and Java roared back shooting his fiery breath out at Takar. This time, however, Takar was waiting for it and like lightening, he jumped out of the way of the dragon's fiery breath, holding out both his arms he let go shooting a huge ball of fire from his deadly fingertips at the dragon's head and yelling something incomprehensible at the beast.

Serina was enraged – she kicked Takar's legs out from under him so hard that he stumbled backward losing contact with the dragon. In his rage he turned on Serina shooting his deadly flame at her as she lay on the ground. She held up the emerald just in time to stop the fatal flame from reaching her. The emerald caught the lightening strike reflecting it back at Takar. He took the full force of it in the chest knocking him backwards about ten feet where he stood looking at Serina for a moment with unbelievable shock on his face then he fell to his knees, blood trickling from his mouth.

Serina got to her feet and inched forward staring at Takar.

"Wh... wa... did your mo... mo-ther ge tha eme..."

"Oh... I think she said something about..."

"It came from your scepter Takar."

Serina looked up into the face of her mother.

"Mother!" cried Serina. She looked beyond her mother and saw Koori, Frog and Zarf with Amil bringing up the rear; he was wearing some shiny piece of heavy armor around his chest.

"In case you did not hear me Takar, I said I stole it from your most precious drinking cup, you know your family heirloom, the emerald that is supposed to reverse things Takar..."

"You?"

"That's right Takar, me! I stole it replacing it with a fake one. I knew that was the only way Serina stood a chance of winning against you and now she has done it, we are free at last."

Takar tried to get to his feet but fell back to his knees, he held out his hand toward Serina pleading with her.

"Serina, please spare my life, I... I would not have killed you, I need..."

"Need me."

"Ye, yes, help me, you have won – you have beaten the Great Takar. Serina you are the victor."

Takar reached out his hand toward Serina but Amil pushed it back.

"I don't think so, you have caused enough problems, and it's over now."

Amil reached and pushed the hood from off Takar's head and stepped back in shock at the long jagged scar running down the side of the man's face.

"Does it frighten you little boy?" panted Takar, his voice was low almost a whisper.

"No, I just wanted to see the face of the man that everyone was so afraid of," stated Amil matter-of-factly.

Somewhere behind her Serina heard Koori's rather large intake of breath at seeing Takar's face for the first time and Frog and her mother soothing her.

Serina did not say another word to Takar; she just left him there on his knees pleading as she walked over to her friend and hugged her. "I bet you're glad to finally get out of that tower," said Serina while hugging her ever so tightly.

She released her and then turned to her mother and embraced her with all the love she felt surging inside her. "It's over mother; Takar has been beaten by his own hand," Serina shouted happily – everyone was happy.

Yes, it was all over and they could now go home to their cherished little village...

Chapter 27

In all their excitement, no one was watching Takar, they were too busy shouting about their freedom. No one that is, except for a rather large pair of yellow eyes. Java was sitting back on his haunches watching, waiting. He knew the Master Takar. He knew better than anyone what he was capable of, he knew from past experiences not to turn his back on him, he had the scars to prove it. In fact, Java did not have to wait long for retributions to befall him.

Slowly, quietly Takar rose to his feet, he could hardly wait to see the look of shocked surprise register on their faces – this was going to be worth the pain he was feeling. Without a sound, he crept toward Serina and the others. He would gladly get rid of them. But Serina, ah, she was going to be his at last. He rubbed his burning chest with the palm of his hand soothing the pain away. Yes, he thought this was going to be soooo good, he could hardly contain his excitement, just a few more feet and victory would be all his.

Serina and the others heard the dragon screeching and all turned together to see Takar standing right behind them his arms stretched forth, Serina sucked in her breath, screaming at the others to run. *Damn, what will it take to rid us of this monster!*

Takar stood laughing at them – an ever so hideously evil laugh.

"Oh Serina, did you think that, that little burst of fire was going to do me in? Surely you should know by now that it will take more than that to kill Takar the Master of evil."

He laughed pointing to the others who were still standing behind her.

"I thought I told you guys to run, now get out of here," yelled Serina

"No Serina, we all fight together," said Amil and Frog simultaneously.

"Don't you mean die together?" corrected Serina.

"Whatever," said Koori.

Serina turned back to Takar who was perilously close to her now.

"To the victor go the spoils, Serina. I will have my fun destroying your precious mother and friends. I'm so excited about it I can hardly wait."

From the corner of her eye Serina saw the dragon; he had moved a little closer behind Takar and was now standing on all fours in a hunched position.

"Oh yeah Takar, who says you're going to win this little battle?" Serina challenged, she wanted to keep his full attention on her.

"Me Serina, only someone with powers as strong as mine could have withstood the blast of both the dragons' and my own powerful lightening bolt. It would have killed twenty mortal men, yet here I am standing without a scratch."

Serina felt the emerald clutched tightly in her hand giving her renewed strength.

"Takar don't you wonder about me and my powers."

"Well, I was concerned at first about the emerald that is but its power is only good to reverse things, with that and the measly little powers you hold – you still do not stand a chance against me Serina."

"I would not be so sure of that Takar, I took your blows earlier and am still here, I think I can handle whatever you dish out," taunted Serina, she was surely bluffing because she felt she could not win against him, he was far too powerful.

"I will deal with you later Serina I have to take care of a couple of things," he added dismissively shrugging his shoulders and pointing in the direction of the others.

Zarf started toward Takar but Senora held him back, she knew he was strong but still he was no match for Takar.

"I can't let you do that Takar," Serina stepped in front of Takar. "Leave them alone, they have nothing to do with this, this is between me and you Takar."

"Let me at him," stormed Frog, but Koori grabbed him pulling him back as well.

"Ah yes the little dragon saver, how touching of you to run into a burning barn to save a creature that will toast you up for a midnight snack the next time you're near him."

"I noticed you were in no hurry to save him," Frog countered angrily, "and he's your dragon."

"Dragon's are easy to come by; I can always get another as I will soon have to do. I can not keep him around now, I do not tolerate disobedience."

"Doak!" yelled Takar.

"Oh he can't hear you, I took care of him earlier," said Amil with a smile.

Serina turned to face a grinning Amil then back around to Takar.

"Well I guess I will have to do this by myself won't I?" Takar said in feigned resignation.

Takar raised his arms but Amil lunged at Takar before he had time to toss another of his fatal blows at anyone. He knocked Takar off balance, the both of them tumbling to the ground. Takar got to his feet first – the heavy armor vest was weighing Amil down enough that he had difficulty getting to his feet so he grabbed Takar around the legs instead pulling him back to the ground with him, the two tossed each other about. Amil was trying to keep Takar's hands busy enough that he could not use his most deadly weapon on him. Finally Takar, who was much stronger than Amil broke loose from Amil's grip and the both of them got to their feet, Takar wasted no time in striking lightening at Amil hitting him square in the chest knocking him back about fifty feet, right under the dragon's legs and there he lay very still, too still.

Not knowing if Amil was dead or just unconscious Serina started to run to him but Takar seeing what she was up to quickly grabbed her, stopping her from going any farther.

"Don't be wasting your time; I'm sure he is dead."

He pulled Serina around up close to his chest forcing her to face him he looked down into her young innocent face and whispered, "There's a lesson for you Serina, do not go up against the Great Takar, you will not win."

He shoved her back and held her at arms length for a few seconds more, glaring at her trying to spook her with his intent stare. This was too up-close-and personal for Serina whose whole body was trembling. She did not like being this close to Takar let alone him touching her. She could feel the evil surging through him; pulsating through his fingertips, which were wrapped tightly around her small wrists.

"Now where were we, oh yes I remember now, I think I was going to take care of your little friends there and your dear mother," said Takar grimacing in demonic delight.

"You know Serina you only have yourself to blame for all of this, if you had not been so pig-headed and accepted my offer from the beginning this would never have happened. You are mine Serina, face it." Takar glared down at Serina, his eyes had taken on an even darker glow. He appeared to be somewhere else as he stared at Serina, he peered deep into her eyes, hypnotizing her. Suddenly she felt herself succumbing to his thoughts, her thoughts becoming his thoughts, his grip tightening more and more around her wrists as he held her there. Serina felt herself slipping away; she was falling deep into a bottomless pit. Everything began to swirl around her, as she could not resist falling deeper and deeper into a dark place.

"You're mine Serina, mine."

She could hear Takar chanting, although his voice was very faint now. She was somewhere else, far away, all she wanted to do was sleep now; sleep for a very long time, nothing else mattered.

Takar released Serina and she slipped to the ground where she lay in a sleep like trance as the others stood by watching helplessly, fear had immobilized them completely.

Takar raised his arms and began chanting loudly, his head lifted toward the sky, as everyone stepped back – paralyzed with fear. They knew they were doomed but still they stood there staring at the mad man.

Senora, who had witnessed the whole scene in complete and utter despair, was now weeping for her daughter helplessly sobbing. Koori, Frog and Zarf, all tried to comfort her but they were not doing a very good job of it.

"Do not weep Senora, she is not dead, she has just succumbed to my powers, she has finally given in."

"You mean she has been hypnotized by you because that was the only way you could get to her, you are a monster Takar."

"Yes, well... Whatever you wish to call me Senora but she is mine now, isn't she?" Takar boasted.

"She will never truly be yours Takar, you and I both know that."

"Enough! She is mine now and that is all that matters. With her, I shall have all the powers I will ever need to destroy anyone or anything that gets in my way – and that includes you my dear. I should have destroyed you years ago, when I first took you, but alas, I have to say I have rather enjoyed having you around. Your beauty Senora is like none other I have ever known not to mention your spunk."

Takar reached up to rub the left side of his face remembering the scar that ran the length of his face and how it got there.

"Yes I have to say you were untamable Senora. For awhile, I thought I would never break your spirit but at last you... Well I can not say I ever tamed you for you are still feisty, but you have settled down somewhat. That's what I always liked about you Senora, you always gave a good fight. I will miss you terribly... But, now I have your lovely, beautiful daughter."

"You will never have her completely Takar, as you say she is too much like me, she will never give in to you." Saying these words Senora glanced over to where her daughter lay on the ground, then back to Takar.

"Please let me go to her, grant me this one last request Takar."

Takar directed his gaze toward Serina who lay sleeping peacefully at his feet then he turned back to Senora who was staring at him with pleading eyes. He returned the stare for a few moments trying to get into her head, to read her thoughts. Realizing what he was doing Senora glared at him now with a burning intensity, which almost overshadowed her eyes. She figured two could play the same game. Old memories came flooding back suddenly, she was careful not to let her guard down, not to let him in, do not let him win. She stood there, the both of them staring at each other neither one giving in.

"I see you still have that spark of defiance in you Senora, like I said I never really broke you."

"You do not have anything to fear from me Takar, I have no powers, I am just a mother who is concerned about her child, let me at least see if she is okay."

"Oh, very well go. For your last request, as you put it, see Senora, I do have a heart. But you three stay where you are," he yelled stepping closer to Koori, Frog and Zarf when they started to follow Senora.

Senora reached Serina and cradled her head in her lap; she brushed Serina's dark hair from out of her daughter's sleeping face and rubbed her cheeks.

"Oh Serina forgive me, I was so foolish to think you could have beaten that monster, now I have lost you forever."

Serina slowly opened her eyes then they fluttered back closed. She could hear her mother but her eyelids were much too heavy to open, if she could just sleep for a while, *yes ... sleep* she thought, she felt herself dropping back to a happy place, a place where everything was warm and nice...

"Serina, open your eyes, this is your mother."

Serina felt something cool on her face, cool and wet and she could hear voices, soft sweet voices, pulling her back from her warm comfortable place, no, she did not want to leave.

"Serina."

Serina fluttered her eyes open but it was dark and there was someone over her, slowly Serina could feel herself being pulled back and when she opened her eyes, everything came flooding back at once.

"Shuuu Serina, don't say a word, it's me your mother."

"That's enough, get back over here with the others Senora, you've had long enough besides she can not hear you she is in a deep sleep," Takar growled.

Senora laid Serina's head back down on the ground putting her fingers to her lips then placing them on Serina's forehead.

"I love you my dear darling Serina, always remember that I love you."

Senora got to her feet and went back to stand with the others.

"How touching Senora, crying over your daughter, apologizing to her for what you have caused, if you had left her alone and left the stone where it was Serina would never have been the wiser and she would have come to me without a fight."

"You can not blame a mother for trying to protect her child Takar, she is only a child and should not have to go through all of this, can't you just let her be, you are so powerful you do not need her measly little bit of powers, you said so yourself..."

"Enough of all this rubbish, I listened to you once before and let her stay in that little village until now but if I had not listened to you she would have been here all along, being trained and prepared for the day she will become mine in every way, this is all your fault Senora."

He suddenly charged toward them with both hands outstretched, they could see the rage in his eyes as he neared them; he had lost every sign of sanity.

Serina had slowly made it to her feet and was now standing behind Takar when he lunged toward the others. She chased after him and reached out to grab him but all she got a hold of was his robes that were billowing behind him but it was enough to throw him off guard. He whirled around knocking Serina back. She kept her feet on the ground, however, this time lunging at him and hitting him in the stomach, which only enraged him, even more. He came at her with both hands; he grabbed her flinging her to the ground about ten feet away. He then continued to run in the direction of the others, shooting a fiery lightening bolt from his fingertips while the four ran for safety into the trees.

Java came from out of nowhere and was on top of Serina before she knew it; he reached down grabbing her by her dress tail with his huge teeth and flung her up into the air before she had time to scream. To her surprise, the dragon had thrown her on his back and into the waiting arms of Rupert – the crazy loon who had been locked in a cell down in the dungeon next to her mother. He was wearing the breast of armor that Amil had been wearing earlier.

"Rupert? Is that you?"

"Yes Serina it is me," replied Rupert in his deep raspy voice.

"How did you ge, get out of the dungeon and how did you get that armor on? Where is…"

"Your friend?

"Ye, yes."

"He is the one who freed me, he also loaned me his armor," he said, tapping his knuckles against his chest making a clacking sound.

"I th, thou, you were," said Serina breathlessly.

"Crazy?" finished Rupert.

"Ye, yes."

"Not quite, now hang on – me and my friend here, we have some unfinished business to take care of."

Serina grabbed hold of Rupert tightly as the dragon lunged forward covering the gap between him and Takar. After only a few steps Java was on Takar's heels, the dragon made an ear-piercing sound as he stopped behind Takar.

Takar turned around at the sound of Java at his heels. He looked startled for a second. Serina did not know what shocked him the most; seeing her up on the dragon's back or seeing Rupert but he was most definitely astonished.

Without another moment's hesitation, Takar flipped his robes back and shot forth a fiery lightening bolt from both his hands. Evidently, he had no intention of letting Serina get away this time.

Rupert and Serina were waiting for his attack. Rupert maneuvered the dragon around so he could ward off his blows. Serina held out her emerald necklace ready to guard off his attacks, the lightening bolt hit the emerald and the stone reflected the fire back to the ground toward Takar causing him to leap sideways just in the nick of time. Takar was already sending another ensilage of flames at the two but Serina held on to Rupert with one hand and squeezed the emerald tightly in the other, reflecting his flurry of fire as fast as he shot them at her. She had no time to catch her breath, for Takar was too fast for her.

Java was dancing all around Takar; making it difficult for Serina to hold on and fight at the same time but she was holding her own returning everything Takar sent her way.

All at once Takar stopped his ensilage of fire and he stood immobile looking up at them quietly. *He looks small*, Serina thought, from where she sat on the dragon's back, but she knew not to let that fool her. She stared at his hooded face and waited quietly for his next move, watching him, waiting. She would not fall for any of his tricks again, she thought. Whatever he was going to dish out; she was going to be ready for it.

Takar did not intend to give in. He just had to figure out a new plan; one that was sure to get Serina off the dragon's back. Then he could take care of that crazy loon and the dragon at the same time. Finally, a thought came to him – yes, why had he not thought of it earlier – oh well, now is better than never.

"Serina." Takar's face took on a sudden evil grin – he was almost laughing, but he caught himself, holding back. He would have plenty of time to laugh later. Yes, he would most definitely get the last laugh.

"Please, can we talk?"

"I have nothing to say to you Takar."

Fine, he thought, that was the answer he expected from her and he knew she would not just kill him. She did not have it in her to kill in cold blood, that was her weakness and he knew now he could use it against her. "Fine have it your way," he whispered, and then taking aim he quickly shot out a light, none too deadly, fire bolt toward the emerald she was holding outstretched in her hand, when she returned his fire he stepped right into it as he planned, taking it full in the chest. The bolt knocked him to the ground where he laid still momentarily stunned.

Rupert and Serina watched Takar carefully and when he showed no signs of getting up Serina asked Rupert to help her down so she could go check on him.

"No, you stay here on Java and I will check him."

"No Rupert, you have no way of protecting yourself from him but I do, I will go."

Saying no more Serina jumped from Java's back and headed toward Takar where he lay motionless on the ground.

She stepped cautiously toward him, even though he was not moving she had to be careful remembering the last time he was hit by the dragon and his own fire bolt. If only she could see his face, but the hood hid it from her view.

"Just a few more feet," Takar said under his breath, "just a couple more feet and it will be all over Serina my sweet."

Serina reached Takar but was actually afraid to bend down; she hesitated for a moment watching for any signs of life coming from him.

"Is he breathing Serina?" yelled Rupert, from atop Java's back.

"I, I can't tell, I can not see his face."

"Takar?"

Serina inched herself a little closer, took a deep breath and bent down, slowly she pulled back the hood that was hiding Takar's face.

"I, I th, think he is dead, he is not moving and I don't think he is breathing," Serina yelled back at Rupert. She turned back to face Takar, "No, I think he's dead he doesn't appear to be breathing."

Serina closed her eyes feeling sick all of a sudden at the thought of taking someone's life, even if it was Takar as evil as he was and deserving of it too, she thought, but still...

Serina knelt on the ground next to Takar with her eyes closed, silently crying.

She felt it inside first, she knew before she opened her eyes what she would see. She opened her eyes slowly to stare into the ever-menacing eyes of Takar, he was looking at her with an evil grin on his face.

"Oh Serina how touching, you were crying for me," whispered Takar. Her face turned ashen.

She tried to get to her feet and run but he grabbed her prying the emerald out of her hand so quickly she didn't have time to do anything but scream.

Once he had the emerald in his hand, he gave Serina a shove and turned on the dragon and Rupert. "Now we shall see who is more powerful."

Serina lunged for Takar knocking him off his feet before he had time to strike out at Java and Rupert. Takar stumbled catching himself but in the process, he dropped the emerald. Serina scrambled to catch the necklace before Takar could, she reached out trying to catch the stone as it fell but in one quick swoop Takar caught it bringing it up to his chest and turned back to face the dragon.

Java shot a fiery bolt at Takar but Takar reflected it back at the dragon, Java screeched out in pain backing away from Takar.

Takar turned back to Serina laughing.

"See Serina, this is how it is done."

He turned his attention back to the fight, he knew it was just a matter of time before the dragon and the mad man on top of him were dead, then he could concentrate on more serious matters. Now that he had the stone there was no holding him back, he would get what he deserved at last.

What happened next was not what Takar expected; Java with Rupert still on his back stepped forward and stood right behind Takar. With one swoop, the dragon grabbed Takar between his teeth and started flinging him around and around knocking the emerald necklace from his evil hands and across the castle grounds.

Serina scrambled to get the necklace then turned back toward the dragon and Takar, she could hear Takar screaming as he dangled from the dragon's mouth. She quickly backed away from all the commotion and found her mother and the others who had stepped out from the protection of the trees. They all stood staring at Java; fear gripping their throats as he threw Takar down on the ground picking him up again biting down with his razor sharp teeth. They all listened to his bones crunching between Java's forceful jaws. In what seemed like an eternity – in reality it only lasted a few minutes, it was all over; the Great Takar was no more.

When Java was through he turned around to face Serina and the others, they all started backing up toward the trees again including Serina, none of them wanting to be the dragon's next course.

"Java!"

It was Deeker the dragon keeper yelling at Java and Amil right beside him looking a little shabby and frayed; the two had come out of nowhere and were standing near the burning barn.

Chapter 28

Rupert headed the big black dragon toward Deeker and Amil where he climbed down turning the creature over to Deeker and headed back toward Serina and the others.

"I am pretty sure he will not hurt any of you, he really is a gentle creature, just a pet really."

"He likes you to scratch him just behind his ears best," said Rupert leaning over and winking at Frog.

He needed to say no more, Frog leaped into a run toward Amil who was standing with Deeker. The dragon had flopped down in front of the two sitting on his back haunches allowing Deeker and Amil to scratch his head. *More like begging them,* Serina thought as she watched the huge black beast for the first time without feeling any fear of the creature.

They made their way over to Deeker, Amil and the dragon.

"Hey you were right," yelled Frog as everyone came closer.

"Watch him Koori, he really likes it."

Frog was so excited to get a chance to play with the dragon finally; Koori just rolled her pretty green eyes and shook her head.

"Boys!" was all she said as she turned her attention back to Serina and Rupert.

"Rupert, back in the dungeon, I… I thought you… Well, we all thought you were kind of a loon you know."

"Yes as did Takar. That was the only way I could stay alive, he would surely have killed me if he thought I had my wits about me. Sometimes though, I thought I would go crazy locked up in there with the rats."

"What you said about the book and the candle, how did you know these things?" asked Senora.

"Ah Senora, Takar captured me as well, several years ago from my kingdom in the east, he stripped me of my powers stealing my dragon and that emerald from my father King Labort who wrote the book that Toddle gave Serina. It angered Takar when I would not bow down to him, he may have taken my powers but he did not take my will... He threw me in the dungeon to rot, holding me captive all this time using me against my father to rule our kingdom.

"Oh Rupert I had no idea, I knew you had suffered at his hands for a long time but no one knew how long you had been here or from whence you came."

"Fourteen years I have been here away from my family, I was only fourteen years old when he took me. It will be great to see my mother and father again."

"Now he is dead and I have my powers back, my family will rejoice with this news. He was an evil man Serina; do not fret over his death."

"Java is your dragon?" Frog interrupted.

"Yes, I raised him from a baby when his mother died from a fall over a cliff. He was such a little thing and needed tending to very badly. If I had not come upon him he would have surely died but look at him now – no one would ever think that he was an orphan would they?"

"Yo, you are a Prince?" Koori inquired, all starry eyed suddenly.

"Yes, I am Prince Rupert De Leon Mandenazia at your service," Rupert replied, bowing low before Serina and Koori.

"I never met a Prince before, this is just, well, I mean I only read about them before, I never really met one before," Koori blurted out spreading the hem of her dress and curtsying to her knees before him.

"I am just a man Koori, no need for that," Rupert said taking her by the hands and helping her to her feet.

"Serina I remember now," Koori said, "I told you I had read about an emerald like yours in a book somewhere. Well, it *was* this emerald indeed. I remember reading about this king and his kingdom with this family emerald that was encrusted on the kings drinking cup, it was a magical emerald and only good could be done with the emerald."

"That's right Koori it is a magical emerald and it has done well for my family and our kingdom for many years."

Serina slipped the necklace from around her neck and without a moment's hesitation handed it to Rupert.

"Here, I am sure your father will be happy to know you have recovered the family heirloom."

"No Serina, the emerald belongs to you now, you take it and do good with it, if ever a need for the emerald should arise I know how to find you and I am sure you will come to our aid as swiftly as if you had wings."

Rupert placed the necklace around Serina's neck then stepped back with a smile on his face.

"But, your father won't he... Will he not want the Emerald Stone back?"

"No Serina, he will understand and know that it is in good hands."

Rupert looked around at the others, his gaze falling on Senora and Zarf; he gently took Senora's hands in his.

"I will not miss this place as I'm sure you will not either but I will always remember you and your kindness, you are a wonderfully gentle kind woman dear Senora. And what you have done for my trusted friend Zarf, will not go without recall either."

"Thank you Rupert and I will miss you as well... But tell me about Zarf; will he go back with you?"

"Yes, dear Lady. He was my best friend once upon a time, and now he must return to our land where his family will be pleased to know that not only he is alive thanks to your kindness, but well enough to return home." Then looking down at Takar's remains – a pack of bones under a cape, really, Rupert added: "I must get news of Takar's death to my father right away; there will be a huge celebration in *your* honor Serina. You must attend, we are free at last and we have you to thank for it."

"But, but I did nothing, I could not even kill him, Java, did that, I..." Serina's voice faded and her body trembled as she remembered Takar's screams.

"Because you are not evil Serina, he knew that too and played it against you, knowing you would not kill him unless you had no other choice. Do not feel bad Serina that he is gone, he was pure evil, and he even had this whole castle under his spell."

"I don't feel bad that he is dead, it just saddens me to think of all the people who suffered at his hands."

"I'm sure it will be a wonderful celebration but I must go home first, to my own village and see if my father is okay."

"I understand Serina but our paths will cross again someday and I will remember the good you have done."

"Oh Miss Serina," said Deeker quietly.

"Yes Deeker?"

"I know you have the power to reverse things if it's for good, well I was wondering if you could look at my son."

"Your son? What is wrong with your son?"

"He lays in a deep sleep Miss Serina."

Serina turned to her mother and she nodded in agreement. "Deeker I do not think that my powers work like that, I have tried to save someone else already and it did not work."

"Yes, I know, it was Toddle."

"Yes that's right Toddle. I tried but he never woke up, I'm afraid it does not work."

"Oh yes Miss Serina it does work... Toddle, he's alive only we hid him from the Master so he would not know."

"Toddle? Toddle is alive?"

"Oh yes Miss Serina very much so, come I will show you."

They all headed toward an old shack that stood at the edge of the castle grounds. And there, just inside, much to Serina's surprise, sitting at an old make-shift table, was Toddle.

"Toddle!" Serina ran and clasped her arms around the old man's neck nearly knocking him off his chair in her excitement.

"You're alive! I can't believe it, you're alive!"

"Yes Little Princess, I am alive and I am most grateful to you. Takar did not kill me. His lightening bolt knocked me into a coma but your tears slowly brought me out of it."

"Oh Toddle I am so happy, I thought I would never see you again but here you are alive and well, you are well aren't you Toddle, right? No problems huh?" said Serina waving her hands in front of Toddle's face and peering into his eyes for any signs of what he may have wanted to hide from her and gave him close inspection.

"No problems Little Princess," said Toddle laughingly.

"Um, Miss Serina?"

"Oh, yes Deeker?"

"My son, if you would, he's over here."

Serina turned to where Deeker was pointing and over in the corner of the room was a narrow bed and on the bed laid Ju.

"No!" screamed Serina.

She ran to the bedside and dropped to her knees.

"Oh Ju! Ju is your son Deeker?"

"Yes Miss Serina, he is all I have in the world."

"He was so brave," said Serina as she turned back to gaze into Ju's cold expressionless face. She remembered everything about that night, when Ju pushed Serina and her mother behind him, protecting them from Takar's wrath. She remembered seeing him fall as Takar reached forth and struck him down killing him instantly (or at least she thought) with one of his lightening bolts. "Yes," she murmured under her breath, "he was so very brave." She clasped one of Ju's hands in hers and wept silently for the man who tried to save her and her mother from Takar's clutches.

She rubbed his forehead with her wet hand whispering to him as she did. "Ju you were most magnificent standing against Takar, you were so brave to do what you did, you are truly a good man and if anyone should have a chance to live it should be you."

Serina knelt beside Ju for what seemed an eternity, stroking his forehead when finally she felt something inside his chest. The slow beat of his heart picked up rhythm startling Serina; she let out a loud gasp. She stared down at his face as his eyelids slowly began flickering and then opened. He gazed at Serina who was now weeping with joy.

"My son, you're alive! You're alive!" Deeker yelled as he ran to his son's side covering his body with his own, sobbing uncontrollably.

Serina's mother and the others gathered around Ju's bed, staring in wonder.

"Let's step back and give the man room with his son," Senora whispered to the group. She took her daughter's hand and led them all outside the little hut into the night air.

Deeker stopped them at the door.

"Miss Serina, I thank you from the bottom of my heart for saving my son, we will always be in debt to you for this great act of kindness. If ever there is anything that you need please call upon me and my family, we will be there for you whenever you need us."

"Oh Deeker; you're welcome and thank you."

As they stepped out into the twilight, Serina turned to Toddle. "Toddle, how did you know about the rhyme in the book and the candle?"

"That's easy Serina," replied Rupert, "Toddle is my man servant and was captured along with me as well as Deeker and his son Ju. Takar stole the book when he rummaged through our castle and any candle falls under the spell of the riddle when placed into view of the book."

"Yes, and it was Rupert here who requested me to bring you the book down in the dungeon so as to help you escape."

"Something else that puzzles me is why Takar did not just sprinkle some of that memory dust over me so I would not have any memory of my village and life before the castle. I would have done as he said and not known the difference."

"Because Serina, Takar had to have you willingly, you had to want to be here with him of your own freewill, or else he would not have been able to receive your powers. That's why he kept asking you and trying to convince you that you needed to be with him."

"You have done well little princess," said Toddle with a half grin, "very well indeed."

"Thank you Toddle but I don't deserve credit, you know Java is the one who deserves all the credit, and thanks to him Takar is no more."

"Ah yes but Java did not bring Ju or me out of our deep sleep my child, that is something that only you could have done and only then if your intentions were of good instead of evil."

"Well, I guess you're right but I still don't feel like I... I, I'm not sure how I feel right now."

"That's to be understood with everything that's happened to you in the last few weeks but in time you will come to terms with this new power you have inherited and I feel in my heart you will do great things with it."

Toddle hugged her to him then held her back at arms length, gazing deeply into her eyes. "Yes, I do believe you will be just fine my child."

"I believe so too," Senora said stepping up and taking her daughter into her arms hugging her to her chest tightly.

"I am so very proud of you Serina; I knew you could do it all along."

"Well Rupert and Java are my heroes; they gave Takar what he deserved, didn't they?"

"Yeah! Java ate him up like he was nothing, like a suckling pig," Frog rejoined cheerfully.

"Okay!" Koori cut-in. "We do not have to hear all the gory details, right Serina?" She glared at Frog with a disgusting look on her face.

"Ah girls!" exclaimed Amil, "they do not have the stomach for things such as that, they get all squeamish inside Frog, I'm sure glad I'm a..."

"A man?" Toddle put-in.

"Well with everything that we've gone threw tonight I'd say they have earned that title wouldn't everyone agree?" Senora stated proudly.

"Most definitely," agreed Toddle.

"Well they would not have been in all this danger if they would have stayed in the village like they were supposed to do," Koori countered.

"Look who's talking," rebuked Serina, "if I remember right a certain someone who's name I need not mention was supposed to do the same thing. You would not have been here either if you'd only have listened to me," she said grabbing her friend around the neck playfully.

"By the way what was it now that brought you two boys back to the castle grounds anyway?" Koori asked.

Well we couldn't let you two girls have all the fun now could we? I figured as pig headed as Serina was she was going to need some help sooner or later whether she asked for it or not, and knowing Serina she would not ask for it, so we had to come back," Amil said.

"Yeah, and besides that I still had not gotten to see the dragon," Frog added laughingly.

"You risked your life just so you could see a dragon, you stupid boy," Koori scolded. "I tell you Frog if you had a brain you would take it out and play with it. You could have been killed and all because you wanted to see some dumb ole dragon," Koori continued dressing down poor Frog in a motherly fashion.

"Yeah, well dragons only come around every once in a blue zillion years, so yeah I wanted to see the dragon but I had other reasons – that is none of your business so don't even ask me what they were."

This got Koori's curiosity aroused – she whirled around facing Frog who instantly stopped dead in his tracks.

"Oh really, well for your information, I do not want to know what other reasons you had, they are probably just as stupid as wanting to see the dragon."

This stung Frog a wee bit, so he kept the other reason of wanting to make sure she was safe and out of harm's way, to himself.

"Come on Koori, you've got to admit that a dragon is a very rare and beautiful creature and well worth seeing, you know you enjoyed seeing him as well as I did."

"Yes, I'm sure of it now, you have lost the last bit of brains you ever had, what a shame too you could have been a bright young man some day but alas."

"Come on everybody," interrupted Serina. She was unable to keep from grinning but at the same time, she wanted to stop this conversation short before hurt feelings arose. She looked up into her mother's smiling eyes; the two shared a silent moment before she grabbed her mother's hand squeezing it tightly in hers, and then turned back to the others.

"You two stop your bickering and let's go home."

Senora very quietly reached inside her cloak feeling the pouch of silvery blue powder that lay nestled at the bottom of her pocket, with a secret smile etched across her face, she whispered to herself, "Home."

About the Author

As a young girl, D.J. Loomis often fantasized; she was the princess in the storybooks or the little street urchin begging for food. Her vivid imagination took her to the most fantastic dream places. She always wanted to write but the opportunity never seemed to arise until she was injured in 1988. As a means to keep from going stir-crazy, while she was laid up she began writing. She wrote several stories, which soon ended up, most of them unfinished, on a shelf collecting dust and cobwebs while she returned to work to support herself and her young daughter.

She began writing **The Emerald Stone** in 1995 but it too soon lay with the other uncompleted books as her life took another turn and she remarried. She worked on the book whenever the opportunity arose but her busy life did not leave her much spare time.

Her new husband, a passionate reader, suggested she finish her book so he could be the first to read it. She finished it in late 2004 just before he passed away; he never got the chance to read it. D.J. Loomis lives in La Grange, Texas.

Printed in the United States
50449LVS00004B/106-300